"You're not going to invite me in?"

"Not without a warrant, Sergeant Temple." Kara smiled, but there was no mistaking the seriousness of purpose. Sam wasn't getting past her.

"Kara, if you have something to tell me, get it out on the table. Now."

No impact. "It's been a long day," she said smoothly. "We're both worried about Henry and Lillian. So let's not do this. You turn around and go do your Texas Ranger thing, and I'll let you know if I need help."

He had to remember she was a respected attorney. If she was afraid or troubled, she could handle it. She knew where to turn for help.

She also knew how to skirt the truth with him if it suited her. She'd come right up to the line—if not across it.

Sam placed one foot on the threshold and narrowed his eyes on her. He saw her lips part and knew she was thinking he might kiss her. He was tired enough that it seemed a natural thing to do, kissing Kara Galway in the doorway of her little house, never mind that she was trying to get rid of him—hiding something from him.

Instead, he tapped her chin with one finger. "I wouldn't cross me if I were you."

"Neggers's characteristically brisk pacing and colorful characterizations sweep the reader toward a dramatic and ultimately satisfying denouement."

—*Publishers Weekly* on *The Cabin*

CARLA NEGGERS

STONEBROOK COTTAGE

MIRA®

ISBN 1-55166-923-4

STONEBROOK COTTAGE

Copyright © 2002 by Carla Neggers.

Visit us at www.mirabooks.com

Printed in U.S.A.

ACKNOWLEDGMENTS

Special thanks to Christine Wenger (again!),
Fran Garfunkel and her lawyer friends, my lawyer friends
and Zita Christian, for their expertise and willingness to
dig for answers…and to all my friends in Connecticut—
Zita, Leslie O'Grady, Liz Aleshire, Linda Harmon,
Bea Sheftel, Mel and Dorothy and CTRWA gang, for
reminding me that the beauty of your state isn't just the
lay of its land, but also its people.

Closer to home, many thanks to Paul and Andrea for
helping me keep in shape—okay, *get* in shape!

Amy, Dianne, Tania, Jennifer, Meg—what a year it's
been! Thanks for everything!

Sam and Kara's story was great fun to do. Next year it's
Zoe West's story in *The Harbor* (January 2003). In the
meantime, I hope you'll visit me at
www.carlaneggers.com or write to me at P.O. Box 826,
Quechee, VT 05059.

Take care,
Carla Neggers

This one's for you, Joe.

Prologue

━━━∽◦∽━━━

Big Mike Parisi was the first-term governor of Connecticut and a dead man. He knew it even before he hit the water.

He couldn't swim, an embarrassment not a half-dozen people knew.

His big, tough body belly-flopped into the water of his elegant pool and dropped hard and deep, hitting the blue-painted bottom that so beautifully reflected the summer sky. He managed to push up off the bottom and out of the water and yell for help.

"I can't swim!"

No help would come. His voice barely rose above the gurgling fountain halfway down the classic, kidney-shaped pool. His own damn fault. He'd refused to let his state trooper bodyguards out back with him. *If I get stung by a bee, I'll yell bloody murder. You'll hear me. What the hell else could happen?*

Someone could try to kill him.

He'd rented a house for the summer in Bluefield, a picturesque town in northwest Connecticut. Stockwell country. People assumed he wanted to be close to his lieutenant governor, Allyson Lourdes Stockwell, so they could strategize. The truth was, he was worried about her. Allyson had problems. Big problems.

Hadn't occurred to Big Mike to worry about himself.

"Help!"

As he splashed and kicked, he saw the bluebird that he'd been trying to save. It was barely alive, soaked in the chlorinated water, slowly being sucked toward the pool filter.

They were both doomed, him and the bluebird. It was a juvenile, its feathers still speckled. It looked as if it had a broken leg. It couldn't have been in the water long.

Clever. His death would look like an accident. *Michael Joseph Parisi drowned this afternoon in his swimming pool apparently while trying to rescue an injured bluebird...*

Christ. He'd look like an idiot.

Some murdering son of a bitch had dumped the bird in the deep end, knowing he'd bend over and try to scoop it up. Bluebirds were his hobby, his passion since his wife died six years ago. They'd had no children. His desire to help restore the Eastern bluebird population in Connecticut and his personal interest in bluebirds weren't a secret.

Not like not knowing how to swim. *That* was a secret. Hell, everyone knew how to swim.

His mother had regularly dumped his ass in the lake as a kid, trying to get him to learn. It didn't work. She'd had to get his brother to fish him out.

Was the bastard who'd planted the bluebird watching him flail and yell?

It'd look like a goddamn accident.

Rage consumed him, forced him up out of the water, yelling, swearing, pushing for the edge of the pool. It was so damn close. Why couldn't he reach it? What the hell was he doing wrong? He could hear his mother yelling at him. *Jesus, Mary and Joseph, Michael, you're such a wienie. Swim, for the love of God.*

These days a mother like Marianne Parisi would be arrested for child abuse or put on pills or something. Total nutcase, his mother was, though she meant well. She died of a stroke when Mike was twenty-four, still thinking her second son would never amount to shit.

The pool water filled his nose and mouth, burned his eyes. He coughed, choking, taking in even more water. He couldn't breathe.

There'd be a lot of crocodile tears at his funeral.

Allyson would do fine as governor…

Who the hell was he kidding? Allyson had her head in the sand. He'd tried to help her, and he knew that was why he was drowning now.

Murdered.

They'd have to cut him open. They'd find out he hadn't hit his head or had a heart attack or a stroke. He'd *drowned.* The autopsy wouldn't pick up where he'd been poked in the ass. It'd felt like a stick or a pole or something. The pool was fenced in, but the deep end backed up to the woods. His murderer could have hid there and waited for Mike to come outside, then tossed in the bluebird when he had his back turned.

Easier to shoot him, but that wouldn't have looked like an accident.

He stopped yelling. He stopped flailing.

The faces of the living and the dead jumbled together in his head, and he couldn't distinguish which was which, couldn't tell which he was. Thoughts and memories, sounds came at him in a whirl. He could see bluebirds all around him, dozens of them, iridescent in the sunlight.

Ah, Mike, you had it good....

But all of that was done now.

He prayed the way he'd learned in catechism class so long ago.

Hail Mary, full of grace, the Lord is with thee...

His mother came into the bright light now, shaking her head, not with disgust this time, but with love and bemusement, as if she hadn't expected him so soon. His wife was there, too, smiling as she had on their wedding day thirty years ago.

They held out their hands, and Big Mike laughed and walked toward his wife and his mother, and the bluebirds, into the light.

One

Austin was in the grip of its fifteenth consecutive day of ninety-plus-degree weather, a quality of Texas summers Kara Galway had almost forgotten about during her years up north. Even with air-conditioning, she was aware of the blistering temperatures and blamed the heat for her faint nausea. The heat and the seafood tacos she'd had for lunch.

Not Sam Temple. He was another possibility for her queasy stomach, but not one she wanted to consider.

She'd been putting in long hours since Big Mike's death two weeks ago, but memories of their long friendship would sneak up on her no matter how deep she buried herself in her legal work. Kara had met him through her friend Allyson Lourdes Stockwell, now the governor of Connecticut. She and Kara had gone to law school together, before Allyson's husband died of cancer and left her with two toddlers to raise on her own.

Henry and Lillian Stockwell were twelve and eleven now. After Big Mike's funeral, they'd flown back to Texas with Kara, and she'd dropped them off at a kids' dude ranch southwest of Austin, a long-planned adventure that Allyson had decided not to cancel, despite the trauma of Mike Parisi's death. Henry and Lillian had loved him, too. Everyone had.

The kids wrote to Kara, who was their godmother, from the ranch, complaining about the food, the heat, the bugs, the snakes. They never mentioned Big Mike.

Kara tried not to think about him, or his funeral. How he'd died. The Connecticut state police and the state's chief attorney's office were conducting a joint investigation. But none of that was her concern. All she should concentrate on were Henry and Lillian, who would be spending a few days with her after their dude ranch experience, then flying back to Connecticut to enjoy the last of summer and get ready for school.

Seeing them would be a welcome distraction.

George Carter stopped in the open doorway to her office and peered at her. "You sick?"

Kara focused on her boss. "I think I had bad seafood tacos at lunch."

He winced. "There's no such thing as a good seafood taco."

At sixty-two, George Carter was a man of strong opinions, a prominent and respected attorney in Austin, a founding partner of Carter, Smith and Rodriguez, African-American, straightforward, brilliant, father of three, grandfather of two. He was also one of Kara's biggest doubters. He made no secret of it. He said he liked her fine and didn't hold her Yale education or her years as an attorney in Connecticut against her. He'd never even asked her about her Texas Ranger brother. His doubts weren't personal. George was a buttoned-down lawyer who fought hard and played by the rules, and Kara was an out-of-the-box thinker, someone who came at problems sideways by nature, training and experience. She liked to get a fix on the complexities of a problem, understand every angle, every approach, before committing herself to a strategy. In other words, the two of them were polar opposites.

He'd agreed to hire her the previous fall on a one-year contract because, he said, he thought she brought skills and a way of thinking to the firm that it needed. At the end of the year, if the fit between her and Carter, Smith and Rodriguez worked, she'd become a full partner. If not, she'd be looking for work.

"Damn, it's freezing in here." He gave an exaggerated shiver. "I'm getting goose bumps. What's the air-conditioning on?"

"Sixty-eight. I'm still acclimating to August in Texas."

"You're wasting energy and running up the electric bill."

He was six feet tall, his hair just beginning to turn gray, an impressive figure in court with his deceptively understated suits and manner—but Kara didn't believe for a second he was cold. He had on a coat and tie. She just had on slacks and a simple top, and *she* wasn't cold.

She felt her stomach roll over. Maybe she'd developed an allergy to seafood.

She thought again of Sam Temple. She was accustomed to men who preferred to love her from afar. Romantics. Nothing about Sam Temple was from afar—it was up close and personal, immediate. And crazy, inexplicable, totally unforgettable. She pushed him out of her mind because thinking about him was insanity. Having a Texas Ranger for a brother was one thing—sleeping with one was another. George *would* hold that against her.

He shook his head. "A born-and-bred Texan like you, fussing about the heat."

"When I first went up to New England, I was always complaining about the cold. I thought I'd never get used to it, but I did. It's like that now with the heat."

"There's no end in sight to this heat wave, you know."

She'd seen the long-range forecast on the news that morning. It was August in south-central Texas. What did she expect? She pushed back her chair slightly from her desk. Her office was small, with standard furnishings. She hadn't bothered adding pictures and her own artwork, the lack of personal touches giving it a temporary feel, as if she was stuck between the kid she'd been here and the woman she'd become up north.

She smiled at George. "You didn't come here to listen to me complain about the heat."

"No, I didn't. Kara—" He sighed, obviously not thrilled with what he had to say. "You've had a rough couple of weeks. I can see they're taking their toll on you."

She knew what he was talking about. "Mike Parisi was a good friend."

His warm, dark eyes settled on her. "Nothing more?"

"No."

But Big Mike had wanted more. He admitted as much after she'd decided to move back to Texas. He was half in love with her, he'd said, and had been since his wife had died, but didn't want to ruin their friendship by saying anything. Now that she was leaving, he wanted her to know. When she met a man in Texas, he'd told her, don't hold back. Go for it. Life was too short, his own missed opportunities too numerous, too bitter, to contemplate.

Would it have made any difference if he'd told her sooner?

No, she thought. She'd never been in love with Big Mike. Nor had he been in love with her—not really. He knew it that day in Connecticut and so did she.

Kara smiled, picturing him in his cluttered office, a fat cigar stuck in his mouth. "He liked to tell me bad Texas jokes," she told George Carter. "He thinks—he thought we were all hard-asses down here."

"The new governor, Allyson Stockwell, is a friend of yours, as well?"

Kara nodded. Allyson's husband, Lawrence Stockwell, had died ten years ago, now Big Mike. Two strong, powerful men in her life. Lawrence's half brother, Hatch Corrigan, didn't have that kind of magnetism or influence, but he was all Allyson had left.

Allyson had insisted for months Hatch was another

one who loved Kara from afar. Kara, who never noticed such things, refused to believe it until Hatch decided to tell her at Big Mike's funeral. *We were both in love with you, Kara. Stupid as hell, huh?*

No wonder she had a sick stomach.

"Worried about her?" George asked.

"I don't know. Allyson's only thirty-seven—she let Big Mike talk her into running as his lieutenant governor. But she's devoted to public service..."

Kara trailed off, remembering her friend's panicked voice the night of Big Mike's death, not long after she was sworn in as governor. *I'm not ready, Kara. I'm just not.* She'd called on her cell phone to give Kara the terrible news. Kara had just arrived at the Dunning Gallery in Austin for the opening of the Gordon Temple exhibit. Temple was a prominent Cherokee artist, raised in Oklahoma, a former teacher in Texas who was now based in Santa Fe, New Mexico. Getting him for their gallery was a coup for Kevin and Eva Dunning, whose daughter Susanna was married to Kara's brother Jack.

That Gordon Temple and Sam Temple, a Texas Ranger, shared the same last name was, Sam said, just one of those things. Kara didn't believe it.

Every second of that surreal evening was etched in her mind.

"Big Mike was a larger-than-life kind of guy," she went on, aware of George's scrutiny. "He won't be an easy act to follow, but people shouldn't underestimate Allyson. Once she gets over the shock of his death, she'll do fine."

Kara blamed her own shock for her subsequent behavior that night at the gallery. She'd turned off her cell phone after Allyson's call and slipped it into her handbag so she wouldn't have to hear more, know more, and when she swept up a glass of champagne off a passing tray, Sam Temple was there. He was not unfamiliar to her. They'd met a few times at her brother's house in San Antonio—she was not as oblivious to Sergeant Temple's black-eyed charm as Lieutenant Jack Galway no doubt would have hoped.

But she never thought she was crazy enough to go to bed with him. He was so dark and sexy and irresistible, and when he suggested they sneak out for coffee, she'd seized the moment.

They ended up at her house a few blocks away. He stayed all night and all the next morning, and never once did Kara mention Big Mike's death.

She'd had no contact with Sam since. She left that afternoon for Mike Parisi's funeral in Connecticut. She talked to the state detectives about his death and how she'd come to know he couldn't swim, that she'd never told anyone his secret. Although not specifically assigned to the case, Zoe West, Bluefield's sole detective, asked Kara about Big Mike's interest in bluebirds and exactly who knew he couldn't swim. When she questioned Kara on her whereabouts the night of Mike's death, Kara ended up giving her Sam's name and number. It had seemed like the thing to do at the time. She thought Zoe West would be satisfied once Kara offered up a Texas Ranger to corroborate her story.

"It was an accidental drowning," she said half to herself. "Big Mike's death."

"You really called him that?" George's voice was unexpectedly soft, and he tapped the far edge of her desk, not looking at her. "Take tomorrow off," he said abruptly.

Kara was instantly suspicious. "Why? It's been two weeks. I can do my job."

George headed for the door. "You've been putting in ridiculous hours, even for an attorney. You're going to crack." He glanced back at her, none of his usual doubts about her apparent now. "Trust me on this, Kara. I know from experience. Take a day or two off, all right?"

"I'll look over my workload and see what I can do."

He didn't push—at least not yet. After he left, Kara took out the compact mirror she kept in her tote bag and checked her reflection. Pale, definitely on the green side. No wonder George was concerned about her. She looked awful.

It had to be the seafood tacos. A touch of food poisoning—she'd be fine tomorrow.

Morning sickness…

She snapped the mirror shut and shoved it back in her tote bag, but she noticed the white opaque bag she'd stuck in there after an impulsive side trip to the pharmacy at lunch. She'd bought two different home pregnancy test kits. Pure drama. She wasn't pregnant. It had only been two weeks since her craziness with Sam. Surely she wouldn't have morning sickness this early.

She'd throw the pregnancy test kits in a garbage can on her way home tonight. Get rid of the evidence of her hysteria. She was thirty-four years old and had never had a pregnancy scare.

Of course, there were commonsense, biological reasons for that, one being that she'd have had to have sex once in a while. She didn't have blazing, short-lived affairs like her weekend with Sam—she didn't have affairs, period.

Big Mike had often teased her about her love life, or lack thereof. "Kara, a tough-minded attorney like you—what's the matter, are you deliberately practicing abstinence? Or do you just not like Yankee men? Jesus, go home. Take yourself a Texas lover. I know you're not afraid of men."

If she should have been afraid of anyone, it was dark, handsome, black-eyed Sam Temple. There wasn't a woman in Texas who didn't feel sparks flying when he was around. Her brother had told her as much, to the point that Kara had felt compelled to assure him she had no intention of falling for any Texas Ranger, never mind Sam.

"Good," Jack had said. "Don't."

At least Sam didn't know she had limited experience, sex and romance the one area in her life that always made her want to run.

For damn good reason, it turned out. She hadn't run two weeks ago, and she'd ended up in bed with Sam Temple.

Better she should have run.

Sam Temple was driving back to San Antonio after nearly two grueling weeks working on the Mexican border when he checked his voice mail and discovered that a detective from Bluefield, Connecticut, was trying to reach him. "Call me back as soon as possible," she said, then left her name and number.

He pulled into a filling station and dialed Zoe West on his cell phone. He'd heard about the death of the governor of Connecticut not long after he'd left Kara Galway's house—and bed—in Austin. Not one thing about it sat well with him, starting with why she hadn't mentioned the governor's death to him before they'd slept together. She'd known. It was in the papers. *The first call Allyson Lourdes Stockwell made after learning of Parisi's death was to her law school classmate and friend, Kara Galway, in Austin, Texas.*

Sam had checked the times and decided Allyson Stockwell must have called just before Kara had grabbed her glass of champagne at the Dunning Gallery.

At least that explained why she'd slept with him. She'd been distraught. Out of her head with shock and grief at the news and looking to put it out of her mind.

Sam had no such excuse. He'd made love to a woman—his friend's sister—without even realizing she was damn near a virgin. He remembered his shock at her tightness when he entered her. He'd seen her wince and bite down on her lower lip. He'd asked if she was okay, and she told him oh, yes, fine, don't stop, as if she regularly met men for coffee and took them back to her house for sex.

He knew she was lying, but he hadn't stopped.

No excuses.

Even with the air-conditioning blasting, he could

feel the August heat, see it rising off the pavement. A half-dozen eighteen-wheelers idled in the parking lot. He'd had less than eight hours' sleep in three days. He needed a long shower, a dark room and cool sheets.

He didn't need Kara Galway. She was a complication. A mistake. Making love to her had been damn stupid, even if he couldn't bring himself to regret it— not for one second, no matter how hard he tried.

Zoe West answered on the first ring. "West."

"Detective West, it's Sam Temple. I'm returning your call."

"Oh, right—thanks. Just a couple questions. Kara Galway said you were with her at a gallery opening in Austin when she heard about Governor Parisi's death. I'm just following up."

"You've talked to her?"

"Briefly."

Sam frowned. "Why are you following up?"

"Routine."

He doubted it. There was nothing routine about the death of a governor or Zoe West's call. "Isn't this a state investigation?"

"Big Mike died in my town. I'm assisting."

In other words, she was sticking her nose in the investigation, whether the state cops wanted it there or not. Sam said nothing. He had his white Stetson on the seat beside him, his tie loosened, his badge still pinned to his shirt pocket. Two weeks on a serial murder investigation in an impoverished area in near-hundred-degree heat, and here he was on the phone talking about a rich man who'd drowned trying to save a damn bird.

"When did Ms. Galway arrive at the gallery?" Zoe West asked. "Did you see her?"

"She was already there when I arrived around seven o'clock."

"That's eight in the east. We figure Parisi drowned sometime around seven."

Sam could see Kara now in her little black dress, her dark hair pulled back with a turquoise comb that he'd tugged out later, threading his fingers into her thick waves of hair even as he warned himself to leave while he still could.

"Aren't you from San Antonio?" Zoe West asked.

"Detective West, I'm not seeing the point here."

She made a clicking sound, as if she was thinking. "San Antonio's about ninety miles from Austin, isn't it?"

"Yes, ma'am."

"What?"

"I said, 'Yes, ma'am.'"

"Are you being sarcastic, Sergeant Temple?"

"No, ma'am."

"People only call me ma'am when they're being sarcastic."

He almost smiled. "All right, Detective West. I won't call you ma'am."

"It's a southern thing, right? The ma'am?"

Sam realized she was serious. "I like to think of it as a manners thing."

"Oh. Well, yeah, I guess. Okay, back to this gallery. It's in Austin, which is about ninety miles from

San Antonio. It has reduced hours during the summer while the owners—Kevin and Eva Dunning—are at their summer place on Lake Champlain, but they came back special because this was the only time they could get Gordon Temple. Right so far?''

"Right so far," Sam said, careful to avoid any hint of sarcasm. He'd let Detective West ask her questions. Why not? He might learn something about Kara and why she'd acted the way she had that night.

"The Dunnings are the in-laws of another Texas Ranger, a lieutenant, Jack Galway. He's Kara Galway's brother. Your superior, right?" West paused, adding, matter-of-fact, "This was all pretty easy to find out on the Internet. I read a couple articles about that business in the Adirondacks last winter. You got shot, didn't you, Sergeant?"

Sam didn't answer right away. Zoe West had done her homework. In February, he'd gone up north to help Jack sort out a murder investigation that had ended up involving Jack's wife and twin teenage daughters. They'd done snow, ice and bitter cold, and Sam swore he'd never complain about the heat again. And, yes, he was shot.

Kara had slid her fingertips over the scar on his upper thigh.

Damn.

"It was just a flesh wound," he told the Connecticut detective.

"The Galways are doing okay now?"

"Yes."

"Gordon Temple's a famous Native American

painter—Cherokee, lives in New Mexico. You any relation?''

"That's irrelevant, Detective." But he'd spotted Gordon Temple that night and remembered the black hair streaked with gray, the dark eyes and muscular build that were a lot like Sam's own.

Zoe West paused a beat. "So you were there, what, for the art?''

Now who was being sarcastic? Sam watched an overweight man with tattoos on his upper arms carry a bag of food to a big rig. He tried to picture the Bluefield detective in her small-town Connecticut police station.

"Okay, so why you were in Austin is beside the point," she said. "Governor Stockwell called Ms. Galway shortly after seven your time. Did you see her take the call?''

"Yes. We left together about ten minutes later.'' Sam had never talked to Gordon Temple, never complimented him on his paintings or said, "Oh, by the way, I'm your son.'' He shifted, losing patience. "Detective West, you're on a fishing expedition. I have things I need to do.''

She made another couple of clicking sounds. "All right, here's the deal. Kara Galway is one of a very few who knew Governor Parisi couldn't swim. She told you that, right?''

Sam didn't answer.

"Oh. I guess it didn't come up over coffee, huh? If someone wanted him dead and tossed the bluebird into the pool deliberately, hoping he'd fall or seeing to it he did—well, they'd have to know he couldn't swim.''

"Stupid way to kill someone."

"It worked. He's dead. And it looks like an accident."

"Maybe it *was* an accident."

"Too many accidents around here for my taste," Zoe West said.

Sam sat up straighter, hearing something in the Bluefield detective's voice he recognized, maybe just because he was in the same line of work. "There's been another accident?"

"You didn't hear? Allyson Stockwell and her two children had a close call during a Fourth of July bonfire at her mother-in-law's place here in town. A gas can exploded. Someone left it too close to the fire. No one's owned up yet, of course."

"Injuries?"

"Not from the explosion itself. A local guy—Pete Jericho—shoved Mrs. Stockwell and the kids out of the way just in time. He had some minor cuts and bruises. Scared the hell out of everyone."

"Governor Parisi was there?" Sam asked.

"He was. What if someone tried and failed to arrange a fatal accident for him that night, then tried again and succeeded a few weeks later?"

"Is that your theory, Detective?"

"Just the sort of question to keep a law enforcement officer up nights, don't you think, Sergeant?"

"What about the state investigators?"

"They say they don't want to speculate. Hey," she said suddenly, "I'm supposed to ask the questions."

Sam wasn't fooled. Zoe West wanted him to have this information or she wouldn't have given it to him. She might not have wide experience as a small-town detective, but she obviously wasn't stupid.

"I guess it's easier to call the explosion a backyard accident," she went on. "Same with Big Mike and his injured bluebird. I mean, I know he was a nut about bluebirds and everything, but wouldn't you think he'd be careful scooping one out of the drink when he knew he couldn't swim? I would."

"He could have lost his balance."

"Could have." She took in a breath. "Thanks for your help, Sergeant Temple. Keep my number handy if you think of anything else."

Sam promised he would, and she hung up.

He sank back against his seat and shut his eyes a moment, the fatigue crawling at him. He was ten minutes from Jack's house. He could stop in and have a cold beer and not mention Zoe West's call, then head home and sleep.

But that wouldn't be smart. Jack was protective of his entire family, his little sister no exception. Bad enough Sam had slept with her—now he'd just hung up with a Connecticut detective checking out Kara's story from that night. Best to keep some distance between himself and Lieutenant Galway, at least, Sam thought, until he'd sorted out just how pissed he was at her.

Kara knew Mike Parisi couldn't swim. His big secret. She was at the Dunning Gallery when he was falling into his swimming pool and therefore couldn't have been in Connecticut killing him.

Theoretically, she could have hired someone to kill her governor friend. *He doesn't know how to swim. Get him to the deep end of his pool. Make it look like an accident.*

But that didn't fit with what Sam knew about the Galway character, and as far as he could see, she had no reason to kill the guy. It was more plausible, but still unlikely, that she could have inadvertently told the murderer Parisi couldn't swim. Zoe West would want to know if Kara had kept her governor buddy's secret—maybe she'd already asked, when the two of them talked. Kara obviously hadn't seen fit to tell Sam about her conversation with the Bluefield detective or that she'd given Zoe West his number.

He swore under his breath. He didn't believe Kara had anything to do with Parisi's death, but she should have told him about it at some point before he'd left her house that Sunday—preferably before they'd landed up in her bed.

She damn well should have told him she was among a chosen few who knew Michael Parisi couldn't swim.

Sam didn't like being anyone's alibi.

Two

$\sim\!\!\infty\!\!\text{)}\!\!\infty\!\!\sim$

For the first time in weeks, Allyson Stockwell felt almost normal. The late-afternoon shade soothed her taut nerves as she swung gently on a hammock strung between two maple trees on Stockwell Farm in Bluefield, deep in the Litchfield Hills of northwest Connecticut. The taste of her iced tea, the smell of her mother-in-law's roses, the sounds of birds in the nearby trees—all of it seemed so blissfully normal.

She felt like such a phony. She'd never lusted for power and title. She'd been content as lieutenant governor, half believing people when they said Mike Parisi had urged her to run only because she was Lawrence's widow and he needed the Stockwell name behind him.

No…I won't think about that now.

She'd had a postcard that morning from Henry and Lillian in Texas. They seemed to be enjoying themselves at the dude ranch. She felt good about her decision to send them. She wanted them to carry on as normally as possible as they adjusted to all the changes in their lives. Big Mike had been an enormous, charismatic presence in so many people's lives, her children's included.

If not for Lawrence, Allyson wondered, would she ever have met Mike Parisi? He and her husband were such unlikely friends—Lawrence, the Connecticut blueblood, and Big Mike, the self-made man from a working-class neighborhood—but they'd suited each other. Lawrence, dedicated to public service, preferred to work behind the scenes and appreciated Mike's passion and drive, just as Mike had appreciated his wealthy friend's genuine concern for the people of his state.

Twenty years older than Allyson, Lawrence was just forty-seven when he died ten years ago. She never thought she'd make it without him. She didn't lack for anything material, just for the man she'd fallen in love with at twenty-one. Use your law degree, Big Mike had told her. Use your brain. Don't wither away. Do something.

She had, and now she was governor. And alone again, on her own with so many responsibilities. Children who needed her, grieving friends, a grieving state.

She breathed in the warm, clean summer air. She hadn't been out to Bluefield since Mike's death. Lawrence had grown up out here on Stockwell Farm, the sprawling estate set amidst rolling hills and fields that his grandfather had purchased and expanded. His mother still lived here, but, as was the case with Allyson, Stockwell Farm would never be hers. Madeleine Stockwell could live in the white clapboard, black-shuttered house for as long as she chose—no

one could throw her out but it and the grounds, all of
Stockwell Farm, were held in trust for Lawrence's
children.

Allyson had never wanted the main house. She and
Lawrence had converted the barn on the edge of the
fields, and she continued to take Henry and Lillian
there. Allyson thought they liked it better than the
main house. The barn, too, would go to them. But
Stonebrook Cottage, across the fields and through the
woods from the main grounds, was Allyson's and Allyson's alone, a bit of Stockwell Farm that Lawrence
had carved out for her. She liked having it for guests
but planned to leave it to her children, too.

Once they got back from Texas, they'd all move
into the Governor's Residence in Hartford. Henry and
Lillian would continue to attend their school in West
Hartford, and Allyson had no intention of getting rid
of their permanent home there.

At least the kids were having fun at the dude ranch.
They loved it out at Stockwell Farm and would have
liked nothing better than to run loose there all summer, but that was out of the question. Madeleine
wouldn't stand for it. Allyson remembered Lawrence
telling her how his father had fancied himself a gentleman farmer and had horses and apple trees and gardens. He would have Madeleine and Lawrence cart
jugs of water from a spring in the woods just so
they'd know where it was and how to do it. He
wanted them to be self-sufficient, capable, never helpless or idle.

When Lawrence was eight, Edward Stockwell cut
his femoral artery with an ax and bled to death before

his wife could get him to a doctor. Madeleine remarried three years later, beginning a string of marriages that ended with her divorce from her fourth husband five years ago. She vowed never to take another. Allyson believed her mother-in-law when she said that if Edward had lived, the two would have grown old together.

What a horrible blow to lose Edward's only child to cancer ten years ago.

Now Lawrence and Mike both were dead, Allyson thought, and she was governor.

I don't want to be governor.

It complicated everything. She had secrets of her own she wanted to protect.

Her heart raced, and it felt as if someone were standing on her chest. Her doctor was encouraging her to learn stress reduction techniques. Kara had dragged her to a yoga class last year before she left for Texas and demonstrated a simple breathing technique she used before trials. Allyson tried to remember it. In through the nose to the count of eight…hold for eight…out for eight…

She got to four and coughed, nearly dumping herself out of her hammock.

Her cell phone rang, almost paralyzing her. She'd forgotten she'd left the damn thing on, but since it was the number Henry and Lillian would use to call her she hated to turn it off. She sat up, her blond hair snagging in the knotted rope as she threw her legs over the side and groped for her phone in her canvas bag. With Mike's death affecting them so deeply, the children's counselors at the dude ranch had agreed to let them call home more often than was ordinarily permitted.

Allyson anchored herself with her feet and fumbled for the right button on her cell phone. *It might not be that sick jackass who's been calling.*

But it was. She could tell by the quick intake of air on the other end. "Ah, Governor Stockwell. You like the sound of it, don't you? What would the people of Connecticut think if they knew the truth, hmm? Their slut governor, screwing her working-class ex-con in secret. Do you think they might wonder if Big Mike had found out?"

Click. The call was over, the voice was gone.

Allyson shook. She'd never said a word to the caller. Never. She didn't want to do anything to encourage another call or escalate the harassment into action. She just wanted the calls to stop. Each time she received one, she tried to convince herself it was the last.

The first one had come a few days before Big Mike's death. *Ye shall reap what ye sow.* That was it. She'd dismissed it as a crank call, political harassment, nothing worth mentioning to anyone, never mind Mike or her security detail. Then, after Mike's funeral, she received another one. *Do you really think you can keep your ex-con lover a secret now?*

And she knew. Someone had found out about her and Pete Jericho.

Pete was the salt of the earth, a man of the land. His family had owned the two hundred acres on the south border of the Stockwell Farm for generations. They used to be dairy farmers, but now they sold cordwood and Christmas trees, and for the past three years had worked a gravel pit. They plowed driveways and built stone walls and managed their rich neighbors' properties, the mini-estates that had sprouted around Bluefield.

Pete had served six months in prison eight years ago for a stupid barroom brawl that should have been settled, and stayed, among friends—he wasn't anyone's idea of an ex-con. Yet Allyson had kept their affair a secret, begging the question of what *she* thought of his past. He'd undoubtedly saved her life—her children's lives—when the gas can exploded during the Fourth of July bonfire. She could still feel his strong arms around her, his body covering hers, as she'd tried to protect Henry and Lillian from the blast.

Somehow an illicit affair with Pete Jericho was different now that she was governor. The anonymous calls didn't make figuring out what to do about him any easier.

Mike had known. He'd given her an ultimatum a few days after the near disaster at the bonfire. He wanted her relationship with Pete out in the open or over and done with. No secret affairs. Period.

"But what will people say?" she'd asked.

"What the hell do you care? We're not talking about your position on capital punishment or gay marriage. We're talking about who you love. You do love the guy, right?"

"Yes, but—"

"But what? He served six months in the pokey for a bar fight." Big Mike had laughed, amazed. "Come on, Allyson. People'll be thrilled you're not just another rich, watery-eyed WASP.''

She hadn't taken that very well, but Big Mike loved to tease—it didn't matter who. Kara was the one who could always give it right back to him. Allyson had enjoyed watching the two of them. She was more reserved herself, more formal by upbringing and temperament. Kara was a Texas hard-ass with a big heart, a combination that'd probably get her hurt one day.

But Mike hadn't been teasing that day. He could be judgmental, calculating when it came to political advantage and appearances.

Did her caller know about the ultimatum? Would he—or she—try to make people wonder if she'd had something to do with Big Mike's death?

What did the bastard *want?*

She jumped to her feet, knocking over her canvas bag, the contents spilling into the cool shade. She saw a state trooper, a woman, make a move toward her and waved her off. The special unit in charge of guarding the governor had come under heavy criticism for "letting" Big Mike die. Allyson had defended them. She knew what Mike could be like. He'd told her countless times he'd never get used to people hovering.

She squatted down, scooping up her wallet and Rolaids and Palm Pilot, three tubes of the same shade of lipstick. She was shaking uncontrollably now, crying. *Ridiculous.* She was overreacting to the cryptic phone calls, reading into them something that wasn't there. There was no real threat, and harassment was part of being in the public eye. Even if she mentioned the calls to her bodyguards, what could they do? The caller hadn't even made a request for any action one way or another on her part. Get rid of Pete, keep him. Tell the world, don't tell the world. Give money, support a particular piece of legislation—nothing. Maybe the calls were designed to soften her up—maybe they were just to get under her skin.

"Allyson!"

Hatch Corrigan ran across the shaded lawn toward her. Lawrence's half-brother was always on the move, a hothead like his father, Frank Corrigan, Madeleine's third husband, whose early success as an actor hadn't panned out the way either one of them had hoped. Madeleine raised their son largely on her own—she hadn't wanted Frank's help after their divorce. Hatch and Lawrence both had their mother's rangy build and sharp nose, but Hatch had his father's clear blue eyes, auburn hair and dimpled chin, his notorious flair for drama. Hatch, though, was content to remain behind the scenes, like his older half-brother. Not Frank, who'd wanted the stage and an audience, but died five years ago when he fell off scaffolding in a rundown off-off-Broadway theater, dead drunk.

Hatch didn't stand to inherit a dime of Stockwell money, but Allyson couldn't remember him ever complaining about it. His mother had some wealth to hand down, but not a lot, not compared to her first husband's family fortune. Hatch loved Stockwell Farm and spent as much time as he could with Madeleine at the main house, when he wasn't cooking up political schemes and gathering information, plotting, strategizing, advising. He'd been indispensable to Big Mike and, now, to Allyson.

He slowed slightly as he approached her hammock. It wasn't uncommon, she thought, to see Hatch Corrigan in a rush, grim-faced and focused.

She grabbed on to the edge of the rope hammock and pulled herself to her feet, brushing away her tears. In time she might come to feel like a governor, but right now she felt like the thirty-seven-year-old mother of two middle-schoolers, a widow who could never again have romance in her life.

"Allyson," Hatch repeated, breathing hard when he reached her. "We have a problem. That damn dude ranch in Texas just called. The kids—"

"Hatch!" She clenched his upper arms, her chest constricting, her knees going out from under her. "What's happened? What's wrong? Henry and Lillian—they're okay, aren't they?"

"Let's hope." His expression hardened, reminding her that he was forty-seven and childless, not a man who got along easily with children, even his only niece and nephew. "They took off on their own this afternoon. They're on the loose somewhere in Texas."

Susanna Galway called Sam at home, waking him up, and invited him to dinner, refusing to take no for an answer. He didn't argue. Under the circumstances, showing up for dinner would be less provocative than not showing up. He buttoned his shirt, pulled on his boots and headed out.

Dinner was hell. He hated hiding anything from his

friends, but if Kara hadn't told her brother and sister-in-law about her weekend with Sam, he didn't feel it was his place to open his damn mouth. He was being a gentleman, he decided, not a coward. It wasn't as if he'd taken advantage of her. Kara Galway was in her thirties, and she'd wanted their night together as much as he had.

Jack, his wife and their twin daughters didn't seem to notice he was suffering. Susanna was a slim, graceful, dark-haired, green-eyed financial whiz who'd tried to keep millions and a murderer showing up in her kitchen a secret from her Texas Ranger husband, not that there was keeping anything secret from Jack Galway, something that Sam knew he should keep in mind. Susanna was smart, and she liked her secrets. In her own way she was as protective of her family as Jack was. All four of them had come close to losing each other in a harrowing experience in the Adirondack woods six months ago. These days, Susanna seemed content with her work and her life in San Antonio. She was redecorating their suburban home and restoring a historic building downtown that nobody quite knew what she'd do with—including, apparently, her.

The twins were getting ready to head to college in a few weeks. Maggie had decided on Harvard, following in her father's footsteps, Ellen on the University of Texas, which she liked to say was following in the footsteps of no one in her family.

They didn't bring up the subject of Kara tonight, but Sam knew they all had welcomed her move back to Texas, teased her about losing some of her accent

during her years up north. They expected her to take
up with another lawyer or a University of Texas pro-
fessor, maybe one of the artists who hung out at the
Dunning Gallery. Not a Texas Ranger. Not Sam.

He hadn't taken up with her, he reminded himself.
He'd slept with her that one night and one morning
two weeks ago.

After dinner, Susanna and Jack made espresso using the espresso machine Maggie and Ellen had given
their father for Christmas. The girls retreated to the
family room to watch television. Whatever the lingering effects of their ordeal this past winter, the
twins were handling them, just a couple of high-
school graduates excited about college.

Susanna handed Sam a tiny white cup and saucer
and eased onto a chair at the new, glass-topped table.
She smiled over the rim of her own steaming cup,
which didn't look out of place in her slender fingers.
"You look as if you're afraid you'll break the china.
Relax, Sam. You like espresso, don't you?"

"I can drink it."

Jack downed his espresso in about two sips. He was
one of the finest law enforcement officers Sam knew,
a big, broad-shouldered man, a Harvard graduate, a
dedicated Texas Ranger who tried to maintain a pre-
carious balance between work and family. He was
fifteen and his sister just nine when their mother was
killed in a car accident. Sam knew some of the details.
How mother and daughter had gone out shoe shop-
ping and were hit broadside on the driver's side by a
speeding delivery truck.

Kara had had to sit still, covered in shattered glass,

splattered with her dying mother's blood, until the paramedics could get her out. She'd suffered only minor physical injuries. After the accident, her father had encouraged both her and Jack to stay busy and excel, apparently believing the less time they had to think about their mother and grieve, the better. At eighteen, Kara headed north to Yale, not to return until last year.

If she hadn't moved back, would Mike Parisi be dead now? Sam wondered if that was a question Kara had asked herself, one she'd been running from that night when she'd landed in his arms.

Susanna set her cup down after the tiniest of sips. "Sam, I understand you were at the opening of the Gordon Temple exhibit a couple of weeks ago. You've been so busy, I haven't had a chance to talk to you about it. Mum and Dad are thrilled to have him at the gallery. Jack and I couldn't make it to the opening. He's an incredible artist, isn't he?"

Sam shrugged. "The paintings looked fine to me. I don't know that much about art."

"My mother said you didn't stay long. They're curious because you two have the same last name."

Jack shifted in his chair. "I wondered about that, too. Sam, you're part Native American. This guy's Cherokee. He used to live in San Antonio. What's the story?"

"No story."

It was a true answer, if not a complete one. Sam had known for the past five years that Gordon Temple was his father. Biologically. He had never had a real father. His mother, an elementary-school art teacher in a poor section of San Antonio, had finally told him the truth when Gordon's fame was on the rise. Sam had already known his mother and Gordon were briefly married when they were both twenty. Gordon left after a year. Loretta Temple said she never expected him to stay. He was a nomad, an artist who needed his freedom. It was a rationalization, maybe, but Sam didn't resent her for it—she wasn't the one who'd left. She didn't find out she was pregnant until a month after Gordon Temple had withdrawn from her life. She thought it would be easier on him, and ultimately their child, if she said nothing and didn't tempt him to come back.

Thirty-five years later, she admitted she wasn't sure she'd made the right decision in not putting a father's name on her son's birth certificate, but it had been the only choice she'd felt she could make at the time.

No, no story, Sam thought. Just a string of simple facts.

Susanna fingered the delicate handle of her espresso cup. "Did you run into Kara at the opening? I understand she didn't stay long, either. She got the call about Governor Parisi's death and left quickly. Mum didn't realize what was going on at the time or she'd have made sure she was all right." Susanna fixed her vivid green eyes on Sam. "I hate to think of Kara dealing with such a terrible shock all alone."

Sam sipped his espresso, which was very hot and very strong, and offered no comment. This explained the invitation to dinner. Susanna was suspicious of what had happened at the opening, but she would be. She was convinced women fell all over him. It happened, but not every time—and it hadn't happened with Kara. Her grief and shock had more to do with their night together than any attraction to him. But Sam couldn't be sure his preoccupation with Gordon Temple hadn't affected his own judgment.

Jack shook his head, finished with his espresso. "You following this governor's death?" He didn't wait for an answer. "I can't get Kara to talk about it. She's buried herself in her work. She went up to Connecticut for the funeral. The new governor's a friend, as well—Kara's godmother to her children. They flew back with her to go to a kids' dude ranch."

"We sent Maggie and Ellen to a dude ranch that one time, remember? Ellen loved it, Maggie thought it was hell on earth—"

But Jack was not to be distracted. "I don't like reading my sister's name in the paper in conjunction with the unexplained death of a governor. At least she was in Austin and not up there when Parisi drowned. I'd hate to see her get involved in something like that."

Sam understood Jack's reaction, but decided it wasn't his place to bring up Zoe West's call checking Kara's story. Let Kara tell her brother two weeks after the fact that she was one of the few who knew Mike Parisi couldn't swim.

"Dad!"

The panic in Ellen's voice instantly brought Jack to his feet, Sam a half beat behind him. Susanna rose unsteadily, grabbing the back of her chair, her dark hair catching the glow of the white dinner candles. Her face was pale, as if she were back on that day six months ago with her daughters at the mercy of a killer.

Jack caught Ellen by the shoulders in the doorway, strands of dark hair matted to her cheeks. Her breathing was shallow, rapid. "Dad, it's Aunt Kara. Something's wrong—"

Jack swore and pushed past her into the family room, but somehow Sam reached Kara first. She was standing, ashen-faced, Maggie Galway at her side. Sam managed not to touch her, but she clutched his upper arm, her fingers digging into his flesh, her dark eyes wide. "Sam..."

"Kara," Jack said sharply. "What the hell's going on?"

She shifted her gaze, focusing on her brother. "Henry and Lillian Stockwell are missing." Kara took in a breath, obviously trying to calm herself, but she maintained her death grip on Sam's arm. "They took off from the dude ranch late this afternoon. At first everyone thought they were hiding somewhere, or misunderstood instructions—"

"The ranch is about an hour from here," Sam said.

Jack nodded. "These kids are what, twelve?"

"Henry's twelve, Lillian's eleven." Kara's voice was tight with fear. "Allyson called me a few minutes after I left work. I was south of town, anyway, meeting friends. I decided to head straight here, in case you'd heard anything."

"We haven't," Susanna said gently. "Kara, why don't you sit down? Tell us what you know."

She seemed to give herself a mental shake, some color returning high in her cheeks. She released her grip on Sam. "I held it together all the way down here and sort of fell apart when I walked in the door."

She brushed her hand through her hair, pulling out the turquoise comb she'd worn the night of the opening. She gave no sign she remembered him taking it out of her hair. She cleared her throat. "I'm sure they're fine."

Sam glanced at Jack. "The two preteen kids of the governor of Connecticut on their own in Texas—I don't like it."

"Sit," Jack told his sister, firmly but gently. "Catch your breath. Tell us everything. Goddamnit, I was just saying I didn't like any of this business."

Ellen started for the kitchen. "I'll get her a glass of water."

"Come on, Aunt Kara," Maggie said, taking her aunt's hand and pulling her onto the couch beside her. Maggie had her mother's build and her father's temperament, her Dunning grandparents' creative flair. She was wearing one of her bizarre outfits, a vintage loud-striped dress from the 1960s and turquoise sneakers. "It'll be okay. Ellen and I ran away once. Mom, Dad, you remember, don't you? We were going to take a bus to Hollywood, but we got hungry and came home."

Sam didn't share her optimism, possibly because of Zoe West's call. Susanna smiled reassuringly. "Maggie has a point. Kids don't usually run off for long. It's barely nightfall now—"

Kara nodded, calmer. "Allyson said someone would call me if they turn up. There's still time."

Jack grunted. "How the hell could this dude ranch lose two kids? Did they have the same schedule?"

"No, and they were in separate cabins," Kara said. "They must have had a plan to meet and sneak out.

The ranch isn't superremote. Allyson said there's no reason to suspect foul play or think they're lost—''

"I'll drive out to the ranch and see what's going on," Jack said. "We can put out an alert—"

Kara frowned. "Allyson doesn't want law enforcement to get involved at this point."

"Not her call. She's the governor of Connecticut not Texas."

Sam could sense the escalating tension between brother and sister. So, obviously, could Susanna. She licked her lips and touched her husband's arm. "Kids this age do impulsive things, sometimes for reasons only they understand. The important thing right now is to find them."

"They *have* to be all right," Kara said, half under her breath. She withdrew a small stack of postcards and letters from her handbag. "The kids wrote to me from camp up north earlier this summer, then from the dude ranch. Lillian more than Henry. She got me to read the Harry Potter books."

Sam had seen them stacked on Kara's nightstand.

She shoved the stack of letters and cards at her brother. "Here. Go through these. Maybe there's something I missed, some clue as to what they're up to. If you find anything, tell me, and I'll call Allyson."

Jack took the cards and letters. "Do you think they'll come to you?"

"How? They don't know where I live, they have no transportation—"

"They have your address."

"But they're *kids*."

Jack and Sam exchanged glances. Kids were capable of a lot. Sam said, "Do they know how to get in touch with you?"

She nodded, not looking at him. "I gave them all my phone numbers when I dropped them off at the ranch."

Ellen returned with the water, her dark eyes huge as she handed the glass to her aunt. "You don't think someone snatched them, do you, Sam? The Stockwells are rich, and Henry and Lillian have been in the news because their mother's a woman governor and so young—"

Kara gasped, though, Sam knew, it had to be something she'd considered on her drive south to San Antonio. "Ellen, no one…I'm sure they haven't been kidnapped."

Jack slung an arm over Ellen's shoulders. She was strongly built, a rugby player with a big heart. "Let's not get ahead of ourselves," her father said, the professional in him taking over. "Kids sneak off from camp from time to time. They didn't like lunch, they're homesick, they're mad at some other kid. Henry and Lillian are probably emotionally volatile right now. It's still not too late for them to turn up on their own tonight."

Kara sipped her water and let her gaze drift to Sam, and she asked tensely, "Did Zoe West call you?"

Her brother's eyes flashed with suspicion, and Sam knew the question was Kara's way of giving him permission to do what he planned to do, anyway. He saw Susanna wince, confirming what he already suspected—that she knew that something had happened between Kara and Sam at the Gordon Temple opening.

"Who's Zoe West?" Jack asked his sister. "Why would you know anyone who'd call Sam?"

Sam decided to get straight to the point. "Zoe West is a detective in Bluefield, Connecticut. She's doing a little solo investigating of Governor Parisi's death. She called me this afternoon."

Jack's arm dropped from Ellen's shoulder, and he straightened, drawing himself up to his full height. Behind him, Susanna sat on an armchair and exhaled, as if she'd been waiting for this particular shoe to drop. Maggie stayed at her aunt's side, Ellen next to her father. Jack kept his eyes on Sam.

"She was checking my story," Kara said.

Jack turned to her, his eyes steel. "What story?"

"Allyson Stockwell called me at the Gordon Temple opening and told me about Big Mike's death. I didn't say anything to Sam about it, but he sensed something was wrong. We went out for coffee." She untwisted her hands, some of the renewed color going out of her cheeks. "This heat. I don't know if I'll ever get used to it again."

Her brother didn't let up. "Kara, why would Zoe West want to know where you were when you heard about Parisi?"

"She's not convinced his death was an accident. If it was murder—well, whoever did it presumably would need to know he couldn't swim."

Jack hissed through clenched teeth, understanding the implication of what his sister was saying, just as Sam had when he'd heard it from the Bluefield detective. "Jesus Christ. You knew?"

Kara nodded. "He told me several years ago. It was his one secret."

"Detective West doesn't like the injured-bluebird theory," Sam said.

Susanna rose, gesturing to her daughters. "Let's try that new gadget that makes frothy milk. I think it's *café au lait* all around."

Mother and daughters retreated to the kitchen. Sam remained on his feet. Jack tossed the stack of cards and letters on the coffee table and swore once, viciously. Kara suddenly looked flushed and self-conscious, and Sam wondered if she was thinking, picturing, remembering everything about their hours together two weeks ago. He was, but he pushed the images out of his mind, not letting them distract him now that two children were missing.

He glanced at the top postcard, which was lying facedown, noted the graceful handwriting. Eleven-year-old Lillian Stockwell. *Dear Aunt Kara, I saw a snake today. I hate snakes!*

Anything could have happened to Allyson Lourdes Stockwell's children. Anything. Sam knew it, and he knew Jack did, too. And Kara. They were all in professions that taught them that ugly reality, but they didn't need knowledge or experience to tell them the obvious, only common sense. Two middle-schoolers were out there somewhere, thousands of miles from home. It didn't matter if they'd left the ranch on their own. They needed to be found.

"All right," Jack said heavily. "Tell me what's wrong with this damn bluebird theory."

Three

～❦❦❦～

Kara couldn't get out of her brother's house fast enough. She ignored the heat and her spinning head, her queasy stomach, and ran down the walk to her car parked on the street. She'd just been interrogated by two Texas Rangers, one her older brother, one a man she'd slept with in a moment of sheer insanity. The more they talked and got into Ranger mode, the less comfortable they were with the events in Connecticut. A near-fatal July Fourth bonfire, an accidental drowning and now two missing middle-schoolers, all involving the political elite of a wealthy New England state—none of it sat well with either Lieutenant Jack Galway or Sergeant Sam Temple.

Their instructions to Kara were simple: stay out of it.

Jack found the injured-bluebird theory unpersuasive. Was the pool deck wet from rain, someone swimming, watering the flowers? What was Big Mike's blood-alcohol level? Who else was at his rented house that day? Who owned the house? Kara had to explain Big Mike's passion for the Eastern bluebird, a native species that had lost ground to the more aggressive starling and English sparrow non-native species that were also cavity nesters and competed with bluebirds in an increasingly scarce habitat. Mike had been a big promoter of bluebird trails, uninterrupted networks of bluebird houses suitable for nesting, thus encouraging a resurgence in the bluebird population.

Her brother had listened to her, dumbfounded. "A bluebird with a broken leg ends up in the pool of a man who happens to have a thing for bluebirds and can't swim? I don't buy it," he'd said. "Not for one damn second."

It was obvious his fellow Texas Ranger didn't, either. Kara had tried to insert her own professional opinion into the conversation. "The police need proof of a crime."

Jack was unmoved. "It's not going to drop out of the sky into their laps. It's their job to investigate."

"They *are*—"

He'd turned his dark gaze onto her, but she'd never been intimidated by her brother. "Then why did a local detective check your story instead of one of the state detectives on the case?"

"Zoe West is new to Bluefield, but I understand she's like that. Very independent. I'd bet the state cops would slap her down hard if they knew she was meddling in their investigation. It doesn't mean a thing that they haven't called me themselves—I'm the last person anyone would suspect of killing Big Mike."

She'd hated even saying it. *Killing Big Mike.*

''Who else knew he couldn't swim?'' her brother asked.

''I don't know.''

Jack didn't like that, either. There wasn't anything about the events in Connecticut that he or Sam liked. ''No one wants the unsolved murder of a governor on their hands. I understand that. If it's an accident, it's over. Everyone can move on. What toes do the investigators have to step on even to look into this as a possible homicide?''

Kara saw his point, but disagreed with it and didn't mind saying so. ''If you and Sam were in their place, would you worry about what toes you stepped on? Not a chance. You wouldn't give up until you were satisfied that you knew exactly how Big Mike died. Give Connecticut law enforcement some credit. I think they're inclined to regard what happened as an accident because that's what the evidence suggests—''

''Then they know something we don't know or they're idiots.''

Sam concurred. ''Jack's right. This thing stinks.''

Kara knew it did, too, but she couldn't resist arguing with them. Maybe it was the attorney in her— maybe it just gave her something to do instead of worrying about Henry and Lillian. More likely, it kept her from looking at Sam the wrong way and alerting her brother to what they'd done after they'd had coffee two weeks ago.

''Lord,'' she muttered as she reached her car, ''no wonder I have a bad stomach.''

She'd forgotten about the two home pregnancy test

kits still in her tote bag when she'd dug out the kids' cards and letters. She could just imagine the scene if either man had spotted them.

"Kara—wait up." Susanna trotted down the walk to Kara's car, coming around to the driver's side. "Are you all right? That was a little rough in there. I'd like to strangle those two. You'd think you were a murder suspect."

"I'm fine, Susanna. Thanks. I put up with that kind of attitude all the time in my work. I didn't tell anyone Big Mike couldn't swim. I didn't push him into his pool. End of story. I just want to find Henry and Lillian."

"I know. But do you think Governor Parisi was murdered?"

"I'm trying hard not to get too far ahead of the facts. Anyway, I have no say—it's up to the investigators."

Her sister-in-law crossed her arms on her chest, the milky, humid darkness deepening the green in her eyes. "You hid it well tonight, Kara, but I know something happened between you and Sam at the Gordon Temple opening. Come on. I *know*. I admit he's one of my favorites, but he's not—well, you're not stupid. You know what Sam's like."

Sexy, straightforward, independent, dedicated to his work as a Texas Ranger. Ambitious. People liked him—Jack often said Sam could be governor if he ever wanted to quit the Rangers and go into politics. But who knew what Sam Temple wanted? Kara remembered him smiling at her over coffee, so unexpectedly easy to talk to. Her heart had jumped, and something more than superficial desire seemed to suffuse her mind and body, awaken her to a longing so deep and complicated she didn't know how to describe it.

Since that night, she'd tried to dismiss what she'd felt—what she'd done—simply as a by-product of the shock of learning about Big Mike's death. But it was more than that, only it didn't matter now. Whatever Sam Temple had been to her, those sixteen hours were over. She didn't have to understand what had happened between them because it would never be repeated. Their lovemaking was like some kind of out-of-time experience that would stay with her forever—she didn't hold it against him.

But her brother would.

"Sam's the classic dangerous man," Susanna went on.

"Yes, I know." Kara managed a smile. "I promised myself when I moved back here that I'd stay away from Texas Rangers. Having one for a brother is bad enough. They're all know-it-all rock heads."

Susanna laughed. "Well, if it's a question of rock heads, you fit right in, Kara. Honestly. *Sam?* What were you *thinking?*" She held up a hand, stopping Kara from answering. "Never mind. You weren't thinking."

"What happened was just as much my responsibility as Sam's."

"Jack won't see it that way."

An understatement. "He doesn't suspect—"

"No. He hasn't thrown Sam out a window." Susanna dropped her arms, shaking her head with affection. "You were away a long time, Kara. A part of Jack still sees you as his naive little sister, not an experienced, thirty-four-year-old professional."

Not so experienced when it came to sex, Kara thought, stifling a surge of awkwardness. At least Sam didn't know *how* inexperienced. "Jack can mind his own damn business. I haven't seen or heard from Sam since we—since the opening." She paused, the heat settling over her, making her feel claustrophobic, unable to breathe. "It's over."

Susanna eyed her sister-in-law knowingly, skeptically. "Nothing's over. I saw you two tonight, Kara. Don't kid yourself." She pulled open Kara's car door, touched her shoulder gently. "Go on. See about those kids. I hope they're back in their beds at the ranch by now. Jack's getting ready to saddle up and go over there—"

"He doesn't have to."

"I wouldn't try to tell him what he has to and doesn't have to do right now. He's on a tear."

"What about Sam?"

"Ditto, I would think."

Kara nodded, holding back sudden tears. Nausea burned up into her throat, cloying, bringing a tremble to her knees. Maybe it wasn't nausea—maybe it was fear. But she rallied, easing behind the wheel of her car. "They're scrappers, those two." She hesitated. "Susanna—I don't have to ask you to keep this conversation between us, do I?"

"Absolutely not. Jack's mad enough as it is about the kids and this bluebird theory."

It was a ninety-mile drive back to Austin, an hour

and a half for Kara to obsess on where Henry and Lillian could be, the dangers they could encounter, whatever the hell had possessed them to run off. The clear, deep water of the ranch's lake, the possibilities of rabid animals, hundreds of acres of trails and hills, reckless drivers, pedophiles—the list of dangers was endless. It didn't matter that they were smart, clever or rich, that they'd run off deliberately. They were *kids*.

And Sam and Jack were on the case. Her fault.

God, what was she to do about Sam Temple?

"Nothing," she told herself as she pulled into her short driveway. There was nothing for her to do because he was running as fast from their weekend together as she was.

She locked her car door and headed up the short walk to the front porch of the little Craftsman-style bungalow she'd bought in Hyde Park not long after she'd moved to Austin last September. It was just a few blocks from the historic house Susanna's parents were renovating, another few blocks from their art gallery. Kara liked the tree-lined streets and diversity of the neighborhood, so different from the 1830s house she'd rented in a Hartford suburb on the west side of the Connecticut River. She'd never bought property in Connecticut. That should have been a sign to her, but it wasn't—it took Big Mike to get her finally to admit it was time to go back home.

She'd met him in law school, on a weekend visit with Allyson and Lawrence to the Stockwell Farm. Her friends were deeply in love, the twenty-year age difference never seeming to matter to either of them.

Big Mike was already a force in Connecticut politics, wealthy, blueblood Lawrence Stockwell an unlikely friend and ally. Lawrence had guessed Kara and Mike Parisi would hit it off, and they had. When Big Mike said something factually incorrect about the law, Kara corrected him, arguing her point with all the hubris of a first-year law student—Mike insisted it was because she was a stubborn Texan, too. They became instant friends. He was her mentor on so many things, but not politics—she wasn't interested. She wouldn't even tell him whether she'd voted for him.

When June, Big Mike's wife, was charged with driving while intoxicated, he asked Kara to take the case, and agreed when she insisted she do it her way and he stay out of it. June admitted to her alcoholism and entered treatment. Mike stepped back and let his wife, whom he loved so much, take responsibility for her recovery. The incident could have undermined his friendship with Kara, but instead it deepened it.

June died six years ago, and not until he came out and told her did it occur to Kara that Big Mike was half in love with her.

He'd tried to make light of his admission. "Christ, don't tell me you're going to fall for Hatch, after all."

"Hatch? He doesn't have a thing for me."

"Ha."

Mike Parisi and Hatch Corrigan. Instead, she'd ended up in bed with Sam Temple.

This, she thought, was why she had her problems with men.

Mike had always known she'd go back to Texas.

"No bluebonnets in Connecticut," he'd say, then pull up every stupid stereotype he could think of about Texas and Texans, just to goad her—just to make her realize she was chronically homesick.

Maybe he'd known telling her he was in love with her would seal the deal, his way of making sure she didn't get cold feet. "You have demons to lay to rest, Kara," he'd told her, his worn, lived-in face without any hint of humor, "and you can't do it here. You need to go home."

In her months back in Texas, she'd only managed to stir up new demons. She hadn't laid any of the old ones to rest.

The night air was still hot, without even a hint of a breeze. Her little house had a decent front yard that needed reseeding and a front porch that needed scraping and painting—well, the place was a fixer-upper. She didn't know why she'd bought it. Why not a brand-new condo? She didn't have time to cook, never mind scrape paint and strip hardwood floors. The previous owners had kept the place clean and tidy, maintaining the original woodwork and floor plan, giving the house, as her Realtor had put it, potential.

She heard someone laughing down the street, music from a nearby house. She unlocked her front door, feeling less panicked. If she didn't hear anything more tonight, she'd call Allyson in the morning and drive out to the ranch herself. She knew she wouldn't sleep.

When she pushed open her door, the cool air from inside washed over her, but she stopped abruptly, hearing something. And when she glanced in her living room, there on the floor, eating microwave popcorn and watching television, were Henry and Lillian Stockwell.

The missing children of the governor of Connecticut looked up at Kara from their bags of popcorn. They were blond, blue-eyed and well mannered for eleven and twelve. Even sweaty and tired, they were obviously well off. They had on neat khaki shorts and polo shirts, and Lillian had tied a western-style red bandanna on the end of her single long braid, wisps of white-blond hair sticking out of it. Henry had dirt smudges on his chin.

He spoke first, his tone everyday casual. "Hi, Aunt Kara. We found your spare key under a flowerpot."

"*I* found it," Lillian said. "Henry was looking under the doormat."

"Does your mother know where you are?" Kara walked into the living room from the small entry and raked a hand through her hair, debating how to handle the situation. "How did you get here? What did you do, hide in a hay wagon? Steal a horse? Come on, you two. Fess up."

"We took the ranch shuttle to the Austin airport," Henry replied calmly. "It makes the trip twice a day, once in the morning, once in the afternoon."

"The shuttle? How? Didn't anyone ask questions?"

He shrugged. "We were prepared."

Lillian flipped her braid over one shoulder. "Henry arranged everything on the camp computer—he even printed out a form we needed. The driver thought we were meeting Mom. When we got to the airport, we pretended to see her and jumped out with our backpacks. It was easy.''

''It's not like we're little kids,'' her brother added.

Kara stared at the two of them. ''You mean you conned your way out here. At the very least you owe this poor driver an apology.'' She could think of two Texas Rangers who'd be interested in the kids' story. ''How did you get from the airport to my house?''

''Taxi,'' Henry said.

''When?''

''A little while ago.'' His chin was thrust up at her, as if he was daring her to try to pin him down to an exact time or tell him he'd done anything seriously wrong.

Kara paced in her small living room, its cozy fabrics and woods having no soothing effect on her. The kids' backpacks were leaning up against her couch, unzipped, water bottles and CD players poking out. Who wouldn't believe anything they said?

''Did the cab take you to my door?'' she asked.

Henry stretched out his legs and dipped his hand into his popcorn bag. ''We had him drop us off on the corner.''

That wouldn't divert Jack and Sam for half a second. ''You left a hell of a trail. I'm surprised I got here before the police. You know they're bound to be looking for you by now, don't you?'' She groaned at the mess these kids had made for themselves. And they no doubt thought they were so smart. ''You're calling your mother *right now*.''

Lillian glanced at her brother, and his mouth drew into a straight, grim line. "She knows we're here."

"No, she doesn't. I talked to her earlier—"

"Then she lied to you because someone was listening and she couldn't tell you the truth." Henry gazed up defiantly, Lillian following his lead. Given her years as a criminal defense attorney, Kara could sense fear behind defiance, bravado, loud, false protests of innocence—and she did now, with her godchildren. There was a quaver to his voice when Henry went on. "Mom told us we had to get out of the ranch as fast as possible and go to you. She couldn't come for us. We had to get away on our own. She knew we could do it."

"Henry. Lillian." Kara continued to pace, her head pounding. The smell of popcorn turned her stomach. "Your mother would not have asked you to run away like that. No one in their right mind would. She'd call me and have me go pick you up—"

"She *didn't*," Lillian said.

Kara sighed. "You two have put me in a hell of a position," she said, not unkindly.

"We know." Henry spoke softly, but his eyes—a clear, pale blue almost identical to his father's—grew wide and serious. "Aunt Kara, we're in trouble."

Lillian nodded, gulping for air. "Big trouble."

There was no bravado now, no pride in having slipped off to Austin on their own, with no one the wiser. Kara stopped pacing, staying on her feet as she waited for them to continue. Their fear was palpable.

"That's why Mom's acting so weird," Henry said.

Lillian reached into her backpack and withdrew the

first of the Harry Potter books, its cover greasy and
torn. She opened up to a page marked with a twig
and stared down at it, her braid flopping down her
front, hands greasy from the popcorn.

"Mom sent us a letter to give to you." Henry unzipped the outer pocket of his backpack and pulled
out a grimy water bottle, a CD player, two fruit-bar
wrappers, a compass and, finally, a limp, rumpled envelope. He handed it to Kara. She noticed it was
sealed, no postmark. He said, "She put it in with
other stuff she sent down for us. We didn't read it."

Kara sat on the edge of an overstuffed armchair a
few feet from her godchildren. She'd gone to a store
decorator with the dimensions and style of her living
room and said go to it. She liked to think she'd have
time one day to fuss with proper renovations and dec-
orating, but this was her life, she thought. Here she
was, listening to two middle-schoolers defend their
inexplicable actions.

Henry had always been precocious and quiet,
skilled at getting people to do what he wanted them
to do without them even realizing it. He wasn't ma-
nipulative so much as an effective negotiator, always
certain of what he wanted the outcome to be. In this
case, apparently, it was to convince his godmother
that he and his sister had run away with their mother's
permission because they all were in big trouble.

Kara recognized the heavy cream-colored stock and
dark green ink, the elegant lettering, of Allyson's personal stationery. Nice touch. The letter inside was
handwritten. Smart. If it had been typed, she'd have
nailed Henry and Lillian immediately. The handwriting was similar enough to Allyson's to pass initial
muster, and whoever had done the writing had even

thought to use her signature black fountain pen. Kara still wasn't willing to declare the letter genuine. She read skeptically:

Dear Kara,

I know this will come as a shock, but you're the only one I can trust right now. Henry and Lillian are in grave danger. We all are. I'll explain everything when I see you. Please take them to Stonebrook Cottage and wait for me there. Tell no one! Don't call me. It's too dangerous. I'll come to you. Please, Kara. I'm trusting you with my children. I have no other choice.

Please believe what they tell you and do as they ask. I'll see you soon.

Love,
Allyson

When she finished, Kara quelled any sense of panic or urgency she felt in response to the dramatic words she'd read. She had to stay calm and reasonably objective, and above all, she had to think. At the very least, she had a tricky situation and two troubled kids on her hands. But if the letter *was* genuinely from Allyson, it was a dangerous situation, confusing, mystifying, illogical...and, still, she had two troubled kids to see to.

Stonebrook Cottage was located at the end of a dirt road on the southern border of Stockwell Farm. Allyson owned it, and Kara had stayed there a number of times during her years up north.

"Henry, Lillian. Listen to me." Kara refolded the letter and placed it back in the envelope. "If this is a forgery, I'm not going to be happy about it. Do you understand?''

They nodded solemnly, their expressions serious, frightened, tired.

Kara was unmoved. These were her godchildren, and she loved them, but she couldn't let that lower her defenses. ''What grades did you get in English?'' she asked. ''You first, Henry.''

He gave her a blank stare. ''What?''

''Language arts, English, writing—what were your grades?''

''A's.''

''He got a D in math,'' Lillian said without looking up from her book.

''What did you get in language arts?'' Kara asked her.

''A's.''

Henry and Lillian are in grave danger. We all are.

The letter didn't make any sense. Allyson was the governor of Connecticut. If she thought her children were in danger down in Texas, why not call Texas authorities? Or send a couple of state troopers to fetch them? At least why not call Kara and ask her to intervene? Why take such a huge risk and have them sneak off to Austin on their own?

If she didn't want to involve law enforcement, Allyson was rich—she could hire a private bodyguard.

Nothing in Allyson's call had prepared her for this development. Her friend had sounded genuinely near panic.

Kara knew how to shoot and had taken a couple of self-defense classes, but that was it. She didn't have the training, the expertise, the weaponry or the mandate of the Texas Rangers, the Austin police. Allyson had to know the entire state of Texas—including Kara's brother—would be on alert for the two missing kids of a New England governor. How did she expect Kara to get them out of Texas on the sly? Allyson's actions defied logic.

For two middle-schoolers to engineer such an elaborate plan and think it made sense—that might not defy logic. The trauma of Big Mike's death, homesickness, isolation and a natural sense of drama could have gotten Henry and Lillian plotting, but there had to be more. Something else had to be going on.

What?

Suddenly hot and frustrated, Kara shot to her feet and turned the air-conditioning up a notch. She heard it hum, felt the rush of cooler air. It was almost ten o'clock. Eleven o'clock in New England. She recalled her brief conversation with Allyson. "I have a million people around right now, so I can't talk, but Kara—please, keep an eye out. I know you're a ways from the ranch, but maybe they'll turn up."

Was that a hint?

Not bloody likely, Kara thought. Henry and Lillian's story had to be bogus. It was the only reasonable conclusion, and it meant their mother and the people at the dude ranch were still worried sick about them. It meant the searches for them would continue. It meant all hell would be breaking loose in Texas and Connecticut until someone tracked them to their godmother's doorstep—or until Kara called her brother and told him what was going on.

Lillian yawned, her book looking heavy on her skinny thighs.

"Don't you two want to call your mother and tell her you arrived safely?" Kara asked.

Henry seemed to know she was trying to trip him up. "She told us not to call. You're supposed to take us to Stonebrook Cottage and wait for her there. Doesn't she say that in the letter?"

He'd know if he wrote it, wouldn't he? Kara tried to keep her skepticism from showing. Her godchildren had gone through a lot of trouble to get her to believe them—it was important to them. She needed to be very careful about how she unraveled their story.

Lillian lifted her thin shoulders. "We're just doing what Mom told us to do."

Kara returned to her armchair, sinking into its soft cushions. She was still hot, the cooler air making little difference, and she was tired and torn about how to proceed.

One thing she knew for certain. The kids' story had a million holes.

"Aunt Kara, you're a lawyer, right?"

She narrowed her eyes on her godson, wondering what was coming next. "Yes, why?"

"I was just making sure. If you're a lawyer, that means everything we tell you is confidential. You can't tell anyone. Right?"

Kara stared at him. "Henry, I'm a lawyer, but I'm not *your* lawyer."

"But that's why Mom sent us to you! She said we can trust you because you're our lawyer. Aunt Kara, you *can't* tell anyone! We *trusted* you!" He balled his hands into fists, his mouth set, his face screwed up with determination. "We wouldn't have said anything if we didn't think you were our lawyer."

"You mean you told me this whole story believing I was representing you? Henry, Lillian—I'm your godmother. I can't be your attorney! Well, I can be, but I'd need explicit permission from your mother, or a court would have to appoint a guardian ad litem for you and then you could hire me." Kara groaned, her head screaming now. "I'm *not* your lawyer, so get that out of your heads."

Henry was near panic. "But that's the only reason we told you—"

"Hold on—relax." Kara got back to her feet, wondering who was in control of this situation, her or the kids. "If you told me this whole tale believing I was acting as your attorney and it was privileged information, then that's what it is. Privileged information. I can't tell anyone."

"We're not fugitives." Lillian was blinking back tears, clearly exhausted. "We didn't break any laws."

Kara studied the two tired, frightened children. Something was wrong. Their story didn't add up, but they hadn't run off just because they were bored. Maybe Big Mike's death was too much for them— maybe they'd overreacted to innocent events and created some wild scenario involving secrets and grave danger and were so wrapped up in it that, at this point, they couldn't distinguish fiction from reality.

Regardless of their motives, however real their fear, they were here now, and they were her obligation. Her *sole* obligation. Nothing else mattered. Connecticut politics, bluebird theories, concerned authorities in two states, not even their mother. If Allyson wrote the letter, she had to be out of her mind. If she didn't write the letter, she would expect Kara to do her best to sort out the situation and get Henry and Lillian safely home as soon as possible.

"We could call your mom on her cell phone—"

"*No!*" Henry yelled in panic, and Lillian almost cried. "We *can't* call her. She told us not to call. We're supposed to have you take us to Stonebrook Cottage and wait. Aunt Kara, *please*, you *have* to believe us!"

"All right, all right. Look, you two need baths and a good night's sleep. I only have one bedroom, but you can share my bed. I'll sleep out here on the couch." Kara hugged them, one arm around each one, as they got up from the couch. "Let's get some rest and come at this fresh in the morning."

Henry looked up at her, his thin face etched with concern. "Then what?"

"I don't know, but I'm on your side. Okay? Do not doubt that for one second." She thought a moment, the bare bones of a plan coming together. One way or another, these kids were going back to Connecticut. "Unless I have good reason to do otherwise—you tell me it's a forgery, or I find out by other means or get new information—I'm going to do what it says in your mother's letter and get you to Stonebrook Cottage." She thought of the trail they'd left and didn't imagine they had much time if they were going to keep this little adventure among themselves and out of the public eye. But she needed to think. Staying a step ahead of Jack and Sam now that she'd enlisted their help—and aroused their suspicions—wouldn't be easy. "Don't be surprised or scared if I have to wake you up in the middle of the night."

Lillian's eyes widened. "Why would you have to do that?"

"Her brother's a Texas Ranger." Henry whispered as if the place was bugged. "Everyone at the ranch probably got nervous when they couldn't find us and called the police or something."

His sister gasped. "Oh! Does *that* make us fugitives?"

"It doesn't matter. Aunt Kara will help us. Big Mike used to say she was the best defense lawyer he ever knew."

"Big Mike exaggerated," Kara said. "Go on, you two. Get cleaned up and get some sleep. I'm not worried about my brother."

Well, she was, but she was more worried about Sam Temple. He'd made it plain he hadn't liked the call from Zoe West. When he found out the missing Stockwell kids sneaked a ride to Austin—and he would—he'd be in full Texas Ranger, by-the-book law enforcement mode. Kara didn't object to him doing his job, but his interests weren't necessarily compatible with her sense of obligation to her godchildren. She needed to get them back to their mother as soon, and as quietly, as possible.

There was nothing by-the-book about this situation.

She led Henry and Lillian down a short hall to her bedroom and the bathroom. Lillian was the first in the tub, Henry next, and twenty minutes later, the lights were out and they were asleep.

Kara cleaned up their popcorn mess and flopped onto the couch, rereading the letter purportedly from Allyson. *You're the only one I can trust right now...don't call me...I have no other choice.*

It had to be phony.

And Henry not mentioning attorney-client privilege until *after* he and Lillian had told Kara everything—what a ploy.

"Smart-ass. He knew what he was doing."

She ground her teeth and placed her palm on her lower abdomen, but her nausea had finally abated. It had to be seafood tacos, the heat, her still-palpable grief over Big Mike's sudden death—she wasn't pregnant. She tried to remember any slips she and Sam had made, but stopped herself short because it entailed replaying every move, every caress, and that was pure torture.

She thought of her towheaded godchildren asleep down the hall. They were so damn young. How could Allyson have sent them on such a crazy trip?

She didn't.

But something was wrong—very wrong. Henry and Lillian weren't bad kids. They wouldn't deliberately scare their mother and manipulate their godmother if they weren't frightened themselves. But of what?

Kara knew she had to think. She didn't have much time, and she had to get this one right. Too much was at stake.

Four

⧉

Fatigue clawed at Sam and had already had an adverse effect on his judgment—after all, he was in Austin, not home in bed—but he continued up Kara's walkway and onto her porch, anyway. A light was on. It was almost midnight, but he doubted he was getting her out of bed. Not that it mattered.

Henry and Lillian Stockwell had apparently conned their way to the Austin airport. Now, why could that be? It wasn't to fly. No flights had taken off with them on board, and their mother was up in Connecticut still sounding the alarm.

Just as Sam started to ring the bell, Kara pulled open the front door. "Sam—scare the hell out of me, why don't you?" She held up a pottery vase and smiled. "Consider yourself lucky. I was going to bonk you on the head. I don't normally get visitors at midnight."

"You don't own a gun?"

"No way. I hate guns." She hadn't changed out of the work clothes she'd worn down to San Antonio earlier in the evening. Sam noticed her crisp blouse was a little rumpled. She set her vase on a small hall table. "Do you have news? I haven't heard a word."

She made no move to invite him in. Everything he knew about body language—and Kara Galway—told him she was trying to keep this exchange simple and short and get rid of him as fast as possible. There could be innocuous reasons for that, sensible ones that had nothing to do with the Stockwell kids.

But he was playing this one his way. "Henry and Lillian conned the shuttle driver at the ranch to take them to the Austin airport."

Kara frowned. "Why on earth would they do something like that?"

Sam rested back on his heels, eyeing Kara. Something wasn't adding up, but she was an experienced attorney, accustomed to not tipping her hand to the other side. And somehow, he'd become the other side. He'd felt it the second she opened the door. "The Austin police are checking with the airport, taxis, buses. The kids told the shuttle driver they were meeting their mother. They claimed to see her and took off. He didn't realize anything was wrong until he got back to the ranch."

"Allyson knows? Someone called her?"

"The people at the ranch. Jack talked to her brother-in-law, Hatch Corrigan. He's some kind of adviser?"

Kara nodded, her dark eyes distant, unreadable. "He must be having fits. I can't imagine what's gotten into Henry and Lillian—" She sighed, breaking off. "What's your involvement? Austin isn't your jurisdiction."

"Wrong. All of Texas is my jurisdiction."

"That's not what I meant. I meant you're stationed in San Antonio—" She stopped herself, squaring her shoulders as she eyed him coolly. "Sam, is this an official visit?"

"Do you mean if you lie to me can I arrest you?" He took a step toward her, aware he was even more intense than usual. She drew back, as if a little shocked at his closeness, but he didn't ease off. "You opened your door loaded for bear. Why?"

"For God's sake, Sam, it's the middle of the night."

"You knew it wasn't an intruder. Your door has glass panels. You saw me."

She took a breath, the light from behind her casting shadows over her face. He saw her intensity, her determination, and knew she had no intention of easing off, either. "Okay. I didn't want you to think I open my door to near strangers unprotected."

As if he was a near stranger and a vase would have protected her. Sam decided not to push his point. "Why didn't you tell me about Governor Parisi's death?"

His question seemed to catch her off guard. He saw her swallow, remembered kissing her smooth throat. She averted her eyes. "I couldn't get the words out. It was as if saying it out loud would have made it real."

"Kara, we were together for a long time."

Her dark eyes lifted to him, met him dead-on. "I know what you must think. It was a weird weekend. Let's just forget it."

"I don't regret what happened between us."

"Neither do I." She took a breath, dropping her hand from the door. "Look, it's late, and I'm worried about Henry and Lillian—"

"I smell popcorn."

"What? Oh—oh, yeah. I didn't have any dinner."

Sam leaned toward her, making no secret that he was trying to peer into her living room. "You're not going to invite me in?"

"Not without a warrant, Sergeant Temple." She smiled, but there was no mistaking her seriousness of purpose. He wasn't getting past her. She had her vase, and she had the law.

"Kara, if you have something to tell me, get it out on the table. Now."

No impact. "It's been a long day," she said smoothly. "We're both worried about Henry and Lillian. So, let's not do this. You turn around and go do your Texas Ranger thing, and I'll let you know if I need you."

He had to remember she was a respected attorney. If she was afraid or troubled, she could handle it. She knew where to turn for help.

She also knew how to skirt the truth with him if it suited her. She'd come right up to the line—if not cross it.

Sam placed one foot on the threshold and narrowed his eyes on her. He saw her lips part and knew she was thinking he might kiss her. He was tired enough that it seemed a natural thing to do, kissing Kara Galway in the doorway of her little house, never mind that she was trying to get rid of him—hiding something from him.

Instead, he tapped her chin with one finger. "I wouldn't cross me if I were you."

She shrugged, unintimidated. "Fine. I won't cross you."

"If you know anything about the Stockwell kids—"

"It's a family matter, Sam, not a law enforcement matter. It's sure as hell not a matter for the Texas Rangers. You're supposed to assist in major criminal investigations. This isn't one."

"Are you sure you never told anyone Mike Parisi couldn't swim?"

"Go away, Sam. I'm tired."

"When did you find out? Did he tell you for a specific reason or did he just let it slip? What was he to you? What was he to your godchildren?"

He didn't expect her to answer his questions. He was simply demonstrating how having the runaway kids of the new governor of Connecticut on the loose in Texas was his business if he decided it was.

Not that it had any effect on her. "Give it up, Sergeant Temple. Mike's death and Henry and Lillian skipping out of summer camp are at most only peripherally related."

He stepped back onto the porch, the hot night air mingling with the cool air coming from her house. He remembered her soft, white sheets, one of Eva Dunning's hand sewn quilts hanging on the wall above her bed. *Kara, Kara.* What had he done?

He pressed two fingers to his lips, then touched them to hers. "I went too fast with you. I'm sorry."

"Sam—"

But he straightened, removing any hint of softness from his expression. "If those kids don't turn up at the airport, I'll be back." He started down the porch steps, his back to her as he added, "You can make more popcorn."

Kara locked her front door behind her and stood in the foyer, her head pounding. A suspicious Texas Ranger was just what she needed. *Now* what? Sam or the Austin police would find the cabdriver who'd taken Henry and Lillian to Hyde Park. Two rich kids on their own—the driver would remember them.

The effects of her long day ate at her nerves, threw her off her normal manner of doing things. She wasn't one to panic. When she was nine years old, she'd had to sit motionless next to her dying mother while they waited for the paramedics. Ranger Temple wasn't getting under her skin. She wouldn't let it happen.

Except it already had. Her reaction to him on her doorstep had been instantaneous and overpowering, a mix of attraction and desire, frustration, a touch of embarrassment, even fear, although not for herself. Having a tight-lipped Texas Ranger at her house gave weight to what Henry and Lillian had done in running off from the dude ranch, what their lives had become now that Big Mike was gone and their mother was governor.

Tell no one…I'm trusting you with my children…

Kara shook off the words in the letter. Replaying

them in her head would get her nowhere, and it was her own damn fault she had Sam on her case. She'd given his name to Zoe West in Connecticut, figuring it couldn't hurt to have a Texas Ranger vouching for her whereabouts. She hadn't expected the Bluefield detective to go to the trouble of checking out her story and actually calling him.

Then, after Allyson had told her about Henry and Lillian, Kara immediately drove to San Antonio in a panic. It wasn't just to see her brother and Susanna and get their moral support. She'd half hoped Sam would be there.

She'd more than half hoped.

She pulled out sheets in the hall linen closet, figuring she might as well make up the couch and at least get some sleep before she had to deal with Sam. Or should she wake up the kids and clear out before he got back here? She couldn't think straight. She started back to the living room with her armload of sheets.

"Aunt Kara!" Lillian called in a panicked whisper, crab-walking up the short hall from the bedroom. Her face was ashen. "Get down! He can see you!"

"Lillian, good God—"

"Get down!"

Doing as she asked, Kara crouched down with her sheets and made her way to Lillian. "What is it, Lil?" The frightened girl was barely breathing. "Did you have a nightmare? Did you see my friend Sam—"

"It's the man…" She faltered, unable to speak. Purple splotches spread across her pale cheeks as she gulped in more and more air, not breathing out.

"Lillian…honey, you need to hold your breath for a couple of seconds. You're not exhaling. If you get too much oxygen into your bloodstream, you'll pass out."

She raised her huge blue eyes to Kara and dutifully held her breath for two seconds, then blew out a sharp breath and blurted, "It's the man from the ranch!"

"What man? Where?"

"Outside. I saw him. Henry said we shouldn't tell you about him until we get to Stonebrook Cottage, but he's *here*. Mom doesn't even know about him."

Kara could feel Lillian's near hysteria infecting her. Wisps of blond hair matted the girl's damp forehead and temples, beads of perspiration formed on her freckled nose. Kara steadied herself. "Lillian, where? Where is this man?"

"Out front. He's in a car. I saw him from the bedroom window."

"Are you sure? This is the city. There are lots of cars—"

"It's *him*. Come on, I'll show you." She tugged on Kara's arm, but when Kara tried to stand up, Lillian gasped and dug her fingernails into her godmother's wrists, almost drawing blood. *"Stay down."*

Whatever was going on with these kids, Kara thought, it was serious and undoubtedly more than she could handle alone. She set the sheets on the floor and tried to maintain an outward air of calm, if only to reassure Lillian, who was scared out of her wits. The girl's hyperventilating wasn't an act. Kara had seen enough faked fear and panic attacks—on the part of witnesses, clients, even young attorneys before a big trial—to recognize the difference.

Staying low, she followed Lillian to the bedroom. Henry was on his knees at the window, peering over the sill in the dark, an angle of light from outside catching his pale face. He silently motioned for Kara and his sister to join him.

"I wasn't going to tell you," he whispered when Kara crouched next to him. "I didn't want to scare you, but Lillian wouldn't listen. He's out there."

"Who, Henry?" Kara asked.

"Do you see the black car? That's him."

She looked up past the neighbor's house, craning her neck, and saw a black sedan parked on the street. Someone was in the front seat, but she couldn't tell if it was a man or woman.

"Look," Lillian said, kneeling down on Kara's other side, "he's smoking a cigarette."

Kara frowned. "I can't see the cigarette never mind who's in the car. How do you two know he's from the ranch?"

"He got out of the car a few minutes ago," Henry said. "He stared right at your house. Lillian and I got a good look at him, didn't we, Lil?"

"Uh-huh. He was under the streetlight."

"Okay, I believe you," Kara said. "So who is he?"

Henry sat down on the floor, leaning back against the wall under the window with his knees tucked up under his chin. Kara noticed a smattering of small scratches and bruises on his tanned bare legs, a twelve-year-old at summer's end. How had his and Lillian's summer come to this?

"We saw him watching us at the ranch," he said. "Well, I did, and I warned Lillian to look out for him. He showed up the first of this week."

"Are you sure he wasn't an employee? He didn't introduce himself—"

"Sometimes he had on a disguise," Lillian said. "I saw him with a fake mustache. I thought he looked stupid."

A fake mustache. It could have been another man altogether and Lillian had just leaped to the conclusion it was her strange man in a disguise. "Did you ever talk to him?" Kara asked.

Both kids shook their heads. "That would have been dumb," Henry said.

"Yeah," Lillian said, "what if he dragged us into the woods and chopped our heads off?"

Kara winced, but realized Lillian was serious. Bad things could happen if you talked to strange men. Why hadn't it occurred to them that bad things could happen if you lit out on your own?

But Kara stuck to the issue at hand. "Did this man ever approach you, ever try to talk to you?"

"No." Henry was remarkably calm. "He just watched us, usually from where no one else could see him. I asked one of my friends who he was, but the man disappeared—it's like he knew I was checking him out."

Kara peered out at the parked car and wondered if the stress of the past weeks—the isolation they'd felt after Mike's death and their mother becoming governor, coupled with the unfamiliarity of being on a Texas dude ranch—had pushed these two bright, imaginative kids over the edge. They had to be making this stuff up.

"You didn't tell your counselors about him?"

"I wanted to," Lillian said, "but Henry wouldn't let me."

He pursed his lips, as if contemplating the logic of his decision. "I was scared to say anything. Then Mom told us to come here. I *knew* something was wrong."

"Lillian says your mother doesn't know about this guy."

"We didn't want to worry her. She was already worried enough."

Kara tried to follow his thinking, but he was twelve years old. "Okay—are you *sure* this is the same guy?"

"Yes," he and Lillian said simultaneously.

They argued over everything—the rules of a card game, television shows, favorite rock groups, where to sit in a restaurant. Kara had put a stop to their bickering enough times to realize that agreeing, without hesitation, about the man outside had to mean something. She sighed, wishing she could be neutral and objective where Henry and Lillian Stockwell were concerned. If they could successfully manipulate anyone, it'd be her. She loved them unconditionally, and they knew it.

Sam would want to know about the man in the black sedan.

Both kids were back on their knees, spying out the

window. The car's headlights popped on, catching them by surprise. Lillian dived to the floor, sobbing and gulping for air, and Henry ducked down low and went stone-still, as if any movement might give away his position.

Kara touched Lillian's trembling shoulder. "Stay here. I'll be right back. *Trust me.*"

She ran up the hall into the foyer, tore open her door and shot out onto the porch, catching the car as it moved up the street. It had a Texas tag, but she couldn't make it out or tell if the car was a rental.

She debated calling Sam. Her brother. 911. Never mind the damn letter—never mind Henry and Lillian's irrational fear. This was her decision to make. She was the prevailing adult here.

When she returned to her bedroom, her godchildren were hoisting their backpacks onto their shoulders, grim-faced, as if they knew exactly what Kara was considering doing and now they had to go find someone else to help them.

She sighed. "What are you two doing?"

"We're getting out of here." Henry spoke calmly, seriously. "He'll come back. We don't want him to find us—or you. We have no right to endanger you, Aunt Kara."

She ignored a sudden, overwhelming wave of nausea and forced herself to focus on the problem at hand. These kids were on the verge of spinning out of control. She had to do something, say something, that would settle them down.

Sam would be back before long. Wouldn't they feel safe with a Texas Ranger?

Henry straightened, as if what they did next was entirely up to him. "Come on, Lil. Let's get out of here. If Aunt Kara won't come with us, we'll just have to manage on our own. We can do it."

Lillian seemed less confident, but nodded.

"Listen," Kara said, "there's someone I can call—"

Henry shook his head, adamant. "No." His face had turned a grayish white, and he started to shake uncontrollably, his self-control crumbling. He stiffened visibly, but the shaking didn't ease. Tears rolled down his cheeks, shining in the light from the street. "Aunt Kara...*please,* you have to believe us. We're in danger."

If they were in danger, there was no question she should call Sam, but she'd never get that far. The kids would bolt. They'd skipped out on the dude ranch and made it all the way to damn Austin on their own— they'd skip out on her, too.

She still had to deal with the letter from Allyson. Did she believe Allyson had written it? Did it even matter at this point? It demonstrated what Henry and Lillian believed was at stake.

And if they didn't release her from attorney-client privilege, there wasn't much she could tell Sam, anyway.

"All right." Kara tried to sound decisive, although her plan was still sketchy, in its early stages—and crazy, every bit of it. "You're going to have to trust me and let me make some decisions. I'll get you to Stonebrook Cottage and your mother, okay? I'll do what she says in her letter."

They nodded, Henry brushing at the tears on his thin cheeks. Lillian was solemn, very pale.

Kara hugged them both, squeezing hard, smelling the rancidness of their fear. The hell with everything. She had to get them safely to Stonebrook Cottage and their mother and stay one step ahead of anyone who might be after them—no matter the reason, good, bad, real or imagined.

She couldn't believe she was cutting out on Sam Temple, Texas Ranger.

She smiled suddenly, and she noticed how reassured her godchildren looked now that she was taking charge—and they were getting their way. Well, what else could she do?

"Let me throw a few things together," she told them. "Then we're out of here."

Five

Pete Jericho regarded the stripped logs piled on the edge of the gravel pit with satisfaction. He'd always liked work he could see getting done. Finish one job, move on to the next. Hard, physical work suited him. He squinted up at the hazy August sky, the humidity on the rise, seeping in from the south. He had a lot of work to get done before the first killing frost. Maybe keeping himself busy would put in check his anger and frustration—his sense of loss since Allyson had stepped up to the governorship.

Stupid to fall in love with her in the first place. He'd known it years ago, when he'd see her and Lawrence up at the Stockwell place, around town. She was a few years older than Pete, but that never mattered to him. After Lawrence died, Allyson was so overwhelmed and quiet, and Pete realized what he felt wasn't just an infatuation. He was truly in love with her.

But Madeleine Stockwell had recognized it before Allyson did—maybe even before he did—and that was his undoing.

He started back to his truck, knowing there was no point in trying to blame Madeleine for his current predicament. Even without the prison record, he suspected Allyson would want to keep their relationship secret. He was the blue-collar guy down the road. He lived on the family homestead and worked with his father chopping wood. The Jericho family had been working their land for seven generations. They used to dairy farm, but now they scraped together a living cutting wood, growing Christmas trees, leasing hay fields to the few dairy farmers left in the area, raising chickens and sheep. Bea Jericho, Pete's mother, handled the chickens and sheep. She was talking about getting some goats and making her own goat cheese, something Pete's father wasn't too keen on.

But these days they earned the bulk of their money managing other people's property, the trophy country houses rich part-time residents built on ten-acre mini-estates carved out of land once owned by people like Charlie and Bea Jericho.

Pete knew his parents didn't know about him and Allyson. Otherwise they'd have said something. Just as well, because it looked as if he'd been dumped; she didn't even plan to call and tell him. He was supposed to figure it out. An affair with Allyson Lourdes Stockwell, lieutenant governor, was difficult enough. Now that she was governor, it was impossible.

Six months in prison eight years ago for a stupid barroom brawl would end up costing him the woman he loved.

He hadn't been involved with Allyson then. Madeleine Stockwell had done her job and made sure he knew her son's widow deserved better than a Jericho. She nipped any romantic intentions on his part in the bud. He remembered that bright, cold afternoon when Madeleine stood out on the patio of the only home she'd known since marrying Edward Stockwell and told Pete he had no ambition, no real prospects. "You'll make a living. You're a Jericho. That's what you do. But it's all that you do."

She knew he had a "crush" on Allyson, a choice of words designed to further diminish him. And if he loved her, he would understand it was in her best interests that he never act on his feelings.

Furious, humiliated, he hadn't gone home and hit the heavy bag or chopped wood. Instead, he'd headed to O'Reilly's Pub in town and intervened when an idiot he'd known from high school harassed a woman. Words were exchanged. Fists flew. A couple of beer bottles. He ended up with torn knuckles and a broken nose, the idiot a cut on his jaw that required five stitches. Pete figured the score was even. O'Reilly went along. He wasn't looking to see an account of a brawl in his pub in the local papers, and he hated cops and lawyers.

Walter Harrison thought otherwise. He was an off-duty cop who happened to witness the brawl. He made a wimpish attempt to break it up, then pushed to have Pete arrested on felony assault charges.

Stories changed. The woman, who was from out of town, said she wasn't really being harassed and begged Pete not to get involved. Not true. The former classmate said Pete threw the first punch and smashed the first beer bottle and was generally out of control. Walter corroborated their versions. O'Reilly stayed out of it. Pete was convinced, then and now, and so was his father, that Madeleine Stockwell had her hand in it. A few greased palms, a little intimidation. A criminal record would make any romantic relationship between him and her daughter-in-law that much more unlikely.

He knew he was screwed, but Mike Parisi, a man who understood barroom brawls and the ways of Madeleine Stockwell, recommended Kara Galway, said she was a hell of a lawyer. Big Mike spent a lot of time in Bluefield even after Lawrence's death, wooing Allyson into state politics; he'd always gotten along with the Jerichos.

Recommending Kara hadn't worked out, at least in Pete's estimation. He'd expected her to find a way to bring out the truth. Instead, she suggested he take a plea bargain when it was offered. The odds were against him if he went to trial, she explained. If he was convicted of felonious assault, he could count on spending three years in a nasty state prison. Plead guilty to a misdemeanor, and he was in and out of the local jail in six months.

Pete took the deal. He didn't like it, but he took it. He supposed it was unfair of him to blame Kara, but he knew he'd lost any hope of having Allyson in his life the minute he heard the jailhouse doors shut behind him. It was as if Madeleine Stockwell had planned it that way.

Then last fall, he ran into Allyson when he was delivering wood up to the barn she and Lawrence had

converted. She was alone, the kids off for the weekend with friends, and it was like two old friends suddenly seeing each other for the first time, that old
cliché. Since then, they met each other when they
could, content to watch television together when she
was at the barn alone on weekends. Pete would sneak
through the woods so Madeleine and Hatch wouldn't
find out. That was no longer possible now with round-
the-clock security.

And a secret affair wasn't what he wanted. It
couldn't last. He didn't want it to. He wanted to tell
everyone—the whole world—that he was in love with
Allyson Lourdes Stockwell. But it was different for
her with her high-profile life, her responsibilities, the
commitments she'd made.

Madeleine was right, after all. He and Allyson just
weren't meant to be. He was a goddamn jailbird. It
stuck to him like rot.

He hadn't heard from Allyson since Big Mike
drowned. Now that she was governor, she was probably wishing she'd never gotten involved with him in
the first place. She tried to pretend she wasn't ambitious, but she was—he liked that about her. She sometimes ranked on her abilities, her self-doubt always a
surprise to him, because he believed in her to his core.

Charlie Jericho drove up on his old tractor, and
Pete waved at his father, a bandy-legged man in his
early sixties. He and Madeleine Stockwell had been
feuding for as long as Pete could remember. Lately
she was mad at him about the gravel pit, accusing
him of having dug it on the border of Jericho-
Stockwell property just to goad her. Charlie said he

wouldn't go to such trouble, it just happened to be where the gravel was located. The gravel pit would play out in three years and the land would be restored. She'd just have to live with it.

Charlie climbed off the tractor, wearing his habitual navy work pants and pocket T-shirt. "Madeleine wants us to deliver her cordwood early this year. Says to make sure it's super-dry. Like we've ever given her green wood. The old bat." He coughed, pulling out a pack of cigarettes as unconsciously as someone else might grab a handkerchief. "We should charge her double for being such a pain in the ass. Call it combat pay."

Pete laughed. "Why not? She keeps saying she gets screwed by the locals. It'd give her something real to bitch about."

His father tapped out a cigarette and stuck it in his mouth, fished out his lighter. He had a bad, wet cough, but he had no intention of quitting. He liked to smoke, he'd say, and you have to die of something. When Big Mike drowned, Charlie Jericho had said, "See, would it have made a damn bit of difference if he'd had a two-pack-a-day habit?"

The cordwood was still drying in the August sun. They'd cut the trees over the winter, trimmed them in early spring, before the leaves sprouted, then dragged the logs out here with a tractor and cut them into eight-foot lengths, setting them up on wooden platforms, off the wet ground, to dry. When the weather cooled off after Labor Day, they'd cut them into cordwood, mostly sixteen-inch lengths. It used to be they could sell four-foot lengths and people would cut them down themselves, but that wasn't the case anymore. Some people even had Pete stack it for them. Hauling it to the wood box was enough of a chore, he guessed.

"Madeleine pays on time, I'll say that for her." Charlie puffed on his cigarette and grinned. "And her checks never bounce. Listen, I was out talking to the gravel guys this morning and noticed somebody's been up on the ridge above the pit. Hunters, kids. Looks like they've built some kind of platform in an oak. If it's kids, it's dangerous up there. One wrong slip, and they're in the pit. That sand and rock is unstable."

"I'll check it out and dismantle whatever's there," Pete said.

"Good. I don't want anyone getting hurt."

Pete nodded. "It's a long way to get help."

"A short way to the nearest lawyer. People get hurt, they start thinking lawsuits."

"Pop," Pete admonished.

Charlie waved a hand and climbed back on his tractor, his cigarette hanging from his lower lip. He could have walked out here, Pete thought. The exercise would have done his father good, but Charlie Jericho's attitude toward exercise was similar to his attitude toward quitting smoking—not for him.

After he finally puttered off on his tractor, Pete headed across the barren landscape of the gravel pit. No one was working it today. They'd finish taking out the last load of sand and rock this fall, then restore the land in the spring. Right now it looked awful, a gaping hole dug out of the hillside, a desolate stretch of stripped ground, with huge piles of sand and rock, the dump truck, backhoe, rock-crusher and sifter all idle today. Pete could picture what it would look like in a few years, when nature had reclaimed the land.

He made his way into the light, untouched woods on the edge of the pit and walked up the hill, the steep, unstable descent into the gravel pit to his right. He pushed through ferns and ducked under the low branches of pine and hemlock, staying in the shade of small maple and oaks. This was the northernmost corner of Jericho land. Their house was back in the other direction, past the gravel pit, through the fields to the main road. The endless acres of Stockwell land stretched out over the rolling hills to the north.

Straight down the hill, to the south and west, the mini-estates started. Charlie had fits every time he saw evidence that the estate owners had been through the backwoods with their horses. He kept talking about putting up No Trespassing signs, a bother and an expense he'd never considered before and probably wouldn't at all if the worst offenders hadn't plastered their own property with them. "What's mine is theirs, and what's theirs is theirs," Charlie would grumble.

Pete came to an old oak, the tallest tree on top of the hill, so close to the near-vertical edge of the gravel pit, some of its massive roots were exposed to the sand and erosion. A crude ladder of skinny, split cordwood led up the trunk on the safer side, above a cushion of fallen leaves. Saplings of maple, beech and ash grew densely on the south side of the hill, which led down to the mini-estate Mike Parisi had rented for the summer.

High in the tree, Pete spotted a platform tree house, a half-finished mishmash of old boards.

Kids. Had to be.

He climbed up the crude ladder, which barely held his weight, and at the top, grabbed hold of a branch above his head and swung onto the platform. It was sturdier than he'd expected, built across two branches above a V in the tree, maybe four feet by four. Some-one had left behind a rusted hammer, a few nails, a water bottle and an old pair of binoculars.

A white polo shirt hung stiffly from a branch. Pete plucked it off and noted the label in the collar. *Henry Stockwell.*

He grinned. There was hope for the kid yet if he was building tree houses. Lillian was a scrapper—she'd probably helped. They must have worked on it over the summer.

The binoculars were grimy from exposure to the elements. He cleaned the lenses on his shirt and trained them on the view. Nothing much to see down in the gravel pit, but he supposed Henry and Lillian would have enjoyed watching the work going on there. He turned, the view to the southwest much more impressive with the faroff rolling hills and end-less summer sky.

He brought the binoculars down lower, focusing the lenses on what he quickly realized was the roof of Big Mike's rented house. He scoped out what all he could see, adjusting the lenses.

"Jesus Christ."

Pete suddenly felt cold, as if it were midwinter instead of midsummer.

With the binoculars, Henry and Lillian had a limited but unimpeded view of the swimming pool. The kids could have been up here with their snacks and water bottles, amusing themselves with their binoculars, when Big Mike fell into the deep end of his swimming pool. They had been in Bluefield that weekend.

Had they seen their friend fight for his life?

Jesus, had they watched him drown?

Even if they saw him go into the water, they'd never have made it down the hill in time to save him.

What did they do? Run to help him? Watch, paralyzed with horror?

Why hadn't they said anything? But Pete had a feeling he knew. If they saw what happened, the police would want to talk to them, answer any nagging questions they had about how the governor had died. Instinctively, Henry and Lillian must have understood that no one, except perhaps their mother's worst enemies, would want to hear that the children of the new governor had witnessed his death.

Pete swore to himself and swung down to the crude ladder.

He was jumping the gun, he told himself. Ten to one, the kids hadn't seen a thing.

Six

~~~~~~~⚬⚬⚬~~~~~~~

"**G**et a warrant." Nothing in Jack's voice on the other end of the phone suggested he had even a shred of patience left for his sister, a feeling Sam shared. "Or wait until I get there, and I'll break into her damn house myself. I'll be there in an hour."

It was 8:00 a.m. in Austin, and no Stockwell kids. Past the point of exhaustion, Sam had stopped in a twenty-four-hour diner for coffee and eggs. A lot of coffee. A cabdriver remembered dropping off two children meeting their description near but not on Kara Galway's street. They'd pointed at a big house, presumably at random, and told the driver that was where they were headed. The man had thought nothing of it, but he definitely remembered them. They were polite, they had Yankee accents, and they'd overtipped him with a crisp twenty.

Sam had gone straight back to Kara's little bungalow in Hyde Park, but he was too late. She was gone. Lights out, doors locked, car not in the driveway. No note. She was a defense attorney. She wasn't about to leave behind any evidence that could be used against her or her godchildren should push come to shove—which it would, Sam thought, if he had anything to say about it.

No one was panicking yet in Connecticut. The kids' uncle and their mother's adviser, Hatch Corrigan, had told the Austin police that he and Allyson trusted Kara completely and weren't as worried now that it looked as if Henry and Lillian Stockwell were with her. Corrigan was sure Kara would get in touch. Nor was he surprised his niece and nephew had made it to their godmother's house on their own—they were smart, worldly children accustomed to being on their own.

Sam didn't share Corrigan's optimism. Neither did Kara's big brother. It all could be spin to keep Texas law enforcement at bay and control what went public. The kids' mother, after all, was already in a touchy situation, with her predecessor dead in his pool. Her people would want to keep this escapade quiet now that it looked as if Henry and Lillian were in responsible hands. Sam didn't know about that. Kara's actions struck him at best as requiring further explanation. Jack agreed. He'd checked in with Sam and hit the road after learning the Connecticut governor's kids were technically still on the loose and his sister had cleared out in the middle of the night.

Sam sipped his coffee. He should have taken off his badge before knocking on Kara's front door last night, said he was there on personal business and walked right past her.

The popcorn wasn't her damn dinner. It was a snack for those kids.

She hadn't lied to him outright, but she'd come close—and she'd deliberately misled him about two runaway minors. He hadn't said as much to her brother. Jack was good at putting together the pieces. Maybe too good, if he started thinking about the gallery opening, coffee, his sister's alibi and Sam beating a path to Austin last night.

"Where do you want me to meet you?" Sam asked.

"My in-laws' gallery. Let's keep this unofficial for now."

He hung up, and Sam set his cell phone on the table next to his plate. His eyeballs felt as if they'd been rolled in hot sand. He pushed his eggs around on his plate, not hungry. He was trying to work the facts and not jump to conclusions, never mind the uncertainty he'd sensed in Kara last night, the fear he'd seen hovering in her dark eyes.

His cell phone trilled again, and he hoped it was the Austin police telling him they'd located Governor Stockwell's children and they were nowhere near their godmother.

It wasn't. It was Susanna Galway. "Sam—where are you?"

"Diner out by the Austin airport."

"Good, not too far. Meet me at my parents' gallery as soon as you can. Fifteen minutes? Do *not* tell my husband—"

"He's on his way there."

"*Here?* To the gallery?"

"That's right. He should be there in an hour."

She swore. "All right, we still have enough time. Get over here, Sam. *Now.*"

The hairs on the back of his neck rose up. "Susanna—"

But she'd disconnected. Sam paid for his breakfast and headed out, wondering if he should just throw his badge in the nearest garbage can and get it over with. Before this was all over, Lieutenant Galway would be feeding it to him. The women in Jack's life gave him fits. His wife, his daughters, his sister. Sam could see why—he'd seen it six months ago in the Adirondacks, and still he'd waded in with Kara.

He drove over to Hyde Park and found his way to the shaded street where Eva and Kevin Dunning had opened their gallery almost eight years ago. It was in a renovated 1920s frame house painted cream with white trim, just enough yard out front for a pecan tree and asters in a half-dozen colors. On the night of the champagne reception for Gordon Temple, the place had sparkled, people wandering inside and out as they chatted and oohed and aahed over his artwork. Even before he'd found a spot to park his damn car, Sam had known he shouldn't have come. He had a similar feeling now, gnawing at him, warning him away.

Susanna met him at the door, refusing to speak as she led him through the main showroom. He barely noticed his father's paintings on the wall, mostly landscapes, some with animals native to North America—bison, eagles, river otters. An Eastern bluebird. Out of the corner of his eye, Sam caught sight of an oil painting of a desert sunrise, haunting with its vibrant colors, but he didn't allow himself to stop and look at it.

When they came to a small, tidy workroom in the back, Susanna shut the door and leaned against it, as if Sam might try to escape and she meant to stop him. "Thank you for coming." She had on a sundress and sandals, no makeup, no jewelry, her hair pulled back with a rolled-up orange bandanna. Last winter Sam had seen fear in her green eyes—it was there again now, mixed, he thought, with a certain measure of anger. She sucked in a breath. "Sam—*Jesus.*"

"Susanna, what's wrong? Are you all right?"

She held up a hand. "I'm okay. I need to ask you a favor. And you can't say no. You can't, Sam."

His eyes narrowed. This was a woman who loved her secrets. "I'm listening."

"Yeah, and you're suspicious as hell." She struggled to smile, then gave up. "First you have to promise—"

"No promises in advance."

"All right, all right. Forget it. You won't squeal to Jack. That would be stupid, and you're not stupid. Well, you *are* stupid about some things, like my sister-in-law, but that's—" She was talking more to herself than to him, her forehead creased as she put one heel up against the door and seemed ready to kick it. "There's no reason to believe a crime's been committed, so you won't be compromised on that score— I'd never ask you to cover up a crime. A real one, anyway."

"Susanna. Start talking or I tie you up and we wait for Jack to get here."

"Yeah, right." Her green eyes fixed on him. "Like it's me you'd like to tie up."

So, she knew. Sam kept his face expressionless.

She peeled off the bandanna and wiped her forehead with it, sighing heavily. "I'd love to babble my way out of this mess, but I can't. Sam—Kara stopped by the house this morning at six, not five minutes after Jack left for work. She must have been around the corner waiting for him to leave."

"Was she alone?"

"She came into the house alone. I didn't think to check her car. She looked terrible. I know she's working too hard, and she's still upset about Governor Parisi's death—and now these runaway kids…"

"Just tell me what happened, Susanna," Sam said, his tone neutral. "We can deal with the emotions later."

She eased away from the door, steadier but by no means calmer. She was an intelligent woman who'd earned an MBA part-time when the twins were little and through skill and luck turned several choice investments into a multi-million-dollar fortune. She'd kept the money a secret from her husband, although he knew about it, anyway, but she thought it'd destroy their marriage—and it nearly had. Not the money, the fear of it. She came to see that the hard way. Nothing important had changed in her and Jack's lives, at least not because of money.

Sam had seen how much Jack loved his wife six months ago in the killer cold of an Adirondack winter, and before that, during the Galways' long months of separation, forced apart because of their unspoken fears—and an unsolved Texas murder. Now that she'd returned to San Antonio for good, Sam saw how much Susanna loved her husband, too, and he'd come to realize he wasn't capable of that kind of love himself. There were reasons. He supposed Gordon Temple was one of them.

As much as Sam liked and admired Susanna Galway, he knew she didn't think the way he did. They'd been arguing with each other ever since he'd become a Texas Ranger five years ago. Her love for her family was the only thing she saw in black and white. He was just the opposite. He saw everything in black and white—except for his love for his family.

"She was pale and sick to her stomach," Susanna went on. "She wouldn't let me give her anything. She got a bottle of San Pelligrino from the fridge and said she had a lot on her mind and couldn't sleep, so she got in her car and just started driving."

"And happened to end up at your house?"

"That's what she said."

Five minutes *after* her brother had left for work.

"Maggie and Ellen were still in bed." Susanna hooked her bandanna on the back of a tall stool at a drafting table. "Kara and I chatted for a few minutes, then she took off."

"You must have headed up here not long after that. It's not a planned trip, is it?"

Susanna shook her head, splaying her fingers in front of her and staring at them, obviously not wanting to tell him what came next. Sam didn't prod her. She hadn't driven here to tell him her sister-in-law had stopped by for San Pelligrino. "Sam, I—" She opened and closed her fingers, as if trying to keep them from stiffening up on her. "I was worried. So I drove up here to check on her. I stopped by her house, but she wasn't there. I tried her cell phone—I just got her voice mail."

"I did the same."

She nodded absently and sat on the stool, the drafting table in front of a window that overlooked a small yard filled with sunflowers. "On my way to Austin, the airport where Jack keeps his plane called me on my cell phone."

That was one of their indulgences now that they had money—a small plane that could make the trip north to Susanna's grandmother in Boston and their cabin on Blackwater Lake in the Adirondacks. She and Jack were both pilots, but by mutual agreement, this was his plane.

When she drifted into silence, Sam decided she needed a little prodding after all. "The longer you wait, the more likely Jack's going to walk in here—"

"The guy at the airport had a routine question and mentioned that Kara had gotten off the ground safely. He said she was a good pilot."

Sam could suddenly feel the heat, the closeness of the small workroom. "Susanna—Jesus Christ. Kara took off in Jack's plane? Without his permission, I presume?"

"Of *course* without his permission. It's not a problem with the airport—she's cleared to fly the plane as far as they're concerned. It's a problem with Jack. I called Maggie and Ellen and had them check my keys. Kara must have swiped the key to the plane

while I was pouring the San Pelligrino. Borrowed,''
Susanna amended. "She borrowed the key.''

"That's not borrowing. That's stealing.''

"It depends on how you look at it. Jack's her
brother.''

"He'll see it my way.''

Susanna sighed and nodded, and she grabbed her
bandanna and put it back in her hair. Her sister-in-
law was out of control, and Susanna had at least to
sense it. But she leaned back on the stool and folded
her arms on her chest, tilting her head back and eyeing Sam as if he were a teenager who'd missed cur-
few. "Am I going to have to play hardball with you,
Sam?''

"You haven't told me what you want me to do.''

"Find her.''

He didn't react.

"I'm not worried about her flying the plane. She's
taken it up several times. Her father made her take
flying lessons in high school, just as he did Jack. He
thought it'd be good therapy after their mother died.
He was always after them to push themselves, take
on more. Harvard, Yale, law school, the Texas Rangers. He didn't want them succumbing to their grief.
He thought of it that way, too. Succumbing.'' She
raised her eyes to Sam, softening just a little. "But
you know all this already.''

Sam chose to say nothing.

"Come on, Sam. For God's sake. I *know*. Okay,
don't admit it. Don't tell me you're at least half in
love with her and have been since long before the

Gordon Temple opening—I don't care. Just find her and bring her home.''

He felt the burn down deep, the tight coil of emotions he didn't dare let loose. ''Do you have any idea where she went?''

Susanna smirked at him, shaking her head. ''You really aren't going to admit anything, are you? I talked to my mother about you two. She said she could feel the sparks. Last night—Sam, the chemistry between you and Kara is hard to miss. Jack didn't notice only because it'd take a bolt of lightning, especially with his sister. He can't imagine anyone wanting to sleep with her.''

''Christ, Susanna.''

She slid to her feet, graceful, determined. ''She filed a flight plan for the airport we use outside Boston. She could change it en route, but it's a good bet that's where she's headed.''

''The Stockwells are from Connecticut.''

''I know. It'd be logical for Kara to land in Hartford, but she's flown into Boston with Jack and me. She knows the airport we use there. She sometimes spent the holidays with my grandmother, when we couldn't get up there and Kara couldn't come home. Gran's never been big on traveling.''

Iris Dunning was a fixture in her working-class neighborhood near Boston and one of the more amazing old ladies Sam knew. But like her granddaughter, Iris was also a stubborn woman of many secrets. ''Iris would hide the kids under her bed and lie through her teeth about it if Kara asked her to.''

"Especially if she thought they were in any kind of danger," Susanna added.

"Don't get ahead of yourself," Sam said quietly.

Susanna nodded, but worry was etched in her angular face, bringing out the fine lines at the corners of her eyes. "No one at the airport will think twice if Kara parks the plane there for a few days, and Henry and Lillian are much less likely to be recognized in eastern Massachusetts."

Sam could feel his chest compressing, the reality of what she was asking sinking in. "You want me to fly to Boston."

"I've got you booked on a flight out of Austin this afternoon. By my calculations, with a stop for refueling, Kara should arrive in Boston by midafternoon. She'll have a pretty good head start on you." Susanna stood in front of him, close. At almost forty, she was attractive, confident and not a woman who liked to be thwarted once she'd made up her mind. "Something's not right, Sam. I don't want her hurt, and I don't want her doing something stupid because she's not in her right mind."

Long before Sam had fallen into bed with Kara Galway, her brother had said she was always getting herself bloodied as a kid defending the kids who were picked on, marginalized, troubled, not believed. She'd turned her zeal for fighting for the underdog into fighting for her clients, understanding the legitimate role of a defense lawyer, the presumption of innocence, the burden of proof, how all of it worked together to preserve a system of justice.

Or so Jack had explained it. He didn't necessarily believe it, though. "I think my sister's just a soft touch," he'd once said with an affectionate smile.

Sam's head was spinning with fatigue, his eyes burning, aching. He needed a shave, a shower, clean clothes. He needed rest. "I haven't packed—"

"I've got a suitcase for you in my car. Jack has the key to your apartment, remember? I took the liberty of packing a few things for you." She smiled, a little nervously, he thought. "I also threw out the chicken you left to thaw on your kitchen counter a million years ago. Jesus, Sam, what a smell."

Something about her story wasn't adding up, and he wondered if she'd spotted the hole in it herself and was trying to distract him. He was too damn tired to think.

Susanna started shoving him back out the door, chattering again about flight plans and refueling and his flight north. She threw numbers at him. A defense mechanism. She didn't want him thinking.

"Why don't you ask Jack to go after Kara?" Sam asked.

"Because he'd just call the Boston police and have her arrested the minute she lands."

It seemed like a good idea to Sam. He might yet do it himself.

They reached the main showroom, where the air was cool and the walls dancing with the bright signature colors of Gordon Temple's work. Susanna smiled coolly, any nervousness gone. "Besides, I don't expect you want Kara explaining to her brother why she's not thinking straight."

"Think you have me by the short hairs, don't you, Mrs. Galway?"

"I know I do."

"If she does have those kids—"

"Then thank God, because then we know they're

safe.'' Susanna touched his arm, all the coolness going out of her. Her eyes were warm, and she seemed
near tears. ''Sam, I know you have responsibilities as
a Ranger, but this is a personal favor.''

''No kidding,'' he said dryly.

''Kara, the kids—losing Mike Parisi was hard on
them. You'll go to Boston, won't you?''

''You knew I would when you dialed my number.''
He was putting his career on the line—everything.
''So, Mrs. Galway, you're so smart. What the hell do
I tell your husband?''

She smiled, her spirits renewed. ''Leave that to
me.''

Sam found Eva Dunning out back in the sunflowers. She had on a floppy, wide-brimmed cloth hat, not
much help against the hot Texas sun, and a shapeless
denim jumper and sport sandals, which she somehow
managed to wear with a creative flare. Her dark hair
hung down her back in a long, graying braid. She was
shorter than her daughter, graceful more in manner
than build, and she didn't have Susanna's green eyes.
Those were pure Dunning. Eva exuded genuine caring
and openness, and she was a talented artist, a quilter,
a woman of many talents and hobbies. She was no
art snob. Her husband was an artist, too, both of them
nomads who'd lit in Austin for a time.

Their Hyde Park gallery and their house weren't
far from Kara's bungalow.

''I'd forgotten how hot it can get down here in the
summer,'' Eva said. ''Whew. I'm bushed. Is Susanna
still inside?''

Sam nodded. ''Jack's on his way here.''

''Is he?''

Kevin and Eva Dunning weren't elitists, but they'd probably never get used to having a Texas Ranger for a son-in-law. Sam didn't have Jack's experience with dealing with them—or his patience. No question in his mind that Eva Dunning was up to her eyeballs in whatever Kara had going on. "Have you seen Kara recently?" he asked.

"How recently?"

"Last night."

Eva snipped off a small, dark sunflower and added it to the bouquet she'd collected in a bucket of water. "Why do you ask? Is something wrong?"

"Possibly. I hope not. Did she come here last night by any chance?"

"No."

Sam realized he had to be very precise with her and give her no wiggle room whatsoever. "To your house?"

"Sergeant Temple, is this an official interrogation?" Color rose in her cheeks, but he knew if he pointed it out to her, she'd only blame the heat. "Should I have my attorney with me?"

Bingo, he thought. Kara had slipped over to the Dunnings' place to avoid him, probably got some rest, then headed south to San Antonio.

Sam took no pleasure in Eva's obvious discomfort. His personal and professional lives had collided the minute he'd walked out of the Dunning Gallery two weeks ago with Kara Galway, and now he was paying for it.

"Let me tell you what I think." He fingered a bright yellow sunflower, then looked back at the older woman. "I think Kara showed up at your house late last night and said I might stop by and ask questions.

She wanted you to stonewall me, told you it wasn't anything that'd get you in trouble. You trusted her because she's an attorney, because she's Jack's sister and because she was desperate.''

"Sam—"

He held up a hand, stopping her. "Ma'am, I'm not accusing you or anyone else of committing a crime. I'm just trying to find out a few things before I put my head any deeper into the lion's mouth."

Eva Dunning stood up from her bucket of sunflowers, the hot sun washing out her eyes. "How deep has Kara put in her head?"

"She's up to her ass, Mrs. Dunning."

Eva nodded, a little pale. "I thought so."

"Did she have anyone with her?"

"She wouldn't say. She never came into the house—she asked to borrow my car."

"Did she say why?"

"Hers had something wrong with it, I don't know what."

It had nothing wrong with it. She didn't want the police spotting it if Sam put out an APB on her.

"I gave her my keys, and she said she wanted to get a little sleep before she headed out. I urged her to come in and use one of the bedrooms upstairs. We have loads of room. She refused."

"She slept in your car?"

"Yes. She left about four o'clock this morning. I was going to go out and check on her—Sam, I've known Kara since she was a kid. She's always been very purposeful, devoted to her sense of right and wrong. She can be irritatingly uncompromising." Eva took a breath, droplets of sweat forming on her upper lip. "But if she's in trouble, I will be there for her. I think you should know that."

He took her statement for what it was—a threat. He'd have the whole damn Dunning and Galway clan down his throat if they decided he'd screwed up Kara's life, which was why he'd warned himself off her in the first place. He'd wanted her for months, but she was forbidden territory—Jack Galway's little sister.

Sam could taste her even now, feel her body under his and hear her soft moans as she reached her climax, pulling him deeper into her, any discomfort she'd felt early in their lovemaking gone.

He'd definitely gone too fast with her. Way too damn fast. She hadn't been in her right mind that night. He should have seen it more clearly.

But he hadn't been in his right mind, either.

"Thanks for your time, ma'am," he told Eva Dunning. "I'm sure this will all turn out fine."

He got the suitcase Susanna had packed for him out of the back of her car and tossed it in his front seat, every fiber of him screaming for rest, sleep, at least a quiet place in the shade to think. What was it about Susanna's story that didn't add up? What was it that was still eating at him?

If he just dawdled, he could run into Jack, take his thrashing, then they could work this problem together. But instead he climbed into his car, and when he reached the end of the street, he turned and drove in the opposite direction Jack would take to get to the gallery.

Halfway out to the airport, his brain clicked into gear with such an abrupt force he nearly ran off the damn road. He pulled over, dialing Susanna's cell phone number while he pushed down his annoyance with her and her labyrinthine ways.

She answered on the third ring. Probably knew it was him and had debated answering at all.

"You were on your way to Austin when the airport called you," he said. "Why did you have my suitcase already packed? Why were you coming here if you didn't already know about the plane?"

"Sam, Jack's in the driveway—"

"Then answer me quick or I'm turning around and heading back there."

"All right, all right. I lied. I called the airport myself."

"When?"

"On the road to Austin, after I packed your suitcase. I was double-checking. I already knew she had the key to the plane."

"Did you give it to her?"

"No. She'd never put me in that position. I guessed after she left."

Sam was silent. She knew what answers he wanted.

"Are you driving?" she asked quietly. "You might want to pull over."

"Susanna, you have two seconds. Then I'm hanging up and driving over there and letting Jack deal with his damn family. Last time I tried to protect a Galway, I ended up getting shot."

"Kara broke into Jack's gun cabinet," Susanna blurted. "She told me she was going to the bathroom. I only thought about the plane after I saw she had one of his guns."

"Jesus Christ."

"She didn't break in, exactly. She has a key. She

must have had it with her. She has copies of all our keys, except the one to the plane.''

"What did she take?"

"A .45 automatic pistol. His Colt, I think."

Jack carried a department-issue .357 SIG-Sauer on duty. Sam felt his pulse throbbing behind his eyes. How had he gotten so far down this road? "Does Kara know how to use it?"

"She took shooting lessons in high school, probably on days she wasn't taking flying lessons and plotting how to get into Yale. Her father—"

Sam knew all about her father, a man who worked two jobs and tried to give his motherless children every advantage in life. "She has to have a permit to carry a pistol where she's going. She can't just waltz into another state with a weapon and expect—" He broke off, because Susanna already understood the ramifications of what her sister-in-law had done or she wouldn't have lied in the first place. "Hell, she doesn't have a permit for it here. She stole the damn thing. She deserves to get herself arrested."

"She's afraid, Sam. I could see it in her eyes."

"Then she should call the damn police."

Seven

Kara rented a car in Boston and put Lillian up front, Henry in the back, but neither said much on the trip to Connecticut. They were west of Hartford now, off the interstate, driving along a shaded, scenic road. Lillian had just finished reading the first of J. K. Rowling's Harry Potter books for what she claimed was the seventh time and now was staring out her window, preoccupied.

"What's on your mind?" Kara asked her.

"Will Henry and I have to go to reform school?"

Henry, who Kara would have guessed wasn't paying attention, shot as far forward as he could in his seat belt. "We didn't run away, Lil. We did what Mom asked us to do. Reform school's for delinquents."

And prison, Kara thought, was for people who stole planes and guns and misled Texas Rangers, then gave them the slip with the missing kids of a governor. And that was only a slight exaggeration. She wondered how much of a head start she had on Sam and her brother. Probably not much if Susanna talked. She must have found out about the plane and the gun by now.

"I wouldn't be worrying about reform school right now," Kara said. "Let's just get to the cottage."

It was early evening, comfortably warm and slightly humid in Connecticut. The farther from Texas Kara got, the crazier her actions of last night and this morning seemed to her. She'd let Henry and Lillian's fear and desperation affect her judgment, feed her own anxiety. She was calmer now. She would follow the instructions in the letter and get them to Stonebrook Cottage and their mother. If she pissed off a couple of Texas Rangers in the process, so be it.

The kids were calmer, too, their spirits improved now that she'd demonstrated she was unquestionably on their side and had stopped trying to poke holes in their story and pepper them with questions. What was the point? Their mother could deal with what they'd done and why, figure out if something serious was wrong or they simply needed help coping with Big Mike's death.

The city and suburbs of the state capital had given way to rolling farmlands, then to the wooded hills and small towns of the northwest corner of the state. The air cooled. They passed houses with green lawns and gardens at their peak, hollyhocks and corn standing tall, hammocks strung under shade trees, black-eyed Susans looking as if they were smiling in the small fields. Kara had taken this route countless times out to Stockwell country for the weekend.

Henry and Lillian had sniped at each other on the flight north, their tension and fatigue getting the better of them. Apparently Lillian was cautious about snakes and big horses and Henry wasn't, and Henry had been excused from the fire circle for making rude noises. Kara had been relieved that at least they were talking about something other than the man who'd spied on them at the dude ranch and followed them to Austin. Occasionally, as they drove to the airport in San Antonio, Henry glanced out the back window, worried the man was after them.

Kara's only fresh concern was what was on her voice mail. Or, more specifically, what wasn't. She'd had one message from Sam late last night: "Where the hell are you? Call me." She hadn't called him. She'd switched off her cell phone and expected other messages when she checked her voice mail in Boston—from Sam, from Jack, from Susanna, all telling her to get her ass back to Texas. But there was nothing.

It could mean they'd buttoned this thing down and weren't taking any chances with her now that she'd blown the opportunity to act sensibly. It could also mean they planned to let her swing on her own, although that was unlikely. The two Texas Rangers in her life weren't passive types. Neither was her sister-in-law.

Between landing in Boston and renting a car, Kara had left a trail that experienced law enforcement officers could easily follow. On the other hand, these latest actions suggested she had nothing to hide.

Last night and this morning were another matter altogether.

She regretted appropriating Jack's .45. It had been

a spur-of-the-moment decision on her part—she'd come to San Antonio for his plane—but a crawling sense of panic seized her on her way to the bathroom. What if the letter from Allyson wasn't bogus? What if she and her children *were* in grave danger? When Kara found herself in the study, unlocking the gun cabinet, she went ahead and armed herself, tucking the Colt into the waistband of her pants. Jack would have noticed it when she returned to the kitchen. Susanna didn't. But at least, Kara thought, she'd dismantled the thing, packed it in her suitcase and stuck the clip in her tote bag, reducing the opportunity for mishaps and further stupidity.

If her brother could forgive the plane, she knew he'd have her head on a platter for the gun.

The one potentially smart move she made before leaving Texas was enlist Eva Dunning's help in assessing the credibility of Allyson's letter. Eva was a certified handwriting analyst, one of her many avocations. While she'd packed, Kara had grabbed an old postcard from Allyson and cut off her signature, then ran the letter through her copier and snipped a relatively innocuous section from the copy. She gave the postcard and the sample from the questionable letter to Eva and asked if she could tell if they were written by the same person.

"I can try." Eva had frowned at the snippet from the letter. "It would help if I had more to go on."

Kara didn't dare give her more. Words like "grave danger" would put Eva on even higher alert. The woman was clearly worried, if not outright suspicious, at having Kara show up in the middle of the night. "That's all I can give you," Kara had told her.

If Eva heard any anxiety in Kara's voice, she hadn't responded to it. "I assume you want to keep this between us?"

"Please. But I don't want you to lie—"

"Of course not. After I've taken a look and made my assessment, I'll tear these up and flush them down the toilet. Anything else?"

Kara had promised to call her later for the results, but decided to wait until they arrived at the cottage. If the letter was a forgery and Allyson had no idea where her children were and no intention of meeting them at the cottage, Kara preferred to know it, but not while she still had to get there. She was tired and feeling a little nutty, her on-and-off queasiness a continuing source of anxiety and frustration. Maybe it wasn't nerves or seafood tacos, or her night with Sam Temple—maybe it was a slight bug.

When they reached the familiar streets of Bluefield, instead of becoming more relaxed, Henry and Lillian shrank down in their seats and seemed hardly to breathe as they drove past the small town common, ringed with Federal and Greek Revival houses in muted colors, shaded by huge old sugar maples. The late-eighteenth-century, white-steepled Congregational church was still the tallest building in the village. The old town hall had been converted into a summer theater, and an upscale deli and wine shop and an independent bookstore with an outdoor café had sprung up next to the longtime hardware store and pharmacy.

At the far end of the common, they passed the post office, the fire station, the police station and a run-down diner with plastic flowers in its window boxes—Mike Parisi's favorite hangout when he was in town. O'Reilly's Pub was just past the common, on the corner of a long street of village houses bleeding into a country highway that led out to Stockwell Farm. Kara noticed gated driveways to some of the newer homes, hidden behind screens of trees and high walls.

They came to the Jericho place with its rambling gray clapboard house and sagging red barn. Several stray chickens warbled in the side yard. Charlie Jericho's ancient tractor was parked out front, and Kara caught glimpses of climbing red roses and a crude scarecrow in Bea Jericho's wild-looking herb and vegetable garden. She thought she heard sheep and the crowing of a rooster and wondered if Pete still nursed his grudge against her for the plea bargain that had landed him in county jail for six months.

"Not far now," she said unnecessarily.

Henry and Lillian remained quiet, both peering low out their windows. Just the tops of their blond heads would be visible from outside. There was no one else on the road, no more houses, the woods and fields on both sides of the road belonging to either the Jerichos or the Stockwells.

Kara turned onto a narrow, dead-end dirt road on the Jericho-Stockwell border. A brook tumbled through the woods alongside the Jericho side of the road, across from undulating hay fields that Madeleine Stockwell leased to local farmers. Beyond the fields were woods laced with old stone walls and carriage roads that eventually opened out into Stockwell Farm with its manicured grounds, stone stable, converted barn and beautiful, black-shuttered historic house. But none of that could be seen from here. This was just, for all appearances, a quiet country road.

Stonebrook Cottage, a stone farmhouse with dark red shutters, stood in a clearing at the end of the dirt road. It always made Kara think of Little Red Riding Hood. There were two small bedrooms upstairs under slanted ceilings and downstairs, a living room, eat-in kitchen, bedroom and bathroom. Simple white curtains hung in all the windows. The landscaping was low maintenance, just a mowed yard, rhododendrons, shrubs and a perennial bed. A gnarled, ancient butternut tree loomed over the small cottage, and even in the dirt driveway, Kara was in its shade.

There were no other houses on the road, none in view through the woods or across the fields. She had enjoyed the isolation during her weekend visits. Now she wondered what she'd do if the man in the black sedan showed up—or a couple of Texas Rangers.

Henry and Lillian jumped out of the car and raced to the front door, Lillian locating the key in an unused mail basket. Kara smiled at their sudden high spirits. What a change since last night. She got out of the car, welcoming the cooler air, hoping it would revive her. She'd taken on a huge responsibility when she didn't immediately call Hatch or Allyson after finding her godchildren in her living room.

"Aunt Kara," Henry said from the porch, "aren't you coming?"

"I need to make a call. I'll be right in."

They burst inside, and she could hear them running around, laughing. Kara leaned against her rented car, not sharing their unbridled energy, and dialed Eva's number in Austin. If anyone else answered, she'd hang up.

She sighed with relief when she heard Eva's voice. "Oh, Kara—I'm so glad you called. I've been worried. Is everything all right?"

"Fine, thanks. Are you in a safe place to talk?"

"Yes, or I wouldn't have used your name. Jack says he's trying to keep the Austin police from going after you on kidnapping charges. He's exaggerating, of course, but the last sighting of the Stockwell kids was near your house—"

"Did you tell him you saw me last night?"

"I had no choice."

"Of course not. Don't worry about it."

"I told him you'd stopped by and borrowed my car. Apparently your friend has assured the authorities she's not worried if the kids are in your care, but you know Jack. Kara—"

"Everything'll be fine, Eva. The police don't want a couple of rich kids from Connecticut lost on their turf, that's all. I'm sorry I put you in such an awkward position—"

"Oh, I don't care about that. I just want to know you're okay."

"Thanks. Listen, go ahead and tell Jack we talked, and I said the kids are in good hands—and tell him he and the police don't need to know anything more than that." Kara was suddenly aware of a contradictory mix of apprehension and obstinacy working their way into her system. She had misgivings about the course she was on, but damned if she wanted anyone second-guessing her. "What about Sam Temple?"

"I saw him briefly this morning. Kara—" Eva sighed. "Never mind. There's much to tell but not a lot of time. You're calling about the handwriting samples, aren't you?"

"Have you come to any conclusions?"

"As I think you suspected, they weren't written by the same person. The smaller sample looks like an attempt to copy the postcard sample. The connectors are a dead giveaway. People tend to put all their effort into copying the letters, but forget the connectors. Under a magnifying glass, you can easily see, too, that the pen pressure is different—well, you don't need to know all that. The samples weren't written by the same person. I think even a real expert would tell you that."

At least, Kara thought, she'd had the foresight to cut Allyson's signature off the bottom of the postcard, but given what she'd written and the Hartford postmark, it could be traced back to the governor of Connecticut in about two seconds. Not that it mattered at this point. Henry and Lillian had lied.

"What did you do with the samples?" Kara asked.

"I did what I said I'd do."

She'd flushed them down the toilet. Kara slumped against the car, wishing she'd called the kids' bluff last night. But she'd been so caught up in their fear, which had felt real to her—and she was their godmother. They'd confided in her thinking she was their lawyer. What else could she have done?

A million things.

"Eva—I can't thank you enough. Tell my brother the Stockwell kids are no longer in Texas and they can all just relax."

"He's going to want to know where you are."

"Yes, he will. I'll be in touch as soon as I've straightened out a few things here. Thanks again. I owe you."

"Forget it. It does my soul good to pull a fast one on a Texas Ranger every now and then."

They disconnected, and Lillian burst out the front door, beckoning to Kara. "Come *on!* There's *ice cream* in the freezer! Ben & Jerry's!"

Kara managed a small smile. Ben & Jerry's ice cream—any flavor—wouldn't make her problems go away, but it couldn't hurt.

Sam sat on a stool at the smooth, worn bar that dominated Jim's Place, a popular bar near Boston famous for its clam chowder and neighborhood atmosphere. It was early evening, the place already packed with graduate students, firefighters, construction workers and old people. There was no sign of Iris Dunning, Susanna Galway's grandmother, who lived just up the street. The first time Sam had come here, he'd been looking for a Texas murder suspect. He wasn't thrilled to be back.

Jim Haviland, the burly owner, greeted Sam with a big grin. "I'll be damned. Ranger Temple returns."

Davey Ahearn occupied his habitual spot at the end

of the bar. He was a plumber with a huge handlebar mustache and a tendency to say whatever came into his head. "No hat? No gun?"

"I'm not here on official business," Sam said.

Jim Haviland laid a white bar towel on his shoulder. "I'll bet you're not here for the chowder, though, are you?"

Clam chowder wasn't one of Sam's favorites. He'd rented a car at Logan and had already driven out to the suburban airport where Kara had parked her brother's plane. She'd arrived midafternoon. No one remembered seeing kids with her. While he was en route to Jim's Place, Eva Dunning called at Susanna's request. Meaning Susanna didn't want to talk to him herself. Eva said Kara had been in touch, that she wanted Sam and her brother to know Henry and Lillian Stockwell were in good hands and all was well.

Sam didn't think so.

He had no idea what Eva and Susanna had told Jack. So far, Sam had managed to avoid talking to Jack Galway. Probably his only smart move of the day.

"You know Jack's sister, don't you?" he asked Haviland.

"Kara. Sure. Didn't she move back to Texas?"

"About a year ago. She's a defense attorney in Austin."

"I hear Austin's pretty as Texas towns go," Ahearn said.

Sam ignored him. Ahearn didn't seem to care one way or the other. "Did Kara ever mention her friendship with Allyson Stockwell?" Sam asked.

"Our new governor to the south?" Haviland said. "Yeah, sure. She and Kara have been friends since college. It's a tragedy, what happened to Big Mike Parisi."

"I should have known." Davey shook his head. "No way is a Texas Ranger walking in here without it having to do with somebody who died."

Sam had slept on the flight north or he might have had less patience with the plumber. "Governor Parisi rented a house in Bluefield, Connecticut, for the summer. That's where he died. Does it ring any bells with you as far as Kara's concerned?"

Jim frowned, thinking. "She used to spend weekends there. She stayed in a guest house on the Stockwell estate—out of the way."

"Stonebrook Cottage," Ahearn said without hesitation. "Remember, Jimmy? Bluefield's the sort of town where people name their houses. She said you should come up with a more atmospheric name for this place, and you told her it was a goddamn bar."

"Jesus, Davey, you remember the damnedest things," Haviland said. "But I remember now—she liked that cottage." He eyed Sam with an air of resignation, perhaps mixed with a bit of relief. "You're not going to tell us what's going on, are you?"

"No, sir."

"Do I get to ask why it's you up here and not her brother?"

Sam withheld comment.

"You know, Ranger Temple," Ahearn said, "you've got your hands full if you're going after Kara

Galway. She's smart and hardheaded, she's a lawyer and she knows how to shoot."

Sam didn't disagree, but Jim Haviland scowled at his friend, then turned back to Sam. "What can we do to help?"

"Tell me what you know about this Stonebrook Cottage," Sam said, "and point me to northwest Connecticut."

Eight

❦❦❦❦

Allyson settled down to enjoy a cup of tea in the dining room of her suburban Hartford house, a comfortable home that didn't rival the stately, historic Governor's Residence. It was her first quiet moment in days. Thank God Henry and Lillian were safe and in Kara's care.

Despite his outward optimism, Hatch had spent much of the past two days worrying about seeing *Governor's kids gone missing* on CNN Breaking News, which so far hadn't happened. He was the one dealing with the dude ranch and the Texas authorities. He said Kara's brother, Jack, the Texas Ranger, was hardest to convince that they really did trust his sister's judgment, despite her recent odd behavior. Allyson had met Jack Galway and understood. He was not a man who liked taking anyone's word about anything, never mind that of his younger sister. He wouldn't be satisfied until Kara was back at her desk and he had reliable word that the children of the Connecticut governor were no longer in his state.

When Kara finally called a little while ago, Allyson

had cried. It wasn't just a question of faith now—she *knew*. Henry and Lillian were at Stonebrook Cottage, and they were fine.

"They spun a wild tale to get me to bring them up here without telling anyone," Kara said. "I'm not to the bottom of it yet, but that's okay. You're the mom. I'll leave all that to you."

"God only knows what they were thinking, running off like that." Allyson knew she was breathing too rapidly, but couldn't seem to stop herself. "It was such a relief when we realized they'd gone to Austin."

"I'd have called you the minute they showed up, but I promised them—" Kara broke off, sounding exhausted. "It's their story to tell. When can you get here?"

"I could come now, but maybe it'd be best if I came in the morning. It's a little over an hour's drive, and Hatch and I still haven't told Madeleine about the kids. Let me get my ducks in a row. Is it okay? Henry and Lillian will be okay overnight?"

"Morning's fine, Allyson. Don't worry about it. It's late as it is, and we could all use a quiet night." Kara yawned, and Allyson thought her friend sounded remarkably calm and sane under the circumstances. "We'll hang out here and wait for you. There's food in the cupboards. It's not a problem."

"Kara, I don't know what to say. I'm so sorry this happened. We've had such a terrible summer, and I thought going to Texas would be good for them. They were looking forward to seeing where you lived. I thought they'd like it—"

"I don't think being in Texas is the problem. They're right here. Do you want to talk to them?"

Allyson's heart jumped. "Yes, but I—my God, what do I say to them? They've put us all through hell! If I hadn't put my foot down and insisted I trusted you, there'd be a nationwide alert, it'd be all over the news—"

"You'll know what to say."

And she did. As her children took turns talking to her, Allyson told them not to worry, she loved them, she'd be there as soon as she could in the morning. She tried to sound caring and reasonable, not like a crazy woman who'd lost her children for twenty-four hours. Of course they'd run to Kara. She was their godmother, their mother's best friend, and she was right there in Austin. They would know they could trust her, that she wouldn't judge them. Kara tried to hide her vulnerabilities behind her legal expertise, her keen intelligence, but Allyson knew better—Kara Galway was independent-minded, smart and capable, but part of her was still the little girl trapped next to her dying mother, helpless to save her.

Allyson had smiled through her tears after she'd hung up with her children. She needed to maintain a certain self-control or people would wonder what *more* was wrong with her, perhaps even question her ability to serve as governor. She didn't want that. She was beginning to enjoy her new role and the opportunities it presented, far beyond what she could accomplish as lieutenant governor, in Mike's shadow. She missed him deeply, but she had work to do, starting with figuring out what was going on with Henry and Lillian. Then she had to get rid of her anonymous caller.

If only Pete were here now. He'd be reassuring, unconditionally on her side and everyone else be damned. Allyson couldn't imagine going on without him, but to have him in her life meant going up against powerful forces—her mother-in-law, Hatch, the people who wouldn't tolerate having a governor in love with a working-class guy with a criminal record. And there was how all the controversy would affect her children.

Hatch rapped on the open door to her study, and she motioned him in, inviting him to sit down. He was forty-seven now, the same age Lawrence had been when he died, but he looked older, more world-weary. His reaction to the news of Kara's call was predictable. "She should have gotten in touch with me first."

Allyson smiled. "Kara does things her own way. You know that. I'm just glad the kids are all right and this latest turmoil is over."

"Is it over?" Hatch asked softly.

"Yes, of course."

She tried to sound confident, in control. It would be so easy to let Hatch take over and just do as he told her. He could be the power behind her, make all the tough decisions. He didn't like being out front and wouldn't care if she got all the credit—and any criticism. But even in her darkest mood, Allyson resisted, instinctively preserving her independence.

She gave a small laugh, thinking of her children.

"Those two rascals. They've led us all on a merry chase, haven't they? I can't wait to see them."

"You'll go in the morning?"

She nodded.

"We'll need to issue a statement explaining their little misadventure to the media before word of it breaks loose. We can do it in an open-and-shut way. I think it should come from a spokesperson—"

"No, it should come from me. I'm their mother."

Hatch didn't push her, but she knew it wasn't because he was satisfied. She could sense his concern for her, his questions, and, when he left, his lingering annoyance with Kara. But that was to be expected. Hatch was always annoyed with Kara, and undoubtedly still in love with her.

Pete laughed at Billie Corrigan as she yawned over her first beer of the night in the dive that was O'Reilly's Pub. "Come on, Billie, one beer and you're falling asleep?"

She scowled at him. "I've been on my feet since eight o'clock this morning."

"Wienie hours." Pete raised his beer to her. "I've been working since 5:00 a.m."

"Yeah, well, you're a farmer boy. I'm a city girl."

Pete drank, wondering why the hell he'd come here. He liked Billie, at least. She wasn't nearly as uptight as her big brother. She and Hatch shared the late, unmourned Frankie Corrigan for a father, but had different mothers. Billie was raised in New York by her crazy waitress-actress mother, Hatch in Bluefield by Madam Madeleine. Billie seemed to get a kick out of her brother's lofty upbringing more than anything else. She'd moved up to Bluefield after watching her father fall to his death in a drunken haze five years ago. She had a good reputation and seemed to make a decent living as a caterer and party planner, not that Pete had ever hired her. She was redheaded, blue-eyed and buxom, and he knew he could have her for the asking.

She had stuffed herself into a white shirt and jeans that seemed a size too small. Pete tried not to notice. He seldom went out for a beer since his release from jail, but tonight was different. Charlie had heard word that Henry and Lillian had skipped out of their dude ranch and were on the loose in Texas, probably making their way to Kara Galway in Austin. Pete tried calling Allyson at the Stockwell Farm, as a neighbor who might help, nothing more. He'd decided to tell her about the tree house, in case it had anything to do with the kids' behavior.

But Hatch, that officious prick, answered and said she was back in Hartford, and he was headed there himself. There was no getting around Hatch Corrigan. The guy always treated Pete as if he was beneath the Stockwells—a hell of a nerve seeing how Hatch's old man had broken his damn neck because he was a drunk. Allyson didn't come from big money, although she hadn't grown up poor. Her father was a doctor in New Haven.

The "real" Stockwells were Hatch's half brother Lawrence, who was dead, and Lawrence's children, Henry and Lillian. They were the ones with the money. But Lawrence had treated everyone with dignity and respect. It didn't matter where they were from, who their parents were, what they did for a living. Allyson was trying to raise Henry and Lillian with that same egalitarian attitude—she wanted them just to be regular kids.

But Pete didn't want to be too hard on Hatch. Allyson could have called and told him about the kids if she'd wanted to.

"I hear one more word about fucking bluebirds," Billie said, "and I'm going to scream. I mean it. I'll start dismantling every bluebird house within fifty square miles."

Pete laughed. "You wouldn't. Ethel Smith would string you up."

Billie groaned at the mention of Ethel's name. "I ran into her in town this afternoon, and she was muttering about how long a juvenile bluebird with a broken leg could last in chlorinated water. She was miffed at the very idea of chlorinated water."

"She was my first-grade teacher," Pete said.

"God, she must be a hundred years old."

"She took up birds when she retired. People are going to keep talking about bluebirds until they accept the fact that Big Mike drowned because he couldn't swim."

Billie sighed, shaking her head, her blue eyes filling with tears. "I saw him the night before he died, you know. He had that cocktail party for a few of his political friends—"

"Yeah, I heard about it."

"He was so full of life."

Pete sipped his beer. "That was Big Mike."

She nodded. "I didn't know him that well, but that's what everyone tells me. Well." She smiled, stifling another yawn and looking as if she couldn't stay up another minute. "What're you up to?"

"I'm finishing this beer and hitting the sack."

Something flashed in her shining blue eyes—desire, yearning—but it was gone again in an instant, and Pete wondered if he wasn't seeing what he wanted to see. A few hours in bed with Billie Corrigan might purge him of Allyson. But he felt disloyal even thinking it, as if he'd dirtied himself, her, their love. He knew Allyson loved him. She was just caught between a rock and a hard place now that Big Mike was dead and she was governor. She had things she needed to figure out.

When Billie eased off her stool, her breast brushed against his arm. He could feel the soft weight of it, the nipple straining against her too-small shirt. She must have noticed their contact but smiled at him as if she didn't. "I'm not starting work until nine tomorrow. I guess that's lunchtime for you."

He turned on his stool and watched the swing of her hips as she headed out. He still could feel the touch of her breast. Billie wasn't forbidden. She wasn't a Stockwell, a wannabe Stockwell or a governor. She was a working stiff like he was, and she wouldn't lose a second's sleep if she fell for a man with a minor criminal record. Everything about the way she moved, laughed, dressed said she was available. Why the hell not?

Pete spun back around and finished his beer. Just as well Allyson was in Hartford. If she were here, nothing would have stopped him from sneaking through the woods to her bedroom in the converted barn on Stockwell Farm. He didn't care if she had round-the-clock bodyguards now that she was governor. She'd have to sic them on him.

He couldn't remember wanting her as much as he did right now.

And wasn't that just his tough damn luck? Allyson had dumped him. He was just too stubborn—too in love with her—to admit the obvious.

It took two bowls of Ben & Jerry's Nutty Waffle Cone for Henry to actually admit the letter from his mother was a forgery. Kara hadn't waited for his confession before calling Allyson and explaining at least some of what had transpired in the past twenty-four hours.

When she'd decided to let Henry and Lillian call the shots and operate under the premise that she was taking them at their word, Kara understood she'd have to leave her friend in the dark about the exact whereabouts of her children longer than was necessary. But that was the risk she had to take, because Henry and Lillian were her priority, not Allyson, and something was terribly wrong with them.

The admonition not to call, not to talk to anyone, had been artful on Henry and Lillian's part, Kara had to admit. It bought them time and got them back to Connecticut.

"I had no choice," Henry said. "I had to do it."

"He didn't do it. *I* did." Lillian spoke in a small voice; she was shrunk down in her seat at the wooden table, painted a summery green, in the middle of the kitchen. "His cursive isn't as good as mine."

"It was my idea."

"Let's not argue about who did what." Kara shook her head in amazement. She'd had a spoonful of the rich ice cream, leaving the rest to the kids. "In all my years as a defense attorney, I've never even heard of a couple of middle-schoolers conning their god-mother with a forged letter from their mother."

Lillian protested. "Kids at school forge their moms' names all the time!"

"Because they don't want their moms to know about a detention, not because they want their god-mother to believe they're in danger." Kara couldn't muster any real anger at them. The reasons for what they did were still not clear to her. Why such drama? How had they feigned such real, palpable fear last night? She sighed. "What if I'd been arrested for kid-napping you?"

Lillian's eyes widened, but her brother scoffed. "You wouldn't have been arrested, Aunt Kara. We'd have said something."

"You don't know my brother. He's a mean-assed Texas Ranger. Be glad we got out of Texas a step ahead of him." And a step ahead of Ranger Temple, Kara thought. "Are you two going to tell me what all this is really about? Sneaking off to see me is a big step. Why didn't you just call me and say you needed me? You know I'd have come in a heartbeat."

"We didn't want to risk it," Henry said.

Lillian sputtered into tears. "We miss you. We miss Big Mike—"

"And we *are* in danger," Henry said, fighting back tears of his own. "It's just that Mom doesn't know. We don't want to worry her."

"Oh, so scare the living daylights out of the god-mother instead." Kara leaned back in her sturdy wooden chair, listened a moment to crickets outside in the warm night. What was she doing? These kids needed a kind of help she couldn't offer. She'd moved away on them, and Big Mike had died on them. Two losses in a year. They were reeling. She leaned forward, touching Henry's hand, surprised at how cold it was. "Henry, what kind of danger are you in?"

His clear blue eyes leveled on her, his Stockwell jaw set, as if he was trying to look older than twelve. He didn't. He was a kid. A troubled kid. "What we told you about the man who followed us is true."

"Did you see him at my house last night or did you make that up?"

Lillian's spoon clattered into her empty ice cream dish. "I saw him. I *did.*"

"All right." Kara didn't want to upset them further by arguing. "So you've got some creep on your tail. We'll look into it."

Henry shot up out of his chair. "*No!* Aunt Kara! You can't tell anyone! You promised!"

She held up a hand, careful this time not to get sucked into his emotion. "Okay, *I'll* look into it. You guys were pretty tired last night. Maybe you just think you saw this man. Maybe he's just a regular guy who works at the ranch, and you two got spooked—"

"No." Lillian solemnly shook her head. "He doesn't work at camp."

"And he's not a pedophile," Henry added.

Kara nearly choked. "Pedophile? Jeez, Henry."

He shrugged, matter-of-fact now. "Mom says it's better to know people like that exist than to pretend they don't."

"Forewarned is forearmed," Lillian said, obviously quoting their mother.

Kara shook her head. "I'd never even heard the word *pedophile* until I was in law school."

The kids seemed pleased by her admission of ignorance, even if it was somewhat exaggerated. She'd known a few things before leaving her father's house and heading north—how to fly planes, shoot a gun, run a half-marathon, deal with an older brother and a father who wanted nothing more than to remove the image of her dead mother from her memory. They didn't take that failure, the impossibility of it, well.

What had Henry and Lillian seen? What did they have imprinted on *their* memories forever? Something. She was sure of it.

"I know you two are grieving for Big Mike."

Kara got to her feet, her muscles aching, her stomach rolling over. She felt a little dizzy but hung on to a corner of the table, steadying herself. The kitchen, with its white cabinets and brightly colored dishes, was unchanged from her first visit here in law school. Everything was gleaming, spotless, the country decor deceptively casual and easy. Texas suddenly seemed very far away.

"And it can't be easy having your mother suddenly faced with all the responsibilities of being governor," she went on. "I don't know, I might feel a little swept aside—"

Henry rolled his eyes. "That's not *it*. We're in *danger*."

"Why? You're kids."

"We saw Big Mike drown."

Henry spit out the words as if he was challenging her to doubt him. He had his hands clenched in fists, his lips smacked tightly shut. His face turned red, and he blinked back tears even as he continued to stare at his godmother in defiance. Kara had no idea whether to believe him.

Lillian stared at her empty dish.

Their fear was real. Kara hadn't gotten it wrong last night—it had been real then, too. Whether or not they were spinning another tale, something serious was going on with these children.

She forced herself to stay calm. "Can you tell me what happened?"

"We were up in our tree house, and we saw him through our binoculars. It was an accident." Henry pushed back his hair, spiked with sweat, his breathing rapid, excited. "I saw him first. I yelled, then Lillian looked, and she saw him."

Jesus. Kara fell back on her experience as an attorney. Ask sensible questions, don't react to answers. "Where is this tree house of yours?"

"It's on the hill above the gravel pit," Henry said. "We can see everything from up there. Mostly we watch the big trucks and sifters and things. They're so cool."

"I think they're loud," Lillian said.

"Does your mother know about the tree house?" Kara asked.

"No one knows. It's in a tree real close to the edge of the pit—Mom'd make us take it down. Charlie Jericho almost caught us once. He'd *kill* us."

Kara didn't doubt it. Charlie was a hard-bitten old grouch most people liked in spite of his irascibility, but she supposed he wouldn't want to see the kids get hurt. "You can see the house Big Mike rented from up there?"

Henry nodded. "Only with our binoculars."

Lillian continued to stare at her ice-cream dish. "We saw the deep end of his swimming pool," she said without looking up. "He was floating on his stomach. I thought he looked funny. I didn't know he was in trouble. Henry did."

"What did you do?" Kara asked, not wanting to picture what they must have seen through their binoculars.

"We jumped out of the tree house. We ran and ran and ran." Lillian looked up, breathless now, the words tumbling out on top of each other. "I dropped my pair of binoculars—they have a pink ribbon tied to them. But Henry said never mind, leave them, and I just ran so hard—we wanted to save him."

"But you couldn't," Kara said gently. "You had too far to go."

"He was already dead." Henry's tone was clipped, as if none of this really mattered to him. Denial, Kara suspected. Bravado. A child's uncertain grasp of death. "We couldn't do anything to help him. I told Lil."

Kara leaned against the sink, feeling more than queasy now. She was sick to her stomach at the thought of what these kids had witnessed, the help-lessness and terror they must have felt. The awful grief.

"How far did you get before you turned around?" she asked.

"Almost to the fence around the pool." Henry con-tinued in that flat, matter-of-fact voice. "The fence by the deep end is a few feet in the woods. We saw the state troopers yelling into radios—one of the troopers jumped in the pool."

"I was scared," Lillian said. "I threw up."

Kara could see it now, two children charging through the woods to help their friend, then realizing he was dead, a *governor* was dead, and the situation was way over their heads. "So you left," she said. "You didn't say anything to the bodyguards."

Henry nodded. "We went back to our tree house."

Lillian sniffed, suddenly indignant. "My binocu-lars were *gone*. Somebody stole them! Henry says they're probably under the leaves and I looked in the wrong place, but I know somebody took them. Don't you think so, Aunt Kara?"

She dodged Lillian's question. "Do you each have your own pair of binoculars?"

"They're old ones Grandma gave to us," Henry said dismissively. "I left mine in the tree house."

"Did you go back up into the tree house after you got back?"

"No. We ran all the way back to Grandma's house. We were going to tell her and Mom what we saw, but the police were there, taking Mom to be sworn in. So we didn't say anything." He shoved the heels of his hands into his eyes and rubbed, yawning as if he couldn't stand up another second. He dropped his hands, lifting his shoulders and letting them fall in a world-weary shrug. "We couldn't do anything that'd bring Big Mike back."

Kara rubbed his bony shoulder. "You heard he couldn't swim, right?"

Henry nodded without looking at her, and Lillian said, "We know it wasn't our fault, Aunt Kara, but if we could have saved him…" She trailed off, rising unsteadily. "Will we have to tell the police what we saw?"

"You should," Kara said. "It might not seem like it to you, but you could have information they don't have right now, something that could help them understand what happened to Big Mike."

"Do they still believe it was an accident?" Henry asked.

Something in his voice—indefinable but unmistakable—gave her goose bumps. "As far as I know, yes. Henry, do you have any reason to believe what happened to Big Mike *wasn't* an accident?"

He yawned, his tonsils showing. "I'm tired." He turned to his sister. "Flip you for the big room."

"No, I want it!"

They scrambled out of the kitchen, pounding upstairs to see who could claim the big room first, yelling at each other as if they'd just been discussing Ben & Jerry's flavors instead of the horror of witnessing Big Mike's death.

Kara dismissed the twinge in her stomach as nerves. She had a right.

Henry and Lillian had left her with the dirty dishes. She cleared the table, laying the dishes in the sink, squirting in detergent. A refreshing breeze floated through the open window. She could smell the clean, cool night air.

Those kids *still* hadn't told her the whole story. They'd seen something else that day in their tree house.

Their mother was coming in the morning. Allyson could look after her children and deal with their fears, get them to tell her what they saw and try to understand it. Kara could go home to Texas and see how far she'd get explaining this mess to Jack and Sam before one or the other clapped cuffs on her.

The idea of Sam putting her in cuffs made her smile. She didn't know why. Probably exhaustion. But it was better than thinking about her godchildren up in their tree house with their binoculars, and she focused on an image of Sam as she did the dishes and cleaned up the kitchen.

Nine

~~~~~~~~⚬⚬⚬~~~~~~~~

Kara's cell phone rang twenty minutes after she sent
the kids up to bed. She didn't want to answer it. She'd
collapsed on the couch in the cottage-style living
room, decorated in soothing shades of blue and white
that somehow failed to soothe her. As tired as she
was, she knew she couldn't sleep. She was too wired,
too preoccupied, her mind racing.

She couldn't imagine anyone calling her tonight for
a reason she'd like. But she hit the answer button,
and even to her own ear, her greeting was raspy and
weak, betraying her fatigue.

Not that Sam Temple gave a damn. "Fair warning.
I'm five minutes from Stonebrook Cottage and unarmed. Don't shoot."

"Sam, you're *what*—"

He'd disconnected.

Kara flung the phone onto the couch cushion. How
had he found her? Who'd given him directions?
Stonebrook Cottage wasn't on any map, even one of
Bluefield.

It didn't matter. He was coming.

She ran upstairs. Lillian was already asleep, her Harry Potter book open to the first page next to her on the double bed. Across the hall, Henry was wide awake in the room with the twin beds. Kara tried not to let her agitation show, but she had to warn him. "Hey, Henry, don't worry if you hear a car drive up in a few minutes. The Texas Ranger from last night is on his way. We're friends." That was a stretch, but no way could she explain the complexities of her relationship with Sam to a twelve-year-old. "It's okay. I'll handle him."

He sat up on his elbows. "Aunt Kara, remember your promise—you can't tell anyone—"

"I won't. What you told me last night is privileged."

"What about the tree house? That's privileged, too, isn't it?"

"Yes. I'm treating everything you told me as privileged. All of it." Reassured, he sank back onto his pillow, and Kara kissed him on the forehead. "You'll tell Lillian if she wakes up?"

He nodded, his big eyes shining in the dark room. Outside his window, the three-quarter moon glowed, as if solely on him.

Kara slipped back downstairs and waited outside on the stone step. The uneven granite hadn't yet given up the warmth it had absorbed during the day, and she could feel it on her bare feet. An owl hooted intermittently somewhere in the woods and across the dirt road, the brook gurgled as it tumbled over rocks. She'd never wanted this much country on a permanent basis, but weekends here had been a pleasant respite from her grueling job in Hartford. Even so, work and the occasional break from work weren't enough—she'd needed more balance in her life. Home always beckoned. Texas. Yet, here she was, back up north again.

And the balance she was looking for remained elusive in Austin, too. Maybe George Carter was right and it was a simple case of putting in too many hours for too long without a break.

Headlights approached around a bend in the dirt road, and although she was expecting them, Kara jumped, seized by anticipation, even dread, at her inevitable confrontation with Sam. The lights of his car seemed brighter, more intrusive, against the unmarred night. He pulled in behind her rented car, a deliberate move, she suspected, to impede any predawn escapes on her part. He'd underestimated her last night, and she'd taken off on him. If he'd had any clue she'd bolt, he'd have sat outside her house and dared her to make a move.

Well, she'd have thought of something.

He got out of his car and shut the door, his tall figure casting a long shadow on the moonlit yard. He carried a bag over one shoulder and took his time walking up to the front door, until he finally placed one foot on the stone step and met her gaze without smiling. "Evening, Miss Kara."

He set his slouchy leather bag on the step next to him. He had on cowboy boots, jeans and a soft-looking chambray shirt with the sleeves rolled up to his elbows. He wore an expensive sports watch. No Texas Ranger badge, no white cowboy hat. No gun.

She didn't know what part of his visit was business and what was personal, but supposed she'd find out.

She nodded at him. "It's a beautiful evening, isn't it? A lot cooler than Austin. You didn't have to come after me, you know."

"I wouldn't be telling me what I have to do and don't have to do." His tone was very controlled, but his black eyes were hot, warning her he wasn't so controlled inside. "Jim Haviland and Davey Ahearn in Somerville gave me basic directions. Then I talked to Jack. He remembered visiting you out here once about five or six years ago."

"You could have called me. I'd have given you directions."

"To where?"

"Sam—"

"Hatch Corrigan told Jack you have the Stockwell children here and have been in touch with their mother."

"That's true. It's complicated—"

"Jack says everyone up here's satisfied."

"But you're not," Kara said.

His black eyes bored straight through her. "You made the mistake of committing all your crimes in Texas."

"I didn't commit any crimes."

"Kidnapping, grand larceny, breaking and entering, unlawful possession of a weapon—that's just off the top of my head."

"Give it up, Sam. You're not arresting me for anything."

"Your brother doesn't know about his gun."

"You didn't tell him?"

He let his gaze settle on her, his mouth a thin, uncompromising line. "No."

"There, you see? You're on my side. You're all bark and no bite or you'd have told him—"

"I suggested he talk to his wife."

"Well, guess what? I'm not scared of either one of you. Are you coming inside, or are you going to wait for the mosquitoes to find you?" She pushed open the door and motioned broadly with one hand, refusing to acknowledge her heightened state of anticipation, excitement. The man did not have a calming effect on her. "After you, Sergeant. I assume Susanna put you up to chasing after me?"

"She was worried about you."

"I was worried about me, too. It's been a hell of a twenty-four hours."

He eased his bag over his shoulder and walked past her into the living room, and Kara noticed the narrowness of his hips, remembered the way he'd strode into her house two weeks ago, how she'd known they'd end up in bed. It had seemed inevitable, and she'd wanted it to happen.

She followed him into the living room, letting the door shut softly behind her. "The kids are in bed." She decided a less confrontational approach might be in order. Sam had a right to be grouchy considering he was here instead of in Texas. "They're very special to me, so if I've acted a little nutty, I hope you'll take that into account."

He didn't relent. "Susanna thinks it's because of what happened between us."

"She called you on the carpet, didn't she? Well, she's wrong. It's not."

"Kara, if I hurt you—"

"You didn't."

"I don't mean just emotionally. I hadn't realized—"

He hadn't realized how inexperienced she was. *Damn.* But she pretended not to hear him, the only defense she could think of right now. "Let's not talk about something we can't undo. You've done your duty. You found me. I'm safe, the kids are safe. All's well that ends well, right? It's not that far back to Hartford. You can get a room at the airport and catch an early flight back to San Antonio. On me."

"Not a chance."

She hadn't really thought there would be.

He eased his bag onto the wide plank floor with its blue-and-white hooked rug. "I want to know why the hell you pulled this stunt."

"I can't tell you. Attorney-client privilege."

"Those kids aren't your clients. You'd need a court to appoint you, or their mother's permission. You didn't have time for a court, and Allyson Stockwell didn't even know where they were."

"Formation of the attorney-client relationship is technically privileged as well—"

He scoffed. "Lawyer talk. These are your godchildren, Kara. Why don't you just use common sense?"

She managed a self-deprecating smile. "Too late for that. You really aren't leaving, are you?"

"No, ma'am."

"All right. Henry's in the only room with two beds,

but I don't think it's a good idea for you to sleep up there until you've met—''

''We all could have had popcorn together last night.''

Kara ignored him, a near-impossible task. He seemed to fill up the room with his intensity, his confidence, his experience as one of Texas's elite law enforcement officers. She'd had this same reaction when they'd gone for coffee, even as she was still reeling with the news of Mike Parisi's death. Sam exuded unbridled masculine sexuality, and it had taken very little time or effort to get her into bed with him.

Maybe they'd both been a touch out of their heads that night.

''You can stay in the bedroom down here,'' she said briskly. ''I tossed my things in there, but that's okay—I'll sleep out here on the couch.''

He shrugged, his expression unreadable. ''Fine with me. I've had a hell of a long day. I could use a bed.'' She noticed the muscles in his forearms, the dark, tanned skin as he hoisted his bag higher onto his shoulder. ''If you don't want to sleep out here, just come on in.'' He winked, a twitch of a smile at the corners of his mouth. ''I'll make room for you.''

''That wouldn't be a good idea.''

''That's not a flat-out no. Duly noted for the future.'' He nodded at her. ''You're done in, Miss Kara. We'll take it from here in the morning. I can find my way to the bedroom.''

He headed into the adjoining kitchen, and Kara dropped onto the couch, relieved he hadn't argued over sleeping arrangements. She wondered if she should give him more credit. He must have realized she'd been in a difficult position and had put a lot on the line for her troubled, conniving godchildren, that it wasn't easy for her to be back in Connecticut with Big Mike gone. Sam might go back into bad-cop interrogation mode in the morning, but for now he was letting her off the hook, and she was grateful.

She remembered her brother's .45 and bolted up straight. The hell Sam was letting her off the hook! If there was a gun in the house, he'd want control of it. He'd search her bag and anything else he could find. Now that he was in another state on personal business, he wouldn't give a damn if she threatened him with needing a search warrant to touch anything of hers. He'd just plow right in.

"*Wait!*"

She charged through the kitchen and into the short hall that led to the bedroom and bathroom, pushing past him into the bedroom and straight to her suitcase at the foot of the bed. If he searched her suitcase for the gun, he'd also find her home pregnancy test kits. Then she'd really be sunk. She'd shoved them in there thinking they'd be accessible but not as in-her-face as in her tote bag, reminding her every time she fished for her wallet or lipstick that she'd done something that made pregnancy not out of the question. And it involved Sam Temple.

"I need my things in case you sleep late in the morning," she said. "I'm a crack-of-dawn type."

He leaned against the doorway. "I remember."

He wasn't making this easy on her, but he had no

reason to. Kara scooped up her suitcase, hugging it close to her chest. She was walking a thousand fine lines. She was bound to slip up sooner or later.

"Nice try, Miss Kara, but I want the gun."

Good, she thought. Let him think her panic was over him knowing she had her brother's Colt. "I dismantled it and packed it separate from the ammunition. I haven't touched it since I got here. No prosecutor would bother going after me on a weapon's charge—"

"Maybe not in Connecticut. Wait until I tell a Texas prosecutor you stole a gun from a Texas Ranger."

"Jack'll back me up."

"Not if you don't give me the damn gun he won't."

"I know how to shoot."

His dark eyes flashed. "This is supposed to reassure me?"

"Sam, for God's sake," she said lamely, realizing if she gave in too easily, he'd wonder what else she was hiding. She wasn't about to unload her suitcase item by item for him.

He put out a hand. "The .45, Kara. If it's in my possession, I can show my badge and fall back on professional courtesy. You can't. I'm doing you a favor."

He had a point. Technically, a law enforcement officer who traveled to another state had to follow local gun laws just like everyone else. Sam's jurisdiction was Texas. He wasn't a Texas Ranger anywhere else. If he didn't have a permit to carry a weapon in Connecticut and he wasn't there on official business, he was violating the law. However, local cops would often look the other way if they caught a fellow law enforcement officer discreetly carrying a weapon, provided he or she didn't do anything improper—like fire the thing.

The local cops wouldn't look the other way with Kara. If they were back in Texas, Sam wouldn't look the other way, either.

He *was* doing her a favor.

"It's not as if anyone's going to catch me with an illegal gun in my suitcase," she said.

"I caught you."

She set the suitcase on top of an old quilt folded at the foot of the bed and unzipped it carefully, trying to remember where the pistol parts were in relation to her pregnancy test kits. Sam watched from the doorway as she felt around inside the suitcase, finding the slide first and easing it out. She set it on the bed and then had to dig under one of the kits for the .45's frame and spring, grabbing the mesh holster while she was at it. She nonchalantly shoved the pregnancy kits deeper into the suitcase, in case she ran into a similar problem before she could send Sam on his way.

She rezipped the suitcase, realizing beads of sweat had erupted on her brow as if she were some sort of criminal, and handed over the gun parts and holster. Sam popped the .45 together with a speed and efficiency that reminded her of what his work was.

"The mag," he said.

"You know, Jack would never arrest me—"

"He doesn't have to. Step foot in Texas with this on you and you're mine."

Her knees buckled at the sexy undertone of his words, but she still had one hand on her suitcase and leaned on it to regain her balance. He didn't seem to notice. He was concentrating on her misdeeds, not her reaction to him. At her brother's house, after the Gordon Temple opening, last night, now—it didn't matter when she saw him. Her reaction was powerful, impossible to ignore. She noticed everything about him, the black eyes, the hard body, the straightforward, no-nonsense way he went about his life. Sam was a man who knew his own mind and didn't bother to pretend otherwise, for anyone, for any reason. People liked him, women loved him—but Kara suspected very few people really knew Sam Temple.

She dipped into her tote bag and produced the fully loaded magazine. "I put you and Jack—and Susanna—in an untenable position. I'm sorry."

"They understand. You put those kids ahead of everything, including your good judgment." His eyes softened unexpectedly, and the hardness of his mouth relented slightly. "I understand, too."

He racked the gun, and Kara shuddered at the metallic sound of a bullet entering the chamber. She scooped up her suitcase. "You're just being nice now because you have my gun."

"I'll sleep better, that's for sure."

Ten

As was her custom, Madeleine Stockwell cornered Pete a few minutes after he arrived at her place. She called him over to the stone patio, where she sat at a table sorting through dozens of brightly colored zinnias and asters. She had on flowered garden gloves and snipped the ends of the flowers one by one with her ancient clippers. Pete didn't know why she and his father didn't get along. They were both tighter than ticks.

She didn't look half-bad for eighty years old. She had on one of her country-manor outfits—navy-and-white stripe top, white pants, white flats—and sighed at Pete without looking up. "I suppose you've heard that Henry and Lillian are with Kara Galway at Stonebrook Cottage. Hatch finally told me about their little escapade last night. It's all around town by now, I presume?"

Pete shrugged. "Not really."

"Allyson's behavior is inexplicable to me. She should be here soon. Hatch insists I'm not to go over to the cottage—she wants to see the children first."

Madeleine snipped off two inches from a pink zinnia with surprising force given her bony hands. "If she'd told me what was going on, I might have been able to help. Suppose they'd come here? I'd have been taken completely by surprise."

"You'd have handled it," Pete said. "I imagine Allyson and Hatch decided it was best to keep this thing under wraps. They probably know more than we do—"

"Hatch? This wasn't his decision. His job is to advise Allyson, yes, but he complies with her wishes. Always. She says jump, he says how high."

"Ah, come on, Mrs. Stockwell, he'd be no good as an adviser if he didn't speak his mind. You're just pissed because you were cut out of the loop."

She scoffed, but said nothing. Pete didn't know why Madeleine told him things, but she always had, even when he'd come up here as a teenager to mow the lawn and wash windows. Charlie said it was because she didn't have any friends. Nobody else would listen to her. After Pete got out of jail, she picked up where they'd left off before he'd slipped up and she'd had to teach him his place. She wouldn't have had to do anything overt, just letting the right people know that Pete Jericho was serving time would please her no end.

He wondered what she'd do if she found out he and her son's widow had made love within sight of her dining-room window.

"I don't like being treated like some loose-lipped old woman who can't be trusted," she said half under her breath.

"Maybe they just didn't want to upset you."

"Oh, for heaven's sake, you'd think I'd never dealt

with a crisis before. I watched my husband bleed to death right out there on the lawn.'' She pointed with her clippers. ''I'm not a weakling.''

''I don't doubt it, but if the kids ran away from the ranch and made their way to Austin, then up here, it had to be for a reason. Allyson's their mother. Let her figure out what's going on.''

Madeleine shot him an unfriendly look, her blue eyes reminding him what a force of nature she must have been fifty years ago. Beautiful, sexy, willful, a survivor, according to everyone who knew her then, Charlie and Bea Jericho included. ''You always take Allyson's side.''

''I'm not taking anyone's side. Why'd they light out for Kara's, do you know?''

''You don't think anyone bothered to tell *me* the details, do you? They've always been close to Kara. I thought it might be different after she moved away, but apparently not.''

Pete shrugged. ''Texas isn't on the moon.'' He smiled, ready to get to work. ''Come on, Mrs. Stockwell. You're being hard on everyone. Just be glad the kids are all right—''

''Oh? Just be glad they're all right? I see. I suppose that's what would have happened at your house. Charlie and Bea always let you run wild. I happen to consider this an appalling situation. My grandchildren are now runaways.''

''Ah, they'll be fine. You don't want them to be a couple of Goody Two-shoes.''

She set down her clippers and peeled off her gloves. ''You're impertinent, Pete Jericho. You and your father both. I don't know why I keep finding work for you to do.''

Pete grinned at her. "Because the place'd fall down around your ears if we didn't come up here and help out."

"You don't think I could take care of it by myself?"

"No one could."

She sighed deeply, gazing out at the beautiful lawn and gardens. "My father-in-law bought this place with the fantasy that he and his children could be self-sufficient out here. My husband was never happier than when he was working this land." She smiled at Pete then. "Perhaps that's why I keep you busy. Watching you work reminds me of him."

Pete felt a pang of sympathy for her. Edward Stockwell had been the love of her life, no matter how many husbands and lovers she'd had since his death. "Mrs. Stockwell, I need to be getting to work—"

"Yes, yes, go off now that the old woman's getting maudlin. Stop and talk to Billie first. She's down by the pool. She's planning a cocktail party I'm having. I want to get people back up here, enjoying themselves, as soon as possible. They need to put the gas can explosion and Mike Parisi's death out of their minds."

"They were both accidents—"

She looked up at him, cool. "I know that."

Billie had arranged the bonfire party, where the explosion had occurred, but even Madeleine, apparently, didn't hold her responsible for the accident. All the papers had reported that Pete had saved Allyson and the kids. That, he knew, didn't sit well with old Madeleine.

He headed down the stone steps to the pool, where Billie was plopped on a lounge chair with her clipboard, markers and a soda. She grinned up at him. "Madeleine gripe to you about those kids? She forgets she's a million years old. She'd have had a frigging heart attack if she'd known her grandchildren were on the loose. She doesn't know how to show it, but she loves them." She took a drink of her soda. "You know Kara has those little shits at Stonebrook Cottage?"

Pete nodded. "That's what Madeleine told me."

"I don't know what they were thinking. Kara might be a defense attorney, but she's also a kick-ass Texan. They're lucky she didn't throw them in the klink down there."

He shoved his hands into his jeans pockets, not wanting Billie to read anything into his expression. Neither Kara nor Allyson was a good subject with him right now. "Madeleine said you wanted to talk to me about something?"

"Right, yeah." She shot to her feet in a sudden burst of energy. "This cocktail party—I originally thought I'd do a bonfire, but that's out because of the accident on the Fourth. Madeleine totally freaked when I even mentioned it. Man, that was a close call." She gave a mock shudder, a gleam in her blue eyes. "Can't be blowing up the guests, right?"

"Billie—Jesus."

"Sorry." But she didn't seem that embarrassed. "I guess I'm an all's-well-that-ends-well type. Anyway, I'm wondering about stringing lights around the pool. You know, those little white Christmas lights. I can get 'em for a buck or two down at the junk store. And candles—I'd like to do those candles in paper bags. What're they called?"

"Luminaria," Pete said.

She laughed and jabbed him in the stomach playfully. "Big word for a blue-collar guy. Think you can help me out?"

Her enthusiasm was contagious. "Sure. Just let me know what you need."

"I will." She beamed up at him. "Thanks."

After that, he got to work. He needed to patch a retaining wall out by the barn. As he walked across the sloping lawn, he pictured himself out here on a dark night, sneaking through the tall, dew-soaked grass in the fields. The barn was painted red, its tall windows looking out on the fields and woods. It wasn't that fancy, just a loft and a big open room downstairs with a separate bedroom and bathroom. But the views were spectacular, and everything inside gleamed, expensive, always spotless.

Pete examined the retaining wall and headed back up to his truck to unload what he needed. Allyson would be here soon, but today wasn't about him. It was about the kids and why they'd run away. If Allyson asked his opinion, he'd give it—he'd tell her to ask them about the tree house. But if she didn't, he'd stay out of it.

Hatch and Madeleine both protested her decision to walk over to Stonebrook Cottage alone, but Allyson didn't care. The state troopers responsible for her security weren't pleased, either. They were all gathered on the patio, the air still and humid, adding to her sense of tension. If she didn't stand her ground now, nothing she said from here on out would carry any weight. She'd be rolled at every turn, ignored, dismissed. She'd be a puppet for operators and handlers and those who didn't like to work out in the open. Everyone would assume she'd finish out Big Mike's term and disappear into obscurity. If she couldn't establish her authority in matters that affected her own children, what could she do?

Henry and Lillian needed her. She was going to them. Alone.

"I intend to walk through the woods as I have hundreds of times before I took the oath of office, and will again hundreds of times after I leave office." She spoke clearly, firmly, without a hint of the anxiety burning through her. "I'll carry my pager and cell phone. If I need help, I'll let you know."

Hatch made a sour face while his mother, sitting across from him, oiled her clippers, pretending she really wasn't a part of this discussion.

Allyson sighed. "It'll take me fifteen minutes. I'll buzz you when I get there."

Hatch almost snarled at her. "Allyson, for the love of God. Mike's only been dead for two weeks."

She understood his concern, but she needed to see Kara, and especially her children, alone, without an escort, without any reminders of her new role as governor. "Trust me, if I fall and hit my head on a rock, the state of Connecticut will survive. I'm wasting time. I'll be back before too long."

She walked off the patio, across the sloping lawn to the fields and woods that would lead her straight to Stonebrook Cottage. She ached to see her kids. She didn't care who she had to thwart to do it her way. She could feel Madeleine's steely, disapproving stare. Five minutes back in Bluefield, and her mother-in-law had already tripped her inadequacy switch. She was being childish, foolish, reckless. She wasn't good enough for Lawrence—if she weren't so selfish, she'd have realized something was wrong sooner and gotten him to a doctor, found the cancer when there was still hope.

Madeleine never actually said as much. She didn't have to.

"Wait up," Hatch called.

But Allyson didn't slacken her pace. He caught up with her, breathing hard, his graying auburn hair matted to his forehead, the steeliness in his eyes reminding her both of Lawrence and his mother.

He softened. "Go on. Walk to the cottage on your own. I'll take care of it. Everyone's extra-cautious after what happened to Mike, that's all."

"I know." Some of the energy went out of her anger. "Please make sure the troopers know it's not them. I trust them completely—"

"They know, Allyson. It's not a problem."

Her gait faltered as she thought about how long Hatch had been at her side, smoothing the way for her, taking care of things. "God, Hatch, what would I do without you?"

"You'd manage. You're a survivor—you're like my mother in that way."

She smiled. "I ought to smack you for that."

But he wasn't smiling, and she realized how different they were—he in his slacks and jacket, she in her jeans and UConn basketball shirt. Hatch had found very little comfort in having Henry and Lillian turn up at Stonebrook Cottage with their godmother. "If there's anything I can do, you've only to call," he said.

She thanked him, then set off across a stretch of soft, sloping lawn, almost running when she came to the retaining wall and spotted Pete. She'd seen his truck in the driveway but had pushed all thought of him to the back of her mind. She had to stay focused on her children.

He stood up from his wheelbarrow, dust on his muscled thighs, everything about him scuffed and worn and hardworking. He had tawny hair, the darkest, bluest eyes. Her breath caught whenever she saw him and had, secretly, for years—why was she the last person to know he had fallen for her? She was the blond, blue-eyed doctor's daughter from New Haven who'd married a Stockwell twenty years older than she was, and now all she wanted, everything she craved, was a man four years younger than she was, who had a minor but undeniable criminal record and had never graduated college much less gone to law school.

"Hey, Allyson," he said.

Pete didn't seem to notice how unsettled she felt to see him. Sweat glistened on his tanned arms and face, a black bandanna was tied over the top of his head. His jeans hung low on his hips.

Your blue-collar, ex-con lover.

The burning sensation in her stomach worsened. Why had she insisted on keeping their affair secret in the first place? The caller would have no room to maneuver if she hadn't.

"I saw your truck but didn't realize you were down here," she said, sounding ridiculously formal even to herself.

"Just finishing up this wall for Madeleine." His eyes narrowed, probing her with a sudden seriousness. Most people underestimated him, Allyson thought. They never saw this side of him. She remembered this same kind of mature gravity when he'd saved her and the kids on the Fourth of July. "I heard about Henry and Lillian. They okay?"

Allyson nodded. "I'm on my way to see them now."

"Word's getting out—"

"It's bound to, but I hope the media won't pounce on this one. Henry and Lillian are only eleven and twelve—it'd be unfair to plaster their names all over the news."

"People'll want to know why they didn't have 24/7 protection."

"Because they didn't—and don't—need it unless there's a specific reason. There wasn't one." Her voice quaked, and she fought sudden tears. "I have to go."

Pete leaned against a long-handled shovel. "What about you? Are you okay?"

"Yes," she said without thinking. "I wish—" She choked back tears, lowered her voice. "I wish you could go with me, but that's not…you can't."

He lifted his shovel and drove it into the ground as if she hadn't spoken. Pete was a man, Allyson knew, who heard what he wanted to hear. "Tell those rascals I can put them to work if they get bored and want to skip town again."

She hesitated, watching him as he refocused on his work, and she knew he was giving her this chance to escape. He wouldn't press her about their relationship, not now—but he had to be wondering. And he had a right to know where he stood. Here it was, two weeks since she'd become governor, and she still didn't know what to do about Pete Jericho. She just knew that her body and soul ached for him. As she left him to his work, she felt a stab of loneliness, worse, even, than in the first months after Lawrence died—maybe because it was so unnecessary, a self-inflicted pain.

She climbed over the stone wall and strode out across the field, through tall grass and black-eyed Susans, and finally into the woods, onto an old, overgrown logging road. It was flanked by stone walls and a light, young forest, birches swaying in the gentle breeze. She followed it down a hill, to a stream that was low and muddy this time of year. She jumped across it, landing in a squishy patch of wet moss and mud. The mosquitoes found her.

Off in the woods, a woodpecker banged at a tree, and it occurred to Allyson that she was alone. Alone, unfettered, on her way to see her children and one of her closest friends. She smiled at the normalcy of the moment.

Eleven

Sam nursed his third cup of black coffee that morning and listened to Kara on the phone, explaining herself to her big brother. She'd scowled at Sam a couple of times and motioned for him to go into the living room, but he stayed put at his spot at the kitchen table. He doubted she had the oomph to move. She'd pitched her cookies at the crack of dawn. He'd heard her and had offered his assistance, and she'd told him to go to hell.

Except for the shakes, she seemed okay now. She'd had two bowls of oatmeal for breakfast.

The coffee must have been sitting on the shelf, opened, for a year. It was lousy.

Kara had assured Jack she was no longer in possession of his .45, but took the opportunity to remind him that she did, indeed, know how to shoot. Also that she was a lawyer. Thirty-four. On her own since she was eighteen. Perfectly capable of making decisions without his input.

At a guess, Jack was as persuaded as Sam was, which was hardly at all, because Kara was missing the point. People in their right minds didn't act the way she had since the Stockwell kids had turned up missing. That meant either she *wasn't* in her right mind or she hadn't told them even close to everything. Sam was betting on the latter. She was like her brother in that regard. The two of them were hard-headed and utterly sane, but also close-mouthed and very protective of those they loved. There was no question that Kara loved Henry and Lillian Stockwell, heirs to the Stockwell fortune, the minor children of the governor of Connecticut, the two towheads who'd gasped when they met Sam and asked him if he planned to arrest them.

Kara handed the phone across the table. "Jack wants to talk to you." She stood in the kitchen, arms folded under her breasts. She had on stretchy black yoga pants and an oversize white shirt with three-quarter-length sleeves that seemed to emphasize the shape of her wrists and the length of her fingers.

"You talked to Susanna," Sam said into the phone. "She's still holding back something."

If there was a god, she was. Sam had no desire to explain the night he'd had two weeks ago with Jack's sister, not while brother Jack was still steamed about the gun and the plane and worried about why the Stockwell kids had turned up at her house. Susanna would withhold what she suspected—knew—about Sam and her sister-in-law from Jack—not to spare anyone but because she'd consider it beyond the scope of Jack's legitimate interests. In other words, it was none of his business who his sister slept with.

"You have my gun?" Jack asked.

"I do."

"Allyson Stockwell's on her way to collect her kids?"

"She should be here any minute."

He didn't seem satisfied. "Kara give you that attorney-client bullshit?"

"Still is."

"I can be on a plane today if you need me up there."

"With a little luck, we'll be back in San Antonio ourselves tonight," Sam said.

Jack grunted. "Don't count on it. Keep her safe, okay?"

"Done."

He disconnected, and when Kara cursed under her breath, Sam took another sip of coffee, unsympathetic to her aggravation with her brother. "If you'd called him when you found those kids at your house, if you all'd taken a commercial flight up here and arrived unarmed—"

She didn't let him finish. "We'd have been met at the airport by a swarm of state troopers. They'd have found out we were on that flight. And if I'd called you last night, I'd never had made it out of Texas with them."

"Fair point."

She snatched up her cell phone. "I made a promise to Henry and Lillian, and I've kept it."

"Most people don't keep promises they make to kids that age."

"I do."

She stormed outside, the screen door banging shut

behind her. Sam dumped the last of his coffee in the sink. She was probably extra testy because of throwing up. He followed her out, enjoying the mild air. He supposed it was on the warm side by New England standards.

He sat in an unpainted Adirondack chair in the shade of a red maple in the backyard and watched her get out an old hibachi and set it on a rickety wooden table. She made several trips back inside for a dishpan of steaming water, a sponge, a wire brush, paper towels, rubber gloves. She attacked the hibachi with the wire brush, going after an accumulation of black gunk. Sam offered to help. She told him no.

"Why don't you go back to Texas?" She didn't look up from her hacking and scraping. "The criminals might take over if you're gone too long."

He stretched out his legs, not letting her provoke him. "I just finished an investigation on the border. I have paperwork to do but nothing that can't keep. My lieutenant knows where I am." His lieutenant being her brother.

"Susanna shouldn't have sent you."

"I'd have come even if she hadn't asked me to." Ordered him was more like it, but that wasn't what had gotten him here. Kara was in some kind of trouble, or the kids were and she was being dragged in with them. He needed to be here.

Kara dipped her brush in the hot, soapy water. "You wouldn't have found me without her help."

He said nothing. He'd have found her.

The brush wasn't working, and she got annoyed and tossed it into the water with too much force, splashing her expensive watch and her white shirt. "Do you see why I stayed up here as long as I did?" She unrolled three or four paper towels and dried herself off. "No room to breathe in Texas. A big state like that, but two kids show up at my door, and next thing I've got two Texas Rangers on my case—"

"Those two kids happen to be the runaway minors of a New England governor."

"They're *kids.*"

"Precisely." Sam crossed his ankles, enjoying the shade. "You'd have all the room you want to breathe if you didn't provoke people. You made off in Jack's plane. You stole his gun. You put his wife in the position of having either to lie for you or betray you—"

"I have a responsibility to Henry and Lillian that supersedes any minor irritations or inconveniences I might cause you and my family." She glanced at him, and he thought he heard her voice catch. "What else would you have had me do?"

She obviously didn't intend for him to answer, but he did, anyway. "Invite me in for popcorn and let me talk to those kids."

"Oh. I see. Ranger Temple to the rescue. They'd cooperate with you, a perfect stranger—"

"It's what you should have done and you know it."

He thought for a second she'd throw her wet paper towels at him, but she didn't, just stuffed them into her hands and wadded them up into a tight ball. "My role here is different from yours. I'm their godmother and an attorney, their mother's friend. I have to take all that into consideration. Plus,'' she added, turning back to her hibachi, ''I know more about what's going on than you do.''

With her back turned, he noticed the shape of her hips, the breadth of her shoulders. She was slim and strong, and suddenly there was no question in his mind he'd make love to her again. It was inevitable. He said quietly, ''I know what it's like to have a conflict between professional obligations and personal interests.''

''I have a moral obligation to Henry and Lillian as well as a professional one. I love them without condition.''

''No such thing.''

She glanced back at him. ''That's cynical.'' She dipped her wad of paper towels into the soapy water and squeezed them onto the black gunk. ''I'll be fine if you go back to Texas. I don't need you here.''

''You don't need anyone, do you, Miss Kara?''

She didn't answer. He could see the stiffness in her spine, the tension in her leg muscles. When she shifted back to her dishpan, he caught her expression, faintly irritated, worried, not about to give him or anyone else an inch. Maybe a little scared, but she'd try hard not to let him see her fear.

''I'm on your side,'' Sam said.

''You threatened to arrest me.''

''With just cause. It doesn't mean I'm not on your side.''

She sighed at him. ''Sam, you're not on *anyone's* side. It's not in your nature. You're the original lone wolf.''

Lone wolf. He hadn't heard that one in a while. He rose to his feet, taller than she was but not by much. "Why were you throwing up this morning?"

"Food poisoning." She hadn't missed a beat, but fished out her wire brush and attacked the hibachi with renewed vigor. "I'm fine now. It might just have been nerves."

Sam shook his head. "You're not the nervous type, Counselor."

He'd spooked her. She scooped up her cleaning supplies and started for the back door, leaving the dishpan and the hibachi. "I'll let that sit a while and see if the grit loosens up." She paused on the bottom step. "Do you want me to check on flights for you?"

"I'm not going anywhere."

"I could throw you out," she said matter-of-factly.

He shrugged. "Jack said he could fly up here today. It's him or me. Take your pick."

She tore open the screen door. "Forget it. I give up. If I keep pushing, I'll just end up with both of you. Stay. You've got my gun, but if I end up needing it—" She dropped a sponge, swooped it up. "Never mind."

"Kara—"

She pretended not to hear him and slipped into the cottage, letting Sam sink back onto his chair in the shade and contemplate the mess that was her motives, loyalties, fears, desires and duties—and his own. Henry and Lillian Stockwell had released her from attorney-client privilege and let her tell him they'd forged a letter from their mother, but that was as far as they'd go.

Whatever was in the letter had precipitated Kara to depart Texas the way she had. But she refused to show it to him. He pushed. She pushed back, telling him he had no authority to compel her to turn the letter over.

He was thinking about searching her bags for it. Let her try and stop him. He didn't need a search warrant in damn Connecticut. He was the family friend from Texas who meant to find out what was going on, the one-night stand from the night the governor had drowned in his pool.

Except it wouldn't stay a one-night stand. That would change. Sam imagined a lot would change before he got Kara Galway back to Texas.

Lillian ran out the back door and plopped on the chair next to him, and it nearly swallowed her up, she was so slim. She looked every inch the fair-haired Yankee heiress, except for the scratches on her legs and the scowl on her face. "There are a lot of poisonous snakes in Texas, right?" she asked.

"I don't know about a lot, but, yes, ma'am, there are poisonous snakes in Texas."

She giggled. "Why do you call me 'ma'am'?"

He smiled at her. "Would you like me to call you Miss Lillian instead?"

"Just Lillian is fine." She was very serious now, considering her answer. "Or Lil. Henry and Mom call me Lil. Aunt Kara does, too, sometimes, but not very much."

"What do your friends call you?"

"Lillian."

"It's a pretty name. Why're you interested in snakes?"

"I'm *not*. I don't like snakes at all. My friend Cicely likes to catch them. Once she caught three baby snakes, and I screamed my head off. It was *so gross*. They were all squirmy. She tried to get me to pet them." She wrinkled up her face dramatically and stuck out her tongue. *"Blech."*

Sam settled back in his chair, noticing that it hadn't taken long for Miss Lillian to warm up to him. "You probably shouldn't be messing with snakes. You leave them alone, they'll likely leave you alone."

"That's what they said at the ranch. I kept asking and asking, but no one would tell me what kind of poisonous snakes there are in Texas. Will *you* tell me?"

"It depends where you are. It's a big state. We've got cottonmouths, copperheads, coral snakes, six or eight different kinds of rattlesnakes. I don't see too many snakes in the city."

She shuddered. "*Eight* different kinds of rattlesnakes? I *never* want to go back to Texas. Henry says there are poisonous snakes in Connecticut, but I don't believe him. I think he's stupid. Do *you* believe there are poisonous snakes in Connecticut?"

"I don't know much about Connecticut snakes." Sam didn't know what else to do but be honest with her. "I think timber rattlesnakes are up here, but I doubt they're common, and I seem to remember reading about a northern copperhead. I'm sure any poisonous snakes up here are rare."

Lillian didn't like his answer. She hung on to the

arms of the Adirondack chair as if it were a spaceship
about to take off. "Well, Connecticut doesn't have as
many poisonous snakes as Texas does. *I've* never
seen one."

Sam laughed. "That settles it, then, Miss Lillian."

Something caught her eye off in the distance, and
Sam, instantly alert, got to his feet. She did, too, then
gasped as a fair-haired woman waved from out in the
small field, across a low stone wall. Lillian squealed.
"Mommy!"

The girl raced across the yard and scrambled over
the stone wall to her mother. Sam watched Allyson
Lourdes Stockwell scoop up her daughter, hugging
her, swinging her so that the top of the tall grass tick-
led her bare feet.

Henry burst through the back door and got almost
to the stone wall before he slowed suddenly, then
stopped, waiting as his mother set down his sister and
the two of them climbed over the wall. The boy
shoved his hands into his pockets and yawned, as if
nothing unusual had transpired in the past two days.
"Hi, Mom."

"Hello, Henry." Allyson smiled at him and slung
one arm over his thin shoulders, hugging him, kissing
the top of his head. "I'm glad you're here. I've
missed you."

Kara had come out onto the steps. If she was worried she was in as much trouble with her friend as
she was with Sam and her brother, nothing in her
demeanor showed it. All that courtroom experience
had to be coming in handy right now, Sam thought,
observing the scene with interest. His mother was an

art teacher and loved kids, but if he'd pulled the kind of stunt Henry and Lillian had pulled on their mother, he'd have been skinned for supper.

"Mom, I'd like you to meet Sergeant Sam Temple of the Texas Rangers," Henry said, his tone Prince of Wales formal. "Sergeant Temple, this is my mother, Allyson Stockwell."

"Pleased to meet you, Governor," Sam said, shaking her hand. She was an attractive, naturally pale and elegant woman, he thought, but the strain of the past few days was evident.

"Thank you—thank you for everything." She turned to Kara, and Sam could see they were both tense, even awkward, as if neither wanted to say anything that would further upset the other. Allyson managed a weak smile. "I'm sorry about all this. I thought going to the ranch and then visiting you was what they wanted to do—they'd been looking forward to their trip to Texas all summer."

"I'm fine, Allyson. Don't worry about it," Kara said. "We're all here, and we're all okay. Nothing else matters. Why don't you and the kids go inside and visit? Sam and I were just cleaning the hibachi."

Allyson clenched Kara's wrist. "Kara…"

"It's okay, Allyson. Hey—we made up a can of frozen lemonade. There's ice."

"Lemonade would be wonderful." She seemed unaware even of what she'd said, and added, out of the blue, "I released a statement this morning basically saying the kids went to your place on their own, but all's well, we're handling it—I didn't lie, just let it be known this is a private family matter. The media'll still have a field day, but Hatch thinks they won't go too far, not with two young kids involved. I don't think any reporters will come out here to the cottage.''

Henry tugged on his mother's hand. ''Come on, Mom, let's go have lemonade.''

''What?'' She seemed to have forgotten the lemonade, then smiled, ruffling her son's blond hair. ''Sure. Lemonade it is. I want to hear all about this 'wild tale' you told Kara.''

Kara frowned, staring after mother and children as they headed into the kitchen.

Sam understood her concern. ''Something's not right with your friend the governor,'' he said. ''Those kids know it, just like you do. Ten to one they clam up on her.''

Kara clenched her hands into fists, her mouth shut tight, and he could see she wasn't saying anything, either.

''Maybe you should tell me this wild tale,'' he added quietly.

Instead of answering him, she fished the wet, shredded paper towels out of the dishpan and slapped the soaking mess on the hibachi. She breathed out. ''Well, I think all that black gunk's set long enough, don't you?''

Allyson did as she'd promised and let Hatch know she'd arrived safely, then tried to make sense out of her children's behavior. Seeing her hadn't brought forth a rush of explanations—a rush of anything, for that matter. Henry and Lillian refused to go into any detail about their reasons for running away and conning Kara into sneaking them to Stonebrook Cottage. They weren't even subtle about it. They just wouldn't talk.

Allyson was stung. "Is it because you're afraid you'll get into trouble?" she asked.

"No." Henry had drained one glass of lemonade and was at the refrigerator pouring himself another. "Aunt Kara's our lawyer. She'll make sure we don't get into any trouble."

"Henry, Kara's not your lawyer—"

"She says everything we told her is privileged."

"If you thought you were confiding in her as your lawyer, yes, but—" Allyson tried to keep the hurt and impatience out of her tone; she'd hardly touched her lemonade. "You're my children. I need to know what's going on with you. I *want* to know. Lillian? What about you?"

Lillian, sitting across the table from her mother, didn't seem enthusiastic about her lemonade, either. "My stomach hurts."

Allyson reined in her frustration. Insisting on answers was getting her nowhere, and she'd been advised not to pressure them. She couldn't remember by whom. Her mother? Madeleine? The kids' counselors in Texas? She couldn't remember. "I'm just glad you're both okay. You can tell me the whys and wherefores when you're ready. If there's anything I absolutely needed to know, you'd tell me, wouldn't you? Or let Kara tell me?"

Henry sat at the table with his fresh glass of lemonade. "Sure, Mom."

"I can work here in Bluefield for a few days. We don't have to go back to Hartford right away, and you know your grandma would love to have you around."

"When are we moving into the governor's house?" Lillian asked.

"Soon. We're keeping our house in West Hartford, and your school won't change—"

"We know," Henry said.

She was getting nowhere. "I've had a lot to do in the past two weeks because of the sudden nature of what happened—but August tends to be a slow month for state government." God, she thought, she sounded like a stereotypical wire-walking politician instead of a mother who had a firm command of the situation. She smiled, feeling her tentativeness. She didn't know what was wrong with her children, and they wouldn't tell her. And she'd never ask Kara to violate their trust. "We'll work all this out in time. I promise, okay?"

Henry was concentrating on his lemonade. Lillian's eyes had glazed over. She stirred her lemonade, then frowned at her mother. "Mom, does Connecticut have poisonous snakes? Henry says it does, and so does Sam."

The nonsequitur caught Allyson by surprise, and she had to stop herself from making a sharp retort. "There are two species of venomous snakes found in Connecticut, the northern copperhead and the timber rattlesnake, but neither is common. Why were you talking about snakes?"

"Lillian wanted to know," Henry said. "She just likes to pretend she's worried about snakes."

"I know this hasn't been an easy summer." Allyson took her lemonade glass to the sink and dumped it out, her stomach burning. "A lot's happened that none of us planned. That means we all have to make adjustments."

Lillian raised her eyes to her mother. "Why can't someone else be governor?"

"Someone else can be. There'll be another election. For now, I'm the governor. That's part of the job of being lieutenant governor—it's the commitment I made when I was elected. If something happened to Big Mike, I had to step into his shoes. Unfortunately, something did happen."

"Are you glad?" Henry blurted.

Allyson jumped back against the sink, shocked. "No, of course not. He was my friend. He was your dad's friend even before either one of them knew me. *No.* I did not want anything to happen to him."

"I didn't mean it that way." Henry's voice was small, but his huge eyes were defiant, daring her to doubt him. "I meant are you glad you're governor. Do you *like* being governor?"

She was screwing this up on every level. "I don't know yet. It's too soon."

She answered honestly, her shoulders slumping as she realized how exhausted she was.

She didn't know what to say to her children, what to do to keep from making the situation any worse— to keep them from coming to hate her. They only had her. But she would be useless to them if she didn't have some kind of life apart from them. Still, serving as governor…maybe it was too much, especially on top of the shock of losing Big Mike.

Henry seemed somewhat satisfied by her answer. Lillian pretended not to be paying attention, a tactic she used, Allyson knew, when she wanted to avoid confrontation.

"I'll get better at being governor," Allyson said. "I'll be more efficient with my time. These past two weeks have been particularly intense, but it won't always be that way. We'll get used to being without Big Mike, all of us." She paused, but neither child spoke. "I didn't send you to Texas to get rid of you."

"We know that," Henry said, as if she were an idiot and had once again underestimated him and his sister.

Allyson felt a surprising tug of confidence. He was a tough little nugget, her Henry. "If I'm missing the point, tell me what it is."

He got to his feet with his lemonade. "Can we go outside? It's hot in here. I want to put my feet in the brook."

"Me, too," Lillian said.

Her first impulse was to make them stay and to keep at it until they told her everything, explained what possessed them to run away and say whatever they'd said to manipulate Kara into bringing them here. Instead, Allyson nodded. "Don't go far—and be careful."

"Can we stay here with Aunt Kara tonight?" Lillian asked.

"I don't know if she's able to stay—"

"She is," Henry said. "She said she was supposed to take a few days off from work."

Allyson seized on the idea. A few days with Kara might just do the trick, snap Henry and Lillian out of whatever funk they were in—and, Allyson admitted, that would give her a bit more time to settle into her new role and decide how to handle the anonymous calls, should they continue. Either they'd end, or she'd have to tell someone. She couldn't go on pretending they weren't happening.

The kids scooted off to the brook, and she headed out back. Sam Temple politely excused himself, leaving her alone with Kara. Allyson raised her eyebrows as she watched him retreat into the cottage. "Kara, Kara, you do amaze me sometimes."

Her friend was sitting in an Adirondack chair in the shade and deliberately ignored Allyson's remark—but she would. As open as Kara was about so many things, she was deeply private about her intimate longings and desires. If she hadn't moved to Texas, Allyson wondered if she'd have told her friend about Pete Jericho. Probably not, because of their history, but Allyson missed telling Kara everything, missed having her around.

"The kids went mum on you, didn't they?" Kara sighed, motioning for Allyson to join her in the shade. "I thought they might, hoped they wouldn't—and flat out asked them not to."

"It's all right. Well, it's not all right, but I can be patient now that they're here." Allyson sank onto the second Adirondack chair, remembering countless times she and Kara had sat out here drinking margaritas, laughing, watching Henry and Lillian play. They'd built a tire swing for them, just she and Kara together. "They trust you, Kara. Thank God they had you to run to. I know it hasn't made your life any easier—"

Kara waved off her apology. "That's the least of my worries. They're great kids."

"They are. Eleven and twelve." Allyson smiled halfheartedly. "Can you imagine what it'll be like around here when they're teenagers?"

Kara laughed. "Why do you think I moved back to Texas when I had the chance?"

"You're *awful*. They've missed you—so have I. Hatch has, too." Allyson paused, but she knew Kara wasn't going to respond. "He'll want to see you."

"He doesn't like how I handled the situation, does he?"

"Of course not, but that's because he doesn't like anything about the situation. You should have heard him pleading with that Texas Ranger brother of yours to keep this quiet." Allyson stretched out her legs, feeling more relaxed, more comfortable with Kara. She gave her friend a sideways smile. "I take it you didn't invite Ranger Temple up here."

"He came on his own."

"Ah. He's protecting you—"

"No, he's plotting ways to get me back to Texas so he can throw me in jail."

Allyson smiled. "I don't know, that could be fun."

"Allyson!"

"God, that was my first genuine laugh in days. Big Mike would be pleased—he knew Texas would agree with you.'' But Allyson couldn't sustain her teasing mood and paused, gazing at a bumblebee buzzing in a patch of burgundy hollyhocks under the kitchen window. ''The kids would like to stay here with you for a day or two. Would you mind? It might be a good idea, a chance for us all to settle down after the past couple of days.''

''You know I'll do anything I can to help. And I'd love to spend some time with the kids. I was looking forward to having them for a few days in Austin. We can have our visit here, instead.''

''Your job—''

''I was just instructed to take some time off. I've been pushing it lately.''

''No surprise there,'' Allyson said. ''I knew when Big Mike died you'd end up burning the midnight oil. You always do when you're upset about something.''

Kara didn't argue. ''It's hard, losing him.''

''Damn hard.''

They stood together and walked over to the brook, which was technically on Jericho land. Henry and Lillian were preoccupied with a frog that had escaped them, and they both seemed cheerful and normal when Allyson said goodbye. She explained that they could stay at the cottage tonight—she'd be at the barn if they needed her. That suited them fine. ''I'll bring you fresh clothes later on this afternoon, okay?''

''Sure, Mom,'' Henry said without looking up from his frog-hunting.

Allyson led the way back to the cottage, fighting tears. Why wouldn't they talk to her? What was wrong? But Kara said nothing, offered no opinion, no comment, as they walked around back. Sam Temple was working on the hibachi. He struck Allyson as a man who wouldn't tolerate stonewalling or any measure of bullshit, but he couldn't have gotten more out of Kara and the kids than she had.

He offered to walk her back. Allyson shook her head. "That's not necessary."

"You're wasting your breath," Kara said, amused.

"I just fended off my security detail."

"They work for you. Sam doesn't." She smiled. "Trust me on this, Allyson."

Allyson couldn't even begin to guess what Temple was thinking, but saw his dark eyes settle on Kara in a way that made her own knees quake. She relented. "All right, after you—what is it people call you?"

"Sam'll be fine, ma'am."

The half grin and black eyes coupled with the well-muscled physique—Kara couldn't possibly have failed to notice. And Temple obviously had an opinion about Kara's dark eyes and slim physique. The idea of a macho Texas Ranger on Kara Galway's case was Allyson's first genuinely entertaining thought in days, and she was sorry Big Mike wasn't there to enjoy it with her.

Twelve

Kara returned to the brook and crept along a narrow path down to a small, shallow pool amidst rocks and coppery mud. Lillian squatted in the ferns and skunk cabbage and pointed to a frog in the wet moss. "Shh," she whispered. "He's scared."

"Of what?" Kara asked softly.

"I don't know."

The frog jumped and landed in the water with a loud splash, startling Lillian. She rose, brushing mud off her knees. Henry got up from the rock where he'd been sitting and shook his head. "I knew you couldn't catch him."

Lillian tossed her head. "I didn't want to catch him. I wanted him to be free."

"Come on, you two," Kara said cheerfully. "If you're going to spend a few days out here with me, we need provisions. Oatmeal, stale coffee and Ben & Jerry's ice cream will only get me so far."

"There's macaroni and cheese," Lillian said.

"It's orange. Look, you'll be doing me a favor. Sam's walking your mom to your grandma's. I want to get to town and stock the cupboards before he gets back.''

This was just common sense on her part. He'd left her and the kids to their own devices only because he'd calculated that it was more critical for him to get a read on Allyson and her state of mind. The Texas Ranger at work. He wasn't just going to sit around and scrape gunk off an old grill. He wouldn't like Kara slipping off to town without him riding shotgun, but that was too bad. They needed food. Henry and Lillian needed to help out with the grocery list and getting the cottage in order. And, she supposed, she needed to reestablish some measure of autonomy with Sam, even if he did have her gun.

She knew he'd see what she'd seen in Allyson— the strain, the gauntness, the worry. Big Mike's death had taken its toll, the responsibilities of being governor and now her concerns about her children. She'd seized on the idea of having them stay at Stonebrook Cottage. Kara wondered if those who saw Allyson every day even noticed the transformation, the erosion of confidence and optimism that, a year ago, had seemed an integral part of her friend's personality.

Sam wouldn't need to know the details of Henry and Lillian's flight to Austin to recognize that something was very wrong with Allyson Lourdes Stockwell, governor of Connecticut.

Henry relented first, then Lillian, skipping off ahead of Kara. She called to them to jump into Sam's car. It was blocking hers, and she'd found the keys right there on the dresser in the bedroom. No point wasting time moving it out of the way just so she could take her rental.

Henry rode shotgun this time. He stared out the window, looking fairly neutral for a boy who'd just stonewalled his governor mother. "If you and Lillian really are in danger," Kara said, "I should tell someone. You'll want backup if this guy who followed you to Austin comes up here."

Henry lifted his thin shoulders and said nothing, but Lillian leaned forward from the back seat. "Sam will back you up. He's got a gun."

Kara nearly drove off the road. "How do you know? Do you notice *everything?*"

"That's right," Henry said. "Sam can protect us."

For reasons she didn't care to contemplate, Henry's comment went up one side of her and down the other. She decided not to tell him that Sam would play it by the book and sic a dozen Connecticut state troopers on them. "Sam's only carrying a weapon because he doesn't want you to get hold of it." Or her, Kara thought. "Look, he's a professional. He's not some wild-eyed nut who's going to start shooting up the place. He'll only use deadly force as a last resort."

"If you see the man," Lillian said, "and Sam's not around, what will you do?"

"Call the police—"

She gasped. "But you *can't,* you *promised.*"

"Henry, Lillian—listen to me. Your mother's the governor. She has security guards whose job it is to protect her and her family. If you don't feel safe, she can get you 24/7 security, a couple of state troopers who'll watch you like hawks."

"We don't want them," Henry said. "We trust you."

"At least let me tell Sam about the man from the ranch."

"She doesn't believe us." Lillian leaned forward in her seat and whispered to her brother. "If she did, she'd tell Mom everything, and you know what Mom would do—"

"Lillian!" Henry shot her a silencing look over his shoulder. "You talk too much."

"I don't know what I believe," Kara said diplomatically. "I'm keeping an open mind. But Lillian's right, if I believed you were in any serious danger, from this guy or anyone else, I wouldn't be taking you out to buy groceries. It's not that I don't believe you saw a man following you—I'm just not sure what it means. It's a good sign, I'd say, that he didn't do anything to you at the ranch or at my house in Austin and hasn't shown up here."

"You want us to tell Mom about him?" Henry asked.

"I want you to tell your mother everything."

Kara didn't bother to hide her frustration. Here she was, still dealing with Henry and Lillian and their fears and secrets. Everything seemed to be at a standstill, and she couldn't help but think Allyson had sidestepped her responsibilities. Kara glanced at her godson, then into the back seat at her goddaughter. They were so young. She felt a sudden urge to cry.

Damn. Wasn't emotionalism another sign of pregnancy? But her hormones couldn't have changed that radically in just two weeks—the stress of the situation must be causing her volatile emotions.

"If you think your mother is in danger," she said, keeping her voice calm, deliberate, "you need to tell her. You need to tell *me* and let me tell her. We can't withhold that kind of information. It's not fair. As for witnessing what you did from your tree house, it's my advice, as an attorney and as your godmother, that you tell your mother that, too, and let her inform the police. You won't get into trouble."

But they'd been through all this before, and their answer was the same as it was last night and this morning. Henry delivered it. "We'll think about it."

"Think hard," Kara told him.

She parked at a small grocery store on a side street near the town common. Both kids seemed delighted to charge through the aisles grabbing food they liked while Kara gathered up fruits, vegetables, milk and bread, and three new flavors of Ben & Jerry's ice cream. She also picked up a bottle of vitamins. Folic acid—if she was pregnant, she'd need to make sure she was getting enough. She'd intended to make use of the pregnancy tests after work the other night, but Henry and Lillian went missing and all hell had broken loose. Now she had Sam in her shadow. Not that it mattered. She *wasn't* pregnant.

She needed to focus on her godchildren. Although she was trying to keep an open mind, she suspected Henry and Lillian had taken bits and pieces of what they'd seen and heard since Big Mike's death and created a scary scenario of conspiracy and danger. They easily could have seen a series of different men at camp, maybe a guy brought in to fix a broken light, another guy who'd come in to remove brush after a storm, a father who'd had to pick up a sick kid—who knew? Given the turmoil of their summer, Henry and Lillian probably needed to talk to a professional, a psychologist or counselor who could help them better understand and cope with what had happened. The accident at the Fourth of July bonfire was enough to deal with, and they'd barely mentioned that to Kara. But their own near escape from serious injury, then their helplessness as they'd watched Big Mike—it had to have had an impact on them.

Allyson, she knew, would resist intervention. Kara remembered her at Lawrence's funeral ten years ago and at Big Mike's two weeks ago—Allyson was of the stiff-upper-lip school of psychology. She'd never see it as repression, simply as being dignified and mature.

Of course, the guy in Texas could be some creep on the kids' tail who had nothing whatsoever to do with anyone in Connecticut, in which case she should tell Sam so he could notify Texas authorities and have the bastard picked up.

Sam wouldn't give a damn that she was caught between a rock and a hard place.

Kara picked up a pound of fresh-ground, knock-you-on-your-ass coffee because she knew Sam Temple wasn't going anywhere. He might appreciate a little warning and a hell of a lot more information, but he didn't have to be in Texas not to take kindly to anyone coming after two children. If this guy showed up, Sam wouldn't need time to adjust.

Kara put the groceries on her American Express card and grimaced at the bags of chips and boxes of cookies and snack bars, the huge box of microwave popcorn with real butter, that Henry and Lillian had dumped into the cart. At least Allyson had never said she trusted Kara to feed her kids properly. They pushed the cart across the parking lot to the car, Lillian taking the keys and opening up the trunk.

"Kara? Hey, there. I thought that was you." Billie Corrigan trotted across the parking lot with two plastic bags filled with what looked like Christmas lights. She grinned at Kara, then at Henry and Lillian. "How are you? Besides keeping Bluefield, Connecticut, in gossip."

Kara smiled. "Billie, it's good to see you. We just slipped out for a few groceries."

"And no reporters have descended on you? You've always been lucky like that, Kara." Billie laughed, her good cheer infectious. Kara didn't know her well, but they'd always gotten along. Billie lifted one bag onto her hip, let the other drop to the pavement. "I was over at the junk store seeing what I could find. If Madeleine Stockwell knew where I get half my decorations, she'd never hire me again. It's all in the presentation. I learned so much from my father, bless his drunken, no-account soul."

"You do great work," Kara said.

Billie squinted at her. "Think I'd make a go of it in Texas?"

Kara laughed. "We'd love you."

"'We.' You really are staying down there, aren't you? Well, I don't blame you. Must be nice to be near family. I know moving up here to be closer to my brother's one of the best things I've ever done, not that I see enough of him.'' She turned to Henry and Lillian, who were lifting the grocery sacks into the trunk. ''What're you kids up to? If you were mine, you'd be chipping rock, running away like that.''

They mumbled a polite greeting and scooted into the car, shutting the doors quickly behind them. Billie shook her head, her expression serious now. ''It's been hell around here since Big Mike died. I don't blame them for acting weird. We've all wanted to run away, I imagine, at one time or another. Anything I can do?''

''I don't think so, but I'll let you know if something comes up. Thanks, Billie.''

''Have you seen Hatch yet?''

Something came into her eyes, and Kara wondered if Billie Corrigan knew how her brother felt about his longtime friend from Texas. ''Not yet.''

''He misses you,'' Billie said.

''I miss everyone, too. Nice seeing you, Billie. I have to go.''

Allyson led Sam along a wide lane through the woods, explaining that it had all been farmland at the turn of the twentieth century. She pointed out the old stone walls that used to mark the fields, the occasional fence post and length of rusted barbed wire, the relative youth of the forest itself. When she thought about the power of nature, she said, she didn't fret so much about the gravel pit out over the hill.

Sam listened and said little.

They came to a stand of poplars, and she continued, unbothered, it seemed, by his lack of response. "Charlie and Pete Jericho will give nature a helping hand, but even if they didn't, it'd happen over time— just too long a time to satisfy my mother-in-law." She smiled at Sam, but he noticed her eyes remained difficult to read. "Madeleine insists the gravel pit's not much better than a strip mine, but that's not fair. There'll be fines and general hell to pay if it doesn't get restored. She'd like it a lot less if the Jerichos chopped up their property into estate lots and sold them for a fortune, I can tell you that."

"What about zoning?"

"It's very strict in some towns, less so here in Bluefield. Connecticut has a forever-farmland program, where the state buys the development rights of a property in exchange for it remaining farmland, but the Jerichos haven't applied. They just keep working the land in their own way."

Sam glanced around him, the shade shifting in the late-morning sun. "It's beautiful land out here."

She smiled. "Yes, it is."

They crossed a narrow, muddy stream. A swarm of mosquitoes found them and followed them out to drier ground. One fat mosquito stayed with Sam all the way out to the end of the lane, where they came to a rolling field of orange and yellow wildflowers and tall, strawlike grass that swayed in the breeze. Across the field, against the bright, clean sky, were the immaculate buildings of what he assumed was the Stockwell estate.

"Madeleine still calls it Stockwell Farm." Allyson

lingered in the shade. "They've never raised stock or grown crops for sale, but they were almost self-sufficient for a while when my husband was growing up here." She laughed suddenly, almost embarrassed. "Do you have this effect on everyone? I'm just yammering on."

"Feel free," Sam said.

"The Stockwells have a great deal of money. I don't. I'm comfortable, but the bulk of my husband's estate is held in trust for our children. Don't get me wrong, as Connecticut goes, they're not super-wealthy. I mean, they're not Rockefeller rich—"

"They never owned land that was turned into a national park?"

She tilted her head back, eyeing him. "Do you have a problem with wealth, Sergeant Temple?"

"No, ma'am. Not me." He grinned at her. "I'm from Texas."

"My God. Have you smiled at Kara like that?"

"Has no effect on her."

"That's what you think, is it?"

He didn't, not really, but he wasn't discussing Kara with the governor of Connecticut, no matter how long she and Kara had known each other. Allyson walked out into the field, and Sam followed, the sun bright and hot, something not at all right with this woman. She'd let her brother-in-law know she was returning from the cottage accompanied, so Sam didn't have to worry about armed guards swooping down on him.

When her cell phone rang, she was so startled she nearly dropped to her knees. Sam caught her by the upper arm, steadying her, and he noticed she was shaking and had bit her lip, drawing blood.

"I forgot I had my phone with me," she said lamely, knowing, obviously, that she'd overreacted to a simple phone call. "It's my private line—I'm sure it's Hatch or one of the kids."

She retrieved her small, expensive cell phone from a pocket and pressed it to her ear, the muscles in her hand visibly stiffening, as if she was trying to keep it from shaking. She said her name and listened a moment. "I can't talk right now. I'll have to call you back." Her tone was cool, almost affected. She shut off the phone and closed her fingers around it. "I shouldn't have had it on in the first place. Sorry for the interruption."

"No problem."

But Sam was still watching her. She couldn't breathe. Her skin color went a pale gray, and purple splotches appeared on her cheeks. Sam was one second away from calling out the troops—he wasn't having a governor pass out on his watch.

She held up a hand, smiling wanly. "I'm okay. A bit of a panic attack. I think I'm allowed, don't you?" She took a shallow breath. "I haven't had one since my first year of law school. Kara was there, but it wouldn't have mattered. I'd have told her. Everyone tells Kara everything."

"Mike Parisi told her he couldn't swim," Sam said.

"He didn't tell me. I didn't know until he drowned. He never confided in me that way." Her speech was too rapid, and Sam had trouble understanding her. She talked Yankee fast as it was. "Kara was like a daughter to him, but I think it was more than that."

"He was in love with her?"

"A little—maybe a lot. But their relationship was strictly platonic. Kara attracts men who love her from afar. They're afraid they'll ruin everything if they touch her." Her speech regulated, and some of the purple splotches faded as she got control of herself. A spark of humor flashed unexpectedly in her eyes. "But you don't have that problem, do you, Sergeant Temple?"

He smiled. "You're a bold woman, Governor Stockwell."

"I'm practicing."

"You want to tell me what that phone call was about?"

"Nothing that would interest you." She continued out across the field, the flowers up to her knees. "I imagine you don't like the idea of Big Mike drowning over an injured bluebird, but it happened. How could his death have been deliberate? It's just about the craziest way to assassinate a governor I can think of. You'd have to find a bluebird, capture it, break its leg, keep it alive long enough to toss it into the pool, get Big Mike out there in time to see it while he'd still have hope of rescuing it—it's just crazy."

"Logic would suggest it was an accident," Sam said.

"That's right."

"Do you believe it was?"

"Let's just walk," Governor Stockwell said.

He stopped, still within a few yards of the cover of

the woods. "You go on from here. I should get back to Kara and your kids."

"You just don't want to explain that gun you're carrying to my security people. I *am* the governor of my state. I know its laws." She suddenly reminded Sam of her son in one of his know-it-all moods, but it didn't last. Her mood shifted, and she gave him a long look, one that told him she was, indeed, governor material and not a woman to underestimate, no matter her current emotional state. "Why are you here, Sam?"

"Kara's sister-in-law asked me to find her."

Allyson smiled. "Kara broke the rules, didn't she?"

"Many."

"Good for her."

"Governor Stockwell, I think your children are in danger. I think they know it, and I think you at least suspect it. You need to talk to your people here."

The ice mask came down, and Sam knew he'd overstepped his bounds—not that he cared. Allyson Stockwell tilted back her head at him, the bright light washing out all the color of her hair. She looked older than thirty-seven, and very tired. "Henry and Lillian have a certain flair for the dramatic. In her own way, underneath all her professionalism and courtroom cool, so does Kara. I'd maintain my objectivity if I were you."

"If you're withholding information from authorities—"

"Need I remind you that you have no jurisdiction in Connecticut?" He didn't answer, and she added crisply, "Thanks for walking me home. I hope you'll let me handle my children in my own way." She spun on her toes and marched three steps, then stopped abruptly, shifting back to him, all her haughtiness gone. Her eyes glistened with tears. "You and Kara— you'll look after Henry and Lillian, won't you?"

Sam took a step toward her. "Governor Stockwell—Allyson, tell me what's wrong. You're right, I don't have jurisdiction here, but if you're in trouble—"

But she'd turned her back to him again and was running now, not a woman of great accomplishment or a New England governor determined to hold her own—she ran as if she was a scared kid herself.

Sam returned to the shade and cover of the woods and decided not to go after her. For all he knew, the Stockwells had dogs. Underground alarms. Razor wire. Allyson Lourdes Stockwell had state troopers guarding her who would, indeed, ask to see a local permit for his weapon. In their place, Sam would, too.

And the governor of Connecticut wasn't telling him anything more today.

About a million mosquitoes followed him back through the woods. As soon as he got back to the cottage, he planned to tell Miss Lillian he'd take eight kinds of rattlesnakes over a swarm of damn Connecticut mosquitoes any day.

Thirteen

❦

When Kara pulled into the cottage driveway, Sam was sitting on the stone steps waiting for them. She'd assumed she'd beat him back, even with her detour to the diner for onion rings. He got up and walked slowly toward the car, his movements controlled but stiff with displeasure. She climbed out of the front seat and popped the trunk. A pissed-off Texas Ranger didn't scare her.

Before she could get back to the trunk, Sam was there, lifting out two grocery sacks and handing one each to Henry and Lillian. "Go on," he said. "Take them inside."

They obeyed without question.

There was one more sack and a gallon of milk. Kara reached for the milk, but Sam touched her elbow, his black eyes narrowed as he gave her his best Texas drawl. "You need to learn the difference between mine and thine, Miss Kara."

"If you hadn't parked behind my car, I wouldn't have had to take yours. I left you a note, so don't get all steely-eyed about me going to town."

"Time you and I got a few things straight."

"Such as?"

But he must have sensed something in her tone—either that or he'd been sitting on the steps thinking dark thoughts for too long—because he took another step closer to her and laced his fingers into her hair, gently drawing her head back so that her eyes were locked with his. "Your brother would shoot me right now for what I'm thinking."

"I might shoot you myself—"

"I don't think so."

He spoke as if he knew what she wanted, and he lowered his mouth to hers, pausing an instant as if to give her a chance to tell him he was wrong. She didn't, and he kissed her lightly, erotically, tracing his tongue along her bottom lip, not at all tentatively, a reminder of how intimate they'd already been.

"Sam…the kids…"

"I think they've seen people kissing before."

"Not *me*."

"Then maybe it's time."

He slid his hands down to the small of her back, then pulled her against him, deepening their kiss, breaking down her natural reserve, until finally she cupped his waist just above his holster and felt the muscles and the heat of his skin through his shirt.

He drew his mouth away from hers, still holding her, still close. "I went too fast with you two weeks ago, but I don't regret it. I can't." His voice was low and filled with an intense, direct passion, a kind of honesty that itself left her breathless. "I'm not afraid of hurting you. I don't want to, but I'm not afraid of it, because that'd mean backing off right now, and I'm not going to."

"You're not afraid of anything." There was no lightness in her tone.

"I am, Kara. I'm afraid of not being capable of the kind of love you want and deserve, the kind of commitment Jack and Susanna have for each other. You've watched them since you were a kid. They're soul mates." He dropped his hands, stepping slightly away from her, his eyes black and hard against the soft summer sky. "I'm not anyone's soul mate."

"Sam..." Kara fought for air, a chance to regain her balance, and tried to adopt a teasing tone. "I don't know, maybe I should sneak off on you more often—"

He touched her nose, then her chin. "One day you're not going to make jokes to cover for how you feel. You're going to tell me." He straightened and stepped back from her, grabbing the last sack of groceries. "Now, let's talk ground rules."

"Who says you get to make the rules?" She didn't know what else to say, how to keep him from holding the high ground now that he'd claimed it.

"All right, Miss Kara." His eyes gleamed, a twitch of humor on the corners of his mouth. "You can have input. Mind if I go first?"

"No. Go ahead."

"You don't leave here without me. The kids don't leave here without me." He rocked back on his heels. "Your turn."

"That's it? That's all you're demanding—"

"Requesting. Yes, ma'am, that's it. What's your input?"

She eyed him and realized he was having fun with her, at least to a certain extent. Well, why not? She smiled. "Do I get my gun back?"

"You must be hell in a courtroom."

"Let's just say you don't want me cross-examining you if your story doesn't hold up."

"Ditto. If we were in Texas, we wouldn't be talking ground rules. We'd be talking bail."

She snatched up the milk jug. "Bet I could have disarmed you while you were kissing me."

"You were too busy kissing me back."

"You're cocky as hell when it comes to women, aren't you?"

He grinned. "I know you'd rather kiss me than go for my gun. You went to Yale. You're smart."

It didn't take a Yale education to know that, Kara thought with a touch of amusement. Sam Temple was not an ordinary man, and this was not an ordinary situation.

His grin faded, and he lifted out the last grocery sack and held it in one arm. "What's wrong with your governor friend?"

Kara shivered despite the warm air. "I don't know."

He seemed to believe her. "Come on, let's fire up the hibachi and throw some dogs on. You can tell me who the players are in this state." He started across the lawn, peeking in at the groceries. "A lot of junk here."

"I didn't think it was the time to enforce good nutrition."

"Probably not." He put one foot on the bottom step and glanced back at her, no hint of humor in his expression now. "One more thing, Kara. If you throw up again for no good reason, you and I are taking a trip to the local drugstore."

"There's a well-stocked first-aid kit in the cottage—"

"Does it include a home pregnancy test kit?"

His black eyes drilled through her, but she managed a scowl. "It was food poisoning."

He didn't say a word as she pushed past him, her mouth still tasting of his, her head spinning.

Pete Jericho drove out to Stonebrook Cottage after lunch and found Henry and Lillian playing barefoot on the tire swing out back like a couple of ordinary kids. He greeted Kara politely, and she responded with her usual warmth, pretending she didn't know he still resented her for the plea bargain. He knew he wasn't being fair. Allyson had told him as much. He sometimes wondered if Allyson would have taken up with him had Kara stayed in Connecticut, if somehow Kara's presence had helped stall things between them.

He'd worked hard all morning and smelled it. Kara introduced him to her Texas Ranger friend, and Pete could tell right away Sam Temple knew about his jail time. Either Kara had told him or Temple had some kind of cop radar that pointed out the ex-cons. Maybe both. Pete groaned inwardly. Maybe he was just paranoid.

He wanted to get the kids alone to ask them about the tree house, but the opportunity didn't present itself. He didn't want to say anything in front of Kara or the Texas Ranger and cause trouble for the children, or come off as overdramatizing. So he just let it go.

He wondered about Temple. The Texan didn't seem Kara's type, but who was? Hatch Corrigan had a thing for her, and Big Mike had, too, if Pete wasn't totally off base about what he'd seen and heard before she'd headed back to Texas. They were both a lot older than she was. Temple looked to be about the same age, and he was a law enforcement officer, armed, definitely not a Yalie.

Well, who knew with Kara Galway. She and Allyson had been friends for years, very different people who loved and trusted each other. Pete figured that sort of friendship wasn't something that went according to logic. It was there, and he had to live with it.

"Would you like some lemonade or iced tea?" Kara offered.

"No, thanks. Just wanted to stop by. Kids are hanging out with you here for a day or two?"

She nodded. "I haven't seen them in quite a while."

"If you need anything, you know where to find me."

He adjusted the rope on the tire swing and left, feeling vaguely foolish for having come in the first place. What made him think he could be a stepfather for those kids? He'd known them since they were babies, but he was someone they'd hire after Madeleine died and they inherited Stockwell Farm. He could see himself in thirty years, like his father, puttering up on his tractor, arguing over cordwood. Henry and Lillian couldn't really remember their father. Lawrence had been so much older than Allyson, and maybe that was part of the problem—she was looking for a father figure. Pete was just a handy romp in the hay.

He headed up the road to finish work on the retaining wall, but Madeleine cornered him out on the patio. She had a tall glass of iced tea and a full pitcher, but didn't offer him any. "I can't get used to having state troopers around whenever Allyson is here," she said, but Pete thought she was secretly pleased at all the activity. "She's been on the phone or in conference with Hatch most of the afternoon. She says she has state business to conduct. I understand, of course, but what state business could be more important than her own children?"

"I just came from the cottage. They're fine."

"They're *not* fine. They can't be fine if they took the trouble to run away. Allyson's doing nothing to get to the bottom of it."

"Maybe it's not a mystery to her—"

"Nonsense. She just doesn't want to know the truth. She's not one for discipline, you know. In my mother's day, they'd be in for a good buggy-whipping."

Pete grinned at her. "Your *mother's* day, Mrs. Stockwell? You're not that old. A buggy-whipping's more like your grandmother's day."

"I'm eighty. I never thought I'd live this long."

She was on a roll, but Pete decided he'd gone in deep enough with her. "Maybe Allyson's taking advantage of having Kara here and clearing the decks so she and the kids can have some uninterrupted time after Kara leaves."

Madeleine looked at him over her frosted glass, and he could see he'd surprised her. "You're so sensible, Pete. I'm not sure I knew that eight or ten years ago."

He wondered if that was an apology for what she'd done to escalate the charges against him and land him in jail, but he didn't ask—she'd only deny she'd done anything. She'd say she never thought ill of him or wanted to stymie his affection for her daughter-in-law in any way. She'd say *affection,* too. Even when she talked about her four husbands, she never said she'd loved them. She'd had great affection for them. There'd been lovers on the side, too, from what he'd heard, but Madeleine liked to pretend lust and sex were for commoners.

He got back to work. He waved to a state trooper posted outside the barn. No wave back. No sign of Allyson at all, but Pete knew she was in there, and he pictured her in the moonlight, her head thrown back as she climaxed. His heartbeat quickened, and his chest felt as if it were being squeezed, his future, hope, everything he'd ever wanted and cherished slowly being choked out of him.

Kara slipped into the bathroom and locked herself inside, shakily opening one of her pregnancy test kits and easing out its contents. She was dizzy, probably just from nerves, but if she passed out and hit the floor with a loud klunk, and Sam had to beat down the door—well, she wouldn't pass out.

She followed the directions on the kit. While she waited for the results, she took a shower, rubbing soap over her abdomen, wondering what she would do if she were pregnant. Did she want to be? How would she proceed with Sam, her family, work? What would a baby feel like moving inside her? Would she be a good mother?

She thought of her own mother, reaching out a bloodied hand to her. *I'll take care of you, Kara...*

When she stepped out of the shower, she made herself wrap up in a bath sheet and take a calming breath before she looked at her test stick.

One pink line.

Negative.

It was the damn seafood tacos. Nerves. A bug.

She sank onto the edge of the bathtub and cried softly into her towel.

Lillian, who'd had hot dogs for lunch, informed Sam that she'd decided to become a vegetarian. She plopped onto the Adirondack chair next to him. "Did you know that some people eat *frogs?*"

"Not the whole frog. Just the legs."

"That's so gross."

"Like orange macaroni and cheese isn't?" They'd had that for lunch with the hot dogs.

She giggled. Their mother had stopped by for another brief visit, bringing fresh clothes and, incongruously, a bouquet of asters and zinnias from their grandmother. Henry and Lillian showed her where

Pete had fixed their tire swing and told her about catching frogs and about Kara buying them onion rings. Sam didn't think Allyson Stockwell looked any better than when he'd left her in the field, but her children didn't seem to notice.

"Some people eat snake, too," he told Lillian.

She gasped. "They do *not*."

He smiled. He thought she was enjoying being appalled by meat-eaters. "I've tried it. It's not my favorite. I like 'gator better. The tail's nice and tender."

"You mean you eat *alligators?*" She jumped up from her chair and ran up the back steps, calling for her brother. "Henry! Henry, Sam eats the *awfulest* things!"

"And you wonder why they have funny ideas about Texans." Kara walked around from the front of the cottage, her hair damp on the ends, her feet bare. She had on shorts and a lightweight sweater. Her cheeks were raw and red-looking, her eyes puffy as she sank into the chair Lillian had vacated. She stared up at the maple leaves flickering in the late-afternoon sun, and she said without looking at him, "I don't care if you can tell I've been crying. Everything suddenly got to me. Big Mike's death. The kids and their problems. Allyson and how overwhelmed she is. *You.*"

"Say the word and I'll take you back to Texas."

"I can't run—"

"And you can't solve these people's problems for them."

"I'm not trying to. I'm trying—" She sighed up at the tree, as if she was trying to make sense of its branches, the shifting light taking some of the worry out of her face. "I can't leave Henry and Lillian, not right now."

"Because they came to you for help," he said.

She nodded. "Come on, Sam. You get this. There's nothing complicated about it. I made a promise that I intend to keep."

Sam was entirely unconvinced. "If I had all the facts, I might agree with you. Since I don't, I will remain skeptical."

"You were born skeptical."

"Helps."

She rose, agitated, maybe a little stir-crazy. Kara Galway was not a woman who would handle idleness well. She walked in front of him, and he threw out one leg and caught her at the knees. When she lost her balance, he pulled her onto his lap and held her close. "Take me off your list of things that make you cry." Her shirt had raised up, exposing the smooth, taut skin of her lower abdomen. He placed his palm there. "If you're pregnant, I'll take care of you."

He expected her to bristle and tell him she could damn well take care of herself, but she didn't. She whispered, "I know you would," and her body went slack, her forehead resting against his shoulder as if she just wanted to stay there in his arms for a while. Forever would suit him.

It didn't last. He felt her muscles tense, and she exploded to her feet. "I don't like needing anyone."

"I don't, either, but I didn't say you needed me to take care of you. I said I would."

"Well, it's all a moot point." Her eyes shone with tears, undermining the fierceness of her words. "I'm not pregnant."

Sam was silent and very still for a moment. He was

surprised at the emptiness he felt, sudden but unmistakable. "We'd have cute babies together, Kara. Black-eyed, stubborn, independent as hell."

"Listen to us. A couple of damn romantics, and you a Texas Ranger and me a defense attorney. We've seen too much." She gave a small, mirthless laugh, the tears still unspilled. "A wife and a child would be a ball and chain for you right now. Don't think I don't know it. You're ambitious, Sam. You've taken on every bit of hard training you can, you earned your master's part-time—Jack says you could be governor if you decided to quit the Rangers."

"I'm not going to quit." He watched her, could feel the doubt in her, about him, who he was, what he wanted. He was aware of emotions surfacing in her that she usually kept carefully at bay, not all of them pleasant emotions involving duty and honor and love, but fear, inadequacies, secret wants and desires. "Kara, you don't know me at all."

Her dark eyes settled on him, unrelenting. "Tell me why you'd take care of me."

"I don't want a child of mine to grow up without a father." But that wasn't all of it, except he didn't know what the rest was—or just couldn't explain it. Family. Responsibility. Commitment. Love. Easier to keep it simple.

"Fair enough," she said. "Do you know what I want, Sam? I want a soul mate."

"A soul mate's a rare thing."

"You don't believe in unconditional love, do you?"

"There are always conditions."

"Name one," she said.

"Fidelity."

She gave him a half smile. "Not an issue with a soul mate."

He settled back in his chair, his legs outstretched, and he noticed her gaze drift to his thighs. He smiled. Soul mates. Right. "Rousing good sex at all hours. That's a major condition, don't you think?"

"You're an evil man, Ranger Temple." But color rose in her cheeks, pushing out some of the rawness from her tears. "I knew the score when we went out for coffee that night. We had ourselves a pretty good weekend fling, didn't we? If it's any consolation, I fantasized about sleeping with you before Mike died."

"Was the reality better than the fantasy?"

"It was," she said.

She used the past tense, spoke with finality, as if she'd dismissed any notion of them going to bed together again. But of course she hadn't. Sam knew it.

She ducked out into the sunlight and marched up the back steps, and he realized that in her mind they'd been discussing what might have been—not what could be with time, effort and compromise, even a little common sense. This, Sam decided, needed immediate attention.

He got up from his chair and walked up the steps, pulling open the screen door. She was at the sink, trying to look for something to do. He took her arm and turned her around, then caged her with his arms against the counter. She could have told him to go away, or go to hell, or leave her alone, but she didn't. She didn't meet his eyes, either.

He'd never known anyone like her. "I don't know if I can be your soul mate—"

"You either are or you aren't," she said, not snappish, just stating the facts. The attorney on the case, but he could feel the passion she was trying to hide, the wanting. "It's not something you can aspire to."

"Jesus. Never mind, then."

He didn't bother with a lot of niceties, just kissed her, and there was nothing restrained about it, either. He felt her small gasp, the response of her body as her lips parted and she fell back against the counter, her legs giving out under her. He could feel her slipping and swept her up before she could hit the floor, pressing himself against her, into her.

"I plan to make love to you again, Kara. Soon."

He felt a shiver of desire go through her, the memory of what they'd been together, the anticipation of having it happen again. But she took in a breath, and cleared her throat. "We haven't even been on a date."

"We had coffee."

"Dinner, a movie—"

"Okay. We'll do dinner and a movie sometime." He rubbed against her as if he was making love to her, and she gulped in another breath. He smiled. "We'll see if you can get through them."

"I'll be lucky to make it through the next five minutes...*Sam*..."

"If we didn't have a couple of middle-schoolers about to burst in here hunting for junk food, I'd have you on the kitchen table right now."

"The bedroom's just around the corner—"

He winked, setting her down on the floor. "Table'd make you forget all your troubles." He touched her cheek, kissed her softly, lightly. "It's good that you cried over not being pregnant."

He released her and went back outside, feeling hot

and uncomfortable and strangely exhilarated. Men who loved her from afar. Hell, Kara was the most touchable woman he'd ever met. Touching her hadn't ruined everything—it was damn near perfect.

Lillian skipped back outside and asked him if he'd like to hunt frogs with her—provided he didn't plan on eating them—and he agreed, deciding it wouldn't hurt to put his feet into an ice-cold Yankee stream.

Henry allowed Sam to bunk in with him that night, giving Kara the double bed downstairs. She slunk off early, claiming she was dead on her feet and just wanted to read for a while and go to sleep. Sam sat up in the cute living room and flipped through books on fly-fishing and golf, a bicycle-riding guide to New England, a kayak instruction book and a history of Connecticut. Not a murder mystery to be found in the place.

He searched the kids' backpacks and found nothing of interest. No incriminating letter. Kara probably had it under lock and key, buried, flushed or burned.

Had he wanted her to be pregnant?

The question returned to him again and again, and remained unanswered when he went upstairs and sat on the edge of the twin bed. Henry had given him the bed next to the window, he said, because the moon got in his eyes last night. Sam thought it was something more, a fear he wouldn't acknowledge. For twelve, Henry Stockwell had layers and depths that most people didn't have in a lifetime. They'd make him strong one day, if he didn't fall into one so deep he could never get himself out.

Sam could see the kid was still awake. He took off his boots and stripped down to his shorts and tried to remember if he'd ever bunked in with a twelve-year-old heir to a Yankee fortune. In the dark, Henry Stockwell's hair seemed flaxen, pale and shining as the half moon rose high in the night sky. The boy reminded Sam of a little prince, the weight of the world on his young shoulders.

He rolled over, yawning at his roommate. "What time is it?"

"Ten o'clock." An eternity until morning.

"You really are a Texas Ranger, right?"

"That's right."

"Do you like catching criminals?"

"It depends."

"What if it's a criminal you like?" he asked.

"People are complicated," Sam said, keeping his voice neutral. "I don't judge people. I make arrests based on evidence."

Henry watched him pull back the covers and slide into the skinny bed. "It was hot at the ranch. Aunt Kara says hell's cooler than Texas in the summer."

Sam smiled. "I'll go along with that. Kara put a lot on the line for you and your sister."

"I know." He seemed pensive, his eyes shining as if he was wide awake, but Sam could feel the boy's fatigue and strain. "We made her promise not to tell anyone what we told her."

"She takes attorney-client privilege very seriously." Sam laid back against his pillow. Even at twelve, he hadn't bunked in with other twelve-year-olds. He'd never done camp. He glanced over at the boy, still listening intently. "She knows you trust her, and she's trying to do the right thing by you and your sister, even if it costs her. You don't want to abuse that."

Henry propped his head up with one hand. "She wants us to tell some of the stuff to someone else, so she's not the only one who knows."

"That'd be a good idea. Your mother—"

"Mom has a lot on her mind."

"Is that part of why you ran away? Get a little attention from your mother the governor?"

Henry scowled as if Sam were an idiot. "*No.* I'm almost thirteen."

"Then why did you run away?" Sam asked quietly.

"To see Kara."

"What could she do?"

"Help us. I don't know." He rolled over, so thin under the covers he hardly made a bump. "I don't think she believes us."

"Henry—"

"Lillian's scared to go back to Texas," he said, "because of the snakes. Not me. I want to be a Texas Ranger when I grow up."

"Up to you."

"No, it's not."

He pulled his sheet to his chin, burying himself deep, a stuffed animal slung over his face. He peered closer and saw it was a tiger, most of its fur worn off. Almost thirteen, Sam thought.

Fourteen

Since she wasn't pregnant, Kara indulged herself with a mug of Sam's drop-dead coffee the next morning and brought it outside with her. She did the second test in the middle of the night, and it, too, was negative. Both kits had indicated it wasn't too soon to check.

Butterflies meandered in the beebalm and hollyhocks, the morning dew clinging to the grass, the air warm, slightly hazy with humidity. But autumn was her favorite season in New England, when the days would get shorter, the air crisper and the leaves start to turn as farmers and gardeners rushed to beat the frost, hauling in the last of the tomatoes and corn, bringing out the pumpkins and butternut squash. She could have stayed here. Yet even when her father drove her north at eighteen, she'd known she'd end up home in Texas, eventually.

Last night, waking up from dreams about soul mates, she'd told herself she was meant to be in Austin the night of the Gordon Temple opening, not just for her sake, but for Sam's, too, although she didn't understand why.

In the warm light of morning, drinking the strong coffee, she shuddered at her romantic yearnings. She must have been half-asleep, delusional. Falling for Sam, Sam falling for her. Impossible. She'd had her guard down yesterday, hence the talk about soul mates and lovemaking, the kissing. Today she'd stick to business and find a way to check out the kids' tree house and get them to tell her what they were holding back, whether it had anything to do with Big Mike's death or their amorphous fears about their mother. The trick was to manage any sneaking around despite Sam and his ground rules. It would be easier if she could take him into her confidence, but she couldn't. She couldn't violate the kids' trust, and she couldn't be sure what Sam would do.

The sound of a car on the dirt road brought her around to the front of the cottage, where Hatch Corrigan was pulling into the driveway in a monstrous SUV. He climbed out and waved to her over the gleaming hood, the sun catching his graying auburn hair.

"Kara! It's good to see you."

He laughed, greeting her with a kiss on the cheek, as if he hadn't revealed his feelings for her so awkwardly, so hopelessly, just two weeks ago at Mike Parisi's funeral. But it was like him to pretend he hadn't said a word, if only to prove his point that he didn't want to let anything as messy as romance interfere with how he felt about her.

"A lot's happened in the past couple of days. You're all right? The kids?"

"We're all fine." Kara smiled at him, noticed lines etched into his forehead that hadn't been there a year ago, a thinness to his cheeks, a tentativeness about him.

"I should thank you for handling Henry and Lillian's little rebellion with such discretion. I can understand this all has been difficult for them and they must be feeling shuffled aside, but to run away—well, it's not acceptable." He seemed annoyed even to have to discuss his niece and nephew's behavior. "But, Allyson will deal with them in her own way."

"Hatch, I don't think they took off as a bid for attention—"

"Well, whatever."

Sam walked out the front door with a mug of coffee, but Kara wasn't fooled by his casual air—and she knew better than to think he was just now aware of Hatch's arrival.

"My, my." Hatch's tone was low and amused. "The Texas Ranger."

"Shut up, Hatch," she said.

He laughed, no hint of regret or jealousy in his eyes. "You're blushing. I should notify the media. Kara Galway and a Texas Ranger is a bigger story than the governor's children sneaking off to visit their godmother." His voice lowered, the amusement going out of his expression. "I just want to see you happy, Kara."

She nodded, but said nothing. Sam ducked under a butternut branch and joined them on the driveway. He gave no indication he'd heard Hatch's remark or even guessed the tenor of what he'd said. Kara made introductions. Hatch thanked Sam, too, and apologized for any inconvenience.

"Not a problem," Sam said.

Henry and Lillian wandered out of the cottage and sat on the front steps in clean clothes their mother had brought yesterday. Hatch called them over, but they didn't move. They'd shown no sign of fear of retribution from Allyson, but their uncle, it seemed, was another matter.

Hatch smiled at them without reassurance. "You two have led us all on quite the chase this week," he said as they maintained their position on the steps. "What a show. Very clever, I must say, conning the shuttle driver and getting cash with your mother's ATM card."

Henry and Lillian leaned back on their elbows and said nothing. They'd never had a warm relationship with Hatch, Kara remembered, nor he with them, but they were always polite to each other. This noticeable coolness between uncle and children wasn't something she'd ever witnessed in the past.

Hatch approached them, Kara on his heels as he crossed the lawn. Sam leaned against his car, observing. She knew he was aware of the awkwardness, that the undertone of animosity emanated more from Henry and Lillian than it did from Hatch.

"You're very fortunate nothing happened to you," Hatch said to his niece and nephew. "We all are."

Henry lifted his chin. "I believe you. You and Grandma and Mom don't need anyone else dying on you. That'd be bad publicity. People'd start thinking you're jinxed.''

Lillian licked a finger and absently rubbed at a grass stain on her shirt, focusing on it as she spoke. ''Yeah, you'd be really mad at us if we got hurt!''

Hatch didn't respond openly to their defiance. ''None of this is about what other people think.'' His tone was patient, but Kara sensed his tension and expected Henry and Lillian did, too. And Sam. ''We're only concerned with your well-being. We were worried something terrible had happened and that was why you ran off.''

Henry yawned and turned to his sister, cutting off his uncle. ''Come on, Lillian. Let's go back inside.''

Hatch sucked in a breath through his teeth, but didn't try to stop them. They jumped up, brazenly dismissing him, and charged back through the front door.

He made a hissing sound. ''Damn it. It wasn't *my* idea for them to go to Texas. You'd think this was my fault.''

Kara shrugged. ''They know you're not happy with them.''

''And should I be? They had no business running away like that. They knew what they were doing was wrong. They knew it'd worry their mother.'' He made no pretense of his anger, but he didn't raise his voice. He started back to his car, Sam still watching without a word. ''Maybe I'd have more sympathy if I hadn't seen how terrified Allyson was and yet still fought tooth and nail to keep everyone from overreacting. She trusted them to be sensible, the little ingrates. Do you know what it was like—'' He stopped himself, sighing. "Never mind. I know I'm being too hard on them."

Kara followed him over to his SUV. "I'm not saying what they did was okay—''

"I know, I know." He tore open the driver door, then turned back, shaking his head. "I've never known what to say to them. It's even worse now that they're older—I thought it would get better."

Kara smiled. "Wait until they're sixteen and seventeen."

He returned a halfhearted smile. "Well, I didn't come here to give them grief. I came to let you know that my mother and I have arranged to hire a private bodyguard for Henry and Lillian. It's as much for Mother's peace of mind as anything else. Allyson refuses to request a security detail for them. She insists that all we'd be doing is asking them to baby-sit."

Sam frowned thoughtfully. "She doesn't believe there's a security concern?"

"Correct." Hatch seemed surprised, even put off, that Sam had spoken. "She considers Henry and Lillian's actions a family matter. She's probably right, but if they run away again, it'll be a *political* problem, I can guarantee that. You're a Texas Ranger, Sam. Don't you think it's a wise move to keep these kids under wraps at least until school starts?"

"Not my call."

"Of course not," Hatch said thinly, shifting back to Kara. "I don't mind saying these past few weeks have been awful. First the close call at Billie's damn bonfire, then Mike's death. Allyson's handled herself beautifully, I have to say. This bodyguard business is just a wrinkle—''

Kara saw it now. "She doesn't know, does she?"

"I'll tell her this evening. He doesn't start until the morning. Mother and I thought everyone could use today to relax—she wants you all to come to lunch. Allyson's finishing up some work this morning, so she'll be able to socialize with the children."

"All right," Kara said. "We'll be there."

Hatch seemed satisfied, as if he'd at last done something right, but after he left, Sam sat on the front steps, stretched out his legs and shook his head. "'Socialize with the children'? If I had to deal with that horse's ass on a regular basis, I'd think up ways to stick it to him, too."

"He's under a lot of stress. He's not always that bad."

"Something between you two?"

His question caught her off guard. She hadn't noticed anything in Hatch—or herself—that would have betrayed what he'd told her at Big Mike's funeral. "Between Hatch and me? No, never."

"He wants there to be."

"Maybe at one time. Not anymore."

"I don't think so," Sam said, exaggerating his drawl. "Your friend the governor says you attract men who prefer to love you from afar."

Kara raised her arms and hung on to a thick, low branch of the butternut tree. "Did she tell you that voluntarily or did you drag it out of her?"

"She seems to think we've been sleeping together. She likes the idea. You know, Miss Kara, I'm glad nobody told me I wasn't supposed to want to touch you.''

She lifted herself chin-up style, but didn't let her feet leave the ground. She could feel the stretch in her arms and her back. ''Ask my brother. He'd tell you if he knew it had occurred to you to touch me—''

''He'd shoot me if he knew it'd occurred to me.'' Sam's eyes stayed on her as she swung a little from her branch, giving herself a better stretch. ''He'd find a rope if he knew it was too late.''

''Do you see why I don't have so many men in my life?'' She dropped back to the ground and realized her shirt had ridden up to just under her breasts. She quickly adjusted it.

Sam acted as if he didn't notice. ''You don't need many. You just need one. This soul mate of yours.''

''Who is a figment of my romantic and misguided imagination.'' But she glanced up the dirt road, the dust from Hatch's exit still settling. ''I can see now why the kids won't release me from attorney-client privilege.''

''They don't want to have to listen to that officious bastard demean everything he says and believes.'' Sam got to his feet and grinned at her. ''You done swinging from that tree or should I stay out here a little longer? The view was nice.''

She couldn't resist a smile. ''You should go soak your head.''

He laughed. ''What should I wear to lunch at the Stockwells'? Susanna didn't pack my country club clothes.''

Kara started to answer, then realized he was kidding. Sam Temple was accustomed to going where he wanted, when he wanted, dressed as he chose.

"What does 'officious' mean?" Henry asked, his head outlined in the screened living-room window.

"You can add eavesdropping to your list of crimes," Sam told him, and when he opened the front door, Kara heard Henry grab his sister and run upstairs, laughing, daring Sam to come after them. She felt a tug of emotion she'd never expected, because this wasn't her husband, and these weren't her children, and back in Austin, George Carter had a ton of work for her to do. That was her life. Not this.

Don't tell me you don't give a damn if I tell the world about your ex-con lover. You won't call my bluff, Governor. You'll keep quiet and wait for your instructions.

Big Mike knew about your secret ex-con lover, didn't he?

Do you want people to wonder if you helped him into the deep end?

Allyson dangled her feet in the pool while she waited for her children to arrive for lunch. She'd played back the caller's words in her head a thousand times since yesterday. What did the son of a bitch want from her?

And Sam Temple. He must have noticed she was upset yesterday when she received the call.

She'd gone through the motions last night at dinner with Hatch and Madeleine, then this morning at breakfast. She hadn't slept. She'd prowled the barn wishing the caller would come then, while Henry and

Lillian were safe at Stonebrook Cottage. She could find out what he wanted and give it to him, or sic her bodyguards on him—something, anything, just to end it.

He hadn't come, and he hadn't called.

Big Mike knew about your secret ex-con lover, didn't he?

The caller had to be someone close to her. Someone who knew about her affair with Pete, knew Mike had found out about it—someone who could bide his time not because of patience, but position. But why? What was the point of such harassment?

Allyson shuddered, feeling watched. She didn't dare make a wrong move, tell the wrong person. She had to know more. She had to find out who her caller was, somehow, or at least tell someone she trusted about the calls—but who? She didn't want to put anyone else in a difficult position or place her trust in the wrong person, perhaps even the caller himself—or herself. Allyson had no idea if it was a man or a woman. She had to be patient, careful.

She trusted Kara and her Texas Ranger. But she'd entrusted them with her children—that was enough responsibility. Kara and Temple couldn't be expected to stay in Connecticut indefinitely, but this wouldn't go on indefinitely. Allyson knew she had to do something, and soon.

Pete leaned over the pool fence. "You look as if you could use a swim, Governor. Why don't you jump in?"

"I'm in my shorts."

He grinned. "Be daring."

She laughed up at him, remembered with a jolt how they'd gone skinny-dipping in the moonlight. They'd done it once in early summer, weeks ago, smothering their laughter with kisses to keep Madeleine from realizing what was happening under her nose. "Are you making fun of me, Mr. Jericho?"

"You bet."

Her laughter faltered. "I feel as if I'm over my head even without jumping in."

He nodded. She thought of all she couldn't say out loud. She missed him. She loved him. She wanted to be with him. But right now there was her evil anonymous caller, her troubled children, her responsibilities and duty—the promise she'd made to Big Mike, to the people of the state. To herself, because she wanted to do this job and do it well. She'd been a damn good lieutenant governor. Before the bonfire explosion and Big Mike's death, before Henry and Lillian ran away in Texas—before this summer, she'd been a different woman, almost another woman altogether, strong, competent, so sure of herself. What had happened to her? Grief, shock, fear and the paralysis that came with too much of all three? Or just stupidity. Just not knowing what to do, how to uncover and face an unknown, unseen enemy.

"How're the kids?" Pete asked.

She pictured them, her serious Henry and her big-eyed Lillian, and she knew she'd resign as governor for them. In a heartbeat. But for Pete? Would she do it for him?

"Great." She managed a smile, twirled one foot in the warm water. "They're on their way up for lunch.

I'm inclined to think they got the idea in their heads
that they could make a break for Austin and just did
it. No rhyme or reason. I've been trying to think like
a twelve-year-old, and that's what I keep coming up
with.'' She kicked her feet in the water. ''They don't
have adult brains.''

''Half the adults I know don't have adult brains,
either.''

She loved his irreverence, his wit—and he was so
damn sexy when he was dusty and sweaty from working. ''Where are you off to?'' she asked him.

''Gravel pit.'' He came through the gate, his old,
cracked, dusty boots leaving muddy footprints on the
wet spots on the pool deck. He seemed to want to
touch her. ''Allyson—are you okay?''

Her throat caught. ''It's been a long two weeks.''

They'd made love the night before Mike drowned.
Their last night together. Pete would remember. He
squinted out at the sunlit pool. ''A hell of a long two
weeks. See you around, Governor Stockwell.''

How could she give him up? ''Soon, I hope.''

Pete drove along the gravel pit access road, an old
logging lane that had been widened and improved for
the big equipment required to dig out and haul the
sand, rock and gravel. He parked up at his wood yard.
After his days of wallowing in self-pity, he felt almost
whole again. He'd feel completely whole when he
had Allyson back in his arms. He was such a romantic
nitwit—a paranoid jackass. She hadn't dumped him
at all. He should have had more faith in her. What a
lovesick dope he was.

They all just needed to adjust to Big Mike's death and Allyson being governor. Then he and Allyson could figure out a way to be together, out in the open, not in secret anymore.

The guys had worked in the pit for a couple of hours that morning, but they were off again, the equipment quiet, the huge piles of sand, stone and rock still in the midday heat. Pete admitted he'd be glad when the work was done and pictured the area planted with white pine, green again with brush and saplings. He walked down into the pit from the access road and stood next to a fifteen-foot pile of pea stone. He heard his father's tractor up on the hill, out of view, then watched it come around the long way, which was less steep, less treacherous.

Charlie puttered over to Pete, a fresh cigarette hanging from his mouth, his wooden trailer loaded with scrap wood. These days he did more of what he felt like doing, less of what needed to get done. "I thought you were going to dismantle that damn tree house."

Pete had hesitated, not sure if he'd get into trouble, if the tree house was evidence of some kind. The investigation into Big Mike's death was ongoing—he didn't need to screw things up. He shrugged at his father. "I haven't gotten around to it."

"I'd do it, but I can't get up there with my tractor. Did you take a look at it? Hunters or kids?"

"Kids, I think. Maybe hunters."

"Well, it's dangerous." Charlie grunted, coughed. "Your mother wants you home for dinner. She's making a pot roast and thinks if you're not there I'll eat too much and end up dying of a heart attack watching the evening news.''

Pete grinned at him. ''Is this a dinner invitation?''

''Best you're going to get, seeing how you live with us. Come early enough so you can shuck the corn.''

After Charlie left, Pete headed up the steep route to the kids' tree house, along the edge of the woods above the gravel pit. Maybe he should have said something about it to Allyson when he saw her at the pool, but she'd seemed so distracted—and he'd been thinking of himself, looking for signs she still wanted him in her life. But she needed to know about the tree house. He could just let her come see it and draw her own conclusions.

Better, he supposed, the news came from him than his father. Charlie Jericho had a near-legendary lack of tact.

He was out of breath, almost to the top of the ridge. He'd started work early this morning, diving into it to keep his mind off Allyson. His legs were tired. He grabbed a thin poplar, bracing himself, and gazed straight down into the pit, agreeing with Madeleine Stockwell—who'd never actually seen it—that it was an ugly gash to the land. He hoped to plant at least a thousand white pine, and his mother wanted a small pond, a wetland for the wildlife, she said. Charlie complained that was a waste of energy.

Something rustled in the woods behind him, fairly big, probably a deer or a woodchuck. Pete started to turn, but his work boot slipped on the edge of the near-vertical embankment, sending loose gravel and stones straight down. He heard a grunt—the forceful expelling of air from lungs—and knew immediately it wasn't a deer.

But he was too late, and before he could react, he felt the wallop to the small of his back. A stick, a pole, the toe of a boot. He lost his footing and fell onto his side, kicking out for something to latch on to, reaching up at a tuft of field grass, a tree root. But he was moving too fast, and the drop was too steep. He slid down the dirt embankment, hit a jutting rock with his ribs. He groaned at the pain, kept fighting to find his footing, but he picked up more speed, rolling, flailing. Then, free-falling.

He hit more rock, and he screamed out in pain, still falling.

Fifteen

〜◦⊙◦〜

Henry interrogated Sam on all matters Texas Ranger as the four of them walked through the woods for lunch with the Stockwells. Kara listened with amusement, Henry's ideas about Texas's elite investigative unit rooted in television, old movies and his limited understanding of Texas. Sam, however, was patient, prompting her one contribution to the conversation. "The Ranger motto is 'Courtesy, Service, Protection.'"

Sam glanced at her sideways, as if he wasn't sure she was being sarcastic. But she wasn't. Henry seemed slightly disappointed in such a polite motto. "Didn't the Texas Rangers used to hang horse thieves?"

"There's a Texas Ranger museum in Waco," Sam said. "I'll take you over there next time you come to visit."

Lillian skipped across rocks in a low, muddy stream. "Not me. I'm *never* going to Texas again. People eat frogs and snakes and alligators there."

Sam sputtered into laughter. "Lillian, I think you

and I need to have another talk. You're getting some peculiar ideas about Texas.'' He glanced at Kara. ''Did you put up with this kind of talk when you lived up here?''

Kara smiled. ''You should have heard Big Mike.''

Henry followed his sister across the stream, but was still clearly entertaining his fantasy. ''Do I have to go to college to be a Ranger?''

''It helps,'' Sam said.

''Maybe I'll join the FBI or the CIA, instead, since I don't have a Texas accent.''

Sam let that one go. ''You don't want to go into politics?''

''No way. I can't now, anyway, after I ran away and forged a letter from my mom—''

''*You* didn't forge the letter,'' Lillian said. ''I did. You just helped me with spelling. It was your idea to say Mom knew we were in danger—''

''*Lillian!* Shut *up!*'' Henry, white-faced, splashed the rest of the way across the stream. ''You're going to get us arrested.''

Kara recognized at once Lillian's mistake in mentioning the word *danger*. So, of course, did Sam. He took the stream in one long, easy stride and offered Kara his hand, but she refused it. He was being cocky now that the kids had slipped up. She'd changed into a decent pair of pants and a fresh top for lunch at the Stockwells' and had on slides, but she made it to the other side of the stream on her own. Sam was right there, anyway, placing a hand on the small of her back, steadying her as she regained her balance.

''Sam isn't going to arrest you,'' she told Henry

and Lillian. "He has no jurisdiction in Connecticut, but no one here is going to arrest you, either. So don't worry about that." She hesitated, met Sam's dark look and sighed. "But I think you should tell Sam what's in the letter, what parts are true—everything."

"It's all true!" Lillian was indignant, slapping at a mosquito on her wrist. "We *are* in danger."

Sam's silence was deadly. Kara waved at a mosquito buzzing around her head and frowned at him. "It's complicated."

"Try me. I bet I can figure it out."

She turned to Henry, who stood sullenly halfway up a gentle hill with his arms folded on his chest. Her heart broke for him. He was trying to be so strong, but he couldn't do it anymore. He needed adult help. "Henry—Sam needs to know. If something happens, he's the one with the experience." And the gun, she thought. "You can tell him."

"I can't. And Lillian, you be quiet."

She stuck her tongue out at him. "I don't take orders from you."

Henry scowled at her, then shifted back to Kara. "Aunt Kara, please—what if something happens to Mom because we said anything?"

"That's it." Sam started up the hill. "If these kids believe the governor of Connecticut is in danger—"

"It's not that simple, Sam," Kara said, not moving. "Trust me."

He stopped, glancing back at her, the shade darkening his black eyes, making them seem even more unyielding, and she knew this all was black-and-white for him. Every bit of it. "I'd trust you with my life in a courtroom," he said. "You're a damn good lawyer from all I hear. This is a law enforcement matter. Time to trust me, Kara."

Her head pounded, and she was aware of Henry and Lillian looking intently at her, barely breathing, waiting for her to come up with a solution. She wished she knew what they were holding back, what else had happened to them that day in the tree house, or the day they'd decided to run away from the dude ranch. What *didn't* she know about their troubles?

Frustrated, she pushed up the hill and tried to think. She didn't understand why they wouldn't at least tell Sam about the man who'd followed them in Texas, unless he was as fictitious as their letter. She wondered if some of what they claimed they saw from the tree house was imagined or exaggerated, a psychological response to the shock of Mike's death, then the sudden isolation of Texas, coupled with their mixed emotions about their mother becoming governor. Saying they saw Big Mike drown could be a way for them to fill in the blanks and make sense of what happened.

But it didn't matter. Sam would want to know everything.

If he had his way, Kara thought, he'd put an asterisk by attorney-client privilege and say it could be violated if it involved the minor children of the governor of Connecticut.

Her shoulders slumped, and she realized there was just no easy way out for her. Or the kids. "I'll sit the kids down with Allyson as soon as possible," she told Sam. "This afternoon. We'll talk. But it's up to

Henry and Lillian to reveal what they told me. It's not up to me."

He didn't like it. She could see his displeasure with any sort of compromise in the stiffness of his spine, the hard set of his jaw. "This isn't a courtroom. We're out in the damn woods."

"It's the best I can do."

He clenched his teeth visibly. "Fair enough."

Henry and Lillian seemed satisfied at what must have sounded like a compromise to them and ran up the hill together, Henry yelling at his sister about her big mouth until she hauled off and belted him. He turned to complain but met with Sam's unsympathetic look and gave up, renewing his solidarity with Lillian.

But Kara knew there'd been no real compromise. Sam fell in beside her and, with his attention on the path ahead of him, said his piece. "You have until five o'clock. Then I go to the state police with what little I know."

Madeleine Stockwell had set up lunch on the patio and greeted her grandchildren with her usual starchy reserve. They were polite, but Kara was relieved when no one brought up how they'd ended up back in Connecticut. She introduced Sam and noticed Madeleine perk up. "I met Kara's brother several years ago," she said. "Do you know him?"

"He's my superior officer."

"Ah. That could be awkward, couldn't it?"

Sam didn't answer.

Kara went down toward the pool and intercepted Allyson on her way to the patio. She smiled, but was so obviously drawn and tense that Kara winced at the idea of having her friend hear more troubling news. "I need to talk to you later. With the kids."

"Sure." She spoke smoothly, vestiges of the Allyson of old. "I was hoping to go swimming with them—"

"After that would be fine." She had until five o'clock, Kara thought with a sudden flash of irritation mixed with resignation. Sam wasn't going to be a passive participant. She'd known that the minute he rang her doorbell and detected the smell of popcorn in her living room.

Henry and Lillian followed Madeleine into the kitchen to help bring out lunch. There was no hired help today. Allyson excused herself, hurrying inside to join them, passing Hatch and Billie at the door. Billie was red-faced, arguing with her half brother. "We *can't* cancel. That'd be a red flag. People'd think it's either because your mother doesn't trust me after the bonfire accident or this thing with the kids is a bigger deal than you've let on."

Hatch wasn't backing down. "I just don't think it's a good idea to go forward with a cocktail party under these circumstances."

Billie threw up her hands. "What circumstances? The kids took off from a stupid dude ranch in Texas and ended up an hour or two away at their godmother's. Big deal. Kids do shit like that. They're fine. If you ask me, it'll look worse if you don't go forward."

"You'll be paid for your trouble."

"Hatch, you are such an asshole. I'm not talking

about the damn money.'' She stormed off the patio, her too-small shirt stretched across her breasts, and stopped abruptly, oblivious to anyone else around her. She flew around at her brother. ''Anyway, this is your mother's gig. It's up to her to cancel.''

He grimaced. ''Billie, for God's sake.''

She grinned up at him suddenly, as if they hadn't been arguing. ''Do you like my luminaria idea?''

Kara bit back a smile. Billie Corrigan was so ir-repressible, it was difficult not to imagine what Hatch might have been like if he'd seen more of his father growing up. He sighed at his younger sister. ''I'd pre-fer only electric lights. After the bonfire on the Fourth—''

''Oh, ye of the faint heart. Luminaria are perfect. This'll be a fun party, Hatch. Trust me.'' She smiled at Kara, as if just now realizing she was there, then at Sam. ''My brother is paid to think the worst. I think he earns his salary, don't you?''

Kara laughed. ''I'm not coming between you two,'' she said, then quickly introduced Sam. When he called her ma'am, Billie just about melted. Kara didn't know what it was about him and his effect on women. She turned her attention back to Hatch. ''Are you and Billie staying for lunch?''

''No,'' he said. ''Neither of us.''

He was definitely in a sour mood. Billie rolled her eyes and dragged him down to the pool to press him further on her luminaria idea. Sam stood next to Kara, obviously devoid of patience for any kind of social outing. ''I'm going to take off for a while,'' he said.

"I'll be back when you're ready to leave. Enjoy your lunch."

Kara was immediately suspicious. "Where are you going? How will you know when we're ready?"

"You can call me on my cell phone or ask one of the troopers to take you back to the cottage."

"Ground rules?"

But he was in a serious mood. "Yes."

"Well, you won't want to be later than five o'clock."

He ignored her. She was feeling argumentative, irritated that he thought he could go off without her, without explaining himself, but he didn't want her making a move without him.

Then she realized if Sam was off reconnoitering or doing whatever he planned to do, she could slip out to the gravel pit and have a look at Henry and Lillian's tree house. If they could indeed see Big Mike's pool through their binoculars, she might be able to figure out how much of their story was reality, how much imagination and exaggeration. It would help her understand and counter any further reticence on their part, and she'd know better how to advise them.

It wasn't just a rationalization. It made sense, even if she did have to violate Sam's ground rules.

"It's a beautiful day," she told him. "It's been so hot in Texas, you'll enjoy yourself, I'm sure."

"Give the Stockwells my regrets."

He wasn't past a little sarcasm, either, Kara noted. "Don't skip through the fields. It'd be bad form."

He didn't answer. She watched him head across the lawn and waited until he was over the stone wall and almost to the woods before she scooted up to the patio and excused herself from lunch. She claimed she wasn't hungry and thought they all needed some family time together. No one protested. She debated borrowing a car, then decided she didn't want to risk having a Stockwell vehicle spotted out at the gravel pit. Best to be as unobtrusive as possible.

She knew the shortest route through the woods— or hoped she did. She didn't need to get lost. Explain that to Sam, she thought. It was a warm afternoon, the air humid and still, chipmunks and squirrels scampering over the stone walls and along high tree branches, but Kara didn't linger, moving quickly, almost at a run. She forced herself to keep her attention on what she was doing, not spin it back to the past or to the future. She'd discover what was what at the tree house when she found it.

She veered off the old, overgrown logging road onto a narrow footpath, guessing from its well-worn look that it was the one Henry and Lillian had used. It led to a stone wall that put her onto Jericho land, the path nothing more than where the kids had pushed through the ferns. She came to a wide, muddy spot, probably a shallow spring, and slopped through the middle of it, wasting no time.

The woods opened up into a mass of low wild blueberry bushes, dotted with ripe fruit, and a tall pine tree, its branches sweeping the ground. She picked her way through the brush and pricker bushes, up a sloping hill, through waist-high Christmas trees and, finally, out onto the gravel pit access road. Off slightly to her left, she saw logs piled on wooden platforms and Pete Jericho's rusted truck, and straight on, the gravel pit, quiet in the afternoon sun.

Kara paused on the rough road and tried to catch her breath. She was panting from exertion, sticky with sweat. She didn't relish the thought of tramping up the steep hill above the gravel pit and marveled at the energy and industry of her godchildren. They'd had to lug wood, nails, tools and snacks out here, get them up into their tree, do their sawing and hammering and building. Quite a project. She admired their tenacity and ingenuity, even if they'd broken a few rules. Their lives, she thought, were sometimes too filled with rules.

She heard the crunch of gravel behind her.

Ah, hell.

She swung around just as Sam's shadow crossed hers. He didn't say a word. He must have watched her from the cover of the taller Christmas trees on the other side of the access road.

"Well," Kara said. "I didn't think you went back to the cottage for hot dogs and coffee." She gave him half a beat to answer, and when he didn't, she pressed on. "Don't tell me you followed me out here, because you didn't. I'd have heard you. It's a quiet day, and you just aren't that subtle."

He slanted his gaze at her. "The house Governor Parisi rented for the summer is on five acres that border Jericho and Stockwell land. All three properties come together on the other side of the gravel pit." He took a step toward her. "Provocative to find you here."

"I didn't stay for lunch—"

"I can see that."

"Henry and Lillian needed to be with their mother, without me. Look, you know I have more information than you do. We both want all this to work out. I need you to trust my judgment."

Sam moved half a step, his boots grinding into the hard-packed road. "I'm surprised Hatch Corrigan didn't come with you."

"What? Where did that come from?" Then she realized what he was doing—throwing her off base, confusing her as if she were some damn criminal. "Sam, whatever Hatch had for me is over."

"No, it isn't. He just doesn't want to sully his perfect love by something as common and nasty as sex."

She could feel the anger rising in her. "You're being an ass—"

"Quaint little town, Bluefield is." He didn't seem to notice her anger, or wasn't worried about it if he did. His black eyes stayed on her, unflinching. "A gas can left too near a Fourth of July bonfire nearly kills the lieutenant governor. A few weeks later, the governor drowns. Then two little rich kids are scared enough to run off in an unfamiliar state."

"When you say it like that—"

"It *is* like that, Kara." The sun was hot out here in the open, but it didn't seem to affect him. "Zoe West doesn't like what's going on in her town. Neither do I. Neither do you."

Kara refused to let his sky-is-falling mood affect her, and she remembered she was in Bluefield because of Henry and Lillian. They were her priority, her sole concern. Everything else took a back seat.

They'd told her about seeing Mike Parisi drown, about the man following them, thinking she was their attorney. She could maintain their confidence, but if she believed they really needed representation, she'd go straight to their mother and insist, or go to court, if need be, and get a judge to appoint a guardian ad litem, who would then see to it they had their own lawyer. Kara hoped it wouldn't come to that—she hoped everything would get sorted out when they got together with Allyson this afternoon.

"That's Pete Jericho's truck." Kara pointed toward the stacks of cordwood logs where Pete had parked his old pickup. "Let's go talk to him and see what he's up to. Maybe he knows something he hasn't said."

"Kara—"

"Sam, I'm here. I went behind your back. I did it deliberately, for good reasons that I can't explain to you." She sighed at him. She appreciated his situation, but it was time he appreciated hers. "Decide what you're going to do about it."

His eyes sparked dangerously. "I could cart you out of here right now and put you on a plane for San Antonio."

"Austin," she said, not backing down. "I don't live in San Antonio."

"Your brother could hold on to you while I finish up here." He said nothing for a moment, then exhaled through his nose. "Before this is over, he's going to have both our heads."

She smiled. "We can take him."

But he didn't return her smile, and his unrelenting

seriousness added to her own sense of gravity. They headed across the road and into the pounded grass of the woodlot, where two gray squirrels chased each other across the top of a pile of logs. There was no sign of Pete. "He must be here somewhere," Kara said, looking around.

She didn't want to miss this opportunity to check out the tree house, but with Sam on her heels, she didn't know how to do it and still maintain Henry and Lillian's confidence. The children were moving closer to confiding in him, trusting him, but if she jumped the gun, she didn't know how they'd react. They'd been through too much as it was. She wasn't worried nearly as much about professional ethics as she was doing the right thing by them, keeping her promise to them.

Sam started down to the gravel pit, the same direction she needed to go to get to the tree house up on the hill. Maybe she'd be able to see it from the gravel pit and could gauge from there the veracity of the kids' story. The equipment was idle, the landscape silent and barren, without shade. There were huge piles of pea stone, uncut rock, gravel and sand, all waiting to be crushed, sifted or hauled out.

Kara stood next to Sam on the pounded subsoil. "It's like standing in a desert, isn't it? Allyson and I used to come out here hunting for lady's slippers. It's hard to believe it's the same place. I understand the pit's almost played out—" She stopped abruptly, noticing that Sam had withdrawn the Colt. "Sam? What is it?"

He touched her arm. "Stay here."

Kara followed his gaze, gasping when she saw a body three-quarters of the way down the steepest part of the embankment. It was a man, sprawled faceup in the dirt.

She recognized the tawny hair, the dusty clothes.

"Oh my God, it's Pete."

She bolted for him, but Sam grabbed her and shoved her down next to a pile of pea stone. He pointed at her. "Don't move."

She nodded. "All right. Go."

He made it to Pete in seconds and knelt down, checking for a pulse as he did a 360-degree scan of the gravel pit. Kara didn't see anyone and shot across the open ground, the sun hot on the back of her neck. She crouched next to Sam, alongside Pete's motion-less body.

"He's alive," Sam said. "We need to get para-medics out here."

She saw Pete's bloody arm and shoulder, his torn shirt, the swollen, bloody bruise on the side of his head—the bone sticking out of his wrist. "Pete...we're calling an ambulance." She pushed back her panic, leaned over him. She had no idea if he could hear her. "It'll be okay."

He moaned. "Kara?" His voice cracked, and he winced in agony, his eyes shut. *"Christ."*

"Do you remember what happened?" Sam asked.

Pete tried to open his eyes, but moaned and shut them again without answering.

Sam had out his cell phone and dialed 911, crisply giving the dispatcher their location and describing the situation. "The injured man is Pete Jericho. Someone will want to notify his family."

"Pop—he was out here." Pete seemed confused, trying to figure out what had happened to him. He coughed, moaning in pain, then swore viciously.

"I know it must hurt like hell," Kara said. "Don't try to talk. Help'll be here soon."

"Kara…shit, you always see me at my worst."

She stood up and squinted at the line of trees at the top of the ridge. The tree house was up there somewhere. Had Pete seen it? Was that why he fell? If Sam found it on his own, she wouldn't have to violate Henry and Lillian's trust. He'd figure out on his own what they were hiding.

"It looks like he fell from up there," she said. "Sam, maybe you should go up and look around, just in case."

He glanced at her, already suspicious. "I will after the paramedics get here."

Charlie Jericho arrived first, jumping off his tractor with more agility than Kara would have expected of him. He ran to his son, dropping down next to him. "Bea heard on the scanner," he explained to no one in particular. "What the hell happened? Pete, you okay?" He looked his son over, shaking his head. "You've got a busted-up head, broken wrist, bruises and cuts—how're your insides? You break a few ribs?"

But Pete didn't answer. "Sam and I found him a few minutes ago," Kara said.

Charlie looked up at Sam. "You're the Texas Ranger? You think this was an accident?"

"I don't know, Mr. Jericho, and it's not for me to make that determination. Your son doesn't remember what happened. He might after he gets medical attention."

Charlie got to his feet and pulled off his cap, his gray hair matted with sweat. He ran his forearm over the top of his head. "I'll bet he was dismantling that goddamn tree house, hunter's platform, whatever the hell it is. I knew someone'd get hurt up there. It's too close to the edge of the gravel pit."

"Which tree?" Sam asked, and Kara knew he'd instantly put together the pieces of what Charlie Jericho had said and understood why she was out here.

"Big oak up at the top. You can't miss it."

The ambulance siren sounded out on the access road. Sam looked at Kara, his intensity palpable. And his fury. She already knew about the tree house and he knew it. "You'll be okay here?" he asked tightly.

She nodded. He meant to find the tree house. When he did, he'd see Henry's binoculars, perhaps stumble on Lillian's missing binoculars, and he'd figure out what the kids were hiding. He tucked the .45 back in the holster and set out across the lower end of the embankment and into the woods.

Kara watched him making his way up the hill, along the edge of the steep embankment. Pete could have fallen—he could have been pushed. She thought of Henry and Lillian's man in the black sedan, then dialed the number for Stockwell Farm.

Hatch answered. "We heard what happened. You're there with Pete?"

"Yes. Hatch, I need to see Allyson and the kids—"

"You don't call the shots here, Kara," he said, and disconnected.

Charlie grunted. "Hatch is worse than ever. People worry about Allyson not handling the stress—I worry about that guy." He gestured up toward the woods where Sam had now disappeared from sight. "You go on with your Texas friend. I'll stay with Pete."

The ambulance bounced over ruts and pits by the logging platforms, a police cruiser behind it, and Charlie waved his arms, directing them to his son. Kara leaned over Pete, his face wracked with pain. "Take care. I'll check on you as soon as I can."

"Pop...he can't..."

"Don't worry," Charlie called down to him. "I'm not having a heart attack today."

Pete's eyes flickered open and shut and he seemed to drift into unconsciousness. Kara ran across the pounded dirt into the woods, pushing her way through knee-high ferns and skinny saplings, her energy renewed—probably from the adrenaline rush of having found Pete injured, seeing Sam's reaction. The gun, the deadly look in his black eyes. She had no idea what he would do when he found the tree house.

She came to a tall oak with split cordwood nailed to its smooth trunk.

Sam dropped out of it, landing lightly in the dried leaves and scraggly field grass. "They saw Mike Parisi drown, didn't they? They're witnesses." He bit out each word, nothing slow or easy or sexy about his Texas drawl, so out of place here on the edge of a Connecticut gravel pit. "I figured this out on my own. You're off the hook, Counselor."

"Sam, they're kids—"

"Damn right. Kids who need an adult with some sense. Your pal Pete Jericho could have been killed." His eyes scalded her. "What did they tell you?"

"Not everything. I'm sure of it." She spoke calmly, as if she were in a courtroom. "They're like you right now, suspicious of everything and everyone."

He swung around at her, grabbing the branch above her right shoulder. She fell back against the tree automatically, instinctively, having expected every kind of reaction from him but this intensity, this rawness of emotion. She thought his professionalism might rise to the surface, even if they weren't in Texas.

He leaned in toward her. "I could make love to you right now against this tree. I don't give a damn they're down there loading a man into an ambulance, and I don't give a damn who saw what." He touched her hair with his free hand. "Who are these people to you, Kara?"

"Sam, I can't...not now."

"Now's the best time, when you're off your game, scared, when you're not sure what I'm going to do next. You could learn something from those kids." He traced her mouth with his fingertips, then skimmed them along her jaw, down her throat and over her breasts, outlining first one nipple then the other. "You're too trusting."

"That shows you what you know." She felt defiant, breathless with exertion and fear and adrenaline,

and with desire, hot and undeniable—and inappropri-
ate, she thought. Not now, not here. "I'm not trusting
at all."

He covered her breast with his palm, caressing it
as he lowered his mouth to hers. He knew exactly
what he was doing, and she saw him watching her as
she took in a breath, anticipating his kiss.

But it didn't come right away. He touched his
tongue to her bottom lip, rubbing it lightly, erotically,
before he covered his mouth with hers. He was deliberate, in control. He dropped his hand from her breast
and eased it down her stomach, past the waistband of
her shorts. She felt his fingertips hot on her skin, then
between her legs, his kiss capturing her small cry of
surprise as he stroked her, touched her. He let go of
the branch and took her hand, placing it on him, and
she could feel that he was aroused.

She pulled back from their kiss, ragged and damn
close to letting him take her there, against the tree.
"Sam..." Her voice caught, and she pressed her palm
hard against him, felt his control falter as he grabbed
the branch again. She leaned back against the tree
trunk, letting him withdraw his hand from her, and
she cleared her throat, coughing a little. "Okay. You
made your point. We should be home, sorting out our
own problems."

He patted her on the hip and smiled. "You're a
quick study, Counselor." His smile faded, but no
hardness came into his expression. "You worry me,
Miss Kara. I imagine you always will."

That low, deep drawl and the way he said *always*
made her stomach churn with possibilities, her head

spin, but she pushed that all aside for another time. Right now she had to deal with the crude tree house from where her godchildren said they inadvertently saw a man die. "Sam, I wanted you to know about the tree house because it seemed only fair. But now I'd appreciate it if you'd let me handle—"

"You'll talk to Henry and Lillian?"

She nodded and tried to smile. "I'll tell them a big, mean Texas Ranger is on their case."

"I would be if we were in Texas. I'd be all over those two. And you." He let go of the branch above his head, and it sprang back hard into position, leaves whooshing, indicating how much tension he had in it. "I'd get a prosecutor to subpoena you and challenge your attorney-client privilege."

"You'd lose."

"Just be glad we're not in Texas."

"You, too, Ranger Temple, or you'd be in quite the mess after what you just did."

He smiled without regret. "There's that."

But she regarded him thoughtfully, then looked up at the tree house. They'd done a good job building it, her clever, rich godchildren. They just could never have anticipated witnessing a man's death. A friend. "Do I need to go up there?"

"No. They could see the deep end of the pool through their binoculars."

"Did you leave the binoculars?"

He nodded. "Looks as if they've been up there a while. What did they do after they saw the governor? Run down there to help?"

"Sam—"

"They didn't call the police or there'd be a record, and the police would have talked to them by now." His eyes were half-closed on her, and she could feel his edgy intensity return. "If they'd gone all the way to Parisi's house, by the time they got there his security people would have been at the pool, pulling him out. They turned back, didn't they? They ran up here?"

"You're speculating."

"You know what happened," he said.

She didn't answer. She looked down the wooded hill and pictured Henry and Lillian scrambling to Big Mike's aid, knowing they wouldn't get there in time. And Lillian, dropping her binoculars. She was more than indignant that they hadn't turned up. She was scared. She thought someone had stolen them.

Had someone seen the two kids charging down the hill?

Jesus, *had* someone murdered Big Mike?

Kara kicked at the green undergrowth and the layers of brown, dead leaves. The second pair of binoculars could be anywhere. Lillian was so traumatized, it was entirely reasonable to assume she couldn't remember where she'd dropped them, even what route she'd taken down to Big Mike's pool.

Without a word, Sam left her and started back down the hill. Kara felt a stab of rejection, but she'd made her choice—she had to keep her promise to Henry and Lillian. She was tempted to trace the kids' route to Big Mike's rented house, but she heard the ambulance pulling out with Pete Jericho.

She glanced once more at the tree house, then

called for Sam to wait up. He didn't. She had to run to catch up with him, and when she did, it was her idea to take his hand. He didn't tell her to go to hell or drag her into the bushes and make love to her. He just gave her hand a gentle squeeze and walked with her back down to the gravel pit.

Sixteen

Zoe West was not what Sam expected for a small-town Connecticut detective. She had short, curly blond hair, blue-flecked gray eyes and a runner's body, about five and a half feet tall. She wore a black sundress with black sandals and an ankle bracelet. Her toes were painted fuchsia. She carried a limp unlit cigarette that looked as if it would unravel any second and spill tobacco over her. She wasn't carrying a weapon.

Apparently he was exactly what she expected, because she told him. "What are you, the poster boy for the Texas Rangers?"

Sam didn't respond, which only seemed to confirm her point. She had come out to the gravel pit in time to watch the paramedics load Pete Jericho into the back of the ambulance. Sam asked her if she'd mind if he took a look at the pool where Mike Parisi drowned. She frowned at him. "Just can't resist, huh? Okay, but you ride with me."

Charlie Jericho was following the ambulance in Pete's truck. Kara had jumped in with him. She promised to meet Sam at the hospital and said she assumed Allyson wouldn't just dump the kids back at the cottage until someone was there.

Zoe West drove a bright yellow Volkswagen Beetle and grinned at him when he squeezed into the passenger seat. "I guess no self-respecting Texas Ranger would have one of these."

"Probably not, ma'am."

She sighed at him. "You're making me feel like I'm a hundred years old with this 'ma'am' stuff."

Sam said nothing.

Parisi's summer house had a gated driveway, but its five-acre mostly wooded lot wasn't fenced. West parked in front of the garage and led Sam around back to the pool. The yard was pleasantly landscaped, nothing too elaborate.

"Governor Parisi liked it in Bluefield," West said, "but he never bought here. He owned a triple-decker in New Britain."

There was nothing working-class about this place. Sam noticed the woods came right up to the deck around the deep end of the pool, a five-foot lattice fence cutting into the trees. He pictured Henry and Lillian shooting down the hill, coming to the fence, watching the troopers pull Michael Parisi's body out of the water.

The pool was clear and inviting now, sparkling in the sun. No dying governors, no dying bluebirds.

"I know a man died here, but I wouldn't mind taking a quick dip," West said. "Wouldn't you?"

"Not hot enough."

"You Texans." She narrowed her eyes up at him.

"You're not thinking of sticking your nose in my case, are you?"

"Is it your case?" He knew it wasn't.

"*The* case, then. Jesus."

He shrugged. "I'm just getting the lay of the land."

"Yeah, I guess we wouldn't want you being bored up here. You and Kara Galway found Pete?"

"Yes, ma'am." He smiled, and amended himself, "Detective."

"Zoe'll be okay. Did Pete say what happened? They were running IVs in him when I got there—"

"He couldn't remember."

"That sucks. You see anything?"

He gave her his story and what he knew of Kara's story, leaving out the tree house for now. He had no idea why. Kara deserved to have every law enforcement officer in Texas and Connecticut on her case.

Detective West pressed her thumb against the filter end of her ragged cigarette. "Going out there was part of your 'getting the lay of the land'? Or don't they have gravel pits in Texas?"

He didn't answer.

She squatted by the pool and swept her free hand into the water. "Nice." She looked up at him. "You know Kara and Pete don't get along, don't you? He's still ticked off at her for that plea bargain he took. But," she said, dropping onto her butt on the pool deck, her legs stretched out in front of her, "I guess that's neither here nor there."

"Kara represented Pete Jericho?"

"Bar fight. He took six months in the county jail over a sure felony assault conviction and serious time in a state prison.'' West nodded at the woods. "Don't you think it's a dumb idea to have a swimming pool this close to the woods? I can just imagine the mosquitoes. I guess somebody thought it made for a better ambience.'' She spoke with no detectable sarcasm and leaned back against her outstretched elbows. "How're the Stockwell kids?"

Sam decided it might be smart not to underestimate Bluefield's sole detective. "They're with their mother right now."

"They must be in an emotional mess to run off from camp like that. Do they call dude ranches camp? I don't know. I've never been to Texas. I'm surprised you didn't arrest them, Ranger Temple." She grinned up at him. "Thought about it, didn't you?"

"On what charge?"

"I don't know, I'll bet you could think of something. They tell you what they had on their minds when they ran off?"

"No.'' He wondered what had possessed him to come out here with her. "Detective West, you don't buy this theory that Governor Parisi fell trying to save a bluebird, do you?"

"It's got holes.''

"He was interested in bluebirds," Sam said.

"Smitten. Ethel Smith at the library's been on my case because she insists there are no bluebird nests out here. I don't know how she knows, but she says she does."

"The state police haven't investigated?"

"Bluebird nests? Come on, Sergeant.'' She got up, a lot of leg showing, and dusted off her rear end and regarded her bent, limp cigarette with a sigh. "I miss cigarettes. I really do. It's been seventeen days." She fastened her gray eyes on him. "I'm not as grouchy about it as I was."

"That's good," Sam said, not knowing what to make of Zoe West.

"Governor Parisi and Ethel were working to get a bluebird trail started out here. I mean, a town with the name of Bluefield ought to have a bluebird trail, don't you think? That's where you set out bluebird boxes every three hundred feet or so, the idea being the bluebirds will nest, have babies, and come back year to year, thus restoring the population."

"Why every three hundred feet?"

"Because any closer and they'll drive each other away. They don't like their fellow bluebirds swooping around their nest. They're territorial and kind of fussy—you can't stick up any old birdhouse and expect it to work. If it's not just right, the baby birds can freeze to death or bake to death, or other, more aggressive non-native birds that are also cavity nesters will take over. Starlings and English sparrows, I think, are the worst offenders. Between them and the loss of habitat, the bluebird population declined sharply over the last century."

Sam smiled at her. "You've been working this bluebird angle, haven't you, Detective West?"

"I sure as hell have. Ethel bent my ear two mornings in a row. I haven't told you half of what she rattled on to me about bluebirds."

"They're beautiful birds," Sam said.

"They are. Ethel gave me a bluebird box that I'm

going to put up, under her close supervision, of course.'' West glanced around the pretty, quiet property, the silence a reminder no one lived here now. ''They also prefer a stretch of cleared land and a high place to perch, like a phone line. All the wires are buried here.'' She sighed up at the sky. ''Well, I guess there are worse ways to go than trying to save a bluebird. I'm probably spinning my wheels and it was just a freak accident. For all we know, Big Mike had rescued the damn bird himself and was trying to rehabilitate it when it got away on him.''

Sam acknowledged that was possible. At this point, anything was.

''Unfortunately, I'm good at stirring up my own dust.'' She was matter-of-fact, her tone not the least bit self-pitying. ''I see a reprimand coming my way for taking a Texas Ranger out here.''

''Why did you?''

''Kara Galway knew Governor Parisi couldn't swim. Henry and Lillian Stockwell ran to her not two weeks after their mother became governor. You came up here with her.'' West nodded to the .45. ''And you're armed.''

''I'm counting on professional courtesy,'' Sam said.

''Just don't fire the damn thing in my town. If I showed up in Texas carrying a weapon, you'd extend me the same courtesy?''

''Under similar circumstances, yes.''

She grinned. ''I doubt that. Where can I drop you off, Sergeant?''

''The hospital where they took Pete Jericho.''

"Yeah, I should probably go over there myself."
She unlatched the gate to the pool and glanced back
at Sam, her gray eyes difficult to read. "You believe
he just slipped and fell?"

"No."

"Neither do I."

Through the fog of pain and medication, Pete was
aware of the doctors and nurses running him through
X rays, an MRI and a CT scan, taking blood, setting
his wrist, cleaning and bandaging his cuts. A doctor
told him he had a broken collarbone and two broken
ribs, but his lungs were fine and there was no internal
bleeding.

Eventually they sent him up to a private room,
where plump, gray-haired Bea Jericho came in sobbing and yelling at him for not listening to her and
staying away from that damn gravel pit, it was a death
trap. Now look at him.

Charlie griped because the nurses wouldn't let him
smoke. "It's not like you're on oxygen and I'm going
to blow up the place."

Pete loved his parents but just wished they would
leave. He couldn't make sense of anything. How did
he fall? What happened?

His mother seemed to sense his irritability and con-
fusion. She took one of the tissues from his nightstand
and wiped her tears. "You just rest, Pete. They want
to keep you overnight at least. What were you doing
up on that bank, anyway?"

The tree house. He remembered now. Had he gone
up there to dismantle it? The details wouldn't come,

and he wondered if his father had told anyone about it and if so, would they all be in trouble now, him and Charlie and the kids.

They had him hooked up to two IVs, one for fluids, one for pain medication. A doctor had told him he might not remember how he fell, it was okay, a normal short-circuiting of the short-term memory process. A chemical reaction while the body was under assault and pouring everything into staying alive.

But he might remember more after the pain medication wore off. "It'll take time," the doctor said. "Be patient."

A state trooper entered the room and said that Governor Stockwell was there to see him, if he was up to her visit. Charlie and Bea retreated, promising to bring him clean clothes later, but before he left, his father leaned over Pete and said in a low voice, "Nothing good comes from getting involved with a Stockwell. First Madeleine gets people to lie about a barroom fight, and now—look at yourself, son. You grew up in those woods. The hell you slipped and fell."

Pete couldn't make sense of half of what his father said. "Pop…"

"Don't worry. I'm keeping my mouth shut. That old bat isn't going to find some way to put you in jail for busting yourself up."

He withdrew, and Pete sank his head into his pillow, no idea what the hell his father was talking about. How could he go to jail for falling?

Allyson entered the room with the air of a governor about her, and Pete knew this was a visit from a concerned neighbor, not his lover. He didn't care. He was so damn happy to see her. He wished he could take the fear and worry from her beautiful eyes, but... *fuck*...he couldn't even stay awake.

Sam's mood started to darken on the way back to Bluefield. Zoe West had snooped around the hospital, then took off, leaving him to his own devices to find a ride back to Bluefield. He got one with Kara, in Pete's truck. Charlie Jericho rode back with his wife, who apparently didn't let him behind the wheel of her car.

Kara drove. She looked drained and tired, her dark eyes betraying her worry and tension. "This your first time driving a truck?" Sam asked her.

"Shut up, Sam."

Still some spark in her. That was good. "You want to talk?"

"No."

"Mike Parisi was murdered. You know that, don't you?"

"It doesn't matter what we know," she said, her eyes focused on the road. "It only matters what we can prove. You know that."

It was all she would say.

Two minutes after they arrived back at the cottage, Hatch Corrigan and a state trooper delivered Henry and Lillian, obviously sticking to the original plan to spend some quality time with their godmother.

Hatch reminded Kara that the private bodyguard would be starting in the morning. "I'll bring him by early."

"When will Allyson be back from the hospital? I was hoping to have a chance to talk to her—"

"Not today. She's very upset about what happened."

Kara nodded. "We all are."

But Hatch wasn't interested in anyone else, and he left.

Kara set the kids up at the kitchen table with drawing supplies and answered their questions about Pete, and Sam could see this wasn't the time to grill Henry and Lillian about their tree house. It could wait. First he'd grill Kara. It probably wasn't the time for that, either, but he didn't care.

She seemed to sense what was on his mind and blew out the back door and started heaping charcoal in the hibachi. He offered to help. She shook her head. So he sat in the shade and watched her.

"Interesting scene at the hospital," he said.

She squirted charcoal lighter fuel onto the coals from a rusted can she'd found under the sink. "People always act weird in hospitals."

Sam didn't argue with her point. He tried to sort through the people he'd met since arriving in Bluefield, who they were, what they meant not only to Kara, but to the two towheads in the kitchen who were just trying to keep a grip on their lives. "No love lost between Charlie Jericho and Madeleine Stockwell, is there?"

"On Charlie's part. I doubt Madeleine thinks enough about Charlie to like him or dislike him. He blames her for Pete going to jail. I represented him—"

"Zoe West told me."

"He thinks Madeleine got people to exaggerate their stories, if not outright lie."

"What do you think?"

"I think Pete tore up that bar and thought it'd be a just-between-us-boys deal and it wasn't." Kara set down her fuel can, very focused on her work. "I could have tried to tear apart the witnesses' stories on the stand, but we still had a guy with stitches. Even if the witnesses were exaggerating, Pete couldn't deny he hit someone with a beer bottle."

Sam sat in the grass, extending his legs and leaning against his outstretched arms, imagining Kara in her twenties, trying to sort out lies from truth and be an advocate for her clients. "So the prosecutor offering to knock it down from felony assault to a misdemeanor was appropriate."

"He never should have been charged with a felony, but if he'd gone to trial, he'd have been convicted. It was stupid. The whole thing was stupid, but there we were. I did my best."

"I don't doubt it."

She shot him a look, then gave a small smile. "Thanks."

"Why would Madeleine Stockwell want Pete in jail?"

"To put him in his place."

"Because he was in love with Allyson," Sam said.

Kara glanced around at him, the soft light of dusk bringing out the richness of her dark eyes. "Do you notice everything?"

"He's still in love with her." Sam plucked a blade

of grass and stuck the end in his mouth. "The governor and an ex-con. That might not go down well with the public. Or her advisers, her family. Governor Parisi. A lot of people she wants to please."

"Pete served six months on a criminal misdemeanor. It's not like he killed people. He was twenty-five. He got into a bar fight." Kara set down her can of lighter fluid. "Anyway, Allyson doesn't think that way. If she wanted to see Pete, she would, and to hell with the rest of it."

"Not everyone's looking for a soul mate. Sometimes," Sam went on, "the wrong people fall in love with each other."

"I need matches."

She spun on her heels and ran inside, returning a minute later with a box of short wooden matches. She tapped one out, but dropped it in the grass, and when she knelt on one knee to look for it, Sam could see she was ready to come apart. She located the fallen match, but it was wet. She tossed it onto the coals and tapped out another.

"These people have a lot at stake, Kara. There are too many animosities and ambitions at work here that have nothing to do with you and who you are. You felt the undercurrents a year ago, and that's why you came home."

"I wasn't running from anything." Her back was to him now, tense and unyielding but Sam could feel her vulnerability, her resistance to it. "I stayed out of the politics. Big Mike was complicated, a great guy, but I didn't see that much of him, especially after he was elected governor."

"But he was in love with you," Sam said.

"Half in love. It was just a romantic fantasy. I don't know, maybe he told me to make sure I didn't get cold feet and stay in Connecticut. Not that it made any difference. I came home because it's where I wanted to be."

"What about Allyson?"

"We'll be friends until we're a couple of white-haired old ladies, even if we don't see each other as often. And Hatch, Madeleine, Billie. The Jerichos. I guess in a way they were my northern family."

"And you can't save any of them," Sam said, "any more than you could save your mother."

At first he didn't think she'd react. She struck her match against the box, and when it didn't light, she threw it impatiently onto the coals and got out another. But she didn't strike it. She set the box on the table next to the hibachi and carefully laid the match on top of it so it wouldn't roll. Then she walked over into the shade and, without a word, slapped him across the face. Not as hard as she could have, but hard enough.

Sam could have stopped her, but he didn't. And she'd known he wouldn't. "Tell me I'm wrong, Kara."

She looked more shocked by what she'd done than anything. "I'm sorry. I had no right to hit you." She turned and walked back to her matches and her grill. "I'm staying until I know Henry and Lillian are safe." There was no anger in her voice, just fatigue and that unrelenting determination. "If someone killed Mike, I want his murderer found and brought to justice. It has nothing to do with my mother.''

Sam had no intention of letting her off the hook, never mind the sting of her slap, her resistance to what he had to say. ''The state police and state's chief attorney are investigating. Tell them what you know and let them do their job.'' And he added, ''If you don't, I will.''

''They're not a part of Allyson's inner circle. I am. I went away, so now I have some distance—but I still have a perspective they don't. And I have access.''

She'd looked around at him, reminding Sam of her brother the morning they'd driven through a blinding snowstorm to save his daughters from a murderer.

''Damn, Kara.'' Sam saw it now. ''You think someone in this inner circle is responsible for Parisi's death.''

She didn't say a word. She struck another match and tossed it onto the coals, jumping back as the flames shot up.

Seventeen

————❦❦❦————

Kara lay awake in her dark bedroom, the moonlight creating eerie, shifting shadows as she listened to crickets and an owl outside in the woods and fields, the distant warble of wild turkeys. She tried to concentrate on these sounds and images instead of those in her head. Big Mike gasping for air, the doomed bluebird, Henry and Lillian watching in horror from their illicit tree house. She'd woken up abruptly from a nightmare in which she was the bluebird and Big Mike had died trying to save her, and it all got mixed up with that terrible day her mother was killed.

Then she saw Pete Jericho lying in the gravel pit, bleeding and broken, and she heard his pain-wracked words. *You always see me at my worst.* She remembered him pacing in her office, already not entirely trusting her because she was young and female and not his idea of tough, a friend of the Stockwells, a lawyer Mike Parisi had recommended, a graduate of Yale. He knew nothing about her upbringing in south Texas or how hard she worked, and she saw no need to tell him.

She blinked as if that might make the last vestiges of her nightmare go away, but it didn't. She wondered what time it was, if Sam had gone up to bed. She peered across the room to see if there was any light under her doorway. Maybe. She couldn't tell.

After dinner, they'd all played a game of Risk. Sam was the first one out. He rose, gathering up his pieces. "There, you see? I don't want to rule the world all that much."

They didn't finish the game and called it a draw. The kids just wanted to go to bed. Sam didn't bring up the subject of their tree house or how he planned to go to the Connecticut authorities in the morning with what he knew.

Kara apologized again for slapping him, but he didn't apologize for his unfeeling remark. What did he know about her mother?

Sinking back against her pillows, Kara ran her hand over her abdomen and breasts and imagined a baby growing inside her, a baby nursing, sleeping on her stomach. She remembered the soft skin and infant smells of her twin nieces and, later, her godchildren, their downy hair and tiny hands and feet, the new baby blankets and cute little outfits.

She hadn't realized she'd gotten so caught up in her pregnancy fantasy and never guessed she'd be disappointed, almost bereft, when the test turned out negative. She thought she'd be relieved. An unplanned pregnancy was not what she needed in her life.

She sighed, remembering Sam's response to her, her response to him, up against that oak tree today.

If they hadn't come to their senses, she'd be buying more pregnancy tests in a few weeks.

A crazy business for sure, she thought, if Sam Temple turned out to be her soul mate. A black-eyed Texas Ranger whose idea of compromise was that people didn't argue with him. Lord, what to do?

But her body relaxed as she thought of him, and she must have drifted back to sleep because the smell of coffee woke her. She got cleaned up and dressed quickly, trying not to pay attention to her reflection in the bathroom mirror. But she caught a glimpse of herself in the bedroom mirror on her way out, and she saw the strain, the tension that had gripped her since Allyson's call the night of the Gordon Temple opening.

Sam was easing onto a chair at the table when she went into the kitchen. He hadn't buttoned his shirt, and she remembered with a jolt how, sometime during their long night together, she'd run her tongue down his hard, dark abdomen, felt his sharp intake of air when she'd gone lower. Her boldness had surprised her—yet everything they did in those hours seemed right, as if a bond already existed between them, one that went beyond sex and time, at least in her own mind.

He drawled a good morning, and she poured herself a cup of coffee and sat across from him. He had the Colt in its holster, nothing about him casual. She needed to remember that. Sam Temple was sexy, witty, even cocky—but he was always serious when it came to violence, the potential for violence. Pete's accident yesterday, the tree house and seeing where

Big Mike died would all have reminded Sam that this was not a normal summer weekend in the picturesque northwest Connecticut countryside.

Henry wandered in looking for breakfast, and Sam helped him fry up some bacon. Lillian, off her vegetarian kick, asked for them to fry her some, too, then slid onto Kara's lap. "Will you help me fix my hair?"

They retreated to the bathroom, where Kara combed Lillian's long blond hair and did her best to fashion it into a single braid down her back. "Did your mother fix your hair?" Lillian asked.

"When I was a little girl, yes," Kara said. "She liked to put it into French braids."

"She died, didn't she?"

"We were in a car accident when I was nine and my brother was fifteen."

"Do you still miss her?"

"Yes."

"Does it make you sad that she died?"

"It did. I accept it now." Kara knew they weren't talking about her mother, but about Big Mike. "She's still a part of my life."

"I talk to Big Mike sometimes," Lillian said.

Kara smiled and kissed the top of her head. "He'd like that, don't you think?"

"Henry says Pete fell from up at our tree house. He says we'll really get into trouble if people find out about it now."

"Lillian, that's not true. You didn't commit a crime—"

"We were *trespassing*. The tree house isn't on our land."

"But you and Henry didn't push Pete."

The girl shook her head solemnly. "We were swimming at Grandma's."

"Then it'll be okay. Trust me. It's unrealistic to think people aren't going to find out about the tree house and figure out what you saw. They'll climb up there and realize you could see Mike's swimming pool—"

But Lillian was done. "I don't think I want any toast with my bacon."

Her braid was lopsided, but she didn't seem to mind and skipped back to the kitchen, instructing Sam and Henry on how she liked her bacon crisp not soppy. They all sat at the table, Sam with a fresh mug of coffee, and Henry asked Kara about the bodyguard Hatch had hired. "Lillian and I don't want a bodyguard," he said. "We're fine on our own."

"Hatch and your mother will feel better—"

"Uncle Hatch will. Mom doesn't care. She just wants us to be quiet and perfect and not get in her way."

"Is that why you haven't told her everything you told me?" Kara asked quietly.

Henry refused to answer. Lillian said, "He's mad at Mom because she wouldn't let us go to the hospital and see Pete. She made us stay with Grandma and Uncle Hatch and that state trooper."

"Kara and I were at the gravel pit yesterday." Sam sipped more of his coffee, his shirt still unbuttoned. Deceptively laid-back, he spoke calmly, without drama. "You know we're the ones who found Pete, right? Kara stayed with him, and I walked up to the top of the hill to see if I could figure out how he fell. I ran across your tree house.''

"Pete's going to be fine," Henry said and jumped up. "Come on, Lillian, let's go upstairs."

She wrapped two pieces of bacon in a napkin and followed her brother out of the kitchen. Kara leaned back in her chair. "That went well."

"I see what you're up against—they're just hearing what they want to hear." But Sam's mind was clearly elsewhere, and he set down his mug and placed one foot up on the opposite knee, his chair pushed back from the table. "Why two weeks before they took off from the ranch? Why not bolt the first week if it was because they were upset over seeing Parisi drown?"

Kara went to the counter for more coffee.

"There must have been a trigger that second week." He studied her, then took another swallow of coffee. "There was, wasn't there, Kara?"

"Sam, I can't—"

"You are not those kids' attorney. You're their godmother."

"I know what I am."

"I'm still going to the authorities."

She nodded.

They heard cars out on the dirt road, and Kara looked out the kitchen window and saw first Billie Corrigan pull up in her old station wagon, then Hatch in a sedan with a gray-haired man at the wheel. At first she didn't recognize him, but when he got out of the car, she winced. Of all the people he could have hired as Henry and Lillian's private bodyguard, Hatch had chosen Walter Harrison? Why? Wally was the off-duty Bluefield cop who'd wreaked such havoc on Pete Jericho's life. He was retired now, paunchy, obviously available for the job.

Sam joined Kara at the window. "This looks encouraging."

"Wally Harrison. He would *not* be my first choice." Kara sighed. "Well, it's out of my hands."

They went out through the front door, and Hatch made the introductions while Billie popped her trunk, rolling her eyes privately at Kara, as if she knew Wally Harrison was the wrong choice.

"Obviously Wally can't stay awake twenty-four hours a day," Hatch said, "but I think he'll provide Henry and Lillian with the extra level of protection we feel they need right now, without overdoing it."

"Wally, it's good to see you." Kara smiled, trying to be polite. "We've all just been hanging out here at the cottage this morning."

Wally had the look of a man who spent a lot of time down at O'Reilly's Pub. His face was ruddy, and he was out of shape, his Hawaiian shirt barely covering his paunch. "It's been a while, Kara. You're keeping the criminals on the streets down in Texas, I hear."

Kara bristled, but said nothing.

"Wally will be as unobtrusive as possible," Hatch said quietly. "He won't interfere with your time with the kids."

She could sense that Sam didn't like this development, but he left her to Hatch and Wally and helped Billie unload several small boxes from her trunk and set them in the shade. "I'm driving Hatch back up to his mom's,'' Billie said, ''so Wally can stay here with his car. I had some fun stuff kicking around I thought the kids might like while they're here.''

''That's great, Billie,'' Kara said. ''Thanks. I'm sure they'll appreciate it.''

Billie lifted out the last box, the largest, and held it on her hip. ''I see Charlie's fixed the front steps. I almost broke my damn neck on them the last time I was here. I love it that they call this place a cottage.'' She grinned. ''It's bigger than my house.''

Hatch grimaced at his sister's words. ''Where are Henry and Lillian? I want to introduce them to Wally. He hasn't seen them since they were toddlers.''

His imperiousness was getting to Kara. She snatched up a small box from the shade and headed for the front door. Billie was already on the way with her big box. They set the boxes on the living-room floor. Kara noticed cheap feather boas and Mardi Gras beads, drawing pads, a shoe box of crayons, glitter glue, gel pens. She smiled at Billie. ''The kids'll love this,'' she said. ''I'll give them a yell and get them down here.''

She called them from the bottom of the stairs. ''Henry and Lillian—come on down. Hatch is here with someone he wants you to meet, and Billie's brought you some goodies.''

They didn't answer, and there was no sound of footsteps.

Kara sighed. ''They must have on their Walk-mans.''

''I can go up and look,'' Billie said.

''It's okay—I'll do it. Thanks.''

Sam came in through the front door with the last box. He set it on the floor, then placed a foot on the bottom step and watched Kara, his intensity unsettling. She continued up the stairs and checked Henry's room first, then Lillian's.

They weren't there.

"Kids? Where are you?"

Maybe they'd gone sullen and uncooperative on her and were hiding. She looked under the beds and in the closets, then peered out Lillian's window and checked the backyard. No sign of them.

She stood on the landing and, stemming any sense of panic, shouted down the stairs. "They're not up here!"

But Sam had already disappeared. Kara ran down the stairs two at a time, almost barreling into Sam as he returned from the kitchen. He shook his head. "They're not back there. I checked the bedroom and the bathroom as well."

"I'll tell Hatch," Billie said, white-faced, and ran out the front door.

Kara charged past Sam and raced through the kitchen and out the back door, sweat already trickling between her breasts from fear and exertion. She could feel the humidity in the air, the dew point higher than yesterday. There was a light bluish-gray haze on the horizon. She cut across the backyard into the woods, but Sam eased in behind her as she ducked down to the brook. But the places where Henry and Lillian had dunked their feet and looked for frogs were undisturbed, humming with mosquitoes on the hot summer morning.

"They didn't like the idea of a bodyguard," Kara said, "but I never thought they'd run off on me. Maybe they were more upset than I realized when you told them you'd found their tree house. I don't know...damn it!"

Sam touched her elbow. "Let's go on back before Corrigan overreacts. Henry and Lillian know this area. No one came in and snatched them." He didn't smile. "I'd have known it."

She thought of the man the kids insisted had followed them in Texas, and blood pounded behind her eyes, her throat tightening. But Sam had a point. If someone had tried to take the kids right out from under his nose, he'd have known it. Kara pushed a hand through her hair and started back up to the dirt road. "We need to find them."

They returned to the cottage and found Hatch pacing on the driveway, kicking at the dirt and cursing his niece and nephew. Billie winced as she watched her brother losing control. "Come on, Hatch—"

"Those damn kids! Where the hell are they?" He gritted his teeth. "I've had just about enough of their nonsense. We have important work to do, but they keep insisting we focus all our attention on them. *Christ!*"

Wally Harrison had drawn his weapon, a Smith & Wesson .38. Sam nodded at it. "There's no reason for that, Mr. Harrison."

"And who the fuck are you—"

"Holster the damn gun, Wally," Hatch said. "We don't need a goddamn shoot-out right now. Let's just find Henry and Lillian."

Kara regarded Hatch with fresh insight, noting the spittle on the corners of his mouth and his flared nostrils, the redness in his face. He was losing it. Hatch Corrigan, the cool behind-the-scenes operator. But she didn't have time for shock or contemplation and decided simply to say what had to be said. "Hatch, you and Walter can find Allyson and ask her what she wants to do. Sam and I can look around here. They can't have gone far—"

"You'll take Wally with you," Hatch said.

"No," Sam intervened, speaking with finality. "Mr. Harrison will only slow us down."

Wally snorted. "Just who the hell—"

"We're from out of town," Sam said, nothing about him softening. "We can't give Governor Stockwell the kind of advice you two can. Henry and Lillian didn't run off until you got here. Maybe we can calm them down."

Hatch backed off, and Kara saw what Sam had done. Not only had he pointed out Wally's inadequacies and Henry and Lillian's volatility, but he'd played on Hatch's desire to control events. Better to keep the Texans out in the woods than influencing Allyson's decision-making. And if anything went wrong and things got out of hand with Henry and Lillian, the Texans could also take the fall.

Billie tugged on her brother's arm. "What do you want me to do? I'd just get lost if I tried to find them—"

"Stay here in case they come back." But Hatch didn't even look at his sister, his unpleasant, nervous gaze on Kara. "We'll stay in touch by cell phone.

Wally,'' he said, not taking his eyes off her, ''you're with me.''

Wally spat in the grass. ''You're the boss.''

After they left, Billie exhaled in a whoosh and shook her head. ''Go on, you two. I'll call Hatch if they turn up here. He can let you know. Wouldn't want to step on his toes.'' She smiled feebly. ''Those poor kids are major-spooked, aren't they?'' But she didn't wait for Kara to answer. ''Good luck,'' she said and headed inside.

Sam was all business. ''The tree house?''

Kara nodded. ''That's what I'm thinking.''

Eighteen

～❦～

"**W**e're not coming down!" Henry was on his feet, shouting down from the tree house. "Go away!"

Lillian lay flat on her stomach on the platform, her chin just over the plywood edge. Kara had a strange sense of vertigo as she looked up at them, with the gravel pit descending sharply to her right, the woods off to her left and the clouds and haze shifting, making it seem as if the oak were moving and they'd all fall at any moment.

"He's the man from Texas," Lillian said, spitting out her words as if Kara should have known. "That man with Uncle Hatch. He keeps following us."

Sam cast Kara a quick, hard look but said nothing.

"He's not here now." She could hear the tension in her voice, her breathing still labored from the fast pace she and Sam had set to get here. "I'll talk to Hatch and your mother, and we'll get this straightened out, once and for all."

"No!" Henry was having none of it. "They'll all lie to you. They'll say it wasn't him. They'll say we made it up."

"We don't want him for our bodyguard," Lillian shrieked.

Kara swallowed, her neck aching. "All right. Consider him fired."

Sam placed a palm on her back and looked up at Henry and Lillian. "Here's what we're going to do. Kara will call and make sure any search parties are called off. We know where you are. People don't need to be worrying about you. Then she'll walk back to your grandmother's house and find out what she can about this Walter Harrison character. She won't break any promises to you." He paused, but the kids didn't interrupt him. "I'll stay here with you."

Henry shook his head. "No way."

"Sorry, kid. That's the way it's going to be."

Henry fumed but didn't argue. Lillian scooted up onto her knees and sat down with a plop, dangling her feet over the side of the platform. Kara shuddered at the thought of the two of them hauling wood and nails and junk up there, the plunge to the gravel pit just one wrong step away.

"You'll be all right walking back on your own?" Sam asked her.

"Of course. This is Connecticut. No lions, no tigers, not many bears and just one kind of rattlesnake."

He didn't even come close to smiling. "You've known all along Walter Harrison followed Henry and Lillian to Texas."

"I knew they *thought* someone followed them. I didn't know if it was for real, and I sure as hell didn't know it was Wally."

"I could have checked out their story. Jack could have followed up—" But he bit off a sigh. "We'll go there later. You'll be all right?"

She refused to give in to the quiver of fear she felt and tilted her head back, nodding. "I'll carry a stick and remember my self-defense lessons. You keep the gun." She forced a smile. "You might need it with those two."

"Kara—"

"I can shoot a target," she said quickly, "not a real person. I don't have your experience or training."

His eyes sparked. "A Galway admitting to a weakness?"

She almost smiled. "Who says it's a weakness?"

"Be careful." He touched her lips, then started up the rickety ladder. "I'm coming up. You two try knocking me out of this tree, it'll just piss me off."

They didn't protest, and no rocks fell on his head. Kara started through the low undergrowth along the edge of the pit, stopping partway down the hill to call Hatch on his cell phone. "We found the kids. They're fine. I'll be there in a few minutes." She hesitated. "I need to talk to Allyson."

"Henry and Lillian aren't with you?"

"They're with Sam. Look, I can't tramp through the woods and talk at the same time. I'll break my fool neck. Billie's at the cottage—she'll want to know the kids are safe. See you soon."

He sputtered, but Kara disconnected, continuing down the hill. She thought of Pete Jericho's body sprawled at the bottom of the gravel pit and kept her eyes open for the biggest stick she could find.

* * *

The tree house held Sam's weight—not because of its quality construction but because Henry and Lillian didn't weigh as much as a pair of gnats. They seemed impressed by his mobility and agility in getting up there and swinging over to them. He sat cross-legged on the edge of the platform closest to the gravel pit.

Lillian gazed at him thoughtfully. "Are you an Indian?"

"Why do you ask? Because I can climb a tree?"

She giggled, no sign she and her brother had just run off in a blind panic. "Henry and I were just wondering. I have a friend at school whose father's Narraganset. He's awesome. My friend's name is Brook. Isn't that a pretty name?"

"My father is Cherokee," Sam said, surprising himself. "He's a painter. I've never known him."

"Is he dead?" Henry asked. He was standing, leaning casually against a branch, close to the oak's trunk, no indication he was aware of the gaping hole of the gravel pit to his left.

Sam shook his head. "He and my mother were divorced before I was born. He moved to New Mexico, and she never told him about me."

"My dad's dead." Lillian was matter-of-fact, neither cavalier nor morose. "I don't remember him. Henry does, a little."

Her brother's brow furrowed as he thought a moment. "I remember riding on his back when we went swimming."

"Your mother's never remarried," Sam said, neutral.

Lillian sighed heavily, dramatically. "I think she wants to marry Pete, but she's worried about us."

"Lillian!" Henry groaned in disgust. "It's a secret." He turned to Sam, speaking gravely. "Mom doesn't think we know."

"I won't say anything unless I have no choice," Sam said. "Kids always know more than the adults around them think they do. I'll bet nobody realizes what all you know about Walter Harrison. Did you think he was from Texas?"

"We didn't know. We never saw him before, not until he followed us around at the dude ranch." Henry looked at his fingers, a white, bloodless scrape along the side of one hand, probably from scrambling up the oak. "I saw him first. I didn't want to scare Lillian, but I had to warn her. Then she saw him, too."

"Sometimes he wore disguises," she added.

Sam pictured these two kids, mourning their friend, isolated at a Texas dude ranch thousands of miles from home. "You didn't say anything to your counselors—"

"Kara asked us that, too," Henry said. "No, we were too scared."

"Because you'd seen Governor Parisi drown from up here?"

They both nodded, saying nothing more.

Sam suspected there was more, suspected Kara did as well, but he could see how frightened and troubled these kids were, how difficult it was to get them to talk. "You're sure it was Walter Harrison in Texas?"

"Yes! We *saw* him." Lillian managed to be defensive, excited and indignant, all at once. "He parked in front of Aunt Kara's next-door neighbor's house. We saw him get out. He was smoking a cigarette.''

"It was the same guy," Henry said calmly.

"When did you see him at Kara's house? Do you remember the time?"

Henry glanced down at him in that Prince of Wales way he had. "We looked out the window when you were there and saw him. I wasn't going to say anything, but after you left, Lillian went and got Aunt Kara.''

"Kara saw him?"

"Only his car. He drove away while we were watching.''

Sam kept his reaction to himself. He was right there, on Kara's porch, and her two godchildren were in her bedroom scared out of their minds, the man who'd followed them from the ranch a few yards from Sam's car. If he'd known, he could have acted that night.

But Kara didn't realize that her runaways believed they had a man following them until after Sam left. It was only a small point in her favor, because when she found out and saw how terrified Henry and Lillian were, she smuggled them over to Kevin and Eva Dunning's, then to San Antonio and on to Boston and Stonebrook Cottage.

It wasn't what he'd have done, Sam thought.

He got out his cell phone. "If I can get through from up here, I'd like to make a call to Jack Galway, Kara's brother. He's another Texas Ranger.''

"We know," Lillian said. "We met him a long time ago."

Sam wondered what a long time ago was to an eleven-year-old. He dialed Jack's number in San Antonio.

"What's up?" Jack asked.

"I need you to check on a retired Bluefield, Connecticut, cop by the name of Walter Harrison—find out if he's been in Texas in the last week or so. Probably flew into Austin, maybe San Antonio. He could have stayed somewhere near the Stockwell kids' dude ranch."

Jack was silent a moment. "Where are you?"

"You don't want to know," Sam said. "Harrison probably also rented a car."

"That's all I'm getting?"

"For now. I'll get back to you when I have more."

"My sister?"

"Like I told your mother-in-law, up to her ass in the lion's mouth. I think that's the way she's used to living. I'm doing what I can."

"I'm catching a flight in the morning," his lieutenant said and disconnected before Sam could try to argue with him.

He stretched out his legs along the edge of the platform. "You have a nice view from up here. One pair of binoculars between you?"

"I have my own," Lillian said, "but I dropped them and lost them."

"That's too bad."

She seemed to think so, too. "Big Mike taught us

how to recognize bluebirds. Do you know they're related to robins?"

"I'm learning a lot about bluebirds," Sam said.

"Big Mike said they like mealworms." Lillian made a face. "That is so gross."

Henry shared her distaste. "He tried to get Grandma to feed mealworms to her bluebirds, but she said no."

"She has bluebirds?"

"Uh-huh." Lillian nodded vigorously. "Big Mike got her to put up boxes, and two bluebirds built a nest and had babies this spring. They were so fun to watch."

"*Two* sets of babies," her brother said.

She sighed. "Grandma says she can't get worked up about bluebirds."

"I'll bet your friend, Governor Parisi, was excited about them," Sam said.

"Oh, *yes*." Lillian beamed, then her eyes filled with tears that she bravely blinked back. "I miss him so, so much."

Sam nodded. "I know you do."

Neither child spoke, and Sam realized there was no need to have them confirm or deny what they all now knew. Henry and Lillian Stockwell, ages twelve and eleven, saw their friend fight for his life from their tree house.

"After the accident on the Fourth of July, it must have been pretty scary out here that day." Sam kept his tone calm and neutral. "But you saw someone else, too, didn't you? Someone besides Governor Parisi and the state troopers who pulled him out of the water.''

Lillian gasped. ''How did you know?''

But her brother dropped down beside her and shoved her by the shoulder. ''Shut up, Lillian! Don't say anything.''

Sam glanced down at the gravel pit, the vertical drop deadly, Henry and Lillian's initial reason, he thought, for not telling anyone about their little project. Maybe it was why they'd picked this tree, because they knew it was dangerous and the preoccupied adults in their lives wouldn't approve.

''You haven't told anyone who you saw, not even your Aunt Kara.'' He kept his gaze leveled on the gravel pit, not on the two kids. He didn't want them to make any assumptions about what he was thinking because of how he looked at them, a wrong gesture, a leap of logic on their part. He needed them, simply, to tell him what they saw that day. ''That's a big burden. I'd like to share it. I don't know anyone from Connecticut except you two—I can be objective. I won't jump to any conclusions.''

Lillian whispered to her brother, ''We should tell him.''

''He's not a lawyer,'' Henry said. ''Aunt Kara says he can't arrest anybody outside of Texas, but he'll tell the police—''

''What if we're wrong? What if Uncle Hatch—''

''Lillian!''

She started to cry, and Sam shifted, saw that Henry was close to tears himself. ''Hey, you two.'' His voice was gentle, more so than he expected. "Relax. I left my thumbscrews in Texas."

Lillian tried to smile, wiping her tears with her forearm. "I don't know what a thumbscrew is."

Sam smiled. "I don't know if I do, either. Look, you don't have to tell me anything. We can sit here and wait for Kara to call or come back and fetch us, or you can tell me where you want to go, and I'll take you there."

Henry sniffled, sitting on the platform with his back to Sam, his feet hanging over the edge. He kicked out one leg and put his sneakered toe on a high, skinny branch. "Uncle Hatch and Big Mike were fighting. I saw them through my binoculars. They weren't punching each other, but they were really mad. They were out by the pool."

"I saw them, too," Lillian said quietly.

"Did they fight often that you know of?" Sam asked.

"All the time," Henry said, "but not like this. Uncle Hatch thumped Big Mike on the chest. I thought one of his security guards would come out and tell Uncle Hatch to leave, but nothing happened."

"But Big Mike never touched Hatch?"

Henry shook his head. Lillian, her ashen face smeared with tears and dirt, fastened her big blue eyes on Sam. "Uncle Hatch stomped off. He was still mad. I could tell."

"At first we thought it was funny," her brother admitted.

"Because you were up here spying on them—"

"Yeah."

"How long before you saw Governor Parisi in the pool?"

"I don't know," Henry said, his back still to Sam. "We ate snacks and stuff. Then I heard something down on the hill, and I got my binoculars. I thought it was just a deer—it might have been a deer."

"This was *before* Governor Parisi was in the water?"

Henry nodded. "I saw him a couple of minutes later. He was already in the water. I was still looking for the deer, so I didn't see how he fell in."

"Henry screamed," Lillian said, "and I was so scared I almost fell, but I looked in my binoculars, and I—I—I saw—" She couldn't say it.

Sam brushed a knuckle over a fat tear on her cheek. "It's okay, kiddo. You can cry."

"Mom doesn't like us to cry," Henry said stiffly. "She says it makes her cry, too."

"Is that what she said, or is that what you think?"

The boy turned his face toward Sam, tears dripping down his cheeks and off his jaw onto his shirt. "I know it."

Sam nodded. "When you saw Governor Parisi in the pool, did you climb down and run to help him?"

"We didn't have our cell phones," Lillian said, as if all kids carried cell phones up to their tree houses. "We couldn't call 911, so we ran as fast as we could—"

"The security guards were already there when we got to the bottom of the hill." Henry reached up with both hands, grabbed a thick branch above his head and pulled himself easily to his feet. Then he wiped his face with the hem of his shirt. His eyes were puffy, but he seemed calmer, less defiant. "They didn't see us. We stayed in the woods."

"It was really, really hot," Lillian said, "and there were *millions* of mosquitoes."

Sam pulled one knee up to his chest, picturing these two kids on that hot summer day. "So you decided not to stick around. You didn't see him fall. The state troopers were dealing with the situation. There wasn't anything you could do."

"We didn't want to be in the way," Lillian said.

"And you didn't want to have to talk to the police and have everybody tramp up here and find out about your tree house. You were afraid you'd get into trouble." Sam leaned back against the tree trunk. "I understand what you were thinking. What happened on your way back up here?"

Lillian was blinking rapidly, uncertain of what she should say. "It wasn't an accident," she whispered. "What happened to Big Mike—it wasn't an accident. Somebody pushed him. That's what we heard in the woods. It wasn't a stupid deer."

Jesus, Sam thought. This was what Kara had dreaded, sensed, hoped wasn't true—that her young godchildren had experienced the unique and terrible fear that they'd brushed up close to a murderer.

"It was leaves rustling," Henry said. "It could have been a deer."

Lillian was having none of it. "But my *binoculars*. They stole my binoculars!"

"What would anyone want with your stupid old binoculars? Come *on*, Lillian. Aunt Kara says we have to look at the facts and not jump to conclusions.'' Henry frowned down at Sam. "Right, Sam?"

Sam didn't answer him. "Did you and your sister look for her binoculars?"

Henry rolled his eyes. "We looked *everywhere*. It was all she could think about. 'My binoculars, my binoculars.'" He imitated Lillian's whining that day and gave a long-suffering huff. "I told her I didn't care."

His sister stuck her tongue out at him. He looked as if he wanted to kick her.

"It must have been a rough time for the two of you," Sam said diplomatically. "Kara's a pitbull when it comes to you two. It must have felt good to get out of here after the funeral, fly down to Texas with her. You liked the ranch okay at first?"

They both nodded, and Henry said, "The horses were the best. Some of the other kids teased me about my accent, but I don't have an accent."

"I made a friend from El Paso," Lillian said, then added knowledgeably, "It's in west Texas."

"So that first week or so was okay? Then you started seeing this man, Walter Harrison, and you didn't know what to make of him." Sam paused, but neither child responded. "You made your plan to clear out and dump the whole mess on your Aunt Kara. You thought she could help you because she's your godmother and you know she loves and believes in you, and she's a lawyer."

Both kids nodded, agreeing for once.

"But you didn't tell her about your uncle's argument with Governor Parisi," Sam said.

Henry swallowed. "She and Uncle Hatch..."

When her brother trailed off, Lillian said, "He likes her, but she doesn't like him."

Sam nodded. They weren't sure of her objectivity, and they knew, on some level, it'd raise the stakes if they told Kara they had information suggesting Mike Parisi's death was no accident. As it was, Kara hadn't known what to believe.

"You two can't change the facts of what happened, what people did," Sam said. "The facts are what they are. If Governor Parisi's death was an accident, it was an accident. If someone killed him, someone killed him. Nothing you can do."

"I don't want him to be dead at all," Lillian said.

"I can see that, and I think Michael Parisi was a lucky man to have you two miss him as much as you do. As for your uncle—here's the deal. Do you think he killed Governor Parisi?"

They gasped in horror. "No!"

"Then you've kept quiet about him because you think he might get into trouble. Well, let him worry about that. He's a smart guy." Sam could feel the tree house hard on his rear end, its confines starting to get to him. "But you know that. So here's what I think is really going on. I think you're afraid that whoever you heard in the woods saw you and will come after you if you say anything. That's why you were so upset when you saw Harrison watching you in Texas, because you figured he was either the murderer or working for the murderer—"

"We jumped to conclusions?" Lillian asked quietly.

"You did, but you paid attention to your instincts, and that's good because they can keep you safe. Let me put it this way, kids. I don't like this Walter Harrison character, either, and I've jumped to a number of conclusions about him." He winked, noting how relieved they looked now that their story was out in the open. "Now, do you want me to help you look for Lillian's binoculars, make sure they're not under the leaves or a rock or something?"

They weren't too enthusiastic about the idea. Sam wasn't, either, but they agreed to it, and at least it got them out of the damn tree house.

Nineteen

Kara didn't know if it was the uncompromising presence of Sam Temple or the shock of Henry and Lillian's secrets—or some combination of both—but no one interrupted Sam when he told their story, with their full permission and occasional interruptions to edit.

They were all gathered on the patio. Hatch, Allyson, Madeleine, Sam, the kids. Two wary state troopers stood near the pool. Billie had whisked Wally Harrison into the kitchen, but Kara had already got Hatch to admit that he'd secretly hired the retired cop to keep an eye on the kids in Texas, never expecting him to do such a poor job. She'd called Sam on his cell phone and told him while he was walking back to Stockwell Farm with the kids.

Allyson, in particular, listened to him without comment, her chin held high, her eyes shining with tears. Henry and Lillian watched her, as if to see how she'd react to what they'd done, what they'd seen. And she didn't react well. She tried to, Kara thought, but she didn't. Allyson Lourdes Stockwell had the look of a gaunt, terrified woman who wanted to run and hide.

When Sam finished and no one said anything, his dark eyes settled for a moment on Kara, then shifted to her traumatized godchildren. His face was expressionless. "I'll leave you all to get your heads around what I just told you. I'll be down at the pool if you have any questions."

Henry and Lillian slid off their chairs and ran after him, each on one side of him, taking his hand.

"Honestly," Hatch hissed in disgust when they were out of earshot, "I don't know how this all got so out of control. It's ridiculous. I never realized what vivid imaginations those two have."

"I didn't realize you and Mike had argued," Allyson said quietly, her eyes cool.

Hatch snorted. "We always argued. My visit is long on the record with the police. His security guards saw me come and go. There was no way I was going to hide it, even if I'd wanted to. I was undoubtedly the last one to see him alive, and we had a whale of an argument." He shook his head and added sourly, "It never occurred to me to inform Henry and Lillian. It was nothing. I left assuming it'd blow over like all our other arguments and we'd be toasting each other's brilliance that evening."

Kara's position at the round table gave her a clear view of the pool. Sam stayed close to Henry and Lillian as they wandered from chair to chair, aimless, and she felt a tug of emotion at how her godchildren had taken to Sam after what must have been a difficult scene in the tree house.

"What was the argument about?" Allyson asked.

Madeleine shifted in her chair. "It hardly matters now, does it?"

Hatch waved a hand. "I don't even remember—well, I do, but it seems so pointless now. Policy nonsense. We were yelling and beating our chests, and it was all over nothing."

Allyson, clearly exhausted, didn't push for specifics, and Kara saw the strain of the past days in her friend's face, the way she twisted her hands together and pushed at a ring. "Why did you go behind my back to hire Walter?"

"That's a loaded question, Allyson. I didn't think of it as going behind your back." Hatch looked uncomfortable, but didn't back away from her question. "First the bonfire, then Big Mike drowning—I suppose I was spooked. Mother mentioned she was worried about the children, having them in Texas with no protection now that you were governor—"

"Don't put Wally off on me," Madeleine said sharply. "Hiring him was your decision not mine."

Kara had noted that Sam hadn't mentioned the kids had seen the black sedan in front of her house. If it *was* Wally Harrison in Austin that night, she thought, it meant he'd either followed them to her house or guessed they would come there. Either way, why hadn't he said anything? Or had he?

Allyson squeezed her eyes shut, grimacing in pain, but when she opened them again she seemed more composed, even managed a small smile. "At least Henry and Lillian's behavior makes sense, given their point of view. Now that I know what's going on, I can deal with them.''

"Wally was just supposed to check on them from time to time," Hatch said, "not prowl around and scare the hell out of them. Allyson, if I'd had any idea—"

"What's done is done, Hatch," Allyson said.

Sam sat on a lounge chair at the shallow end of the pool. Kara watched Henry and Lillian splash water at each other, then at Sam. He must have threatened to come after them, because they scampered out of his reach, laughing. Kara could hear their squeals.

"Of course," Hatch said, "I didn't know about this tree house of theirs and this whole fantasy they spun around what they saw—not to mention what they *think* they saw."

Madeleine shook her head, looking every minute of her eighty years. "Charlie Jericho stopped by this morning, early, and told me about the tree house. This was before we heard Henry and Lillian had run off again. I assured him it couldn't possibly be their tree house." She sighed, settling back against her chair. "Charlie told me he liked the idea of my grandchildren building a tree house on the sly, just not on his property, because he didn't trust us if anyone got hurt. He implied we—*I*—was lawsuit happy, when I've never filed a lawsuit in my life. He thinks Pete fell on his way up to dismantle it."

"How's Pete doing?" Kara asked, noticing a tremble in Allyson's hands, slight enough no one else probably saw it.

"He was released from the hospital this morning,"

Madeleine said. "Apparently he's cranky and complaining about the herbal teas Bea's making him drink. I think she's picking things out of her garden for them." She smiled faintly, some color coming back into her pale cheeks. "Charlie says Bea's hoping to corner Pete now that he's laid up and talk to him about getting goats. Of all things. I'm sure she's just teasing."

Allyson got to her feet and said abruptly, "No more bodyguards. Wally Harrison proves my point that Henry and Lillian just need to live their lives as normally as possible. If there's a specific threat—" She broke off, raking one hand through her hair as she looked down toward the pool. "I'm sure the missing binoculars and the rustling in the woods have an innocent explanation."

"Allyson," Hatch said, "the investigators—"

"Henry and Lillian will stay with me at the barn tonight." She turned to Kara, smiling graciously, distantly. "You and Sam have been wonderful. I can't thank you enough."

The governor of Connecticut walked off the stone patio, two state troopers falling in behind her as she headed toward the barn, without even a sideways glance at her children.

But Kara knew why. She recognized how Allyson held the back of her head with one hand, how, in a faltering gait, she picked up speed, almost running. She'd completely lost it—she was crying, and she didn't want anyone to see.

Down at the pool, Sam scooped up Lillian in one arm, Henry in the other, and gave them the heave-ho into the shallow end. They went under, all skinny arms and legs, and popped back up, shouting and laughing, splashing him mercilessly now that he'd dunked them.

"My husband used to throw Lawrence in the pool like that," Madeleine said quietly, getting unsteadily to her feet. "He'd run out, wanting more. *Do it again, Dad,* he'd say. Dear Lord, but I shouldn't have had to outlive both a husband and a son." She smiled, unabashed by her tears, and gave Kara a quick, startling hug. "Thank you for looking after my grandchildren. Allyson will come around. She can't possibly blame you for being there, having them put their trust in you."

Hatch got up, his chair screeching on the stone, and went inside without a word.

Madeleine glanced after him. "He thinks he loves you, but he doesn't. Not really. He doesn't know who he is. How can he know who he loves? Don't feel sorry for him. You're convenient, Kara. He picked you because he knows he can't have you." But before Kara could get her bearings enough to respond, the older woman smiled. "Why don't you go to your Texas Ranger?"

She headed inside, calling to Billie about finalizing plans for her cocktail party. Kara was alone on the patio. She walked toward the pool, Sam wet now from the knees down, water droplets sparkling on his dark hair. He was breathing hard from tossing the kids. She grinned at him. "Want me to throw you in there with them?"

His eyes sparked. "That could be fun."

But she looked out toward the barn, Allyson still rushing toward it with the troopers on her heels. ''I think we're free to go back home.''

''Not a chance.'' None of the merriment he'd had with Henry and Lillian was evident in his expression now. ''Your friend the governor's hanging by her fingernails. I'm staying until I know these kids are safe.''

''Sam—''

He tilted his head back slightly, staring down at her, his eyes slits. ''Do you want to go back to Texas?''

''It doesn't matter what I want. Allyson's got the damn National Guard at her disposal—''

''Ask her about Pete Jericho.''

Kara nodded, remembering the tremble she'd seen in her friend's hand at the mention of his name. ''It's on my list.''

Lillian got out of the pool behind Sam, her wet clothes clinging to her and dripping onto the deck as she carried a plastic beach bucket of water with both hands. Henry pressed one finger to his lips, begging Kara not to tattle as he fell in beside his sister. She knew Sam could see their shadows, or just sense them trying to sneak up on him, but he let them dump the bucket of water over him, catching him from the waist down because they were too short to get him any higher up.

He feigned surprise and roared after them, and it was into the pool again with both Lillian Stockwell and her brother.

* * *

Henry and Lillian took a long afternoon nap in hammocks in the shade by the barn, under the watchful eye of Sam Temple and Kara Galway, who sat in the grass with tall glasses of iced tea and wondered, no doubt, why Allyson didn't come out. She stayed inside, pacing, writing and rewriting her letter of resignation in her head.

She couldn't go on, not with her children in this shape, not without Pete—why had she ever let Big Mike talk her into running for lieutenant governor?

Because you wanted it. Because you thought you could make a difference.

She lay on the couch in the barn, tall windows looking out on the fields and wildflowers and hazy summer sky, but she was looking, instead, at her favorite picture of Lawrence on the piano. She'd taken it at Stonebrook Cottage, and he'd been smiling at her, thinking, as she was, that they had all the time in the world. But the cancer was in him even then, not yet discovered. Now he'd been gone for ten years, frozen in time, and Allyson knew she'd catch up with him one day, overtake him in age. She was thirty-seven now, already a governor. She tried to project herself ten, twenty, thirty years into the future and found she couldn't.

And Henry and Lillian…Lawrence would have been so proud of them for building a tree house, charging through the woods to save Big Mike.

Kara was probably on her way to the barn now. She'd promised to help make up the beds for the kids. A pretense. It was still early, and she'd obviously needed some reason to get Allyson alone.

Twice during the afternoon Allyson had gotten all the way to the door to bring in the state troopers and tell them about her anonymous calls. But what could they do? Her caller had access to her. Even with round-the-clock security, how could anyone protect her and her children from someone they knew and trusted?

She needed to lure the bastard out into the open. Somehow. If only she could think. But there'd been no call since yesterday when she was walking back with Sam Temple, and she wondered if she even dared hope there wouldn't be another.

If so, she might never know who it was. Maybe he'd bide his time, wait for a better opportunity to try again. The uncertainty and fear could go on indefinitely, leaving her to suspect everyone, trust no one.

Would her resignation end the problem?

Only, she thought, if that was what the caller wanted from her. And even then. Would that just be the beginning?

No. She needed to figure out who was doing this to her and stop him, or her. Them. Whoever it was.

Her cell phone rang, and Allyson pounced on it almost with relief. "Yes?"

"Eager to talk tonight, aren't you?"

The voice was well disguised, weird-sounding, almost disembodied, neither male nor female. She had no idea who it was, recognized nothing about the syntax, the tone. She sat up, clenching her hand to keep from dropping the phone.

"We've played this game long enough," Allyson said. "Tell me what you want. Money? My resignation? What is it? You can't be doing this just for your entertainment.'' She suddenly felt steadier than she had in days. ''I don't care if you tell the world about Pete and me. Go ahead.''

''It's not going to be that easy, Governor. You know that. People're going to think you killed Mike Parisi. And don't be stupid, okay? No matter what you do, I can get to you.'' There was a short laugh, almost a grunt. ''I can get to your children.''

Allyson staggered to her feet. ''Don't even think you can get near my children. Do you hear me? I swear to you—''

''Pete Jericho had himself a hell of a day yesterday, didn't he?''

She couldn't breathe, but refused to let her panic show. *I can get to your children.* ''Did you push him?''

''I'll call you in the morning, Governor. You're a little feisty tonight.''

''Wait—''

But the call was finished, the connection ended.

She sank back onto the couch, aching suddenly to see Pete, confide in him all her troubles. He'd give her his solid, commonsense opinion and stand by whatever decision she made. He wouldn't let her second-guess herself. How could she have let this situation escalate? She'd thought her actions made sense, were reasonable and responsible—and now here she was, terrified that, if she made the wrong move, Henry and Lillian would suffer for it. She was paralyzed.

The trooper, a woman, let Kara in, then retreated

without comment. Kara crossed the wooden floor and smiled. "I'm here for the great bed-making adventure."

"Oh, bullshit, Kara, you're here to grill me." Allyson laughed to take the sting out of her words, forced herself to push back her fears, compartmentalize them. She had until morning to figure out what to do, but she knew she couldn't go on alone. She had to trust someone, sometime. *I can get to your children.* "Come on, let's go up and do our mom work. Do you think any of the guy governors make beds?"

"I don't know if they'd do it for an eleven- and twelve-year-old. They're old enough to make their own beds—"

Allyson laughed. "You are *such* a hard-ass."

They took the spiral stairs up to the loft, where two twin beds shared a narrow space beneath slanted wooden ceilings. Even now, ten years later, Allyson felt how terribly Lawrence had been cheated, never knowing his children—he never saw them fall asleep up here with their stuffed animals, never heard them having pillow fights and yelling over the railing for their mother to come up quick, one of them was sick.

One reason she hadn't acknowledged her relationship with Pete, she knew, and kept him secret even from Henry and Lillian, was that she didn't want to give up that loss, that ache she had for what her husband had been to her and all he'd missed. Keeping it meant he stayed close to her, and perhaps to the children who could hardly even remember him. Didn't she owe him that much?

"Allyson, I wanted to talk to you alone." Kara sat

on the edge of one of the beds. "I'm almost positive Henry and Lillian know about you and Pete. Or at least they've guessed. I know it's none of my business, and I'd never intrude under normal circumstances—"

"Hell. They know? *You* know?" Allyson pressed her back against a chest of drawers, facing her friend. "Sam?"

Kara nodded. "*Suspect* is probably a better word. It's not as if the kids have been spying on you—"

"God, I hope not," Allyson said wryly, but couldn't sustain even that small amount of humor. "I'm surprised this doesn't fall under your attorney-client privilege." But her bitterness was short-lived, too, and she added quickly, "I'm sorry. That was uncalled for. I'm so grateful for all you've done, and I know it hasn't been easy."

"My first impulse was to tell you everything."

"It's okay. Kara—my God, I don't know if I can stand one more thing. Give me a category 5 hurricane blowing up the coast—I'd be a damn good governor then. Just nothing more involving my children."

But Kara seemed unperturbed, her ability to stay self-contained one of the qualities Allyson most admired about her. Kara had always had a knack for grasping a hundred different strategies at once, seeing all their ramifications and contradictions even as she insisted on plodding through them, airing each one out, until she settled on the best. Allyson had never had that kind of keen, creative mind. She wasn't a particularly good strategist, or even a good listener. She was drawn to public service for what she could do, but even so, she wasn't much of a politician. Kara, she thought, would be an awful one, and she smiled at the thought, feeling some of her irritability ease.

She got sheets and two flannel blankets from one of the chest of drawers. "Pete and I are doomed—I guess we knew that from the start."

"Are you kidding? Pete doesn't know now. He's an optimist."

"An incurable romantic is more like it. Knowing and accepting are two different things. He knows the score, but he doesn't want to accept it." Allyson turned, setting the stack of linens on the mattress next to Kara. "He still thinks we're going to get married and have a couple of babies."

"Why not? You're just thirty-seven. Of course, after this week with those two rascals you already have—"

Allyson groaned, her love for her children suddenly overwhelming her. "Oh, Kara, what were they *thinking?*"

"They weren't thinking. They're in middle school. They have no brains." She grinned, irreverent. "Even if they are Stockwells."

Allyson dropped down beside her friend, as if they were back in law school with nothing more pressing on their minds than how they'd do in moot court. "Pete has been incredibly patient. If he decided to go public with our relationship, there's nothing I could do—but he won't. I was about to tell the story to the whole world, come what may." She didn't mention how Mike had forced her hand, the anonymous calls. "Then all this mess started. It's different now that

I'm governor…I don't know, a man with a criminal record…"

"As criminal records go, Allyson, Pete's isn't much, and he hasn't had any scrapes with the law since then. It was a while ago. He was young. People will take that into account."

She leaned back against her outstretched elbows. "We're so different…"

"Then you want to break it off with him?"

"No!" Allyson was surprised at her response, the depth of her passion. "I love him, but being governor—Lawrence Stockwell's widow…" She sighed. "It's not just a question of what I want. I have responsibilities."

"What about Pete? What's your responsibility to him?"

"He deserves the kind of life he wants." She sat up straight and stared down at her hands, remembering how he'd taken her up here and sat her right in this spot, where she was sitting with Kara, and asked her much the same questions. What did she want for herself? What did she want for him? He thought it was all so simple. "He loves it out here, Kara. He doesn't want to expand his horizons—he thinks that's idiotic and patronizing, that it presumes his life here is limited somehow. I don't know, it might have worked if I'd stayed lieutenant governor."

Kara frowned at her. "You're confusing the hell out of me, Allyson. First you say you knew all along it couldn't work—now you're saying it could have. So are you giving him up or what?"

Allyson smiled. "Cut-to-the-chase Kara."

"If you love each other, the rest will sort itself out."

"You're one to talk," Allyson said gently. "Every time someone falls for you, you run."

She managed an irreverent smile. "Well, geez, when it's Hatch—"

Allyson grabbed a pillow and smacked it into her friend's shoulder. "You're *awful*. Hatch is a great guy—"

"He's been a pain in the ass from the get-go with this business with Henry and Lillian. I don't know why I haven't strangled him. Then I wouldn't have had to listen to him today."

"He's tense," Allyson said inadequately. "Although I have to admit, if I had a choice between going to bed with Hatch Corrigan and that Texas Ranger of yours—"

Kara gave a mock shudder. "I've *never* been tempted to go to bed with Hatch, and he just likes to pretend he's been tempted with me. Makes his life easier. Nothing quite like unrequited love to take you off the hook."

"Never mind Hatch—am I to take it you *have* been tempted to go to bed with the Ranger?" Allyson paused, studying Kara's expression, then laughed at her friend's obvious discomfort. "Ah, I can see I'm way behind. You've already been to bed with our Ranger Temple."

"Allyson...I thought I was the one who was supposed to do the grilling."

"I love this. I'm the repressed New Englander, but who's sitting here *squirming* with awkwardness?"

She got to her feet and moved to the other bed with a stack of sheets, shaking the fitted bottom sheet out over the mattress. "Big Mike knew there was someone in Texas for you. I know he had a special place in his heart for you, Kara, but he never wanted anything for you but your happiness."

Kara's dark eyes filled with tears. She nodded.

"And your Ranger. He was good with the kids today."

"He's also a damn fine law enforcement officer, and his instincts tell him—"

"I know what they tell him."

Allyson felt her cheerful mood dissipate. She focused on smoothing out the sheet, tucking in the ends, welcoming the normalcy of the chore. She imagined for a moment she had nothing more at stake tonight than putting her children into a clean, freshly made bed. And what, she thought, could be more important?

Keeping them safe, she thought.

"My instincts tell me the same thing." Allyson spoke quietly, continuing with her bed-making. "That Henry and Lillian didn't hear a deer that day. That they aren't safe. But it's okay for right now—we'll have state troopers here tonight. We'll be fine."

Kara shook her head, staring at her friend in a mixture of shock and despair. "Allyson, what's going on? How did you become this passive? You didn't get to be a governor by acting this way. You're one of the strongest women I know."

"You have no idea what it's been like," Allyson said simply.

"Then tell me. Talk to me—talk to *someone*. I know what you're like, Allyson, and this isn't it, no matter what you're not telling. The public might not see it yet, but they will—and Big Mike would be disappointed as all get out in you." Kara was on her feet, snapping open a sheet, not letting Allyson off the hook, glaring at her, demanding answers. "Damn it, I can see now why Henry and Lillian have gone to such lengths to keep me from telling you what's going on. They knew it wouldn't make any difference."

But Allyson couldn't take it, not tonight. "Go to hell, Kara."

She didn't back down. "They love you, and they're worried about you. They see *everything*, Allyson. If you know something is wrong, if you even suspect—"

"I don't." She grabbed the top sheet and stopped herself just short of balling it up and either stuffing it down Kara's throat or falling into it in a useless heap.

I'll call you in the morning, Governor.

She wasn't taking any chances. She'd wait for that call. Then she'd decide what to do. That was the best way she knew to protect her children. She didn't care what it cost her.

"I don't know anything."

Twenty

〜◦⑤◦◦⑤◦〜

Sam's pants had pretty much dried by the time Kara was finally ready to head back to the cottage. It was late afternoon, the heat and humidity getting to everyone but him. Compared to August on the Mexican border, this little Connecticut heat wave failed to impress him. Billie Corrigan had assured him it would blow out this evening. Thunderstorms, she said, were on their way, along with a Canadian cold front.

Henry and Lillian weren't too enthusiastic about spending the night with their mother, but Kara promised them she'd be back first thing in the morning. Sam didn't blame them—Kara's friend or not, their mother the governor was in trouble.

Wally Harrison had slunk out earlier, his ass fired. Sam approved. Not that Hatch Corrigan gave a damn. He and his mother and sister had argued cocktail parties and luminaria out at the pool, then Madeleine abruptly excused herself and slid behind the wheel of a huge, fifteen-year-old Mercedes. She drove herself down the road to visit Pete Jericho, taking him asters she'd picked herself. "I'm not as awful as people think I am," she'd told Sam.

Billie had overheard and laughed. "Yes, she is, but nobody cares. Just don't tell her that."

When Madeleine Stockwell returned from the Jerichos a little while later, she was beside herself. "I thought Charlie wasn't serious, but Bea Jericho *is* getting goats! She told me so herself. What on earth does she want with goats? They'll get out of their pens and come up here and eat my roses."

She was still fuming when Kara emerged from the barn and headed back through the woods with Sam. He told her about the goats, and she laughed, some of the worry going out of her face. "Madeleine wouldn't know what to do with herself if the Jerichos weren't annoying her. They've been more of a constant in her life than any of her husbands."

"Is that part of the reason Allyson is keeping her relationship with Pete under wraps?"

Kara shrugged. "I wish I could tell you. She wouldn't talk to me."

"Tough, isn't it, when you know someone's holding back on you?"

"I had no choice. Henry and Lillian boxed me in—"

"Maybe Allyson has no choice, either."

But Kara didn't like that, and she pushed on through the wildflowers and tall grass, oblivious, he thought, to the heat. A good sign. She was more Texan now than northerner. Then he wondered why he cared, or noticed—his life had been a hell of a lot simpler when Kara Galway was practicing law in Connecticut.

She spun around in a shady spot just into the woods and waited for him. "I can't believe Allyson would dump Pete because it's too complicated to be in love with him. That just doesn't make sense to me."

"It's hard when a love seems forbidden somehow."

Kara gave him a sharp look, as if he'd said something disturbing or profound, or maybe both. Sam ignored it and started along the lane through the woods, his pants legs stiff and smelling of pool water. He'd have gone back to the cottage for a clean pair, but the kids were not to be trusted—they'd have seen an opportunity for more mischief upon his return.

"The kids are better off for getting that story off their chests," he said, glancing at Kara as she came up beside him, matching his pace. "You did right by them. Don't let anyone tell you otherwise."

"No, I was just lucky. Sam, if it *was* Wally in Austin, why didn't he tell anyone? Why didn't he knock on my door and ask me if the kids were there? He was supposed to be keeping an eye on them. What if he followed them from the ranch? Why didn't he stop them from running away in the first place?"

"Good questions."

"You've thought of them, too? I should have called you when Henry and Lillian said they saw him. Well, not *him*. They didn't know who it was, a man in a black sedan, the same guy who slunk around the ranch. I didn't know what to believe."

"Still should have called me."

She made a face. "I just said that."

"Henry and Lillian were scared?"

"Terrified. You know, Wally must have been discreet with everyone while he was in Texas *except* them."

"Makes you wonder, doesn't it?"

Sam thought of the kids konked out in their hammocks, their bony legs hanging over the sides, and he remembered his own mother trying to keep him safe in a rough neighborhood, fashion a life of her own through her work as an art teacher, even as she had to be everything to the son she was raising without a father. He didn't want to be too hard on Allyson Lourdes Stockwell.

The heat and humidity brought out the damp, earthy smells of the woods, as well as more mosquitoes. He started down a long, easy grade, aware of Kara still pondering what he'd said as she walked alongside him. Finally, she took a breath. "Are you thinking Wally deliberately let Henry and Lillian see him? He *wanted* them scared out of their minds?" She shook her head, obviously not able to accept it even as a hypothesis. "That's cruel. There's no good reason for it. You didn't say anything to Hatch, did you? He's furious with Wally as it is—"

"Don't get carried away. It was just a thought."

She scoffed. "You don't just have thoughts, Sergeant Temple. Regular people have thoughts. You think in terms of criminal conspiracies." She frowned up at him. "And your pants are about as stiff as stovepipes. How can you walk?"

He noticed her legs and hips as she crossed the

muddy stream, their footprints still visible from their earlier jaunt through the woods. Nothing stiff about her. He winked. "I can't wait to get out of them."

Her brother picked that moment to call on Sam's cell phone.

"Walter Harrison was on a flight that left Austin the same morning my damn sister was stealing my gun and plane in San Antonio," Jack reported. "He dropped off a car rental at the airport."

"Black sedan?"

"Four-door Ford Taurus. He had it for a week. You want to tell me what the hell this is about?"

"At best this guy's a moron," Sam said. "At worst—I don't know."

"Sam?"

He could hear Jack's concern, laced with just enough irritation to remind Sam who was the lieutenant and who was the sergeant. "It's not a good situation up here."

"Get Kara out of there."

"Easier said than done."

"No, it isn't. Knock her on the head and tie her up."

Sam glanced at her and deliberately didn't picture tying her up in case her big brother could read his thoughts.

"Give me the phone." Kara snatched it out of Sam's hand and put it to her ear. "Jack? Everything's under control. Sergeant Temple here is just in full paranoid, suspicious Texas Ranger mode. I'm being the cool, sensible lawyer who sees all sides." She listened a moment, then scowled. "Who put you in charge? Forget it. You're not *my* boss.'' She tossed the phone back to Sam. ''What was I thinking? Your turn.''

Jack wasn't finished with Sam, either. ''You wouldn't be taking advantage of my sister while she's half out of her head over those kids, would you?''

Sam didn't hesitate. ''No, sir.''

''I left you wiggle room in that question, didn't I? Sam—Kara is one of the smartest people I know and as cool and professional in a courtroom as you'd ever want to see. You have to have your act together when she's the defending counsel. But when it comes to men…''

Susanna came onto the line. ''Jack's done, Sam. I'm going to remind him before we fly up there tomorrow that his sister isn't nine anymore. Who knows, a fling with a Texas Ranger might do Kara good.'' Jack roared in the background, and Susanna laughed, then told Sam to take care, a note of worry in her voice as she disconnected.

''How long before he shows up?'' Kara asked.

''Midafternoon tomorrow, the latest. Susanna's coming with him. Kara, it was Harrison in Austin.''

''It was? It just doesn't make sense. Why did he drive off like that? Why didn't he call Hatch?''

''Maybe he did call.''

''My head's spinning. We need to tell Zoe West, don't we? She can let the state guys in on our pal Wally. They can talk to him.''

Sam nodded. ''I'll call her after we get back.''

Kara stopped and gazed up at the sky, low gray clouds moving in from the west, then smiled suddenly and cut her eyes around at Sam. "If my brother and his dear and lovely wife aren't showing up until tomorrow, that at least gives us tonight."

"I think that counted as a date," Kara said later, after they'd finished dinner and had the dishes cleaned up and were sitting in the cottage living room, the curtains billowing in a warm breeze that brought with it clouds and the smell of rain. She could almost taste it.

Sam was in a wooden rocker across from her. He'd left a message for Zoe West, asking her to call him on his cell phone, and Kara could tell he wanted to get that conversation over with. She sat on the love seat and picked through one of the boxes Billie Corrigan had left, enjoying the baubles and paints and fun things.

"What?" he said. "Tuna sandwiches for dinner?"

"Sure, and the walk. That's two dates. Chasing after Henry and Lillian this morning doesn't count, and neither does gathering around the patio to hear you tell their story. That was very well done, by the way. You must make a good witness."

"Unflappable," he said.

"Watching you at the pool with the kids almost counts, because I enjoyed it so much, but I think I'd have had to get wet if it was going to count as a date." She felt heat rise to her face. "I mean…"

He smiled. "Kara, where is this leading?"

"To bed, I hope." But the humor went out of her, and she swallowed, feeling a little light-headed. "Allyson says I run from men, and I think she might be right—Sam, I don't want to run from you.''

"You can't. I'm a damn good Texas Ranger.''

"I lost my mother, Allyson lost her husband—I wonder if it's easier for us just not to put it all on the line, not to risk that kind of loss again. So I run, and she hides…'' She looked up, realizing Sam was on his feet, walking toward her. "What are you doing?''

"Well, Miss Kara, I believe I am going to sweep you into my arms and carry you to the bedroom and make mad, passionate love to you all through the night.'' His eyes flashed with a deep, dangerous desire, and he stood tall in front of her and smiled "How would that be?''

"That would be fine,'' she said, and threw back her head, letting him scoop her up and carry her Rhett Butler style down the hall.

She was reminded of old romantic movies, but the urgency and intensity in him soon eradicated all thought of that. He laid her on the bed and began to undress her slowly, unbuttoning her shirt, smoothing it off her shoulders, saying nothing as he paused to gaze at her breasts before unclasping her bra. She couldn't speak, and he eased the straps over her shoulders the way he had her shirt, then skimmed his palms over her nipples. Sensations poured through her, the breeze cool on her hot, bare skin.

"You've done enough talking and thinking for one day,'' he whispered. "So have I.'' And when she raised her hands to work on the buttons on his shirt, he smiled. "Not yet.''

She stopped, and he moved his palms downward

over her stomach, unfastening the button on her shorts, sliding down the zipper. The anticipation shortened her breath, but she could see him pretending not to notice as he drew her shorts down over her hips, leaving her underpants.

"Sam..." She licked her lips and managed to say his name again, before he had her shorts at her ankles and finally cast them off. She lay before him in just her scrap of underpants, sexy little things she'd picked up on a lunch-hour lark, never imagining this moment...or maybe she had.

But he left them, coming to her, whispering her name as he lowered his mouth to hers and kissed her slowly, deeply, his tongue mingling with hers, probing, and just when she thought she'd melt, he kissed her throat, skimming his mouth down to her breasts.

He took one nipple between his lips, licking, teasing, then the other, until she threw her arms over her head and moaned softly, and outside the rain came. She smelled its cool wetness as his mouth drifted lower, and he raised up suddenly, casting off his clothes—and it was as if she'd never seen him naked before, his body dark and hard in the glowing light, his erection thrusting, wanting.

She paid attention to every nuance of him, what she was experiencing, feeling, at this moment, refusing to avert her eyes or her mind from any of it. She wouldn't run, not any part of her.

"Kara...I don't want to hurt you..."

"You won't," she said. "You didn't before."

He came back to her, easing his body between her legs, helping them to open to him, to relax at the feel

of him there. He caught her panties with his thumbs
and pulled them slowly down over her thighs, and
when she was fully exposed, he stopped, touching her
with his fingertips. She jumped with a mix of pleasure
and surprise—and the newness of it, a man seeing
her, touching her most intimate places. He explored
her, slipping into her crevices, her slickness, until she
was panting, tearing at her underpants. But he pushed
her hands away and finished the job himself, and if
he wanted her to touch him in the way he had her,
he wasn't waiting.

Once her legs were free, he drove into her, knowing
she was ready, wanting him. She pulled him deeper
into her, no tentativeness this time, no pain, just searing need—she felt the climax upon her, couldn't slow
it or control it. He did nothing to help her, thrusting
fast and deep as she dug her fingers into his arms,
quaking, crying out. His eyes locked with hers as if
he knew this would happen, planned it, and he didn't
let up, his own climax coming now, mixing with hers,
endless.

She threw her hands above her head, and he held
them, raising up off her, but still inside her, still moving, as the rain beat against the window and filled the
room with dark, unsettled shadows.

Twenty-One

Charlie Jericho sat at the cluttered kitchen table with a fresh mug of coffee and shook his head. "You and Allyson Stockwell. Christ, Pete. She's the goddamn governor."

Pete got to his feet to look for his truck keys in the black hole that was his mother's kitchen. "That doesn't faze me."

"It fazes everyone else."

Pete couldn't see straight. He lifted a stained, ragged flour towel on the counter and found his keys. A cold front had moved through overnight, leaving the morning bright and cool, the air drier. He hoped it'd clear his head.

"You don't want a relationship you have to keep secret," his father said. "Nothing good can come of that."

"You're right about that. Wish I'd seen it sooner." He stuffed his keys in his pants pocket. The damn cast on his wrist was a nuisance. His mother had offered to help him get dressed, but Pete had refused. She was out in the yard measuring for her goat pen.

"I'm thirty-four years old, Pop. Time I moved out of the house."

"Where you moving to, the governor's mansion? Maybe Stockwell Farm?" Charlie crushed a half-smoked cigarette in an ashtray. "You can pour Madeleine tea while you wait for an audience with the governor."

Pete pulled out a chair and sat across from his father, pushed aside a stack of magazines. "You need to quit smoking. You've got a bad cough. You're going to kill yourself one day."

He shrugged. "We all have to die of something."

"Pop…" Pete sighed, wondering how he could explain himself to this crusty old man, why he even bothered. "I don't want to lose Allyson. I've loved her for as long as I can remember. It's not a schoolboy crush. I've had time to think since I took that fall—"

"You've been doped up."

"I need to do this."

Charlie took a sip of his coffee. "You look like a banged-up kid to me. What if someone pushed you into the gravel pit? What if someone doesn't want you carousing with the governor?"

"I don't remember what happened, how I fell. It won't change anything."

"Zoe West has been up there scouring around for clues. Nothing so far. But Pete—"

He got back to his feet. "I have to go. You going to wish me luck?"

"What kind of luck?" Charlie looked up from his coffee, his gray hair sticking out, his age and years of smoking showing in his eyes. "The luck that's good for you or the luck you think is good for you?"

Pete didn't answer, and when he went out to his truck, he could feel the pain in his broken ribs. If he didn't move the wrong way, the collarbone wasn't too bad. He wanted to get off pain medication as soon as he could. Maybe his father was right—maybe it was affecting his thinking. But it didn't matter, he knew what he had to do. He knew it before he fell.

He sat behind the wheel of his truck and realized he couldn't drive standard one-armed. Hell. He'd have to borrow his mother's car. She'd plastered it with goat and herb bumper stickers.

Sam would have liked to lock the doors to Stonebrook Cottage and make love to Kara all day, but her brother was on his way north and she wanted to go back out to the gravel pit. "I'm not taking that as a compliment," he told her over coffee. "Choosing a pile of dirt over me."

She smiled, a hint of the intimacy they'd shared last night in her dark eyes. "I'm thinking of all the rock out there. Then it's not such a big difference." She took her coffee to the sink and stared out at the cool, bright air. He could feel her seriousness, the weight of what the people up here were into affecting her. "Zoe West hasn't found evidence that someone pushed Pete?"

"Not yet." The detective had returned Sam's call a little while ago. "She says everyone in Bluefield knows about the tree house now. Charlie Jericho's not keeping it a secret. Allyson's talking with a state detective this morning.''

"Then they're on the case. That's good.'' Kara continued to stare out the window, the morning air refreshing after yesterday's humidity. ''You told Zoe about Wally Harrison turning up at my place?''

"Yes.''

"I still want to go out to the gravel pit.''

Sam drank some of his coffee. It was hot, strong, but it didn't cut his mood, his certainty that this woman had penetrated all his defenses. He'd watched her sleep in the midst of the thunder and lightning, her dark lashes against her creamy skin, a strand of hair on her cheek. Soul mates. In the light of morning, in a rich woman's cottage kitchen, he knew it was crazy and there was no such thing.

"You want to look for Lillian's binoculars,'' he said.

Kara nodded, her back still to him. ''Maybe she dropped them farther down the hill than she remembers. Sam—'' She swung around, arms folded tightly on her chest. She was in khakis and a little blue V-neck top that outlined her breasts, reminded Sam of making love to her. But her mind was a million miles away from their night together. ''Something's not right with Allyson. *Really* not right. I think she wanted to tell me yesterday at the barn, but she just couldn't.''

"Do you think it involves the kids?''

"It must.''

"Zoe West is talking to Harrison this morning.

Maybe his story will unravel and we'll get to the bottom of this thing.''

"I hope so." Kara dropped her arms to her sides. "I can run out to the gravel pit and then meet you back here, or at the Stockwells' if you want to go on and see the kids." She smiled suddenly. "Don't worry, I'll be careful."

Sam slid to his feet. "You won't just be careful—you'll have me with you."

She nodded absently, as if she'd expected his response. "Well, you won't want to trip out there." She dumped her coffee in the sink and headed out back, adding as the screen door shut behind her, "Your gun might go off and you'll end up shooting yourself in the ass."

"Not my gun." He followed her outside, down the steps, still wet from last night's rain. "Jack's gun. Don't think he's forgotten."

"Jack never forgets anything. None of you Texas Rangers do." Her irreverent mood, he knew, was a cover for her darker thoughts. She ran a foot over the top of the grass. "It's soaking wet out here. We should drive. We can take your car. That way, if we wreck the suspension bouncing over rocks and ruts, it'll be on your tab."

"No, ma'am. Yours. You're paying my expenses for coming up here after you, remember?"

"I said that?" She smiled, walking past him and back up the steps. "Good thing I'm a well-paid criminal defense attorney." She emphasized criminal, as if there wasn't much difference between him and her clients.

Sam followed her into the kitchen, got his keys and beat her into the driver's seat. "I think maybe you didn't get enough sleep last night."

She slid into the seat next to him, cut a glance over at him, a wicked gleam in her eyes. "Maybe I got too much."

He grinned. "Be careful what you wish for, Miss Kara."

He'd sensed no hesitancy in her last night. There was no question of her inexperience, but also none of her passion and openness—and that had rocked him to his core. It made him feel vulnerable, shaken, this need mixed with desire, this heart-stopping yearning not to possess or protect but to give himself entirely to her, empty himself into her and become one with her.

Scared the hell out of him.

When they reached the access road, he negotiated the pits and ruts as best he could and drove into the gravel pit itself, pulling in behind an idle dump trunk. A crew was working today, the sifting machine running loud.

Kara winced. "I wouldn't be surprised if Madeleine can hear that up at her place." She climbed out of the car and met Sam around front. "I suppose somebody could have tossed Lillian's binoculars into one of these piles of sand and rock. We'd never know it."

Sam looked at her. "What else is on your mind, Miss Kara?" he asked quietly.

"When you and Zoe West were talking this morning, it occurred to me that Wally Harrison could be playing both sides of this thing—looking out for the kids for Hatch and at the same time making sure they kept quiet for whoever killed Big Mike.'' She tilted her head back, squinting at Sam. ''But you've already thought of all this, haven't you?''

''Not as soon as I should have.''

Kara balled her hands into fists. ''I hate crooked cops—I don't care if they're ex-cops.''

The loud rattle of the machinery made conversation difficult. She started past the pile of tiny, polished, smooth pea stone, toward the spot where they'd found Pete Jericho. Sam watched his footing in the slick dirt, wet from the overnight rains. Huge puddles had formed in the various holes and ruts, rippling in a stiff, dry breeze. Kara sank almost to her shoelaces in the light-colored mud, but she pressed on at an angle toward the woods.

Sam glanced back at the work crew and pictured Henry and Lillian sitting up in their tree house, watching the big machinery in their private little world. He noticed that the pea stone looked as if it had shifted during the night, probably because of the rain. He went to turn back to Kara, but saw something and stopped, peered closer.

A foot, or just a cast-off work boot. He couldn't be certain. He took a couple of steps to his left, and he went very still inside, seeing an arm this time, sticking out of the stone.

''Sam?'' Kara slid beside him. ''What is it?'' But she followed his gaze, and he felt her stiffen, heard her gasp. ''Oh, no…Sam…''

He moved quickly now, Kara skidding next to him

in the mud, shouting and waving at the work crew. Sam stepped onto the pea stone, the arm at shoulder height, and he reached for it, felt for a pulse. No point. The arm was grayish in the bright sun, covered in wet dust from the stones, lifeless.

Kara got the crew's attention. They shut off their equipment, and three men leaped onto the dirt, running toward the pea stone. "Holy shit—we gotta dig him out. *Jesus!*"

A bearded kid jumped into a front-end loader, but an older man, probably the foreman, shook his head. "There's no way he's alive. You get on top of this stuff, it shifts and you start to sink. You can't get your footing, and pretty soon you're sucked down deep. It's worse in the smooth rock. The rough rock doesn't move around on you as much. Probably suffocated." The man's face reddened, his frustration and horror making him angry. "Goddamnit, what was he doing here? You know, we tell people it's not safe out here—you know who it is?"

"I have an idea," Sam said.

Kara was grim beside him, breathing hard. "We should call the police."

Sam took out his cell phone and dialed Zoe West directly. She answered on the fourth ring, silent as he relayed what had happened. "A body? As in a dead body? *Who?*"

"Walter Harrison if I'm right."

"Damn it. You're sure he's dead?"

"Yes."

She was fully alert. "What, it's just his arm and foot sticking out? All right, look—go ahead and let the work crew dig him out. You never know with suffocation. Maybe there's a chance he's still alive. I'll get an ambulance over there.'' She swore under her breath. "I'm on my way. Secure the damn scene, will you?''

Sam hoped he didn't need to remind West that he had no jurisdiction as a law enforcement officer anywhere in the state of Connecticut. He hung up and nodded at the foreman. "Detective West says to dig him out.''

They all moved out of the way of the front-end loader as it gingerly knocked the top off the pea-stone pile, exposing more of the body. It was Walter Harrison, and there was no doubt he was dead. The foreman passed out shovels from the back of his pickup, and Sam took one and helped dig at the small, smooth, shifting stone. There weren't enough shovels to go around, but Kara dug with her hands.

Harrison's body rolled toward them, and Sam and the foreman grabbed him and got him down on the wet ground. Kara, who must have seen countless crime scene photographs, breathed in shallow gulps, but the two younger men turned and vomited in a puddle. The foreman swore viciously and kicked some of the stones that had come loose from the pile.

Kara stood back, her face pale, her dark eyes hollow. "He didn't just crawl up there and accidentally suffocate to death. What was he doing here, anyway?'' she asked no one in particular.

Sam squatted next to the body. "I'd say, no, Mr. Harrison did not just accidentally suffocate to death.''

Blood had coagulated on his chest where, obviously, he'd been shot. Kara leaned over the body and touched Sam's shoulder, her fingers icelike. "Ah, hell, Sam."

He rose and asked everyone to sit tight until Zoe West arrived, and the men nodded without speaking, the foreman leaning against the bumper of his truck, scowling. The one who'd dug out Harrison climbed down from the front-end loader and grimaced. "Wally Harrison. That lying SOB finally got his own."

His boss told him not to speak ill of the dead, but it was apparent all of them knew Walter Harrison and none had anything good to say about him.

So, why, Sam thought, would Hatch hire such an unpopular character to watch after two children? He glanced back down at Harrison. From the looks of him, the cause of death likely would be suffocation, although the bullet might eventually have killed him. Sam pictured the scene out here last night, at dawn, before the storms. Wally Harrison up on the pea stone, maybe hoping for a clear view of whoever was after him, maybe in an attempt to find cover. Maybe just in a blind panic. He could have lost his footing on the stone after he'd already been shot, or in reaction to the bullet tearing into him. And once he started down into the pile, he couldn't get out.

If Kara drew any of these same conclusions, she said nothing, her mouth clamped tight as she turned away from the body.

Zoe West finally arrived in her bright yellow Volkswagen Beetle. She had on purple running shorts and sneakers and, as far as Sam could see, again carried no weapon. But this time, her cigarette was lit.

Twenty-Two

Allyson stormed into the barn, sick with fury, bristling with frustration and indignation. Madeleine had turned Pete away! Not the troopers—her damn mother-in-law! An hour ago! He'd dragged himself up here, injured and in pain, only to be sent home. "He can't work in that condition," Madeleine had said, unrepentant. "I did him a favor. He needs to get well."

Liar. She'd known he was there to see Allyson and decided to keep it from happening. She must have sensed that the attraction between him and her daughter-in-law had gotten out of hand. She'd long made her position known. Pete Jericho wasn't right for her son's widow. It was as if Allyson falling for Pete somehow diminished Lawrence.

She didn't have the guts to stand up to Madeleine, as if her approval was tantamount to having Lawrence's approval, neither of which Allyson needed. Lawrence was *dead*. He'd been a vital part of her life, she'd loved him, but he'd been gone for ten years. She was just twenty-seven when she lost him. Was she supposed to go on forever without love in her life?

She turned the water in the kitchen sink on full force and splashed her face. She couldn't find Hatch. He could talk to Madeleine, rein her in—Pete must have been mortified about being sent home like a naughty ten-year-old. But would Hatch approve of Pete? She thought of the argument he'd had with Mike, doubted it was over policy differences. Not here, not in the middle of the summer. Had they argued about Pete, Mike's ultimatum?

I can't think...I don't want to think...

Through the window above the sink, she saw Kara with one of the troopers and sighed, not really pleased to have her friend show up. Allyson turned off the water, dried her face. She was feeling too vulnerable and out of control—Kara would see it right away.

She'd hoped to have heard from her anonymous caller by now. Get that over with. Find out what he wanted, tell her security people.

She opened the back door and waved to the trooper that it was okay to send Kara over, and her friend came running. "Allyson, all hell's about to break loose. Sam just dropped me off—I can't find Hatch." She was pale, clearly upset. "We found Wally Harrison at the gravel pit. Allyson, he's dead. He was crushed under a pile of rock. He'd been shot."

"Shot? He's dead?"

"The police will want to talk to you. I didn't say anything to the troopers outside, but, Allyson—"

"You can't find Hatch?" She sank onto a chair at her round oak table, her gaze falling on the blown-glass vase of zinnias Madeleine had sent over. She could have had a normal life. Where had she gone wrong? "He must be here somewhere. He'd have told me if he was leaving."

"I didn't really look for him that hard. Where are Henry and Lillian?"

"Upstairs." Allyson couldn't seem to focus on her surroundings, wondered if she was disassociating, if she'd had one shock too many. How could Wally be dead? What did that mean? She added dully, "They wanted to sleep late."

Kara paced, a caged lion, and finally she swore and grabbed Allyson by the shoulders. "Allyson, for God's sake, snap out of it. *Tell* me what else is going on. This isn't like you. You're not one to sit here passively. People are getting *killed*. Mike's dead, Wally's dead—Pete was nearly killed. And you and the kids. What if that damn explosion on the Fourth wasn't an accident?"

"Go to hell, Kara."

"I'm not going anywhere. The police will be flooding in here any minute now, putting themselves on the line to protect you—"

"Stop it!" But Allyson groaned in self-disgust, collapsing back against her chair. "Oh, God, Kara. You're right, you're right. I've been such a self-absorbed *ass*. I thought I was doing the right thing— that I could control everything. Pete and me, how Henry and Lillian handled Mike's death, being governor, Hatch—these goddamn calls I've been getting." She blinked back tears, born more out of frus-

tration now than fear. Kara had cut through the fear. "I didn't want them to mean anything—"

"Allyson…" Kara pulled out a chair and sat on its edge. "Tell me about the calls."

"I'm supposed to get another one this morning with instructions—I thought they were political, and I know—" She broke off, thinking she'd cry, but she didn't. She was past crying. Sick of herself. She cleared her throat, and she quietly, succinctly told her friend about the calls.

Kara listened without interruption, but Allyson knew her lawyer mind would be spinning with all the possibilities and theories, no matter how outlandish. That was Kara, and if she had an opinion on Allyson's decision not to tell anyone about the calls, she kept it to herself.

"Could the calls be Wally's doing?" Kara asked. "He's had it in for Pete for years. He hated the plea bargain—he wanted Pete to get state prison for a year or two. Then Hatch goes and hires him to check on Henry and Lillian. What if Wally stumbled onto your affair with Pete and decided to freelance? Soften you up, threaten to get people thinking you'd killed Mike, then at the right moment make his demand. Knowing Wally, he'd want money."

"Hatch could have told him about Pete," Allyson said quietly. "He tends to think he has to protect me from myself. If he found out Wally was trying to blackmail me—" She shook her head. "No, Hatch wouldn't kill anyone. He just wouldn't."

Kara struggled to smile. "Sam would get on our case for speculating and getting ahead of the facts.

But you said it yourself—it's not a stranger making those calls. If you were supposed to get another one this morning and haven't, and Wally's dead—'' She didn't bother finishing her thought. "Allyson, you have to tell the police about the calls. You have no choice.''

"I don't, do I?" She smiled thinly. "Henry and Lillian are so much smarter than I am. They managed to manipulate you into attorney-client privilege." But she nodded, more to herself than Kara. "I'll tell the police everything as soon as they get here. Where's your Texas Ranger?"

"On his way to talk to Charlie and Bea, and Pete, about Wally. He dropped me off here—reluctantly, I might add.''

Allyson smiled. "I've got two state troopers up here, but he's not going to trust anyone else to protect you.''

"That's stifling and old-fashioned.''

"Ha. You love it." Allyson saw the gleam in her friend's eyes, the trust there for Sam Temple, even if she couldn't admit it. "And I have a feeling you can more than handle your Texan. Oh, Kara—'' She choked back sudden tears. "Where did I go wrong?''

"It doesn't matter. It's what you do now that counts." Kara was on her feet, and she touched Allyson's shoulder. "You'll be okay?''

She nodded, feeling some of her old determination well up in her. "It's time I got to the bottom of this mess.''

"I'll fetch the kids and take them back to the cottage or up to the house with Granny. You've got enough on your plate right now.'' She gave a reassuring smile. ''When you're finished with the police, Henry and Lillian will enjoy having their mom back.''

''I can resign—''

''For their sake? They don't want that. They just want *you.*''

Kara left it at that and headed up to the loft, and Allyson returned to the sink for a glass of water. She would handle this situation herself, directly, not through Hatch or any of her other advisers. She might not even bother with the state detectives—she might go straight to Zoe West, a skeptic from the start about the summer ''accidents'' in her town.

Suddenly Kara yelled from the loft, then pounded down the spiral stairs and charged into the kitchen, her face ashen. She held up a sheet of drawing paper. Allyson recognized Lillian's handwriting in a filmy purple gel ink.

''They've gone back to the cottage,'' Kara said. ''On their own. They say they don't want to be 'in the way.'''

''But they were just up there—I checked on them a little while ago.'' Allyson couldn't seem to think straight. ''Kara, they were fine. They never indicated they felt they were underfoot—my God, I don't want them out in the woods by themselves, with Wally—''

''I'll go find them. I'll tell them the score.''

Allyson nodded, unable to grasp what her children had been thinking, how terribly wrong they were about her. She suddenly grabbed Lillian's note, found a pen on the counter and jotted at the bottom, *You're never in my way. Listen to Kara and do as she asks. Love, Mom.*

She thrust the note at Kara. "I'll come when I can. If they just left, you might catch up with them in the woods."

Kara looked at the note and smiled. "You know, Lillian really did do a pretty good job of forging your handwriting."

Allyson almost laughed. *"Go."*

Kara gave her a quick hug and ran back through the living room and out the door, Allyson following to the big windows. She watched her friend climb over the stone wall and head across the field, moving fast, black-eyed Susans at her knees. Allyson sat at the piano a moment, touched Lawrence's face as he smiled at her.

Her cell phone rang, and she thought—my God, maybe Wally *wasn't* her anonymous caller. She grabbed it off the coffee table, sank back onto the piano stool as she answered. "Yes?"

But it was a different voice, unrecognizable but not as elaborately disguised. "Walter is dead. He was an idiot."

"Who is this?" A horrible thought struck her, and her heart seemed to stop. "Do you have my children?"

"Where are you, Governor?"

The venom on the other end shocked her, her elbows banging down on the piano keyboard.

"Ah, the living room. Perfect."

The connection went dead.

Allyson rose unsteadily, the silence enveloping her.

She walked to the tall windows and felt an over-whelming sense of impending doom. Something was wrong.

Ah, the living room. Perfect.

She ran toward the kitchen, yelling for her security guards. "Help me!"

She dived for the door, saw the troopers racing toward her, but she was suddenly in the air, blown off her feet, and she heard glass shattering…a thunderous explosion…felt the heat…her chest compressing. She couldn't breathe.

Thank God the kids aren't here.

The words didn't form, just a thought, a wish, as unconsciousness claimed her.

It was against Sam's better judgment to leave Kara at all. Henry and Lillian had it right when they ran off to their godmother and told her they all were in danger—it just took a while for everyone else to catch up with their instincts.

He found Pete Jericho slumped in his kitchen, sullen because Madeleine Stockwell had given him the boot. "Christ, I'm such a jerk. I'm out of my league with those people. I was never good enough for Allyson—she's still under Madeleine's spell."

"Ever think you're reading this wrong?" Sam had little patience with the guy. "Could be Madeleine's being overprotective and just doesn't want Allyson to make the same mistakes she made after she lost her husband so young."

"Four husbands? Marrying a commoner?"

"Quit feeling sorry for yourself. A man just died in your gravel pit."

But Pete already knew about Harrison. He just wasn't ready to look at the situation from any angle but the one that made him the victim. "Wally was another one under Madeleine's thumb. He was always thinking he'd find a way to make his fortune off her. Pop nailed it. Rich people find a way to hang on to their money."

Sam shook his head. "I'm tempted to haul you out to the gravel pit and let the work crew pound the rocks out of your head. Time to step up to the plate and be a man, my friend." And that was all Sam intended to say about this nonsense. "Where's your father?"

"I don't know, out on his tractor." Pete lifted his chin, his eyes glassy with pain, medication and embarrassment. He managed a self-deprecating smile. "Thanks. I was getting sick of myself."

"You're in love. Hard place to be."

Charlie Jericho burst into the kitchen, peeling off his cap and raking a hand over his gray hair. He was out of breath and looked both relieved and awkward at seeing his son. "I thought you were up with Allyson. Christ." His face lost more of its color. "I'll just give it to you straight. There's been an explosion at the Stockwell place. Some kind of bomb. The barn's on fire."

"Allyson?" Pete asked, staggering to his feet.

"She's hurt, Pete. I don't know how bad. A trooper's down, too. They've got ambulances on the way." Charlie turned to Sam, who'd gone still inside;

he knew what was coming. The older man's eyes softened. "Kara and the kids might be in the barn. They don't know."

"It's a volunteer fire department?" Sam asked.

Charlie nodded. "Pete and I are supposed to meet the trucks up at the house." He licked his lips, catching his breath, and glanced over at his son. "Pete—you coming?"

He inhaled deeply. "Damn straight. Let Madeleine fucking try to throw me out now."

The three men headed outside, a gust of cool wind a reminder to Sam that he wasn't on his home turf. Two ambulances and a state police cruiser screamed past the Jericho house, their sirens wailing.

Pete climbed into the passenger seat of his father's truck, and Charlie went around to the driver's side. A fire truck blasted past them on the main road, Billie Corrigan in its wake. The portable emergency light flashing on her dashboard identified her as a volunteer firefighter. She pulled in behind Charlie, her window rolled down. "Charlie, Pete—you heard? Need a ride?"

"We're going in my truck," Charlie told her.

"See you up there. Temple? What about you?"

No way would he get through security in his car, Sam thought. He jumped in with her. She tore back out onto the road, driving with one hand as she fiddled with her radio. She was in touch with the fire station. Governor Stockwell was unconscious with cuts and burns, maybe broken ribs. One state trooper had the wind knocked out of him. Another was down with smoke inhalation after charging into the barn looking for the Stockwell kids. They weren't there. There was no sign of Kara.

Billie glanced sideways at Sam, her eyes shining with excitement and fear. "Reporters have been camped out at the diner since Big Mike took a header in the deep end. This'll be on as breaking news before we get the fire put out."

Sam didn't give a damn. "Who stands to gain if Allyson and her kids are out of the way?" he asked abruptly.

"What? What an awful question!"

But he didn't care who he pissed off. He had questions. A lot of them. And he was going to get answers. It was past time. "Your brother? Would he inherit as Lawrence Stockwell's only surviving immediate family?"

"You've your nerve." She raked a hand through her auburn hair, her blue eyes hot with irritation. "Hatch isn't a Stockwell. His mother would inherit before he would."

"I don't think so."

Billie scowled at him. "You're an arrogant bastard, you know that? I give you a ride, because I can see you're worried about Kara, and here you make these insinuations about my brother."

Sam didn't relent. "You two share a father, right?"

"Frankie Corrigan. He fell off stage scaffolding, drunk as a skunk, and broke his neck. I was right there and couldn't do a thing. His number-one helper, he used to call me. So what?"

"Hatch grew up here in Bluefield?"

"On Stockwell Farm with Ms. Madeleine, thinking

he was one of them.'' She careened up the road, the picturesque hills outlined in sharp relief against the clear summer sky. ''I grew up with my no-account mother and knew better. And am happier for it.''

''You don't like the Stockwells,'' Sam said.

Billie tried to laugh, her instincts always, he thought, to make people feel comfortable around her. The life of the party. But her laugh didn't quite materialize. ''Jesus, are you intense or what? I don't have much of an opinion one way or the other. They're Hatch's family, not mine.''

''What do you know about Walter Harrison's relationship with your brother?''

''Nothing. It's terrible, what happened to him. I guess Zoe and the state detectives'll be getting their butts up to the Stockwell place. A bomb going off at the governor's is a bigger deal than some poor retired cop nobody liked turning up dead in a gravel pit.''

Sam didn't bother explaining the procedures the law enforcement officers would follow. Billie Corrigan had her own view of how the world worked. ''I'm surprised your brother picked Harrison to watch two kids—''

''Why, because they're Stockwells? Wally was a jerk in a lot of ways, but he was solid. I think, anyway. What do I know?'' She gave Sam a sideways glance, a small grin. ''What is this, Texas Ranger comes to Connecticut?''

He said nothing, and she veered onto the long, pretty Stockwell driveway and pulled alongside Charlie Jericho's truck. The tracks of the emergency vehicles had dug into the soft, wet lawn. ''The police're buttoning down this place. I need to check in and see what I'm supposed to do. Are you going to get yourself into trouble?"

Sam got out of her car. "If you get any word on Kara or the Stockwell kids, I'd appreciate it if you let me know."

"Will do, Ranger Sam." She hurried off, then stopped and turned to him as she walked backward. "Did I pass my interrogation?"

He didn't answer. A yellow VW bug turned up the driveway, and he decided to hear what Zoe West had to say. He could smell smoke, hear more fire trucks, their sirens blaring as they approached.

As he passed Charlie Jericho's truck, he spotted a pair of binoculars on the dashboard and stepped in closer, peering through the passenger door. They were old binoculars, clunky, expensive, just as Lillian Stockwell had described them to him a dozen times yesterday out at the tree house. They even had the pink ribbon she'd mentioned, tied to the strap.

A car door shut nearby. "I don't know what good I'm going to do up here," West muttered. "My chief's on his way. Lordy, lord. What a day. Sergeant?" He turned, saw her frowning up at him. "What are you looking at?"

"Lillian Stockwell's missing binoculars."

West got it instantly. "Ah, hell."

"Get a warrant," Sam warned her.

"Hell with that. They're in plain sight. I'll just ask Charlie what he's doing with the damn things in his truck. He's here playing firefighter? There's Pete." She waved him over before Sam could stop her. Another fire truck barreled up the driveway, and West looked as if her ears hurt and she'd rather be elsewhere. But she rallied, and she told Sam, "You know those binoculars are a plant, don't you?"

"Yes."

"Wally, probably. Plant Lillian Stockwell's missing binoculars in Charlie Jericho's truck, go get yourself shot in the gravel pit." She shook her head. "I'm missing some pieces here."

Pete sank against the front of his father's truck, his face gray, his shirt covered in sweat. His breathing was ragged, and he clearly was in pain. "I can't get near her," he said, and Sam knew he meant Allyson. "They're taking her out in a minute. She's conscious. Apparently she said Kara left before the explosion. She was heading to the cottage after Henry and Lillian."

Zoe West frowned. "So the kids aren't here? They're at the cottage?"

Pete coughed, wincing in obvious agony. "I guess. This is all secondhand." He held his broken wrist up to his chest, looking as if each breath caused him pain. "I suppose you two have your knickers in a twist over the binoculars. Pop said they were in his truck this morning, on his seat. He put them up on the dash out of the way."

West groaned. "Oh, come on. Who'd be that stupid?"

"And I'll bet when the arson squad gets here," Pete said, "they'll find shit from our house was used to make the bomb."

West still was unimpressed. "As frames go, Pete, it's pretty flipping weak."

Sam agreed. Pete stared out at the immaculate lawn, smoke rising over the main house, the burning barn beyond it. He sniffled, near tears. "Whoever set that bomb didn't care if they got the kids—they didn't care if they were there—"

"No." Sam straightened, wishing they were in Texas where he had jurisdiction, authority. "Henry and Lillian were the main target. Someone wants those kids dead."

Pete started sinking, and Zoe West shot over to him and kept him from landing face first in the dirt. She looked at Sam, thrusting her keys at him. They hung from an antique spoon. "Take my car," she said, balancing a half-conscious Pete Jericho between her and the hood of the truck. "People recognize it—you'll be able to get out of here without a lot of red tape. I'll grab a trooper and my chief and get some people down to the cottage."

"Keep an eye on Billie Corrigan," Sam said.

She nodded. He could see she was with him. "I intend to."

"Detective, you're not armed—"

"Yeah, well, everyone else here is."

Sam got behind the wheel of the little yellow car and found the right key on West's spoon. Before he got the ignition started, Pete managed to get the passenger door open and was falling into the seat, smelling of sweat and fear, the fingers poking out of his cast purple and cold-looking. "I love those kids like they're my own," he said. "No one's fucking touching them."

Twenty-Three

❧∾❧

Henry and Lillian had their backpacks loaded and a list of 800 numbers for different airlines ready when Kara found them at the cottage. They were torn. On the one hand, they said, they hated to leave their mother and scare her again. On the other hand, she still trusted Hatch, and they didn't.

But learning that the explosion they'd heard came from the barn changed everything. They set their backpacks by the back door and stared at Kara, all the drama and indignation gone out of them. "Is Mom okay?" Lillian asked, her voice almost inaudible.

Kara had talked to a trooper on her cell phone and gotten the basics—and instructions to stay put with the kids until a cruiser could get there. "She has to go to the hospital, but she'll recover. I didn't get many details. We need to wait here."

Henry wasn't as willing as his sister to let go of his suspicions, his urge to control the situation. "Hatch isn't coming, is he?"

"Henry, I suspect Hatch made some bad decisions

along the way that affected you and Lillian, but I honestly don't think he killed Big Mike.'' She'd decided to confront the boy directly with what she knew was on his mind. ''Isn't that what you think? That he pushed Mike into the pool, then found your tree house and stole Lillian's binoculars?''

''And he had that awful man follow us,'' Lillian said.

Too agitated to sit down, Kara stood at the kitchen counter. ''I have a feeling Hatch put his trust in the wrong people. That's what you're afraid you did, too, isn't it? Trusted him by mistake?'' She smiled, pulling the kids to her and kissing the tops of their heads, aware of how worried and tired they all were. ''Come on, it's a beautiful day. We don't get weather like this in August in Texas. Let's go out and wait for the trooper. He'll bring us to see your mom.''

Lillian started to cry. ''It was awful hearing the explosion.''

Kara had, too, on her way to the cottage, and had almost turned back. But she knew she couldn't. She had to get to Henry and Lillian. If Allyson was dead or seriously injured, they would need her. She didn't know how she'd made it to the cottage, why she didn't slip in the wet grass. Her pants were soaked from the knees down, muddy and grass-stained. Questions—a million questions—spun through her mind, all of them centered on who would want to set fire to Allyson Stockwell's converted barn...who would want to kill her.

Not just her. Henry and Lillian, too. They were supposed to be there. It wasn't a secret.

Kara remembered the pad and pen Lillian had used to write the note that morning—both from the boxes Billie Corrigan had brought to the cottage yesterday. Billie must have stopped by the cottage this morning after Kara and Sam had left for the gravel pit, grabbed some art supplies and dropped them off at the barn. Allyson wouldn't have thought to mention it. Billie was always doing fun things for people, trying to make them happy and appreciate her talents.

Henry and Lillian eased out of her embrace, and Kara could feel the cool breeze beckoning through the window above the sink. She breathed in deeply, trying to calm herself. Sam would be on the case, never mind that he had no authority and every law enforcement officer in the state of Connecticut would be on alert, as well as the ATF and the FBI.

At least, Kara thought, she had a better feel for what was going on, the dangers and the stakes, the reason for it all. Someone would talk to Billie. Someone would ask her about the drawing materials, what she knew about Wally Harrison. Kara hoped she was wrong—she didn't want Hatch's half-sister to be behind any part of what had happened over the summer.

Kara jerked herself out of her thoughts and turned to join the kids outside. They were at the screen door, but made no move to push it open, as if they were transfixed, frozen. "It's okay, guys," Kara said. "We can go out and wait—"

"Uh-uh," Billie Corrigan said. "Sorry. No way are you coming out here."

Kara saw her now. She was at the bottom of the kitchen steps, her eyes wide and shining, a gun—at a guess, Wally's .38—pointed through the screen door. "Billie, what's going on?" Kara asked quietly.

"I thought you all might end up out here. Isn't that what you say in Texas? You all? Do *not* move. Any of you. I want you to stay where I can see you."

Kara had squeezed between the screen door and Henry and Lillian. "Billie, listen to me. The police are on their way. You don't want to make this worse than it already is."

"You think you're so smart, Kara, but you don't have a clue. Well, in five minutes you'll get the picture. I'll try to save you, of course, and I might even get wounded in the process. But I won't succeed." With her free hand, she brushed beads of sweat off her upper lip. "People like me. They'll believe I acted heroically."

Kara eased her hands behind her back and grabbed up Henry's and Lillian's stiff fingers, holding them in hers as if she somehow could shield her godchildren from Billie Corrigan's violence and desperation. "Billie." Her calmness surprised her, but she knew she had no other choice—she had to keep a clear head. "Billie—Allyson isn't dead. This isn't going to work."

Billie sniffed. "Damn bomb didn't blow up the way I expected. A simple little gas can near a bonfire worked better. If it hadn't been for Pete, this'd all be over. Big Mike'd be alive. He knew Allyson and the kids were in danger—he knew about her and Pete. He wanted their affair out in the open. He told Hatch. He wanted Hatch to pressure Allyson." Sweat stains spread across her white blouse. "They'd argued before—I overheard them from the woods. Big Mike suspected the bonfire wasn't an accident—he practically accused Hatch of being involved. Out at the pool that day—they were really shouting at each other." She shrugged. "But I was ready to act."

Kara tried to think, her mind racing. She knew to keep Billie talking, keep her calm, until she figured out what to do…but she had no time. There was another bomb. There had to be. It was the only reason for Billie to be here. She would want to keep them in place long enough for it to go off—which meant it had to be on a timer. "You found the bluebird at Madeleine's?"

"Broke its little leg myself."

Lillian gasped but said nothing. Kara squeezed the kids' hands gently. "You were lucky, weren't you? It was late in the season for juvenile bluebirds."

Billie glanced at her watch and smiled. "The clock is ticking. Pete, God love him. He couldn't stand there and let the gas can explode and not do anything. He had to act. But he'll see, even if Allyson is alive—he'll see what she is. He's just got a blind spot where she's concerned. He'll see what a selfish bitch she is—"

Henry shot his head around at her. "Don't call my mom names!"

Kara gently but firmly, quickly, shoved him back behind her. "I didn't know you could build bombs," she told Billie. Where had she put the one in the cottage? How much longer before it went off? "You do such beautiful parties."

"Trying to butter me up so I'll let you live? Forget

it. My dad, the old drunk, taught me all sorts of things. He used to fantasize about blowing up the snot-nosed actors and directors. Most of the stuff he put together was for show, but he could do the real thing." She licked her lips, her hand slipping slightly on the .38. "He did love his bombs, my dad. If he didn't drink, I guess he might have been good at it."

A car sounded on the dirt road. Billie raised the .38, cocking it. "Move one step and I'll shoot."

"Kara!"

Sam was at the front door. Pete was with him, calling for Henry and Lillian.

"No," Kara yelled, "there's a bomb!"

Billie's eyes flickered. Kara had the split-second distraction she needed. She shoved Henry and Lillian back across the kitchen, toward the living room. "Go, run, get outside as fast as you can."

Henry hesitated. "What about you—"

"Go!"

They scrambled, screaming as Billie Corrigan tore open the screen door and barreled into the kitchen. Kara grabbed a chair from the table and shoved it at Billie, throwing off Billie's aim as she fired, a sharp, cracking sound followed by another shot. She fell backward through the screen door and down the steps. Kara staggered, wondering how Billie could have fired twice, that fast.

Then she realized she was on the kitchen floor, but couldn't remember falling. She felt a searing pain in her side. She held it, thinking she had a cramp, then saw the blood oozing between her fingers. "Ah, hell..."

Sam was there, scooping her up with one arm around her waist, Jack's .45 in his free hand. He half carried her, half ran with her toward the back door, then kicked it open and dropped her, hurling her down the steps, leaping after her.

She landed hard in the grass, the explosion happening around her, ripping through the small kitchen—not as big a bang as the one at the barn, she thought crazily, feeling the bomb's concussion lift her. She heard a window pop out and crash, the hiss of flames, children yelling and crying. She smelled acrid smoke.

Pete…he had to have gotten Henry and Lillian out through the front. They had to be okay.

Sam got to his feet, and Kara managed to crawl up onto her hands and knees, the wind knocked out of her, pain and dizziness seizing her. Out of the corner of her eye she saw Billie on her stomach, reaching with a bloody hand for Wally's gun.

Kara felt blood warm on her side, dripping through her shirt. Through her haze of shock, she realized Billie would shoot Sam—and she'd had enough. She staggered to her feet, and with one arm swept the hibachi off the table onto Billie Corrigan's head, then felt herself collapsing.

Sam caught her before she hit the ground, and he eased her down gently. "It's okay, darlin'. I've got you."

"You do, don't you?" She winced, dizzy with pain. "Oh, Sam. I told you there was a bomb. Did you listen? Of course not. You came running, .45 blazing. Damn Texas Rangers."

He knelt beside her and tore off his shirt, giving her a wink of pure bravado. "I know where they keep the fire extinguishers."

"The barn and the cottage...what a mess." She was aware of Sam wrapping his shirt around her wound and didn't know why she didn't stop him. "You should have let me keep my gun."

"Probably should have."

"Couldn't you have shot Billie before she shot me?"

"That was my plan until you threw the chair at her."

She smiled, or thought she did. "It was a pretty good move, don't you think?"

"Damn good move. Kara, you saved those kids."

He held her, putting pressure on the wound, and she shuddered with pain, saw her blood spilling onto his hand. She sank against his chest. "If you were the one who got shot, I'd take care of you. I would, Sam. You know that, don't you?"

"Yes. I know."

"I'll defend you if Zoe West arrests you for using your weapon. Hell, it's not even department issue, it's Jack's. Oh, Jesus...he's on his way up here."

She heard sirens, up close now. Sam held her, kissing her on the forehead. She couldn't talk anymore. She shut her eyes, leaning into him, and it didn't hurt so much.

Kara didn't make a very good patient, but one of the paramedics who tended her in the backyard of Stonebrook Cottage knew her from her Connecticut days. Sam gathered he was another reformed criminal. Whoever he was, he told her to shut up and be still. The bullet, he said, had grazed a nasty path just below her rib cage but didn't look as if it had gone in. She was very lucky.

But Sam had to admit she'd probably thrown Billie's aim off with that chair.

Another paramedic crew worked on Billie Corrigan. It wasn't going as well for her. Sam's aim, even with a bomb about to go off and a chair flying, was better. Hatch was with her. The paramedics ran IVs and tried to stop the bleeding as they got her onto a stretcher.

Zoe West stood next to Sam. "Deadly force was called for?"

"Yes." He'd already turned his weapon over to her.

"The Texas Rangers—they going to fire you?"

"Maybe."

She eyed him. "You give a damn?"

"Not right now, no."

"I'd tell everyone I shot her if I could get away with it."

"Thanks, Detective," Sam said. "I appreciate the thought."

"No, you don't. You're a straight arrow, Sergeant. If I were down in Texas and shot one of your citizens, you'd have my gun and my badge."

But she moved away, the volunteer firefighters working on the cottage, the place crawling with town and state cops. And reporters. The media were descending. Sam moved closer to Billie Corrigan. He took no pleasure in watching anyone die.

"Don't say you did this for me." Hatch choked back tears as he held his sister's hand. "Billie...you killed one of my closest friends. You almost killed the only family I've ever known other than you."

"Hatch, don't—I did it for you." Her voice was insistent, thready from fatigue and loss of blood. "Big Mike thought you tried to kill Allyson. He'd have made your life miserable."

"No, Billie. He'd have found out it was you. *I'd* have found out. That's what you were afraid of."

"You deserve some of Lawrence's money," she whispered. "You *do*, Hatch. He was your brother."

"I don't want the damn money. I never have. You *know* that."

She shook her head. "I don't believe it." She drifted a moment, came back. "And Pete. He couldn't love anyone else while he was still under Allyson's spell. Hey, brother. You don't hate me, do you?"

"No. I wish I could. Billie...oh, Jesus, don't die on me!"

"Wally was a dumb idea, Hatch. You wanted him to find out if it was me, didn't you?"

"I wasn't sure—I didn't know what to do, what to believe. I thought he'd at least keep the kids safe—"

"Wally had his own agenda. He found out about Pete and Allyson, started calling her—he threatened to pin Big Mike's death on her. You couldn't have that, Hatch. You'd have turned me in for sure before you let Allyson take the fall."

A paramedic turned to Hatch. "She needs to stay quiet."

He nodded. "Billie…rest, okay?"

"That's why I went after Charlie. I didn't want—" She tried to raise up, but the paramedic gently restrained her. "I didn't want you hurt. Hatch, please say you believe me."

"I believe you, Billie."

"Big Mike…I knew he'd try to save that bluebird."

Her eyes were shut now, and the paramedics lifted her stretcher as she drifted into unconsciousness. Sam doubted she'd make it to the hospital alive. Hatch watched them take his sister away. He seemed rooted to his spot on the lawn, the cool wind catching the ends of his hair.

"I'm sorry," Sam said.

"She can't believe she tried to kill Allyson and the kids for me. For me! So I could inherit." He didn't look at Sam, just stared at the bloodstains in the grass. "I was afraid she was up to something—I hired Wally to keep Henry and Lillian safe while I figured things out, but it turns out he had his own agenda. My God." He raised his head suddenly, fastened his incisive gaze on Sam. "Have you ever had something stare you in the face that you simply refuse to accept?"

"I imagine we all do."

Hatch Corrigan brushed at tears on his cheeks, but his voice was unaffected. "I felt sorry for Billie. She had to deal with our father more than I did. She watched him fall to his death. I thought she was happy here, satisfied with her work. Instead, it ate her up, seeing Pete Jericho mooning after Allyson month after month. That was it, you know. That was what drove her to go after Allyson and the kids. I knew she was in love with him but I never—'' He broke off.

Sam nodded. He'd had people unload on him before after experiencing violence. It was never pleasant. "Then the money was a rationalization?"

"To a degree. Billie knew if I inherited I'd have taken care of her." He exhaled, sniffled, and pulled out a folded handkerchief and dabbed his eyes. He added abruptly, "Kara was never in love with me. But I think you know that."

Sam said nothing.

"I'm not good at close relationships. I think that's why I stayed in love with her for so long. It was convenient, easy, because I knew she wasn't in love with me and never would be." He returned his handkerchief to his pocket. "I preferred it that way."

A state trooper came back and told them they'd heard from the ambulance. Billie Corrigan was dead. Hatch gave a curt nod and turned away, walking out past the charred cottage to a quiet spot in the shade.

Sam's cell phone rang, and he knew exactly who it was.

"We're at the Hartford airport," Jack said. "Susanna and the girls are glued to CNN. They've got the story as breaking news—an explosion at the governor's summer house. She's seriously injured. Damn it...now they're saying there are fatalities."

"The suspect and a bodyguard."

"Kara?"

"She'll be okay. She's on her way to the hospital. A bullet grazed her on the right side. She was telling me everything I did wrong when they loaded her into the ambulance. Jack, she saved those two kids' lives—"

"Where are they?"

"With a friend of their mother's." Pete Jericho, Sam thought. Pete wasn't letting them go. "We're all heading to the hospital now."

"I'll meet you there. What about you, Sam? You okay?"

"I'm responsible for one of the fatalities."

Twenty-Four

Kara tried to focus on her brother and sister-in-law, but her eyes didn't seem to want to work properly. And she wasn't making any sense. She knew it was the medication. Pete Jericho had stopped in briefly and warned her she'd feel a little nuts for a while, but she probably wouldn't remember half of it, anyway. And he'd told her Allyson would be okay. His voice cracked when he said it.

"God, I hurt." Kara wasn't quite sure if she spoke out loud. She didn't know where Sam was. In a holding cell, maybe in custody for shooting Billie Corrigan with an unauthorized weapon. "Jack, what would you do if I married a Texas Ranger?"

"You're delirious on painkillers," he said. He wasn't wearing his badge or his white hat, just a denim shirt and jeans with a big western buckle on his belt. Susanna, as always, looked elegant.

"I'm deliriously in love with Sam."

Susanna winced, but Jack said, "A hard-nosed attorney like you."

"I thought I was pregnant." She couldn't have said

that out loud, not to her brother—she'd tell Susanna, no problem. But Jack didn't see her as an adult, he still saw her as a shattered nine-year-old, remembered how helpless he'd been after their mother died. Her father, too. It was one reason she'd stayed in Connecticut so long.

Jack didn't say anything at first, so she thought she was off the hook—she hadn't spoken it out loud. But Susanna had her hand on his elbow, and finally he said, "You mean you and Sam—ah, hell, I don't even want to go there."

"I wanted to be pregnant. I wanted a baby more than anything in the world." Her head spun, and the ceiling seemed to be moving. "Sam's baby."

"Kara, women fall in love with Sam all the time. He doesn't return the favor."

Susanna smiled down at her sister-in-law. "Jack and I need to go find Maggie and Ellen. I think they're buying out the gift shop for you. Rest up, okay?"

"I love Sam," Kara said.

"I know you do," Susanna said. "You have for a while now."

Kara didn't know if she drifted off, but when her eyes opened again, Sam was there, black-eyed and shaking his head at her. "I don't know what you said to your brother, but he just told me I'm lucky he came into the state unarmed."

"Was he serious? I never know with you two."

Sam grinned. "We like to keep you defense attorneys off balance about us Texas Rangers."

"Don't make me laugh—it hurts." The doctors

didn't think she'd need surgery, but it was still a possibility. "I might have told Jack I thought I was pregnant."

"Ah."

"With your baby," she said.

"Of course. Who else's?"

"I said I wanted to be. More than anything. I know I said that. I've never been good with medication." She tried to sit up, but she didn't have the strength and collapsed back on her bed. "I'm your soul mate, Sam. If you don't think you're my soul mate, that's okay, I'll still be there for you."

"I know you will."

"Do you? Or are you humoring me because I'm mumbling a lot of romantic bullshit? I'm really loopy from this medication."

He smiled and kissed her softly. "I like you loopy."

Hatch Corrigan visited later, when Kara was more clearheaded. Sam had gone off with Jack and the state investigators, and Ellen and Maggie retreated when they saw their aunt had a visitor. Their mother did not. Susanna plopped in a chair by Kara's bed and said she'd just look at a magazine a few minutes while Kara and Hatch talked. "The last time I left you alone, you made off with a gun and a plane."

But that wasn't it, Kara knew. Susanna just thought her sister-in-law needed a solid female presence and intended to step in if she got overwhelmed by a grief-stricken, guilt-ridden Hatch Corrigan.

He looked drained, and Kara could see more of his

mother in his thin, gray face. "I'm sorry about Billie," she said, and he nodded, as if he understood she meant she was sorry about all of it—what Billie had done, that she'd put herself in a position that ended, at that point necessarily, with the loss of her life.

He cleared his throat, his natural formality, Kara thought, helping him now. "It shouldn't have come to this. I didn't see how bitter and angry she'd become, how twisted her thinking was. She felt entitled to whatever she wanted. She hated it that Pete couldn't get over Allyson. Then, when she found out Allyson had fallen for him—I think the downward spiral really picked up."

"People liked her, Hatch," Kara said. "I think most of us believed she had a good thing going in Bluefield."

"I did, too."

"How did she know Big Mike couldn't swim?"

He shrugged, but there was nothing nonchalant about him. He exuded a kind of emotional pain Kara never wanted to experience. "I think she figured it out from watching him at parties. She was good at zeroing in on people's foibles, their secrets and weaknesses."

"Yours?"

"Kara, you know that the Stockwell wealth has never mattered to me. Never. You know that, don't you? Lawrence left me with plenty. I never—"

She managed a small smile. "It's okay. You don't have to explain."

"It was my vulnerability for her she exploited." But he sighed, straightening, his uneasiness with soul-baring of any kind apparent. "Allyson's not as badly hurt as they originally feared. None of the burns is that serious. Pete—good God, he's been incredible. He can hardly stand up himself, but he's there at her side. I thought it was Billie who pushed him, but Sam says it was Wally."

Kara nodded. "I agree."

"I'm sure he'd be pleased," Hatch said wryly.

"No, seriously. Billie didn't want to hurt Pete. She thought he'd turn to her when Allyson was out of the way. Wally was a sneak looking for an advantage. I'll bet he found the tree house and was up there putting two and two together when he ran into Pete and gave him the heave-ho over the edge."

In her chair, Susanna gave up any pretense of reading her magazine. She frowned at Kara, as if she shouldn't be discussing the facts and theories of attacks, murders, bombs going off. But Kara needed to sort it through, needed to come to some kind of understanding, and Susanna must have understood that, because she didn't call for her husband.

Hatch rubbed the back of his neck, and Kara knew that he, too, needed this chance to understand. "Sam thinks Wally stumbled on Lillian's binoculars before he pushed Pete."

Kara raised an eyebrow. "How come Sam told you all his theories?"

He smiled. "I wasn't shot, Kara."

"My head hurts more than where I was shot, I swear. I can't think straight..." She winced in pain, touching her bandaged middle, but rallied when Susanna made a move to throw Hatch out. "Billie probably ran across the binoculars when she was making her escape after killing Mike and realized Henry and Lillian could have seen her. She must have decided to take her chances and left the binoculars in the woods, hoping the kids hadn't seen anything. They were all over the woods, but she might not have heard him—or did and just didn't want them to know she was onto them. But she didn't leave the binoculars where Lillian remembered dropping them.''

"Then Wally finds them and gets in touch with Billie—''

"Right.'' Kara frowned, trying to think and reason it out the way Sam had. "Being an opportunist, Wally figures he's got something he can use to put the squeeze on Billie, maybe get her to give him a cut of the inheritance she's going to get you? Whatever. He arranges to meet Billie at the gravel pit, and she kills him, takes the binoculars and tries to frame Charlie.''

Hatch grimaced, but she thought their blunt talk was helping him accept the reality of what his sister had done, the twisted clarity of her thinking, at least early on. "Billie could have hoped ultimately to pin the frame on Wally—''

Kara didn't like that. "And what, say she killed him in self-defense? No way. Did Ranger Sam come up with that theory?''

"He said it was a possibility.''

"One full of holes. It doesn't explain the bombs, and Billie shot me with Wally's .38 *after* he was dead.''

"She didn't expect to have to shoot you at all,'' Hatch said. "That was an act of desperation. She wanted to keep you in the kitchen until she was sure the bomb went off, then heroically but unsuccessfully try to save you.'' He smiled at her, but his eyes were soft and sad. ''According to Sam.''

Kara sank her head back into her pillow, exhausted now. Pete didn't remember falling, but she remembered getting shot—she remembered everything. ''Oh, Hatch. Big Mike was right, you know. I needed to be home. I needed to go back to Texas.'' She touched his hand, clammy from the shock he'd had. ''What are you going to do?''

He didn't hesitate. ''Go away for a while. Figure out who I am apart from my mother and my dead brother's wife and children. But don't worry, I'll be back. And Kara—'' His smile reached his eyes, but just barely. ''You and Sam Temple are something else together. I can't wait to see your babies. They'll be hardheaded and black-eyed, and you'll both have your hands full.''

Susanna shook her head as if she couldn't believe what she was hearing and yet, somehow, had expected it all along.

Kara tried to sit up. ''Hatch...''

''Be happy, my friend. I'll see you around.''

After he left, Susanna sighed. ''Hardheaded and black-eyed? He doesn't know the half of it.''

''He's dreaming. *I'm* dreaming. Susanna, you warned me about Sam.''

''I warn Jack about a lot of things. He doesn't listen, either.''

A few minutes later, her sister-in-law whispered to her. ''Kara? Are you up to a couple more visitors?''

Kara stirred, and Henry and Lillian waved tentatively at her from the doorway. Susanna, a natural with children, smiled, getting to her feet and encouraging them to come in. "I'm hearing stories about how great you two were today."

"They were," Kara said. "They were pretty damn unbelievable."

But Henry and Lillian weren't interested in themselves. "We brought you a present," Lillian said.

Henry nodded, edging toward the hospital bed with his sister. Kara felt light-headed and not quite there, but she smiled, wondering what they were up to this time.

"We made it ourselves while we were waiting to see Mom," Henry said. "Pete got us the materials."

Lillian pulled something from behind her back, what appeared to be a long, skinny stick covered in multicolored sparkles and glitter and bits of ribbon. Kara wasn't sure what it was, but they told her.

"It's a wand," Henry said.

Lillian giggled. "For our fairy godmother."

Twenty-Five

Allyson spent just three days in the hospital and was released on the condition she take it easy for a couple of weeks. Not that hard to do, she thought lazily in her hammock. Even as governor. She lay on her stomach on a special pad Pete had made to cushion her wounds. He'd moved the hammock from outside the charred remains of the barn and hung it between two sugar maples in the Jerichos' backyard. Allyson could see Bea Jericho in her floppy hat, chickens warbling behind her as she scooped up their droppings and dumped them into an old bucket she'd then carry to the compost pile.

"Your mother seems so normal," Allyson said. "I love watching her."

Pete, sitting in the grass near her hammock, shook his head. "My mother is not normal."

Allyson didn't laugh. She couldn't, not yet. It hurt too much—physically, emotionally. She had relatively minor but still painful burns on her back and arms, three broken ribs, a partially collapsed lung and cuts and bruises, but none of her injuries, mercifully, were that serious. The quick action of the troopers guarding her had saved her life. She'd asked them to her hospital room to thank them, but they insisted they'd just done their duty and wanted no special recognition. Also, although no one else did, they blamed themselves for not knowing the bomb was there in the first place.

But it's difficult, Allyson thought, when it's family trying to kill you.

She should have said something sooner. She knew that now. She thought she was doing the right thing, but, it turned out, the bulk of the calls were from Wally Harrison. The police would have caught him. Or Hatch would have spoken up sooner about his arrangement to have Wally keep an eye on Henry and Lillian.

Still, who knew? Wally had been clever with the calls, and if Allyson had spoken up, she could have ended up triggering Billie to act sooner, with even more disastrous results.

Allyson knew she couldn't let the what-ifs drive her out of her mind. The last call, just before the bomb exploded in the barn, was from Billie. Wally was already dead. They'd played each other, Billie Corrigan and Wally Harrison.

Billie made both bombs with common materials she'd stolen from the Jerichos. She set the bombs on timers. Allyson didn't understand why Billie hadn't set them to go off at night. The investigators believed she already had the bombs in place, but was pushed into setting the timers after she killed Wally Harrison. That was a clear homicide, and Billie would know once his body was found, access to the Stockwells would be cut off, even for her, until his murder was solved. The sand had simply run out of the hourglass. She'd had to make her move. She must have set the timer on the cottage bomb when she picked up the art supplies for Henry and Lillian, the one at the barn when she delivered the supplies. Helpful Billie, always trying to make people happy. Nobody had thought anything of her showing up.

None of them had seen that she was bold and desperate and maybe a little crazy—and also very determined.

"Are you sure you're up for this press conference?" Pete asked, and Allyson could see his concern for her. He had no other agenda. He just wanted to be sure she was okay.

But she didn't hesitate. "Yes."

"Henry and Lillian want to do it with you, you know."

"They're not allowed. They're children. But I'm telling the world that if not for them, God only knows where we'd all be right now." She felt the hot sting of tears in her eyes. "They've been so damn brave."

"Pop wants to put homing devices on them."

Allyson smiled through her tears. "I swear to God, Pete, but Madeleine said the same thing."

He laughed. He was so good for her, she thought. So steady. "Those two. A couple of old cranks. They ran into each other in the hospital waiting room. Madeleine told him she could have done worse for neighbors all these years. I could tell Pop was pleased, but he insisted she'd never called him a neighbor before.

Then she said she had—well, they argued about that for a while, until she finally told him not to get the idea he could just pop over to borrow a cup of sugar whenever he felt like it.''

"They both love the land," Allyson said. "They respect that in each other."

Pete ran one hand over the top of the grass, not looking at her. "Madeleine's blunt and says things she shouldn't, and she's a snob. But she never asked Wally Harrison or anyone else to put the screws to me. They did it to curry favor with her. She's not perfect. She's made mistakes, but we all do." He looked at Allyson now, wisdom in those young eyes. "Even you."

"That's not so easy to admit," she said quietly.

"No. Not for you."

He leaned back on his outstretched elbows, his face and arms tanned, his stomach flat, his legs well muscled, and she knew she could rely on him. He was solid, her rock. They'd rebuild Stonebrook Cottage and live there, make it their home. Pete was excited about doing a lot of the work himself.

"Madeleine'll help Henry and Lillian get through this," he said. "She'll help you if you'll let her."

Allyson thought of Madeleine Stockwell, the joys and the immeasurable grief they'd shared over the years. Could she have endured Lawrence's death without his mother there, ever the survivor? She sighed, listening to Bea hum to the chickens. "You're right, Pete. You like that, don't you? Being right."

He grinned. "It's a switch."

And he rose, agile and surprisingly graceful. Allyson gave a small groan. "I can't believe I'm lying here burned and broken and thinking about the next time we're in bed together."

"Good, because I was starting to wonder what kind of creep I am to be thinking the same thing." He leaned over her hammock and took a strand of her hair and tucked it behind her ear. "You need to rest and use that breathing thing they gave you for your lung. It's okay to cry at your press conference, but if you collapse and have to be carried out of there on a stretcher, that's it. Connecticut'll have a new governor by the six o'clock news."

"They might, anyway," she said. "I might yet resign."

"Nah. You'll stay. You're a do-gooder, Allyson. You love this state. You want to give it your best shot."

"My children need me."

He winked. "Don't tell them that."

She'd set them up with a psychologist who'd asked her to listen to them very carefully and not assume she knew what they were thinking. Help them to feel safe. Make sure they knew she loved them. They'd already made their position on her future very clear. They liked the idea of their mother being governor, and if she wanted to continue as governor, she should. She said it could be rough going for a while, because of the scandal and her own inaction. They'd asked her why she didn't say anything about the calls.

She told them the truth. "Because I didn't believe they meant anything, and I didn't know whether Pete and I would stay together after Big Mike died—I wasn't going to be backed into a corner by some jerk looking for political advantage. Then everything started to happen. I was afraid for you two, for myself. Don't get me wrong. I *should* have said something the minute I got the first call.''

"It wouldn't have mattered," Henry had said sagely. "It was that man who followed us—Walter Harrison—who was calling you. Billie still wanted to kill us."

Twelve years old, and someone had wanted—tried—to kill him and his sister. A reality they would all have to absorb. The news conference was at Stockwell Farm in two hours. Madeleine had insisted. People needed to see the ruins of the barn, she said, see for themselves the depths Billie had sunk to, how close Allyson had come to being killed. Pete had told Madeleine she just wanted people to see her summer roses. She'd almost managed a small laugh. Allyson knew they'd be all right. It would take time, but they'd be okay.

She planned to stand there and talk until the reporters ran out of questions. Then she'd probably have to start over and answer them all again. But they'd be the ones to call it quits, not her. The people deserved to know what had happened to their governor and lieutenant governor this summer. She would tell them everything. Then they would decide if they wanted her to continue as their governor.

Hatch wouldn't be there. He'd packed up and bought a ticket for the Patagonians. He would hike, he told her. He would find himself. Then one day he'd come home.

Allyson became aware that Pete had left, letting her rest, but she could see Henry and Lillian running across the lawn toward her hammock. She sensed their excitement, the resilience their psychologist had already spoken of. "What's up?" she asked them.

Lillian was jumping up and down. "Charlie and Bea are getting us a baby goat! We can each have our own!"

Henry's response was more muted, because, Allyson thought, he had to prove he was older and less prone to wild displays of enthusiasm for anything. But he was pleased, his eyes sparking in a way she hadn't seen since the kids had escaped Billie Corrigan. "I'm helping Charlie build a pen for them."

They talked about the goats for a while. Bea was insisting they learn all about goats and what they needed, how to care for them. Then Lillian, sitting in the grass with her brother, frowned up at her mother. "When can we go visit Aunt Kara?"

Kara had been released from the hospital that morning and had stopped by with her brother and sister-in-law before they all headed to Boston. Sam Temple wasn't there, but Allyson wasn't worried. She smiled at her children. "I think very soon we'll be going to a Texas wedding."

Twenty-Six

—⋙⧼⧽⋘—

It was chowder night at Jim's Place, and Davey Ahearn was complaining. "Jimmy, is that corn in my clam chowder? Why is there *corn* in my clam chowder?"

"I'm trying something new."

"Not with the chowder. You don't mess with the chowder."

Kara laughed, and for once it didn't hurt all that much. She had painkillers in her tote bag, just in case. And her family around her. Jack, Susanna, the twins. Iris Dunning, Susanna's indomitable grandmother, had secured them two tables, shoved them together and made them all sit.

The crowd at Jim's Place was celebrating the birth of Jim Haviland's grandson, Jedidiah James Thorne. Kara thought finally she had all the players straight. Tess, the baby's mother—Jim's daughter and Susanna's best friend in Boston—was doing fine, and Andrew Thorne, the baby's father, and his little girl, Dolly, were beside themselves with joy. So were Jim and Davey, Tess's godfather, except they had an opinion about the name. They thought it should be James Jedidiah. Who'd name a kid Jedidiah?

"We'll call him Jed," Jim said.

Davey sighed. "Like Jed Clampett?"

But the two friends passed out cigars, and some of the construction workers and firefighters had brought booties and little nighties, and the graduate students all insisted they liked the name Jedidiah. Before they flew back to San Antonio tomorrow, Susanna said she wanted to run up to the North Shore and visit.

The baby talk made Kara wistful, and even with her family gathered around her, she felt alone.

Sam wasn't there. He was still explaining himself to the Connecticut authorities. Jack had gone to the mat for his sister and his sergeant, and Kara knew it just about killed him. He was a by-the-rules kind of guy. In another life, he'd have Sam fired and both of them in jail—or at least tossed to the coyotes.

Texas Rangers weren't supposed to go up to Connecticut and shoot people, even murder suspects. And little sisters weren't supposed to get themselves shot.

"I can't believe you stood there *arguing* with Billie Corrigan when she had a gun pointed at you," he said over his chowder. This part of Kara's story had only just come out. He was sitting across from her at the table. "You lawyers. You'll argue with anyone, over anything."

She scoffed. "What would you have done?"

"I don't know. Door swing in or out?"

"Out."

"Kicked it in her face and dived for cover."

Next to him, Susanna rolled her eyes, amused.

"He doesn't know what he'd have done, Susanna. He wasn't there."

"I wouldn't have argued," he insisted. But he sighed at his sister and said to his wife, "Look at her. She's going to slide under the table any minute."

"I'm fine," Kara said.

"Right. Well, when you do slide under the table, we'll just have Sam carry you back to Iris's and put you to bed."

"Sam's not here or you wouldn't be saying that."

He gave her one of his know-it-all looks. "That's where you're wrong, little sister. Sam is here, and he will carry you back. Just one clarification." Jack got to his feet, Susanna and Iris and Maggie and Ellen all following his lead, and he leaned across the table to her and smiled. "It's separate beds at Iris's."

They left her alone at the table, and Sam walked into the pub and sat across from her, tilting back in his chair and shaking his head. He was, Kara thought, the sexiest, handsomest man not just in Texas, but on the planet.

He grinned at her. "You look like you've been shot, Miss Kara."

"I didn't expect you back here. I thought I might end up having to borrow some of Susanna's millions to make bail for you."

"Not me. The state's chief attorney herself told me I was free to go this morning and personally thanked me for saving the lives of the governor's children. I told her you saved their lives, and I saved your life."

"Did you tell her I saved your life?"

"Ah. The hibachi. No, I didn't mention the hibachi."

"It was a good move," Kara said. "Sam—"

"I know, babe."

She took a breath. "Billie was determined to kill Henry and Lillian. I could see it in her eyes. She had it in her head that all her problems would be solved if only they were out of the way. Allyson, too, by that point. Hatch'd be rich and take care of her, Pete'd be free to fall in love with her, Allyson wouldn't be there to resent and be jealous of, the kids to remind her of her own sad upbringing. If you hadn't shot her, she'd have come after them—"

"She'd have gotten her ass blown up by her own damn bomb."

Kara had hardly touched her clam chowder. "What about Zoe West?"

"She'll be fine. She says she wishes she had a picture of me charging to the rescue in her yellow VW."

Kara smiled. "The whole of the Texas Rangers will wish she had that picture."

Sam ignored that one. "I don't think she's going to last much longer in the Bluefield Police Department. Her chief's pretty mad at her for letting me run loose with a gun, but it would have been a hell of a lot worse if he'd had another governor turn up dead in his town."

"She'll take the fall," Kara said.

"She knows it. She told me she's been trying to get fired for the past year. I gather she doesn't like guns."

"Why doesn't she quit?"

"Her father was a police chief in Maine, killed in the line of duty."

"I didn't know," Kara said quietly.

Jim Haviland offered Sam chowder, a beer, a cigar—whatever he wanted. But he shook his head, and Kara knew she had to tell him what Susanna had told her just that morning.

"Gordon Temple called Susanna's mother after he saw what happened on the news. He wanted her to tell you he's sorry you and he didn't get to talk at the opening. He hopes to have that chance one day soon."

"He's my father," Sam said.

Kara nodded. "What you said before—you're right. Not every love is meant to last forever. Sam, about what I said when I was in the hospital—"

"It scared the hell out of me."

"I understand."

He leaned across the table and put one finger under her chin and lifted it, raising her eyes so they had to meet his. "You should jump on my testimony, Counselor. I used the past tense. Scared, not scares. I never believed I could love one woman with all my heart and soul, forever." He smiled, tracing his fingertip over her lips. "But I do. I do love you with all my heart and soul."

Her throat caught. "Sam—"

"How loopy were you in the hospital when you said you were my soul mate?"

"Pretty loopy to have said it out loud."

"Did you mean it?"

She didn't look away, didn't even think of running. "Yes."

"Good, because I'm your soul mate, Kara. Forever."

Up at the bar, Davey Ahearn groaned. "Jesus, I think I just cried in my chowder. Jimmy? Champagne all around. On me. It'll help kill the taste of the damn corn." He slid off his stool, a big man with an enormous heart, and he clapped a powerful hand on Sam's shoulder and pointed at Kara. "She isn't going to make it through champagne, Sarge. She'll be on the floor in about thirty seconds."

Sam nodded. "Rain check?"

"Sure, although you're running out of places up here where you're welcome."

"You'll always be welcome here, Sam," Jim Haviland said.

Davey scowled at his friend. "That's what I said."

Whatever they said next, Kara was lost—her bullet wound and the medication and fatigue and the delirious feeling that came with knowing Sam Temple loved her, loving him as much as she did, all had her falling off her chair.

Davey Ahearn and Jim Haviland made a move for her, but it was Sam who got around to her first. Although she said she could walk just fine, he carried her out of the bar into the warm summer night and up the street to her family.

CARLA NEGGERS

66845	THE CABIN	___	$6.50 U.S.	___ $7.99 CAN.
66790	THE CARRIAGE HOUSE			
		___	$6.50 U.S.	___ $7.99 CAN.
66582	THE WATERFALL	___	$6.50 U.S.	___ $7.99 CAN.
66541	ON FIRE	___	$5.99 U.S.	___ $6.99 CAN.
66485	KISS THE MOON	___	$5.99 U.S.	___ $6.99 CAN.
66266	CLAIM THE CROWN	___	$5.50 U.S.	___ $6.50 CAN.

(limited quantities available)

TOTAL AMOUNT	$_____
POSTAGE & HANDLING	$_____
($1.00 for one book; 50¢ for each additional)	
APPLICABLE TAXES*	$_____
<u>TOTAL PAYABLE</u>	$_____
(check or money order—please do not send cash)	

To order, complete this form and send it, along with a check or money order for the total above, payable to MIRA Books®, to: **In the U.S.:** 3010 Walden Avenue, P.O. Box 9077, Buffalo, NY 14269-9077; **In Canada:** P.O. Box 636, Fort Erie, Ontario, L2A 5X3.

Name:_____

Address:_____ City:_____

State/Prov.:_____ Zip/Postal Code:_____

Account Number (if applicable):_____

075 CSAS

*New York residents remit applicable sales taxes.
 Canadian residents remit applicable GST and provincial taxes.

MIRA®

Visit us at www.mirabooks.com

MCN0802BL